HIGH PRAISE FOR HAYWOOD SMITH,
WINNER OF THE *REVIEWER'S CHOICE* AWARD
FOR BEST FIRST HISTORICAL AND WINNER OF
THE CAREER ACHIEVEMENT AWARD FOR
INNOVATIVE HISTORICAL ROMANCE, FROM
ROMANTIC TIMES.

dangerous gifts

"Haywood Smith's newest is another jewel in her crown. . . .
The characterizations are wonderful. . . . Those looking for a
medieval romance won't want to miss this."
—*Publishers Weekly*

"Haywood Smith crafts unusual and intriguing romances that
weave history and passion together in a remarkable tap-
estry. . . . Fans will devour DANGEROUS GIFTS."
—*Romantic Times*

"Warm your heart with DANGEROUS GIFTS, a haunting,
medieval love story."
—*Playgirl*

"A novel of adult reality that leaves a warm afterglow, and
brings insight into the frailty of life and the strength of human
nature."
—www.newandusedbooks.com

"The love story . . . is one that will grab a corner of your heart
and never let go."
—Writers Club Romance Group on AOL Reviewer Board

more . . .

damask rose

"[Smith constructs] strong, complex characters, and this dark tale of vengeance and redemption is splendidly told!"
—*Publishers Weekly*

"Haywood Smith crafts a tale that grips you and never lets go. You'll be mesmerized by the magical and mystical qualities of the story and left spellbound . . . A tale for the discriminating reader searching for the ideal mix of history, mysticism, dreams and romance."
—*Romantic Times*

"A beautifully woven tale . . . Ms. Smith delivers a rich fascinating plot. Splendid!"
—*Bell, Book, and Candle* (4½ Bells)

"DAMASK ROSE proves that with faith and love, all things are possible. Once every year or so I read a story so compelling, so moving, that the characters stick with me for months afterwards. Such is the case with DAMASK ROSE. Add this keeper to your personal library."
—*The Old Book Barn Gazette*

"Don't miss this first-class read!"
—*Belles and Beaux of Romance*

secrets in satin

"Will appeal to readers who love characters that show faith, strength, and courage while learning to build a lasting relationshsip."
—*Compuserve Romance Reviews*

"A beautiful tale . . . entrancing and amazing. Just sit back and let Haywood Smith draw the world of 17th-century England around you."
—*The Literary Times*

"Haywood Smith continues to shine as a bright new star of the genre. Her rich historical novels are marvelous and her impressive talents truly shimmer and shine."
—*Romantic Times*

"Haywood Smith always provides her fans with an exciting, extremely powerful historical romance. . . SECRETS IN SATIN is a winner!"
—*Affaire de Coeur*

shadows in velvet

"Rich in history, romance and fine narrative drive, this is an impressive debut that explores new territory for readers who may be growing tired of the usual plots and settings."
—*Publishers Weekly*

"Haywood Smith's novel stimulates fans of this genre . . . This tale is an exciting, fast reading experience that readers simply must purchase for their collections."
—*Affaire de Coeur*

"A superb romance as rich in history as it is in passion. SHADOWS IN VELVET will not only fascinate but enthrall readers. Splendid . . . a wonderful debut."
—*Romantic Times*

"An outstanding tale from a great storyteller."
—*Rendezvous*

St. Martin's Paperbacks Titles
by Haywood Smith

SHADOWS IN VELVET
SECRETS IN SATIN
DAMASK ROSE
HIGHLAND PRINCESS

Haywood Smith

St. Martin's Paperbacks

NOTE: If you purchased this book without a cover you should be aware that this book is stolen property. It was reported as "unsold and destroyed" to the publisher, and neither the author nor the publisher has received any payment for this "stripped book."

HIGHLAND PRINCESS

Copyright © 2000 by Haywood Smith.

All rights reserved. No part of this book may be used or reproduced in any manner whatsoever without written permission except in the case of brief quotations embodied in critical articles or reviews. For information address St. Martin's Press, 175 Fifth Avenue, New York, N.Y. 10010.

ISBN: 0-312-97496-5

Printed in the United States of America

St. Martin's Paperbacks edition / July 2000

St. Martin's Paperbacks are published by St. Martin's Press, 175 Fifth Avenue, New York, N.Y. 10010.

10 9 8 7 6 5 4 3 2 1

This book is dedicated to Mama,
Anne Crane Pritchett,
my confidante, my boon traveling companion,
my sister in Christ,
but most of all, my friend.

acknowledgments

Whenever my life has been especially hard, the Good Lord always sends me some really special people to help ease the load. Betty Cothran is one of those people. Without her, I would never have been able to write this book, so I would now like to thank her publicly for her friendship, her patience, her encouragement, and her brilliant critique. Thanks, Betty. Couldn't have done it without you.

I would also like to thank my brother-in-law, Ron Carlsson, who loves my books and buys them as gifts in his travels all over the world. With Ron in my corner, how could I fail? I'm international!

Thanks, too, to Kay Grier, Stephanie Hauck, Carmen Green, Jill Jones, Victoria Barrett, Delia Parr, Bonnie Bruce, Betsy Allen, Susan Carlsson, and Lisa Cross. All these women are rays of light in a sometimes dark and hurtful world, and I am privileged to call them friends.

As always, thanks go to my editor, Jennifer Enderlin, publicity manager Walter Halee, and our publisher, Matthew Shear, for making St. Martin's Paperbacks the best publisher in the world to work for.

in the land of
caledon
(now known as scotland)

during the time of
princesses

chapter one

June, on the training field of Pitlanric Castle

The breath of God blew warm across the heather-covered hills of Caledon, driving puffs of cloud from west to east beneath a vault of azure blue. But Bera gave no heed to sun or sky. All her strength and concentration focused on the writhing mass of muscle beneath her blade.

She'd beaten him, the last and strongest of the twelve!

Well, almost. If only the great blockheaded lummox would admit it and yield.

"Yield!" Bera tightened her legs around Angus's barrel chest and brought her blade harder against his throat. She leaned closer, grinding the thick double links of her silver princess chain into her own neck, but she did not feel the pain. Nor did she care that she was muddied, bruised, and drenched from the contest. All she felt was the purging power of the fight.

Abruptly, the afternoon sun disappeared behind the clouds of an advancing storm, and a fresh blast of wind rippled across the stands of bracken and heather that carpeted the vast slopes beyond the training ground.

A storm.

A good omen, for it meant that her protector, Lachna, mother of storms, had come to watch.

Bera's brothers were watching, too. All eleven of them moved in closer and murmured amongst themselves. She knew they wouldn't interfere. Doubtless, they relished the sight of their eldest brother where each of them in turn had been: shamed and defeated by their only sister, the youngest of them all.

"I said yield!" Bera couldn't hold out much longer against Angus's superior size and brute strength. "I've defeated you, well and true. Admit it!"

"You didn't beat me," her eldest brother snarled. "You tricked me, slithering like an eel." He thrashed again, in vain. "Glomming onto my head like an octopus. That's not what I call fighting!"

"Call it what you will, I've beaten you." Pushed to the limit, her muscles burned. She lifted her eyes to the roiling clouds overhead and called upon her spirit-mother for help. *Tempest Mother, grant me the power of the storm.*

The Tempest Mother answered with a rare growl of thunder and a gust of benediction that cooled the skin exposed by Bera's brief training tunic.

Heartened, Bera pressed the edge of her blade even harder against the bulging muscles of her brother's neck, breaking the skin. "Yield, I said!"

Angus's enormous fingers groped for a hold on the offending weapon, yet could not get a grip to pry the blade from his flesh. But when he felt the sticky warmth and drew back his hand to find the fingers red and dripping, he stiffened in surprise.

Blood had been spilled.

A tense murmur of alarm went through Bera's eleven watching brothers even as a stab of fear slashed through her. She willed the fear to strengthen instead of weaken her. What had begun as a challenge had now become a blood matter. She couldn't give up now, even though tremors told her that her muscles were failing already. "Yield!" she shouted with a conviction she did not feel.

She felt her brother hesitate, sensed his relentless mind weighing out the alternatives. Then, to her amazement, he eased his struggle and choked out, "All right, blast it!"

Bera's strength was born anew in triumph. Now that she had won, she had no intention of letting him off so easily. "Say it!"

"Insolent little flea." Angus's pale skin mottled with rage, but he said the words Bera had so long dreamed of hearing: "I yield."

Instantly, she withdrew her blade and leapt back safely out of reach.

The rest of her brothers erupted into gleeful hoots and jeers, pounding each other in the way of men.

"Good work!" her brother Evan called. "I knew you could do it!"

"Ah, shut up, Evan," Angus railed as he lumbered to his feet. "It took her ten years to get the best of me. She beat you in only seven!" He glowered at the lot of them, then stomped toward the fortress with as much dignity as he could muster.

"My prize!" Bera called after him. "You promised me the stallion!"

Angus kept his back to her, but motioned to his left, where his twin brother Airell was leading forth the skittish roan stallion.

Exultant, Bera lifted her diminutive sword toward the approaching storm. "Tundarr is mine!"

Her outburst sent the stallion rearing, but Airell quickly brought him down again. He halted a safe distance from Bera, acknowledging her victory with a wry half-smile and a brief nod. Praise came scarce from any of her twelve big brothers, and he was no exception.

"You've won him, Little Bit, but can you ride him?" Clearly, he didn't think she could.

"No horse shall get the best of me," she retorted, stung by the diminutive nickname her brothers all insisted on using. She was a middle-aged woman of twenty-six, not a child. "Especially not after I've beaten the man who is his master." She closed the distance between them.

"*Was* his master." Kegan, the handsomest of the lot, came forward. After only a few steps, his gaze shifted to something behind her. "Look sharp, Little Bit," he warned. "Just this moment, I'd say the stallion was the least of your worries."

Bera turned to see that Angus had thought better of retreat and was now advancing toward her, his blue eyes almost as dark as his black hair, and his skin as flushed with anger as his neck was red with blood.

Evan stuck his fingers in the bowl uninvited, as usual. "There's a time to fight and a time to flee," he cautioned. "I'd advise the latter."

"Well said." Airell handed her the reins and bent over so she could use his back to vault astride the huge animal.

Bera wasted no time in doing so. But the stallion, testing this small and unfamiliar rider, immediately began to writhe and fight against the reins.

"None of that now!" She tugged with renewed vigor to subdue the beast, but both she and the stallion knew she had neither the strength nor the bulk to win the war of wills.

As always, she was forced to rely on cunning and speed. Angus was almost within reach, and there was murder in his eyes.

"You *will* obey me, horse!" Quick as a flick of Tundarr's tail, she flipped her sword and caught it by the blade, then whacked the mutinous stallion decisively between his flattened ears with the smooth ball at the end of the handle. Bera regretted the need for such brutal measures, but the tactic got Tundarr's attention.

The steed staggered briefly, his ears askew, prompting another outburst of hilarity from all but one of her brothers.

Angus halted. A warrior of his stature would rather die than utter a word of complaint about a defeat, but a man's steed was another matter. No self-respecting prince of Caledon would allow anyone to discipline his warhorse without protest, so Angus directed all his anger to this lesser insult. "How dare you strike my steed?" he bellowed up at her. "I'll not have you abusing my horse!"

As if in response to his former master's voice, Tundarr resumed his struggle.

"He's *my* horse now," Bera shot back. "And he must obey me." In a blink, she flipped the sword's handle back into her grip, then whacked the flat of the blade decisively on the rebellious animal's arched neck. At last, the stallion settled enough for her to urge him toward the gray curtain of rain advancing across the highland, erasing everything in its path.

"Rraaah!" She kicked the beast to a gallop, hoping a good run would settle him down.

"He doesn't like storms," Angus shouted after her.

"He will when I'm finished with him," she shouted back.

Now that she'd defeated both man and beast, she began to feel the cost of her victory as her skin bloomed with bruises. But she did not care, for she had won.

Her filthy tunic felt clammy and constricting, though, and she wished she could strip naked so the Tempest Mother could wash her clean. She wanted to revel naked in the storm, celebrate her victory unfettered.

Tundarr knew every trail across these rolling highlands as well as she, and Bera balanced her own movements to the speed and power pumping away beneath her. As soon as she felt confident of the stallion's rhythm, she leapt to her feet and stood triumphant as they galloped toward the rain.

Reckless, she pulled loose the thongs that bound her auburn braids at the base of her skull, then threaded her fingers through the plaits until her long hair—the last vestige of her femininity—blew free behind her.

If only she could free her body, too. Her tunic felt constricting, as did the clout beneath it.

It occurred to Bera that she needn't wear her clothes if she didn't want to. After all, most male Caledonian warriors trained and fought naked. Her brothers had gone against that tradition only in deference to her modesty, but Bera felt anything but modest now. She had beaten them each in turn. Why accept their restrictions now?

The steed was hers, the day was hers, the storm was hers . . . The whole, wide world was hers.

She gripped both reins in her left hand and threaded her sword securely through the braided leather. With her free hand, she untied her belt and cast it aside. Then she pulled the sodden tunic over her head, transferred the reins to strip it off, then hurled the garment behind her. Now bound only by the clout that covered her most private places, she loosed that and flung it away, too. At last, she was truly free, just in time for the first heavy drops of rain to sting her skin.

As the Tempest Mother wept her clean, Bera turned her face toward the heavens, closed her eyes, and rode as one with the galloping steed beneath her.

Half a mile away, Curran's mount shifted uneasily, moving closer to the low crag that offered precious little shelter from the storm. It was a small movement, but

ne that snapped Curran instantly from the guarded sleep
e stole whenever he could.

Had Voltan heard something above the storm?

Curran tensed, grateful for his helmet and hauberk in
pite of the rain that rusted the iron mail even as he sat.
A man in his line of work could take no chances. Con-
tant vigilance had kept him alive to see this twenty-
inth summer, long past the age when most mercenaries
ad been sent to the Otherworld, and he could ill afford
o be careless now.

He was on his way to an assignment that would earn
im a king's ransom. Lord Drust had promised him a
antastic sum for training his troops, and Curran was
nly a few days' ride from his destination.

He closed his eyes and strained to filter out the din
of rain penetrating his heavy black cloak.

Ah. He *had* heard something: a horse, a big one, com-
ng fast from the north.

He signaled Voltan to silence with a carefully placed
wipe of his mail-covered left hand even as his right
drew his sword.

Something about the hoofbeats seemed odd, too swift
and light to be heavily laden.

Riderless?

Maybe not.

He guided Voltan behind a dark outcropping at the
base of the crag. Secure in the knowledge that his black
steed and cloak would disappear against the rain-
darkened rock, Curran made bold to keep his head above
he crest of the outcropping so he could see what was
coming. Just to be safe, though, he kept his sword at the
ready as he watched and waited, still as the stone that
hid him.

Long seconds passed before horse and rider loomed
out of the rain only fifty paces away.

Curran took one look and, for the first time in all his
years as a mercenary, froze, unable to move.

The rider was a woman, stark naked and standing atop a galloping roan stallion! Dark tendrils of her unbound auburn hair whipped free behind her or molded in stark contrast against the pale skin of her muscular body.

Curran's manhood leapt with such force he almost abandoned caution in favor of sheer lust.

Almost.

Was she a pagan goddess, then, returned from the lore of old?

Tlaguh, perhaps, the mistress of the thunderbolt . . . or Murgan, the deity of war?

She stood with such poise, her feet planted on the huge warhorse's back, the reins in her left hand and a perfectly scaled sword lifted heavenward in her right.

Surely no mortal woman could ride as she did.

But Curran had always thought of goddesses as more . . . *ample* beings. This one was lean as a lad—except for her breasts, breasts as round and taut as a maiden's. Curran's gaze followed the path of a wet tendril molded provocatively over the curve of her bosom before it trailed to the dark vee between her legs, prompting another jolt of desire that almost brought him up out of his saddle.

Goddess or mortal, he didn't care; he wanted her.

But in the instant between impulse and action, he halted. What if she was neither goddess nor woman, but some evil apparition instead—a ghostly seductress without substance sent to lure him to his doom.

Find out! his manhood urged him. Follow her!

But self-preservation held him fast. For now, he watched and waited.

Bera had ridden with abandon until she noted a subtle hesitation in Tundarr's gallop that coincided with a tingle of warning, as if someone was watching her.

She opened her eyes and saw that the land had lev-
d. They had reached Black Crag, the southern bound-
y of her dominion, and Tundarr's ears were back, his
strils flared.

Had he sensed someone, or was it just the storm?

She peered through the rain at the dark, brooding
esence of the crag, but she neither saw nor heard any-
ng amiss.

It must be the storm that's upset him, she told herself.

"Easy, Tundarr. Easy." She slipped back down astride
m and gentled him to a trot, reining him into a circle
cool him down. His broad back was warm from ex-
tion and felt good against her bare skin. "Nothing to
afraid of. Lachna will not harm us. She loves me too
ll."

She leaned forward to confide, "Your fear insults her,
ough. She'll grow angry if you do not trust her."
orses needed to know these things, for the spirits of
rth, air, and elements could be just as capricious with
imals as they were with humans. "So do not be
raid," she reassured the stallion. "As long as you are
ith me, we are safe within the storm." She eased him
a walk.

Tundarr remained skittish. Since he didn't seem to
lieve her, she leaned forward to stroke his neck. "The
oddess will not cast her fire-spear at us. She is my
irit-mother, given to me by God when my own mother
ed."

Odd, how the feel of his backbone against her
oman's parts sent sparks of pleasure through her. She
adn't felt like that since . . . since she'd been a girl of
n and four just coming into womanhood—right before
e night that had changed everything.

She hadn't meant to think about it, but even that brief
collection was enough to resurrect the horror she had
ng since buried. Every hateful taste, touch, smell, feel-

ing came flooding back so vividly she gasped in revulsion.

The sour stench of spirits on her father's breath, the explosion of pain when he'd sent her flying, the sound of her mother's cries as she'd tried to protect Bera, her sire's roar of fury, and the sickening crunch of his fist pounding into her mother's bone and flesh. The smell of blood.

How could it all seem so fresh, even twelve years later?

Why could she still recall every evil sense and sound, yet not remember her mother's worn but loving face before he'd smashed it?

Guilt and grief welled up within her, but Bera had long ago shed her last tears for that night. She and her brothers had avenged their mother, then and there, but they were all still paying the price for what had happened.

Now, even from his grave, her father reached out to spoil her moment of happiness.

This day should have been triumphant. Now it was ashes.

Hard against the crag, Curran watched the naked woman's shoulders slump. Then she collapsed against the roan's withers and gave him his head.

What had happened? Something had snuffed out her pride and assurance as quickly as wind killed a candle flame.

He had no time to wonder further, though, for just as the rain began to subside, a noisy shower of pebbles washed loose from the crag above him.

The woman sprang erect and looked toward the sound. Curran could almost feel the bolt of raw terror that rode her gaze when she saw him.

In one motion, she brought up her sword and kicked the stallion into flight. As she rode for cover in the re eating storm, Curran noticed for the first time the thick lver chain at her neck, and his lust evaporated.

How could he have missed it? His naked goddess ore the emblem of a royal princess of Caledon. She as the enemy.

He watched her disappear into the gray curtain of rain nd wished her good riddance.

Curran turned east, toward Burghead.

Lord Drust was waiting with a timely job for the Dark Varrior.

hirty miles to the southeast at the stone fortress of urghead, Princess Diedre concealed her disgust when er idiot husband started shouting at the two men who tood, hats in hand, before him.

"What do you mean, the ewe is yours?" Lord Drust bared, his pocked skin dusky red and his piggish eyes right with anger. "You said yourself, the ewe is dead! Vho wants a dead ewe?"

A starving shepherd, that's who! Diedre kept her eyes emurely downcast as she rose and approached her low-witted husband. "Pray forgive the interruption, my ord husband, but might I show you the stitchery I've ust completed?"

"Stitches?" Drust bellowed. "I'm about a lord's work, voman, and you dare to speak to me of stitches!"

Diedre concealed her disgust behind a vacant look of urprise. The old fool was so boulder-headed he couldn't ven remember a signal as simple as that one! Diedre ecame the very outward soul of contrition, kneeling before him and taking his huge, scarred hand in her tiny, apered fingers. "Pray forgive me, my lord husband, but live only for your favor. A mere word of recognition rom you, and I am content."

The two supplicants watched surreptitiously, clearly nvious of their brutal master's doting, obedient wife.

If only they knew . . .

Her grip was far tighter than it looked on her husband's crooked, callused fingers. "Pray, *do not forget*
my lord husband, how well I love you. Do you love
me?" Her winsome smile turned genuine as she drove
her needle deep into the sensitive web between two of
his meaty fingers.

Drust let out a howl and tried to retract his hand, but
Diedre would not let go. The Beast, as she preferred to
think of her "lord husband," deserved a lesson for forgetting how things were and chiding her before inferiors.

The two witnesses stepped back in fear, but Diedre
withdrew her needle and kissed the back of his hand,
beaming. "See how well my lord husband loves me. He
shouts it to the heavens. I am blessed above all women."

Drust thunked back into his chair, his brows knitted
in confusion and his thick lips protruding in a monu-
mental pout. "What was *that* for?" he snarled. Then a
dim flicker of recognition dawned in his tiny eyes. "Ah,
the stitching."

Diedre gently turned his hand and pretended to kiss
his palm. The two shepherds looked away in embarrassment at the intimate gesture, so only she and Drust saw
that she wasn't kissing his palm but seductively licking
the blood from the base of his finger.

She had to sleep with The Beast every so often, as
long as she continued with her own diversions. Just in
case. Diedre shot him a lascivious glance, then rose to
whisper moistly in his ear, "Give one lamb to each of
them, but direct them to bring the ewe's carcass straightaway to our kitchens. We can feed it to the slaves."
Suppressing a shudder, she touched her tongue to the
rim of her husband's ear. "Both shepherds will be disappointed, but they'll think you wise."

Drust was all but cross-eyed with lust when she withdrew. "One lamb for each of you," he grumbled distract-

edly to the shepherds. He pinned the first with a baleful glare. "You! Bring the carcass to my kitchens. Now! There's an end to it."

As the men hurried away, Drust lunged greedily for Diedre, but she deftly evaded him.

"Tonight, my beloved," she cooed. "I shall give you pleasure and pain. And you, I pray, shall give me another daughter," she lied. Diedre wanted another daughter, but from any father but Drust. That was why she drank the rank and bloody potion made from dried hogs' wombs and ovaries every day—to keep her own womb from drying up. She wanted another daughter like her precious Alma.

Not like the eight thick-lipped, thick-minded sons she could hardly bear to look upon for the uncanny resemblance they bore their father. If she hadn't carried her eight sons and witnessed their births, she never would have believed she'd had any part in them. They were the image of their father, and one Drust in the world was one too many, as far as she was concerned.

Diedre put on her prettiest smile and left The Beast to muddle through the rest of the afternoon alone.

There was work to be done, and if it was to be done properly, she would have to be the one to oversee it.

chapter two

Six months later—December, Pitlanric Castle

Vikings or no Vikings, Bera couldn't stand being cooped up in the fortress another day.

Four months had passed since Viking raiders had stolen much of their food and half their cattle. Three of those anxious, hungry months had crawled by since her nine eldest brothers had gone to Burghead seeking an alliance with Drust, only to be taken hostage by treachery.

Bera had had her fill of smoke and noise and the smell of too many bodies in too cramped a space. But it was the faces of her nieces and nephews that haunted her most. Hunger had sunken their cheeks and dulled the eyes of even the older, stronger ones, and a season of fear had quieted the children's play, banishing the sound of laughter from the fortress.

Playing rough-and-tumble with the children had been Bera's greatest joy. Now there were no games. And the babies . . . how she'd loved holding the babies, but lately twice as many as usual had died.

Soul-sick with worry and sorrow, Bera feared she would shame herself if she couldn't get away, even if for only an hour or two.

Nothing would come amiss.

She'd made it as far as the outer corridor when an all-too-familiar voice assaulted her in the narrow passageway.

"And just where do you think *you'll* be goin', then, your highness?"

Moina. Of all The Wives to catch her trying to escape.

"Dear Moina." Bera turned in the stone corridor to confront Angus's big, bossy wife and was almost moved to pity. The recent troubles had taken their toll on Moina, too. Her once-substantial bulk now hung flaccid on her frame.

"Tundarr needs exercising," Bera said casually, well aware that most of The Wives cared more about the stallion than they did about her. They could *eat* the stallion. Come to think of it, though, Moina might just love making stew out of her, too. "The horse grows lazier and more obstinate by the day, pent up within the stockades these many weeks."

"Aye," Moina surprised her by agreeing. "Time for some discipline, no doubt." Her close-set gaze met Bera's. "Like all headstrong, arrogant creatures, he must be reminded of his proper place."

Both of them knew she wasn't talking about the horse. As always, Moina missed no opportunity, plain or subtle, to criticize Bera's "unnatural" status in the family. So Bera braced herself for yet another verse of the woman's endless, relentless paean of judgment.

"Horse training . . . 'tis warriors' work, hardly a proper pastime for a *princess*," Moina observed caustically. "Boyd or Connal or Cusantin are better fit to ride my husband's stallion."

"*My* stallion," Bera corrected sweetly. "Won when I bested your husband, remember?" Moina had bullied the rest of the women into submission, but she would not succeed with Bera.

Moina squared with her. "As I *said*, you'd best leave ridin' the stallion to the menfolk."

"The menfolk?" Bera feigned surprise. "Why, Moina, I am shocked. I would be a poor princess, indeed, if I were to risk one of my three remaining brothers with nine already held prisoner in Drust's fortress." She looked the woman straight in her beady eyes and smiled. "Nay. I could not do such a thing. If anyone is to go beyond the walls, better it should be I."

A third voice reached them in the dim passageway. "Good sisters? Has something come amiss?" The question oozed false concern.

Perfect. Bera suppressed a moan. Fenella.

Evan's wife had never fooled Bera. Underneath her meek manner, Fenella would secretly like to eat Bera's liver on a platter, but she would do it in tiny, ladylike bites.

Bera turned to see her gliding toward them with a grace that any woman, even Bera, had to envy. Yet appearances were deceiving. Evan's pale, beautiful wife and Angus's big, brutish one might look like opposites, but in truth, they were cut from the same bolt: devious, resentful, ambitious. And both of them hated their husbands' only sister.

Bera had her allies among the twelve Wives—lame Olwyn, sweet Lavena, practical Melva, strong-willed Ula, and feisty Lyonesse—but Moina and Fenella were pure poison. And now she was trapped between them in this cramped hallway.

"Our *princess* would leave the protection of our stockades." Moina shot Fenella a pointed look of indictment. "To exercise *her* stallion."

Fenella's flawless features registered concern. "Cusantin and Boyd and Connal have made it very clear.

None of the women or the children may leave the protection of Pitlanric." She blinked her big blue eyes at Bera. "It's for our own good."

Horseshite, Bera thought. You don't believe that any more than I do!

She knew better than let Moina or Fenella see her irritation, though. They'd only bedevil her even further, so she merely smiled instead.

Stay cold, she told herself. Feed upon the anger and turn the heat to ice. As long as you hold yourself in check, they cannot win.

She lowered the hood of her dark green cloak and straightened to the full extent of her mediocre height, deliberately exposing her silver princess chain in a less-than-subtle reminder of her superior status. "I won't be gone long."

"But you must not go at all." Fenella spoke with uncharacteristic boldness, an unsettling gleam in her eye. "I did not merely wander up upon you, Bera. I was sent."

Bera stiffened. To be addressed solely by her name . . . Fenella would never dare such insolence, unless . . . Unless what?

"I have a message." For the first time since Fenella had come to them as Evan's wife, she let her wicked slyness show. "The brothers would speak with you—" She paused for effect. "—in the tower room."

The tower room? High above the noise and activity of the rest of the fortress, that chamber was reserved for the gravest of matters.

Suddenly the corridor seemed colder and narrower, and fear gripped Bera's heart. Had Lord Drust grown weary of waiting for ransom?

Had he killed her brothers?

The mere prospect squeezed the air from her chest and stole her equilibrium. Heart racing, she quaked, then shifted to regain her balance. "I shall go, then."

Somehow, she managed to put one foot in front of the other in purposeful strides.

Please, don't let them be dead, she prayed as she went. *Anything but that. Don't let them be dead.*

They weren't dead, but Bera was totally unprepared for what *had* happened.

"Sit down, Bera. Please," Boyd asked her for the third time. "Let us speak of this rationally—"

"Nay!" She didn't want to sit down. She wanted to thrash all three of them! Planting her fists on the table, she leaned forward, her face only inches from her brother's. "How dare you do such a thing? And without even consulting me!" She searched his once-merry blue eyes for some sign of his old jesting ways, but she found none. The past three months had aged them all, especially Boyd.

"There was no other way," he repeated.

Bera turned her attention to Connal and Cusantin, who were studying the rafters as if their very futures were graven there. "Look at me, you cowards!" The insult worked; both twins pinned her with identical warning glances. "You cannot do this!" she challenged. "Our heritage—our place among our royal kinfolk, all we are, all we possess—can pass through me, and me alone, as princess. Would you barter with our very bloodline?"

Connal looked away, but his twin regarded her with grim resignation . . . and sympathy. "We have no choice, Bera, and you know it."

There *had* to be another way. "I am a princess of Caledon, not some wench to be tossed as a sop to any mere warrior who can free our brothers!"

Connal rose, desperate as always to escape a family conflict. "I'm needed at the foundry." The man would happily wade into a wall of Vikings, but let one cross

word pass between brother or sister, and he was off for
the hills.

"Nay, Conn." Cusantin pulled his brother back into
his chair. "Sit you down and face this. We owe her that
much, at least." He turned to Bera with open pity. " 'Tis
a grievous choice we had to make, Little Bit, but we
saw no other way."

Paralyzed by their betrayal, Bera sank into the empty
chair facing her brothers. They had promised her away
as a prize, offered her hand to any man who could free
her brothers, and they hadn't even told her first. They'd
just done it!

"Drust wants food, cattle, gold, and absolute subjec-
tion from us," Boyd explained as if it would make some
difference to her. "Hell, Angus went to Drust in the first
place to barter an alliance for food!" He shook his head.
"There's not even enough here to feed our own children,
and Drust knows it, much less any gold! We've eaten
half our breeding stock already." His handsome face
grew even more haggard. "The bastard means to make
slaves of us, and if he does, I have no doubt he'll happily
let our wives and children starve."

Connal and Cusantin nodded grimly.

"We've argued this out a dozen times before amongst
ourselves," Cusantin said quietly. "We cannot meet
Drust's terms. And we cannot leave our women and children unprotected to try and free the others ourselves."

"Bera, you yourself dictated the words Father Maclin
wrote to ask King Bred for help," Boyd reminded her.
"We knew when we did it there was precious little
chance of aid."

"Aye. The princes are too busy fighting amongst
themselves." Palms flat, Cusantin spread his fingers on
the tabletop. "As we feared, none of them will move
against Drust. He's far too powerful."

"And none of the princes would have me," Bera interjected, her tone both caustic and defensive. She knew the truth. Why not say it?

"How'd she find out about that?" Connal looked to Cusantin in accusation, his coppery eyebrows almost to his hairline. "*I* certainly didn't tell her."

Cusantin elbowed him to silence, but the grouse was already out of the bush.

"I'm not a simpleton," Bera retorted. "It only makes sense that you would offer my hand to the princes before you decided to barter me away like a slave-girl."

"Aye. We tried," Boyd admitted. "Truly, but—"

Conn cut him off with an angry, "Princes, my arse! Weak-livered barley-eaters, all of 'em, callin' our sister a shrew and a she-devil just because she can fight. Why, if I were free to leave, I'd teach those—"

"Shut up, Conn." Cusantin glared at him. "Can't you see you're only makin' it worse? She has feelings, you big, dumb block o' peat!"

"Oh, leave him alone," Bera snapped. "It's true, isn't it?" She could stand almost anything, but not their pity. "I've heard the stories they tell about me. All of them. Moina and Fenella make certain of that."

Boyd shifted the subject back to the matter at hand. "For the good of the family, Bera, the offer has been made. You must marry whoever frees our brothers." He looked on her with resolute compassion. "Our word is given. We are honor-bound."

Frantic for a way out, she argued, "What if I were already married? You'd have come up with another solution then! You'd have had to."

"We'll not play 'what if,' Bera," Boyd answered. "You are not married. That is fact." He did not say that she, herself, was responsible for her single status. He didn't have to.

Bera sagged. "I always meant to marry. It is my duty. I just wasn't ready." She never would be, and all of them knew it. Part of her longed to take her rightful place in the family as keeper of the bloodline—her sons would have the right to stand as kings, and in her daughters would lie the future of Caledon—but the greater part of her had become accustomed to independence.

Warriors often risked their lives, but they lived those lives to the fullest. Wives, on the other hand, were trapped in drudgery, their lives defined by the will of their husbands, the needs of their children, and the survival of the family.

Even if her husband were a prince among men, Bera would rather fight a thousand battles than lose herself among The Wives.

As if he could read her very thoughts, Boyd said, "I fear we did you no service when we allowed you to remain unwed." The twins nodded. "I must admit, though, you kept us laughing."

"And losing," she shot back with what she hoped was convincing humor.

But there was nothing amusing about her brother's desperate decision. Unless a miracle happened, she was trapped.

"Damn. I never should have encouraged those wild stories about me." She closed her eyes briefly. "At first I was glad of them. They made it easier to chase away the suitors Moina kept forcing Angus to drag up."

Boyd and Cusantin nodded in wry recollection, but Conn blurted out, "Remember that poxed one? Rrrrrr, the little weasel . . ." He waggled his finger at her. "I warned you then, he only came because he'd heard you had horns growin' where your breasts should be. Lost all interest when he saw you were made as plain as any other princess."

"Give it a rest, Conn," Boyd commanded. "Are you tryin' to offend her, then? Keep it up, and you'll have her runnin' from the room in tears!"

"I *do not* run from rooms in tears," Bera huffed. They might force her to become one of The Wives, but she'd rather be bound naked and thrown upside down into a great silver cauldron to drown than *act* like a fragile, manipulative female.

"Useless little weasel," Conn rattled on about the suitor. "Not another word about marryin'—and after we'd got him good an' drunk too, on the last of our best malt spirits." He let out a snort. "A dead waste, that."

Bera turned to Boyd in frustration. "Conn couldn't have come up with a scheme like this," she accused. "And neither would Cusantin. They're followers. It had to be you." She leaned closer. "This was all your idea, wasn't it?"

"Nay." To her surprise, it was Conn who answered, his tone uncharacteristically subdued. "It was all of us, Little Bit. Much as we hate it, it had to be done. For the good of the family."

Bera sank back in her chair.

Marriage.

She had seen what marriage did to her mother and the others. "I know my duty, and I shall do it. But not this way." Desperation forced her to speak of the unspeakable. "Need I remind you why you took me from the women to train as warrior among you? None of that has changed."

"Aye, it has," Boyd countered. "You've learned your lessons well. No man, not even a warrior, could abuse you now. If he tried, we would kill him." He cocked a weary half-smile. "If he tried, *you* could kill him."

"Noble intentions, and sincere, I'm sure," she spat out. "Yet what help were all of you when our father murdered our mother in our very presence? Where was her protection then?" The instant the words were spoken, she knew she'd gone too far. She saw the grievous pain in her brothers' eyes, read it on their haggard faces.

"Dear God, that was unforgivable of me, completely un-just," she breathed out. "I'd give anything to take it back." Sick to the marrow, she subsided into her chair. "I beg you to forgive me."

Cusantin swiped his freckled brow as if to erase the hateful words from his mind, and Conn let out a cleans-ing sigh, but Boyd's voice was pregnant with hurt. "It is in God's hands, Bera. The offer has been made. If any man completes the quest, you must marry him."

Marrying a prince would have been bad enough. But to sacrifice her independence to some nameless, greedy adventurer . . . The bile rose in Bera's throat.

Then a flash of inspiration resurrected her hope. "Wait! There is another way!"

All three brothers regarded her with skepticism.

"I could go to Burghead, free them myself!" She ap-pealed to Boyd as eldest of the three. "If ever there was a time for stealth, this is it. There aren't enough warriors in all of Caithness to bring down Drust by force. But I could insinuate myself into the fortress and help our brothers escape."

"You're all we have left, Bera. We dare not risk you," he countered.

"I can do it, I tell you!" Desperate, she turned to the twins. "You know I can. It could work! No one would expect a woman to rescue them." She turned back to Boyd. "Give me that one hope, at least. It is all I ask. Promise me that if I can free them, I may choose my own husband, at least."

Bera knew she'd been deluding herself to think she could keep her freedom, but her dream of indepen-dence—of safety—died hard. She glared at each of them in turn. "If you do not, I shall make no promises as to what I'll do."

Kill herself. Run away.

The three brothers exchanged looks that clearly said

they had no intention of letting her set one foot beyond the safety of their stockades. But to appease her, Boyd agreed. "Very well. Should you somehow manage to free them, you may choose your own husband. But you must give me your solemn vow that you will do nothing without our consent." He eyed her warily. "Swear it, Bera, for the good of the family."

"You swear first!" she challenged, slapping her hand down on the table to seal the vow.

Her brothers shifted uneasily, but after a long pause, each laid his hand atop hers and voiced a ragged chorus of "I swear."

"Now you," Boyd ordered.

"In time." Bera jerked her hand from beneath theirs, leaping backward as she did. Before they could lay hold to her, she pivoted and sprinted for the door. "In time," she shouted back over the scrape of chairs and rumble of pursuit.

They would never catch her, never find her. Bera knew places to hide inside the fortress that even the rats hadn't discovered. And she knew exactly when and how to get the things she needed for her quest.

Already, a plan was forming.

Too bad she couldn't take Tundarr along. He really needed the exercise.

Four days later at the fortress of Burghead

"A woman, you say." Diedre accepted the folded square of fabric from her maid. She opened it to find a masterfully executed bull woven against an intricate interlocking background. Never had she seen such artistry.

And the backing . . . it seemed of a whole with the front, yet its pattern was not the same at all. Even among the foreign emissaries at court, Diedre had never seen such miraculous artistry.

To have such a weaver in her household would bring honor indeed to her and Burghead. "Bring this weaver to me," she commanded.

Malisande hurried into the hallway. Diedre was still inspecting the mysterious sample when she returned.

"The weaver, my lady."

She looked up and beheld a cloak so magnificent that everything else in the room—even Diedre's priceless tapestries—paled to bland oblivion.

"By Mother Earth!" she breathed, amazed. "You have plucked the very night sky from heaven and captured it with weft and warp." Compelled to touch, she rose and inspected the cloak. The soft wool fabric was dense yet supple, and the closer one looked, the more intricate the arrangement of symbols and backgrounds became. The "sky" was in fact a tight pattern of interlocking dark blue knots outlined in black. The white "stars" were whorling power medallions that radiated daggers of gold and yellow. Magnificent lunar symbols illustrated the phases of the moon around the shoulders.

The effect was entrancing . . . and powerful. By the reckoning of their people, each new day started with the coming of darkness, and the moon ruled the cycles of months and years. "I would have this cloak," Diedre announced, so moved she did not even rebuke the weaver for remaining hooded in her presence. "Name your price."

Two square, callused hands appeared from inside the cloak and drew the fabric tighter. "My cloak is not for sale," an oddly ageless voice spoke from shadow. "But I could make another for your highness. If I were given good food, good wages, and the proper supplies, of course. And a safe place to work undisturbed."

"You shall have it," Diedre agreed all too hastily. Then she thought better of such rashness. "Assuming you are the one who made these marvels."

"I am," the weaver answered with calm assurance.

"We shall see," Diedre countered. "I would have you weave something for me before the morrow. A test." Summoned by a subtle flick of Deidre's fingers, her lady-in-waiting came forward. "Malisande will oversee. If your work meets with my approval, you may make a cloak for me."

"Such a test is reasonable," the weaver answered. "I shall weave for you this night." She bowed, yet what she said next was anything but humble. "And I can promise the princess, she will approve."

Diedre bristled. "We shall see." She peered into the shadow of the hood. "Why do you remain covered in my presence? Are you scarred?" She recoiled. "You're not a leper, are you?"

"Nay, great lady." The weaver drew the hood partway back, and that only briefly, granting a glimpse of narrowed, blinking eyes, an unremarkable face, and reddish-brown hair drawn tight against her skull. "My eyes are weak after so many years at the loom. The light hurts them, so I keep them shaded."

Diedre wasn't convinced, but she played along, her curiosity pricked. It would be fine sport to uncover this weaver's secret—who she really was. "Very well. You have my leave to remain hooded. But my lord husband does not tolerate such disrespect. If you hear Lord Drust coming, bare your head and bow it."

"I shall, your highness," the weaver said. Too glib, too smooth.

There was an odd stillness about the hooded figure— something that didn't fit. Diedre's instincts cautioned her to be ware. "What is your name, then?" she demanded.

"Everyone calls me The Weaver. It is name enough."

"I am mistress here," Diedre reminded the stranger with calculated mildness. "If I ask for your name, you must give it."

The weaver bowed low. "Forgive me, great lady, but I must then beg your leave, for I cannot give what I do not have."

Why was she talking in riddles? Again, Diedre's instincts sounded a note of warning. But the cloak . . . she had to have one.

"Oh, all right then. The Weaver it is," she acceded. "Let us speak of the cloak you will weave for me."

The Weaver nodded. "First, I must study the princess to see if she is sun or moon. The cloak will be a talisman, a portrait of the great lady's very soul."

A chill of foreboding pebbled Diedre's flesh. Beneath her sleeve, she made the sign against the evil eye. "Are you a sorcerer, then, a follower of the Old Ways?"

"Nay," The Weaver answered. "Merely an observer of those who interest me. And a recorder of truth."

Only a fool would take a stranger to the bosom of her household, and Diedre was no fool. She weighed the risks. This Weaver was clearly not what she seemed. If she had indeed crafted such a magnificent cloak, why had no one heard of her? Such an artisan would be known far and wide.

Yet the greatest risk was also the most compelling reason to allow The Weaver to stay. The last thing Diedre wanted was for anyone to discern, much less record, the secrets of her soul. Yet the prospect of seeing such a portrait, of wearing it . . .

What woman could resist?

"Very well." She would keep a close eye on this one, though. "You shall have a room nearby and access to my presence, but only at my convenience, and only after you have been searched."

"Of course, great lady." Bera bowed again, her mind still reeling from the keen intelligence she'd recognized in Princess Diedre. Others might accept the woman's artfully crafted illusion of feminine meekness, but Bera knew a kindred spirit when she saw one. This princess was no more a modest, obedient wife than Bera was a lowly weaver.

To place herself under the very nose of such a deceptive adversary . . .

She could still succeed, but getting her brothers out of here was going to be even more difficult—and dangerous—than Bera had planned. She'd hoped to win the princess's patronage, then manipulate the relationship to her advantage, but now . . . Bera wasn't at all sure who would be manipulating whom.

A knock sounded at the princess's door and Malisande opened it. The servant outside handed her a silver tray bearing a single, jeweled goblet filled to the brim with what looked for all the world like blood. Malisande brought it forward, curtsied, then tasted it for her mistress. A sour smell rose from the murky potion, and she shuddered when it passed her lips.

The princess watched and waited in silence for several minutes, then tossed back the goblet's entire contents, daintily blotted her lips, and turned a stern look on Bera.

What was *that*? Bera wondered before she forged ahead. "I brought a bag with a small loom and my special bobbins and enough wool to demonstrate my skills. Your guards took them from me."

"They will be returned." The princess picked up her own needlework and pretended to be absorbed in it, but Bera could see she was still watching her every move, weighing her every inflection.

An odd pattern, that needlework the princess was doing.

"Once I pass the test," Bera said, "I shall need a large loom and wool, the best quality."

"Granted. If you pass the test," Diedre murmured,

stitching away on the disjointed dots, bars, and swirls of her embroidery.

Bera had saved the biggest—and most important—request for last. She shot a brief, fervent prayer to her mother in heaven for intercession, then ventured, "My dyes are secret, known only to me. If I do not find the roots and herbs I require among the castle's stores, I shall have to forage for them beyond the stockades."

A brief lift of the princess's left eyebrow and a subtle hardening of the royal mouth betrayed her annoyance at The Weaver's boldness.

Bera realized she'd overstepped, but searching for dyestuffs would provide a perfect ruse for finding the best escape from Burghead. She held her breath and waited for the princess's response.

To her infinite relief, the woman agreed. "Very well. If you must leave the stockade, I shall petition my lord husband for a guard to accompany you."

Now she would be able to retrieve the weapons she had hidden beyond the stockade. "Great lady, your generosity knows no bounds."

The princess faced her with surprising candor. "Do not bother to flatter me, Weaver. I love those best who speak the truth."

"My lady is wise, indeed." Bera bowed low, her posture tempered by genuine respect.

"You ask much, Weaver," the princess said, turning her attention back to her to her stitchery. "Take care that my cloak is worth the investment." The silence stretched long between them before Bera was released. "You may go. Malisande will show you to your chamber."

Bera backed a respectful distance, then turned and followed the maid to the corridor.

Outside the door, the guard handed the attendant Bera's colorful woven bag. "No weapons. Just a comb and some yarn and a bushel of bobbins." He hefted the sack and the bobbins clicked against each other.

So far, so good. He hadn't found the silver chain stitched into the bottom of the lining.

The maid hefted the bag. "Heavy." She pulled the drawstring open and reached inside. "Ah. The bobbins." Satisfied, she returned the bag to The Weaver. "Follow me to the kitchens. After you have eaten, I will show you to your chamber."

For the first time since she'd entered this dark and evil place, Bera breathed a little easier, but she kept her senses sharp.

She had made her bed in the dragon's den. Now she must find her brothers and free them, all under the dragon's watchful eye.

And if what she suspected was true, the name of the dragon wasn't Drust. It was Diedre.

Weaving through the night under Malisande's watchful eye, Bera produced an artful sun-square that won her a place at the dragon's feet.

chapter three

Curran raised his sword from Murdoc's neck and offered him a hand up from the frozen earth between Burghead's stockades. "You're getting better every day." Of all the chieftains, Murdoc was most deserving of respect—and fear. "A few more sessions like this one, and it'll be *me* on *my* back."

"Your mouth to God's ear," Murdoc grumbled with as much equanimity as any warrior could after being bested by a man five-stone lighter than he. He gripped Curran's forearm and levered himself to his feet. Drenched by exertion despite the cold, his gambeson gave off faint wisps of heat into the frigid December wind that constantly lashed the peninsula where Burghead stood. "I've never seen that counterthrust before. Where did you learn it?"

"On my way here from King Bred's court at Scone," Curran answered. "The lesson almost cost me my life, though." Breathing hard himself, he removed his iron helmet and camail and sucked in the clean, cold air. "But the brigand who used it against me lived only a heartbeat longer than it took me to learn the move."

A harsh bark of a laugh escaped Murdoc. "So it isn't foolproof."

"No move is foolproof," Curran responded with a

cold slice of a smile. "He was bigger, but I was faster . . . and smarter. So he died and I lived."

"Just as I would have died today, had our contest been in earnest," Murdoc observed dryly. He headed past the groups of men conditioning under the other chieftains' harsh supervision.

Curran fell in step beside him, anxious to check for subtle signs of suspicion. Murdoc was Drust's second-in-command, and the only one of the chieftains clever enough to suspect the truth: that the Dark Warrior was honing their skills as he'd been hired to do, but not well enough to tip the scales when he fought them, as he knew he must eventually.

Two months ago, Curran had taken a message to Scone for Drust, never intending to return. But when he'd learned in Scone of the bounty offered by the family of Drust's hostages, he had come back to Burghead with a quest of his own. He couldn't afford to arouse Murdoc's suspicions, so he played along.

Murdoc stopped a discreet distance from the rest of the men and scanned the warriors with grim assessment. "Our men are the strongest and fiercest in all of Albion. They're bred for war and weaned on beef and beer. They eat red meat from boyhood on. Costly, but it grows 'em big." There was pride in his voice, even affection. "By the time they're trained, they fear nothing. In their battle frenzy, I've seen them rip the heads from slain enemies with their bare hands." His eyes narrowed and his voice dropped to a confidential level. "They obey our lord without question, as do I." A pregnant pause lengthened between them.

Curran knew better than to speak. Murdock was leading up to something—something important . . . and dangerous, if his instincts boded rightly, as they almost always did.

Long seconds passed before the chieftain at last said

what he'd been working up to. "But where once we were three hundred, now we are only a hundred and eighty. In the last year alone, seven of our best chieftains have crossed over to the Otherword in valor." He inhaled, then exhaled heavily. "Which is well enough for them, but damned hard on the rest of us." He faced Curran squarely, his gray eyes piercing. "Our master takes what he wants with no thought of the cost."

With no thought of anything, Curran silently confirmed even as he concentrated on keeping his expression blank. Drust was like a rabid wolfhound: huge, vicious, and dangerously unpredictable. But Murdoc . . .

Why was he confiding in Curran, a stranger? Was he testing Curran's loyalty? Worse yet, was he planning to overthrow Drust and looking for an ally?

Either way, Curran had already heard far too much. But only a fool would insult a man of Murdoc's rank or influence. The only safe way out of this would be to remain neutral and not say anything that could later be used against him.

Murdoc resumed walking and Curran kept apace. "Our numbers are limited, but our enemies are not," the chieftain said. "We have need of the refinements you teach us, the battle tactics and the strategy. Our losses prove that brute force is not always best." He stared down at the cold, hard ground as he walked. "Lord Drust is blessed with an excellent advisor, but of late he will not heed prudent counsel. He often disregards it completely, to the detriment of all who follow him."

"I am honored that you trust me with such frankness," Curran said, "especially regarding matters of import." Just inside the stockades he halted within easy earshot of the sentries, and Murdoc stopped beside him. "Your devotion to your men is most commendable. They are fortunate indeed." He kept his manner light. "I shall make it a point to concentrate on the training elements you have mentioned," he said with absolute conviction, even though he had no intention of doing as he promised. "As for me, my main concern is . . ." He forced himself to grin and clapped Murdoc's meaty shoulder. "It's almost dark and I'm cold to my bones and hungry enough to eat an ox."

The chieftain scowled at the abrupt change of subject, but he did not tighten or pull away. The knot of tension in Curran's chest eased, though only slightly.

"There's no banquet tonight," he went on with forced good humor. "What say we head for the kitchens for some warm beer and hot stew?"

After a tense pause, Murdoc's features lightened. "Aye. Might as well." Together, they struck out for the welcome heat of the cookfires. "Warm beer and hot stew . . . and after that, a willing slave-wench to heat my bed."

A *willing* slave-wench? Curran's blood roiled with secret indignation. A wench must have a choice to be willing, and how much choice did a slave-woman have? None, just as his mother had had none.

His children would have better choices than she, he promised himself for the thousandth time.

If he completed this quest, freed the hostages, and won their royal sister's hand.

He followed Murdoc into the kitchens, sensing the unnatural tension in the room even before he saw the mysterious, much-whispered-about Weaver stirring a bubbling cauldron at the far end of the cookpit. Her shadow loomed huge on the wall behind her.

Both men halted when they saw her there.

Curran had discounted the tales of The Weaver's fabulous cloak as exaggerations, but this was one of those rare occasions when reality outdid even the embellishments of rumor. Dancing firelight caused the symbols on The Weaver's fantastic garment to shimmer, giving a magical aura to her presence.

Little wonder everyone else in the kitchen had fallen into edgy silence.

Maybe it was the cloak, but The Weaver's presence made him feel as if he'd stepped uninvited into the holy of holies of some ancient pagan temple.

His curiosity pricked, he feigned disinterest and strolled to the trestle table nearest the fire . . . and The Weaver. "Bring me warm ale and stew," he directed one of the serving girls. He eased onto the sturdy bench and propped his helmet and camail beside him. It wasn't easy to keep from wincing. Murdoc might have lost, but he'd gotten in his licks, and Curran was beginning to feel them.

Curran glanced back to see that Murdoc had stayed by the door, where a brazen scullery maid rubbed against him, no doubt eager for a chance to sleep in a real bed, even if Murdoc came with it.

Murdoc's huge hands closed on the wench's sturdy upper arms, and he lifted her up so he could bury his face between her ample breasts. "Aarrrgh!" he roared, the sound muffled by her flesh. The wench shrieked with delight, revealing blackened, broken teeth.

Murdoc came up for air and grimaced when he saw her teeth. "Eesh! Keep that mouth closed, woman, and we'll get along fine." He threw her over his shoulder like a slain deer and announced to no one in particular, "It's not her mouth I'm interested in, anyway." He turned to leave, running his hand up her skirt, which elicited another squeal. "Send my supper to my chamber," he called to the serving wenches as he exited.

Curran turned back to stare into the fire. He couldn't muster up much indignation on behalf of the wench, for she had initiated the concourse. But he'd seen all too often the hunger, fear, and desperation that would lead a slave-woman to trade her body for a few hours of warmth and her master's leavings.

It was foolish, though, to waste energy wishing the world were different. The world was as it was and always had been. Curran could only change the way things were for him, and change them he would, but not tonight.

He studied The Weaver from the corner of his vision. This was no slave; that was certain. Marking her proud posture, he figured her to be a freedwoman—a widow of some means, perhaps. She had that assurance.

She definitely didn't seem the type to make merry. But then, neither was he. Idle pleasure was just one of many sacrifices required to survive as a mercenary. But it would all be worth it—the long and lonely years as an instrument of death—if he accomplished his real purpose in returning to Burghead.

His gaze drifted back to the glowing heart of the charcoal fire. The rest of the men would be coming in soon, but for now, he rested his hand ready on the hilt of his sword and enjoyed the silence. Several peaceful minutes passed before two slave-women timidly approached him and bowed, keeping their eyes downcast.

"Would the master wish us to remove his hauberk? We can clean and oil it, and his helmet."

"Aye, thank you." He sat forward, hiking the heavy mesh clear of his hindquarters. Then he drew his sword from his girdle so the women could unbuckle and remove the thick leather strap. They did so swiftly and silently, never lifting their gazes from their task.

Curran wondered if he would find the same angry resentment in their eyes that had once been in his. The same secret hatred that lurked there hidden, still, when he was forced to bow and scrape to beasts like Drust.

"If the goodly knight would lift his arms, please," the elder of the two women murmured apologetically.

He raised both arms so they could pull the hauberk over his head.

As always, he hadn't realized how weighted down he'd been until he was free. "Ah, that's better." Before he could thank them, they scooped up his helmet and camail and hurried away to clean them.

Curran massaged the scrapes and indentations left in the backs of his hands by the hauberk's scallop of mesh.

"Food, master?" Another of the nameless slave-girls approached and set before him a crusty bread-bowl brimming with thick lentil stew. "And drink." She placed the mug of hot beer beside it and quickly bowed out of harm's way.

"Thank you," Curran called after her.

The slave-girl turned, a shocked expression on her face, then scampered away as if he'd cursed instead of thanked her. None of the slaves had gotten used to his treating them with common decency, not even after the months he'd been here.

Out of the corner of his eye, though, he saw the mysterious Weaver pause. After a moment of silent scrutiny, she resumed her stirring.

Curran pretended to take no notice. Instead, he turned his attention to the hearty meal in front of him. And the beer. Only when he was full did he lean back and again stretch his feet toward the fire. He wasn't quite ready to retire to his cold bed amidst the stink and tumult of the warriors' lodgings.

Again, he felt his attention drawn to the silent Weaver, like iron filings to lodestone. Odd, how she made no sound nor any unnecessary movement. Most unusual, for a woman. Her posture erect under the concealing folds of her cloak, she moved her wooden paddle in smooth, graceful figure eights, pausing only occasionally to lift the thick strands of yellow wool from their dye bath to check the hue.

"So Princess Diedre is a sun creature," Curran commented, still staring into the fire.

The Weaver kept right on stirring.

Intrigued by her silence, he pivoted to peer into the shadow that concealed her face. "Are you deaf, then?" he asked politely. "Or merely rude?"

"I am neither deaf nor rude, good sir," a warm, low-pitched voice replied. After an insolently long silence, she added, "No one asked me a question."

Curran smiled in spite of himself. She was right; he'd a made a statement, not asked a question. "Aye," he acknowledged. He'd heard the gossip about why she always remained cloaked and hooded: she was poxed; she was deformed; she was horribly scarred; she was an ancient hag of a sorceress, her body tattooed with wohl in the symbols of the Old Ways.

For some reason, he didn't believe any of it. But he did wonder.

Curious, he decided to risk a conversation—a pastime he usually studiously avoided. Everyone in the room was watching them, listening to every word, he knew. But there was something about this Weaver . . . something indefinable that pricked a nagging hint of recognition.

That was foolish, of course. He'd seen no more of her than her hands, and those were square and functional—more like a lad's than a woman's, which made him even more curious.

He studied those hands now. They were not heavily veined, nor pocked, nor wrinkled, but well used and marked by a number of faint scars. Yet her grip on the wooden paddle was decisive, her wrists delicate.

"I'll ask you a question, then," he ventured. "What brings you to Burghead?"

"I might put the same question to you," she parried, her regal posture unwavering.

Clever, this one. And cheeky. Curran found himself

wondering how old she was. And if she—like he—was not what she seemed. "Everyone knows why I am here," he said casually. "I'm sure you've heard the gossip, as I have heard the gossip about you."

"I hear no gossip," she stated evenly. "What do they say?"

"That I am here to train Lord Drust's warriors, which is true," he lied. Then he improvised. "And that you are not really a weaver, but a mystic come to lure Princess Diedre to her doom."

"Hmph. You lie."

Curran went rigid, his hand tightening on his sword. How had she known he was lying about his reason for being here? No one knew the truth, save he. Yet she had spoken so quickly, with such certainty. " 'Tis a dangerous thing to accuse a warrior of lying," he said smoothly despite the battle-rush.

The Weaver did not flinch. "You lied. Admit it." Just when Curran was about to drag her outside to force the truth from her, she spoke again, her tone wry. "They've said a lot of things about me since I came, but not that."

She'd called his tale about *her* a lie, not what he'd said about himself. Curran was so relieved, he decided to be magnanimous. The Weaver would not have to answer for her insolence. Instead, he forced a smile to his lips. "Ah. You found me out. I confess; I made it up."

Relax. Lean back. Don't let her know how close she came.

He shifted the subject. "Are you dying that wool for Princess Diedre's cloak?"

"Aye." It was just a word, a single syllable, and plainly spoken at that. Yet in that single syllable, she'd somehow managed to convey both disapproval and an air of superiority.

Curran bristled in spite of himself. No warrior would tolerate such disrespect from a mere weaver. "I would know," he said more forcefully. "Will it be a sun cloak?"

"You shall know, good sir," she said with the same faintly disdainful excess of politeness, "if and when Princess Diedre chooses to reveal it." She checked the deepening yellow of the wool. "Until then, I would invite you to mind your own affairs. Questions can be dangerous, especially in this household."

Was that a threat?

Curran rose, incredulous.

It *was* a threat!

He closed the distance between them in a single stride.

She did not pull away or try to flee, but instead gripped the paddle with both hands as one would grip a stave, shifting her weight to the balls of her feet in a wider stance and waiting for him to make the first move. Just as he had been trained to do and in turn had trained so many others.

Again, she surprised him.

Then a flash of inspiration cleared up the mystery of The Weaver.

Of course. "So you're not a woman at all," he mused aloud. Only a warrior would respond as The Weaver had—a small warrior, but a well-trained one.

Hooded eyes jerked upward to regard him. "Why say you such a thing?" the voice snapped. "I am woman indeed."

Curran moved in closer. "Your reaction gave you away," he whispered. "And everyone in this room saw it. They've been watching us all along, hanging on our every word."

Reminded of that, The Weaver immediately substituted his defensive stance with his previously composed posture.

Curran returned to the bench, his curiosity deepened instead of allayed. Why would a lad—or a small warrior—insinuate himself in such a treacherous situation?

The truth came to him with chilling clarity: for the same reason Curran had decided to return to Burghead instead of remaining in Scone after delivering a message from Drust two months ago.

He had competition!

From the other side of the cauldron, Bera looked sidelong at the Dark Warrior and wished with all her might that there was some way to hurry the dye, though she knew there wasn't.

Things had gone awry so quickly, and now the legendary warrior was staring at her with a look as black as the clothes he always wore—a look that seemed to see straight through the cloak in which she hid. In a way, she wished he *could* see her as she was. Then he would abandon the preposterous notion that she was a boy.

Why had she let him pull her into conversation? Why, why, why? It was stupid and impulsive, and she was neither.

But the Dark Warrior had looked so handsome sitting there, his blue eyes brilliant, his strong, fair features reddened by cold and wind, his golden hair glowing in the firelight like some Nordic god. She'd caught only glimpses of him in the days since she'd come, but even those had been enough to catch her fancy.

Many bards, both here and at home, had sung of the Dark Warrior's ruthless valor and superhuman exploits, as well as his harsh, masculine beauty. The truth was, from the moment he had walked into the kitchens, she'd been just as curious about him as he seemed to be about her. But she still should have known better than to allow herself to be drawn into conversation with him, no matter how handsome he was.

Bera scowled, staring down at the coils of wool that swirled in the brilliant yellow dye.

The Dark Warrior was clever. He'd reasoned from the color of the dye that Princess Diedre was a sun creature, and so she was, but not because of her unfailingly even disposition, as everyone seemed to think. Underneath Diedre's carefully maintained air of calm, the "meek and obedient" princess burned with resentment and keen intelligence.

The name Diedre meant "raging," and despite her demure manner, Princess Diedre lived up to her name.

That was the portrait Bera would weave into the cloak while she worked out a way to free her brothers. But she never intended to finish it. God willing, she and her brothers would be gone before all the wool was dyed and the framework set.

The last thing she needed, though, was for the Dark Warrior to get the idea she was a boy! But how could she convince him otherwise without making things worse?

If he hadn't been so arrogant, speaking to her as if she were his familiar . . .

Bera's musings were cut short when the very man she was thinking about loomed beside her, his black-clad body shielding her completely from the others in the room. "Begging your pardon, Weaver, but I must know the truth or I won't sleep a wink. And I need my sleep."

Unseen by the others, he slipped his hand between the front panels of her cloak and slid his palm past her girdle to cup the apex of her legs. Before she could do anything but gasp, he explored the area with practiced precision, then withdrew his hand and stepped back, granting her a courtly bow and a hard smile. "Pray forgive me, good lady. That answers one question at least. But I am left, alas, with many more."

Shaking with outrage, Bera's hands gripped the paddle so hard her knuckles went white. It was all she could do to keep from breaking the tempered oak over the Dark Warrior's insolent head. The scoundrel! He deserved to die for such an intimate violation, and she silently lifted up a fervent prayer that no one else would deprive her of the pleasure.

The handsome warrior looked down at her. "Until we meet again, good lady." He strolled from the room to a whispered hum of conjecture by the servants.

Temples throbbing, Bera forced herself back to her stirring. *Some day*, she consoled herself. *You can kill him some day.*

She spent the next hour in a satisfying daydream of dismemberment, evisceration, torture, and beheading.

Curran slept fitfully that night and dreamed of The Weaver.

He followed her across open ground in a thick mist. Then the mist lifted, and—in the senseless way of dreams—The Weaver became his storm princess, naked on her steed, and he was riding after her, his body throbbing with lust. Over tall, forbidding crags, through huge clumps of bracken, down into steep, narrow gorges— again and again he came within inches of capturing the thick, reddish hair that streamed behind her, but always she eluded him.

When he woke in darkness, he was breathing hard, a mighty aching in his loins and the vivid image of his storm goddess still resonant in his mind.

The next ten days passed uneventfully for Bera. After her confrontation with the Dark Warrior, she ventured down to the kitchens to dye wool only when she knew he would be busy training. The rest of the castle's waking hours she spent spinning thread, planning the pattern for Princess Diedre's cloak, and modifying the large loom that scarcely left room to sleep in her chamber.

As for her audiences with Princess Diedre, she'd quickly learned all she needed in order to design the sun cloak, yet she continued to visit without pattern or explanation so that Diedre and the guards grew accustomed to her coming and going unchallenged.

Bera was just about to end one of those visits when the princess, without looking up from her incessant stitchery, issued a curt order to her pageboy: "Have the prisoner Evan brought to me."

Evan!

Bera stilled, willing herself to blend into the very walls so Princess Diedre wouldn't notice her.

Evan, alive. Here, in the same room.

Her heart pounding, she thanked the God that made her for this chance to see her brother, even as she prayed he wouldn't recognize her. Bera had kept her cloak a secret, but Evan was very observant. He might recognize her style of weaving and somehow betray her.

Then all would be lost indeed.

Even if he only commented on the cloak, it would draw attention to her presence, and the princess would surely ask her to leave.

She needn't have worried.

When Evan arrived—thin and dirty but otherwise healthy—he gave the hooded stranger by the fire only a passing glance before turning his full attention to the princess.

"Your highness." His bow conveyed a most convincing deference.

"Sit." Diedre spoke the order softly, almost as an invitation, and Evan obeyed. Without hesitation, he sank to the upholstered footstool beside his captor and gazed up at her.

What was going on here?

Did Evan know that the princess was behind everything that had happened?

He must not, for he seemed almost smitten.

Bera studied the two figures vignetted by the border of her deep hood. The princess looked down on Evan with open tenderness, and Evan returned her gaze with longing. No, not longing. Lust.

Her breath caught in her throat.

This was obviously not the first time Evan had been summoned. But why would the princess have sent for him in the first place? And why Evan instead of one of the others?

She could see why Evan might try to seduce the princess. Such a liaison would not only give him only influence with his royal lover, but also the power to destroy Diedre by revealing her infidelity to Drust.

Diedre, though, was far too calculating and self-controlled to risk such a dalliance.

Yet when Bera saw the way they were looking at each other, she wasn't quite so sure. She had never seen two people so besotted with each other.

The princess gently stroked his cheek. "Sing to me, Evan," she asked him, her expression unguarded and vulnerable. "I can almost bear it when you sing to me."

Bera bristled. He'd sung for her? How had Diedre gotten him to do that? No one, not even Bera, had been able to coax Evan to sing, not since his marriage to Fenella had gone sour.

But sing he did, at only a word from the dragon princess.

Unable to accept what she was seeing and hearing, Bera watched her brother close his eyes and heard him loose the deep, clear tones of his voice.

Softly, seductively, he began the tale of Saint Fínán's conception. He lingered long and poetic in describing the beauty of the saint's mother as she removed her clothing and waded naked into Loch Léin.

Looking at the princess, Bera was startled to see how

note by note, beat by rhythmic beat, word by sensual word, Evan's song transformed Diedre's longing to open desire. When he described how the magnificent red-gold salmon swam between the woman's legs and impregnated her, Bera's cheeks burned with embarrassment to hear such words come from her brother's mouth.

But when Evan sang of how a star came down from heaven and entered the woman's mouth, filling her bosom with golden light, causing her paps to shine like purest snow, the princess came undone. Her eyes locked to his, she hurled her needlework in Bera's direction. "Leave us," she ordered Bera, her voice harsh with need. "And tell the guards to let no disturb me. No one enters!"

Far from eager to see what came next, Bera hastened to do as she was bid. When she turned to shut the door behind her, though, she could not miss the sight of her brother and the dragon princess locked in a passionate embrace.

Appalled, she shoved the door closed with a thump. "Her highness has given strict orders that no one is to disturb her, not even her maid." She straightened under the protective shielding of her cloak and confronted the guards. "Is that clear?"

"An' who are *you* to give such orders?" one of them challenged.

Bera did not hesitate. She grabbed his larynx and pushed him hard against the wall, the pressure of her fingers immobilizing him. She rose up on her toes to bring her hooded face closer to his ear. "I am merely her highness's weaver," she said softly, "but in this case, I am also her highness's messenger, one who speaks your princess's express orders. You would do well to remember that and obey those orders on pain of death."

By the time the other sluggard had gathered enough wit to protest, Bera had released her captive. "Let no one disturb her highness," she repeated. "Not even Lord Drust."

"Drust?" the still-gasping sentry choked out. "But—"

"Whose wrath would you rather face?" she asked. "Your master's . . . or your mistress's?"

"Ooo. Remember Hastin?" the second guard asked his fellow. "One little slip an' . . ." He grimaced, his hand unconsciously shielding his manhood. "Ugly business, that."

The first guard hesitated, thinking. Then he nodded. "And Torg. Took him three days to die, screamin' all the way." He shot Bera a grudging look. "She's got a point, ya know."

"Aye," Bera confirmed. "So do as you are bid." She turned and headed for her room. Her brother would be safe from intrusions, at least. What Bera didn't know was how safe he would be in the princess's arms.

She winced. One little slip, and Evan could end up like Hastin.

She wondered if he'd sing as deeply then.

Late that night, when all but the sentries were sound asleep, Bera braided up her hair and pinned it out of sight beneath a tattered cap, then donned the ragged tunic, shoes, and gausses of a long-dead slave-boy.

So far, the disguise had worked. On the few occasions when she'd been caught searching for her brothers, the guards had easily dismissed the humpbacked slave-"boy" and his sullen complaints about being rousted from his pallet and sent to fetch a cure for flux for one of the warriors.

Now, when the fortress was dark and still, she completed her transformation, then crossed to the large pile of wool and yarn in the corner. Carefully, she reached deep until she felt the bulging bag she had hidden there.

She pulled it out and brought it to the tiny flame of her oil lamp.

Good. No holes gnawed in the coarse fabric, and the wineskin hadn't leaked. She opened the drawstrings. The bread had gone stale, but she saw no signs of mold on it or the baked parsnips she'd hoarded from her meals.

The princess hadn't even blinked when she'd asked for extra rations, to be eaten in privacy. Bera wasn't sure whether her thinness or the promise of the cloak had secured her request, but Diedre had promptly given the order.

Tonight would be the night she found her brothers, Bera told herself. It would have to be. She'd searched everywhere but the dungeons, and tonight, that was where she'd go.

She couldn't bear to think that her brothers might already be dead, their bodies tossed into a shallow grave or thrown out like offal, carrion for the wild dogs of the moors.

No, she told herself. She would find them, and all of them would be alive.

She dropped in two precious narrow rods of steel for picking locks. Then she pushed the bag up under the back of her tunic and secured it by tying a braided woolen belt across her hips. Checking her shadow, she positioned the "hump," then blew out her lamp and crept from her room into the torchlit hallway.

She managed to reach the stone tower and creep inside undetected, but once she found her way to the dark, narrow hallways within, the hair rose on the back of her neck. The air was thick with the smell of human misery—her brothers' misery. The thought of them crammed into a tiny cell, living in their own waste, brought stinging tears to her eyes, but she fought them down.

Don't take time to feel. Just find them.

Twenty careful steps later, the darkness seemed to lighten, and she heard the sound of snoring.

Thank you, blessed Saint Columba!

The guard must be asleep. Now, if he would only stay that way.

She crept forward, every tiny crick of her bones and scuff of her feet magnified in her own ears to terrifying proportion. But when she rounded the corner to find the guard stretched out on the cold stone floor as peacefully as if his bed were summer moss instead of winter stone, she got by him without a hitch.

Beyond his post, a stair only half again as wide as she was curved down and down to an armored wooden door with an enormous lock. At the bottom step, she looked up to the timbered ceiling fully fifteen feet above her head and saw the only opening, a horizontal ventilation slot so narrow Bera wasn't sure she could squeeze her head through it, even if she did reach it.

She had to try. Her brothers might be on the other side of that door. She had to get them food.

She tried not to think about being trapped in the bowels of the earth, but already, the walls seemed to be closing in on her. Resolute, she freed her precious cargo and hung it by the drawstrings from her shoulder. Then she straddled the space between the walls and began the arduous climb. Wishing she had longer legs, she stretched with all her might, prayed for divine protection, and fought her way to the ventilation slot. With every foot higher, her legs grew weaker and the stench grew stronger, but at last, she reached the stone sill.

It was a tight fit, but she squeezed her head and shoulders far enough inside to whisper safely, "Who's there?"

The darkness shifted far beneath her, intensifying the strong smell of waste and unwashed bodies. Bera knew the smell of those particular bodies, though.

She'd found them!

"Who's there?" a gruff whisper shot back at her.

Angus, taking charge as usual.

The sound of his voice swelled her chest with hope. "One who seeks nine brothers to set them free."

A palpable thrill of excitement set the bodies astir in earnest.

"We are only eight at the moment," another familiar voice said softly. "One of us is elsewhere having a poke."

Kegan, joking, even now!

"Shut up, you dunderhead," Fidach hissed. "We don't know who it is."

"Dunderhead yerself," Kegan retorted. "Don't you recognize your own sister's voice? It's Bera."

Faith, but it did her good to hear them bicker. It meant they were up to that, at least.

"*Bera*?" Roy, contentious as ever, spat her name more than said it. "What in three cauldrons of hell are *you* doin' here?" She sensed more than saw him stand to his feet. "We were expecting Boyd or Connal or Cusantin."

"Oh, aye," Becan countered in an angry rasp, whacking Roy with a dull thud. "I've told you a hundred times: They're men; they can't be spared. Bad enough there are only three to defend our families. It would be certain destruction to leave only two at home."

Only two? A surge of outrage set Bera's neck to throbbing. "And what about me?" she whispered far too loudly. "You don't even count me?"

"Shite, Bera!" Angus's gravelly whisper was tight with alarm. "Pipe down! There *is* a guard out there. You'll do us little good if they catch you, too!"

She dropped back to a more moderate level. "I whipped every one of your big hairy arses well and true, and you don't even *count* me to protect—"

"Oh, shush, Little Bit." She could hear the smile in

Airell's voice. "We'll settle all that later." His voice sobered. "How do you mean to get us out of here?"

All the vinegar abruptly left her. "I'm working on
that," she answered.

The fetid air shifted with an accompanying murmur
of disappointment.

"Are any of you injured?" she asked, ashamed that
she hadn't done so sooner. To her relief, her question
set loose a chorus of dry chuckles.

"They did not take us easy," Angus answered, "but
we're all healed well enough. Just weak from hunger
and bein' penned up night an' day."

Hunger! How could she have forgotten? "Wait, I
have food. And wine."

"No hurry," Airell whispered. "We haven't eaten all
of what you brought us last night."

"Last night?" Bera almost lost her balance.

"And before," Angus added. "But why have you
waited so long to tell us it was you?"

Because it hadn't been Bera!

"I'll explain all that later, once we're free," she said,
wondering who was working already to free them.

Someone had taken up her brothers' offer. She
couldn't think about that now, though. Time was ticking
away.

She hooked her knee on the ledge and eased clear of
the opening only long enough to pull the cords free of
her shoulder and extract her "hump." Then she wedged
herself back into the tiny slot, squeezed the bag through,
and thrust the hand holding it into the stinking dark. "It's
so dark in there. Can you see me?"

"Aye," Kegan answered, his voice thick with emotion. "And the food."

"I don't want to hit one of you—"

"By all the pregnant nuns in Dalraida," Roy scolded,
"just drop the food, woman."

"I put in two steel rods to try and pick the lock from your side. Don't eat them," she quipped. Bera stretched as far down as she could and released the cords. Judging from the time it took to reach the waiting hands of her brothers, the cell's floor was several feet lower than the door.

"Give the first food to Orrin," she heard Kegan say.

Orrin. Deaf, and dark as it was, he had no way of knowing she was there. Next time, she'd bring a flint and candle.

No one fought for food, but she could sense the strained impatience as her brothers rationed the precious sustenance among themselves. Their silence was more chilling than anything they might have said or done.

They *were* starving. The only reason they hadn't eaten what her rival had brought them was probably that they were rationing what little they had.

The silence broke right after Bera smelled the faint scent of wine in the stench.

"Ah. Nectar of heaven," Fidach murmured. She heard them pass the skin. When each man took a sip, every one of them, even Orrin, made some small sound of pleasure. And in that pleasure, there was hope.

She would free them, and soon. She had to. If only she had some inkling of a plan. But she didn't.

"I have to go now, but I'll be back."

"Wait," Kegan whispered. "Hold out your arm."

Bera did as he asked and felt the empty bag land neatly across her elbow. "I'll bring more as soon as I can," she whispered, doing her best to keep the sound of her tears from her voice.

She knew she must leave, but her heart wanted to stay.

"Take care, Little Bit." As always, Airell was concerned for her well-being. "Don't let them hurt you."

"Pity the fool who tries to hurt *me*," she shot back

with as much vinegar as she could muster. Then she realized that if anything went awry, this might well be the last time she would ever speak to her brothers.

"God be with you, Little Bit," the others murmured.

Partings had never been easy for her, but this . . . She forced her voice to remain resolute. "God be with you."

She wiggled back out and began her agonizing descent.

Only when she was safely back on her pallet, her bag and disguise hidden, did she allow the tears to come. *Please, blessed Saint Columba,* she prayed, *thwart my rival and help me get my brothers home again. Get us all back home.*

But their fate was not in St. Columba's hands. It was in Bera's, and she did not have a plan. Not yet.

chapter four

Time to get up. The fortress is stirring.

Bera burrowed deeper under her cloak and blanket. It couldn't be dawn already. She'd only just closed her eyes, which now felt glued shut.

Whoever your rival is, he's probably up already, her practical self prodded. *But you . . . anchored like a sluggard to your bed, when* he *is out there, even now, working to free your brothers before you do. And you will be his prize.*

That was all it took to bring her bolt upright, smack into the frame of the substantial loom that now took up most of her chamber.

"Ooch!" She rubbed the bump on her skull. As the throbbing faded, she realized that last night's foray had left her as stiff and sore as any of Angus's drubbings.

She'd grown soft so quickly here. Too much bread, not enough meat, and too little exercise. She resolved then and there to bring her body back to battle-ready sharpness.

But for now, she broke her fast with stale bread, staler beer, and a bit of cheese. When breakfast was served later, she would save it for her brothers.

After relieving herself, she crossed to the laver and splashed her grainy eyes awake with handfuls of icy spring water. The jolt brought her body alive, but her spirit dragged as if all the standing stones in Caledon were piled upon it.

She'd returned from the dungeon too edgy to sleep and lain awake for hours searching for a plan, trying to find some hope in the dismal realities she faced. They were hard realities. Burghead was all but impregnable, inside and out. There were guards everywhere, and the dungeon seemed escapeproof unless one had a key. How could she possibly get her brothers out alone?

Break it down, she remembered Evan lecturing her. *Set your priorities. What has to happen first, and how can you make it happen?*

Bera listed the tasks before her: most important, she must devise and execute an escape plan for her brothers; equally pressing, to find and thwart her adversary. Meanwhile, she had to fortify her brothers with food and wine without getting caught, and she had to do all this while coloring and spinning wool, then weaving it into a cloak fit for a princess.

Dejected, she scrubbed her teeth with a frayed twig, then rinsed.

For the first time since she had rushed into this desperate, impulsive quest, she wondered if she had only made things worse by coming. Maybe Moina was right; maybe she *was* being selfish, always wanting to do things her own way.

She'd been so sure she would know what to do once she got here, but the fortified peninsula seemed impregnable, from within as well as without. Seasoned guards kept close watch on every inch of the rugged shoreline, and a series of heavily defended gates made it all but impossible to escape by land.

She was only one; she had no horses, weapons, or boats for her brothers; and—much as she hated to admit it—she had to sleep sometime, rest, even if only a little.

Her nocturnal wanderings had taken their toll already.

No. She couldn't let herself think about the obstacles. Somehow, she would find a way. She had to. The lives and future of her whole family depended upon her.

So she completed her morning routines and tidied her chamber. By the time she was done, the flap of oiled parchment over her window glowed faintly with the first promise of sunrise.

Bera lifted the parchment and breathed in the clean, moist breath of the sea. High above in the cloudless winter sky, the brightest of the morning stars still held their place against the growing light. It helped somehow to see those stars, the same ones that greeted every dawn at Pitlanric. Encouraged, she inhaled another long, clean breath, then let it out slowly.

Don't you think it strange, though, she asked herself, *that a mere weaver would be given her own chamber—a chamber with a window—so close to Diedre's?*

It was odd . . . and disturbing. Bera let the parchment fall.

She had sensed immediately that this was an unwholesome place. Superficially, Burghead seemed like any other great chieftain's settlement, but underneath, the air roiled with intrigue and evil, curling coil on coil like a bucketful of deadly vipers. She had to get her brothers out, and soon, before the evil swallowed them all.

She had a jarring thought: What if her mysterious competitor had already worked out an escape plan. If they were to join forces . . .

But then she'd be helping him succeed, working toward her own undoing!

Yet she'd be freeing her brothers. That was all that mattered now. She couldn't think of herself, only that.

She would marry the devil himself, if that was what it took to bring her brothers safely home.

Bera drew on her cloak and raised the hood. Odd, the effect it had. Off the training field when she was simply Bera, she couldn't seem to keep from bumping into furniture, dropping the crockery, and spilling things. But the moment she donned the cloak, she became the mysterious Weaver who glided, graceful as a ghost, from room to room in regal silence.

So it was the smooth, silent Weaver who gathered her distaff and a cloud of freshly carded blood-red wool.

Outside in the hallway, she took only a few steps before she noticed something at the far end of the dim hallway. "Who's there?" she challenged, her dagger in hand.

No response.

It was small, whatever it was, curled into the corner like a hedgehog.

Slowly, carefully, she moved closer and closer until at last she could see that it was a child—a quaking, terrified child clad in rags. Bera crouched near it, but kept her dagger in hand. "It's all right," she soothed. "I won't hurt you."

A dirty little face turned to peer askance at her. Bera's heart ached at the fear she saw in those hazel eyes.

Then she remembered the cloak she was wearing. "Don't be afraid of my cloak, little one. I'm just a weaver, not a sorceress."

The tight knot of child eased slightly.

"What's your name, child?"

"Osann." The voice was small, like the rest of her.

A girl's name. "My chamber is just down the hallway," Bera said softly. "You'll be safe there, and we can talk in private. Will you come with me?"

Osann glanced left and right, unwilling or unable to move.

"I have some rolls and cheese in my chamber," Bera said. "We could eat."

Fear battled hunger, and hunger won out. The little girl stood. She was still wary of being seen, so Bera walked beside her back to her chamber, shielding her from detection.

Osann looked to be about six, but small for her age, and dangerously thin. Her tiny feet were bound with rags. Her brown hair hadn't been washed or combed in far too long, and the clothes she wore looked like castoffs from a churl.

"I'd like to be your friend," Bera offered, but Osann just looked up at her with suspicion. Poor child. Her eyes were those of an old woman.

Once they reached her chamber, Bera closed the door, then turned to find Osann gazing in awe at her loom, yarns, and colorful array of dyed fleece.

"Those are my weaving things," she said as she fetched some bread and cheese for the frail little girl.

When Osann saw the food, she at last reacted like a normal child. Her whole face lit up, adorable dimples punctuating her cheeks. "Oh, thank you!" she said softly. She cradled the food in her lap as if it were some great treasure. "Aren't you going to eat?" the emaciated little girl asked. "There's plenty here for both of us."

Such generosity from one so hungry tugged at Bera's heart. "Thank you, precious, but I have just eaten. Go ahead. We can talk while you eat."

Osann tore a hungry chunk from the bread, then shivered with delight. "Mmmm. So soft," she said through her mouthful. "And not moldy."

"That was a dangerous thing to do, playing so close to the princess's chamber," Bera said with concern. "Your family would be frantic if they knew you'd taken such a risk."

"I have no family," Osann said, working on another mouthful.

"No one?" Again, Bera's heart went out to the little girl.

Osann shook her head. "I never had a papa. My mommie died . . ." Bera could sense Osann's childish mind grappling with time, then giving up. "Sometime very long ago. I try to remember her, but it's harder and harder."

"Who took you in when your mother died?"

Those old-woman eyes looked up at Bera as if she'd just said something very stupid. "No one."

Children could not survive without *someone*. "What is your job, then?"

"I don't have one." Osann took a tiny bite of cheese and closed her eyes, savoring the flavor on her tongue.

Everyone had a job to do, even a child. "But how do you survive?"

"I hide," Osann said matter-of-factly.

The life she described seemed bleak indeed. Some day, Osann would be discovered. And when she was, she would be ill-used. Bera couldn't bear to think of what would happen then.

"I have need of a body servant," she said on impulse. "If I can get the princess's permission, would you like to be my body servant?"

Osann's hazel eyes widened, but she remained suspicious. Little wonder.

"The work will not be difficult, and there will be plenty of food," Bera coaxed, using the tone she would to lure some wild, wounded little creature from its hiding place. Osann had been hiding in more ways than one, and Bera knew that trust would not come easy for the little girl. "We can even get you some new clothes. How about it?"

Osann nodded as if she expected to wake up and find this had all been just a dream.

"Wonderful. I am going to see the princess even

now." Bera picked up her wool and distaff. "Wait here for me. No one will disturb you." She chuckled. "I think they're all afraid of my cloak." She paused. "Are you afraid of my cloak?"

"Nay, my lady."

"Good for you. You are brave. I like that." Bera exited into the hallway and closed the door behind her.

She'd never visited the princess so early. Doing so would be an excellent test of whether or not she'd become as unremarkable a presence as Diedre's cats. She glided down the corridor and was admitted to the dragon's lair without so much as a glance from the guards.

Better still, the princess herself took no notice, too absorbed with scribing at her worktable to look up. Bera would ask her about Osann later. Passing by the princess, she recognized the complicated symbols. Latin.

Years ago she'd badgered Father Maclin into teaching her Latin despite his wife's vocal disapproval. But Bera had never been much of a scholar. The baffling cipher had proved too difficult, so she'd contented herself with Ogam.

It did not surprise her, though, that Diedre had mastered the language of priests and kings. It seemed a fitting medium for the dragon princess's relentless manipulations and consuming ambition.

Silently, Bera settled on a cushion in her usual spot and began to spin. No sooner had she lost herself in the mindless rhythm of her task than her thoughts returned to the one who was working to free her brothers. Someone had accepted Boyd's offer, but who?

None of the chieftains; she had heard enough to know they all had lands and wives of their own.

One of the warriors, then?

Perhaps, but there were almost two hundred of them, and their loyalty to their thane was legend. Every man among them had risked his life time and again in blind devotion to Drust.

Still, one of them might wish to better himself by marrying a princess. But how could she possibly ferret out a single conspirator among so many?

She decided to investigate the warriors last.

The most logical suspect would be a stranger—someone only lately come to Burghead. But the only people besides her who fit that description were the Dark Warrior and Owen the singer.

She ruled out the Dark Warrior immediately. What use would he have for lands and a wife? What reason to settle down to the mundane struggle for survival? His deadly calling had already brought him wealth and fame beyond any she could offer. As for rank, no man who cared about rank would ever take the shameful work of mercenary.

No. It couldn't be the Dark Warrior.

More's the pity, came an unexpected thought, punctuated by the vivid memory of his compelling presence by the cookfires. An even more outrageous notion followed: What would it feel like to handle him as he had handled her? To touch his manhood, cup its weight?

Just thinking about it caused a disconcerting sense of fullness in her secret places.

Ballocks and Banshis! Had she lost her mind? The man must have bewitched her, put a spell on her!

True, he was the handsomest and most fascinating rogue she'd ever seen. But he was also a cold-blooded killer, loyal to no one but himself, a man without a soul, much less a heart. To join with him would be to mate with death.

She shivered at the very thought and hastened to recite a proof against evil spells. Then she directed her wandering thoughts back to a more likely suspect: the bard Owen. He was a small man—nothing like Bera's idea of a knight-errant. Yet his dark, deep-set eyes held a glint of intensity that blossomed to a flame when he brought life to tales of heroes dead and living, and to the legends of the Old Ways.

He just might be the one.

She would investigate later in the day. But for now, she must spin her thread of fire . . . and weave a plan to free her brothers.

Less than an hour passed before Bera heard the sound of heavy footfalls, coarse complaints, whining children, and grumbling men grow louder and louder until a knock sounded at the princess's door.

Malisande rose silently from her seat and went to see who it was.

Bera heard whispers outside in the hallway, then Malisande closed the door. She shot Bera a suspicious glance on her way to murmur her message to her mistress.

The dragon princess's alabaster brow wrinkled, but only momentarily. "Dear me. Can it have been a month already?" She set aside her own handwork and straightened her wimple. "Very well. Show them in."

Eight hulking warriors of various ages—all of them bearing uncanny resemblance to Drust—filed into the chamber. Behind them, a procession of small-eyed, sullen women followed, bringing with them so many dirty, boisterous children, babies, and nurses that there was scarcely room to stand.

Yet none came near where Bera sat. Perhaps it was her cloak, but even the children seemed afraid to get too close.

Seemingly intent on her spinning, Bera watched as one by one, Diedre's sons and their families paid grudging homage to the matriarch of their clan.

Diedre received their tribute as her due, but Bera saw

no affection in her eyes, only thinly veiled contempt for the sons she had borne.

Then a quiet, sad-eyed young woman great with child entered from the hallway. Instantly, the visitors radiated resentment.

Diedre, though, took one look at her daughter and came to life. She opened her arms. "Alma, darling. What a treat."

Alma glanced uncomfortably toward her departing brothers and their families, clearly embarrassed by her mother's blatant favoritism.

Here was the child of Diedre's heart. The transformation was amazing; for the first time since Bera had met the princess, Diedre seemed happy. "Sit, dearest, and tell me all about how you're feeling."

Malisande brought a chair and set it close for the princess. Heavily burdened with child, Alma put her hand to her lower back and plunked to the seat. "Oh, Mother. I can scarcely breathe. And I haven't slept more than two hours at a time since I saw you last."

"Poor darling." Diedre took her daughter's hand between her own. "How well I remember." She cocked her head and regarded Alma with tenderness. "It won't be long now."

Alma shifted in her chair. "I just want to be able to put this baby *down*."

Bera felt like a spy, witnessing the intimate exchange. Then she remembered she *was* a spy.

The two women shared a companionable chuckle, then Alma sobered. "Were you afraid when I was born?"

"Aye." For just a moment, Diedre looked young as a girl, and vulnerable. "Every woman worth her salt is afraid to have her first baby." She smiled. "Perhaps that's why God allows us to become so uncomfortable at the last, so we'll be so grateful to be delivered that we won't be frightened."

"You always know just the right thing to say." Alma struggled to her feet. "Forgive me, Mother, but I must beg your leave. My back is aching so, I think I'll go lie down."

"Malisande," Diedre summoned. "See her highness safely to her bed, then go to the apothecary and fetch her some of my special calming tea."

"Yes, your highness." The two women departed, leaving Bera alone with Diedre.

Oblivious to her presence, the princess picked up her handwork and began to stitch.

"Your highness," Bera said quietly

"Aye?" As usual, Diedre did not bother to look up.

"It has come to me that I could work much faster if I had some help, a child perhaps."

Diedre looked at her then, one eyebrow arched in disapproval. "A servant? For a weaver?"

"Nay, great lady. Nothing so elevated as a servant," Bera hastened to amend. "But I came upon an outcast child this morning. She is frail and would die soon unless someone takes her in. It seemed to me that if I shared my food with her, she might come to some use."

"A girl-child?"

"Aye, your highness. I would judge her to be four or five, perhaps six. She is so frail, I cannot really tell her age."

"Why would you want such a frail thing, then?" Diedre countered, clearly suspicious. "How could she possibly be anything but a bother?"

"She is bright, your highness. She could fetch things for me while I am at the loom. And I could teach her to set my bobbins."

"You eat as much as two grown men already," Diedre said, resuming her handwork. "I will not grant you more rations."

"I would not presume to ask for such a thing," Bera

said, relieved that Diedre had brought up the specifics of such an arrangement. That meant she would agree. Now all Bera had to do was wait.

She resumed spinning in silence.

Diedre said nothing for a great while, but eventually she acceded. "Very well. You may use the child. But remember, she belongs to me."

"Of course, your highness. Your highness is most generous." Bera settled back to her spinning.

The sun was well risen before Diedre spoke next. "Enough, Weaver. I'm expecting a guest. Gather your wool and leave me to myself."

"As you wish, your highness," Bera answered, but she took her time collecting her things in hope that the guest might again be Evan.

Please, dear Lord, let it be Evan. I'd be grateful for even a glimpse of him. Please.

But the tall figure that loomed in the doorway wasn't Evan. It was the Dark Warrior.

Bera couldn't help staring at the stark silhouette that tapered from broad shoulders to a narrow waist and hips, his powerful legs planted solidly apart, ready for a fight.

A faint shudder rippled through her. Whether it was dread, revulsion, or irrational attraction, she did not know.

"Let him pass," the princess absently instructed her guards.

The short doorway forced him to bow low in order to enter. Seeing him humbled thus, Bera couldn't help wondering if the door's diminutive height was by the princess's design. Drust, too, would have to enter like a suppliant.

But when the mercenary straightened to the full extent of his impressive stature, all thought of the princess fled.

He seemed too large, too angular for this draped and

womblike place. His pale Viking coloring and stark
black clothes were as out of place amid the riot of hue
and pattern as a gleaming iron blade upthrust in a patch
of wildflowers. His very presence radiated power . . . and
peril.

He scanned the room with cold blue eyes as sharp as
any eagle's.

She had not feared him when they bandied words
beside the cookfire. Even when he'd violated her person,
she'd been outraged, not afraid. But seeing him now . . .
Diedre might be a dragon, but this man was shadow
given substance, not flesh and blood but ice and iron—
with the aura of death.

As if he sensed what she was thinking, he fixed her
with a look so piercing she almost dropped her distaff.
Wishing she had left the moment she'd been asked to,
Bera glanced to the princess and was annoyed to find
Diedre smiling, clearly amused by the silent exchange
between her Weaver and her hired killer.

Bera made for the door in a huff, keeping as far from
the mercenary as possible, but when she passed him, he
turned with a salacious smile and granted her an exaggerated bow. "Ah. The *lady* Weaver."

Flushing now from head to toe, she left the room
without acknowledging him.

Curran hated to see The Weaver go. Their conversation
by the fire had raised more questions than it had answered, intriguing him. And he did not relish being left
alone with the princess. He'd rather be thrown naked
into a bear pit.

He fingered the grip of his sword, weighing the risk.
Lord Drust was hunting, but he might return unexpect-
edly and find them together alone. But if Curran's suspicions about Princess Diedre proved true, none of that
would matter.

His hand still on his sword, he watched in silence as the princess abandoned her worktable for the magnificent fur-draped throne by the fire. She picked up her needlework and sat.

"You sent for me," he challenged. "Why?"

She did not chastise him for his rudeness. She didn't even frown. She just stitched away, her manner pleasant. "My goodly lord husband has told me of your directness. 'Tis an admirable quality in battle." She paused interminably without deigning to look up. "But when speaking with your superiors, such an approach might be misconstrued as disrespect."

"A warning well taken, your highness," Curran emphasized the last, more certain than ever he was addressing the true thane of Burghead.

At last, she met his gaze, motioning to a low footstool at her feet. "Pray, sit. You've been working very hard to train our warriors."

Curran's blood boiled, but he kept his outrage buried. "I prefer to stand, thank you." He would rather die on his feet than sit like a child on a Caledonian princess's footstool.

The princess was not amused. "I bid you sit, sir. To do so in my presence is an honor. To refuse ... truly, I cannot fathom the depth of such an insult."

Curran hated intrigue, and the princess's chamber was rank with it. But this was how the game was played, so he sat.

The result was worse than he'd imagined. His sword and hauberk dragged the floor, and his knees were halfway to his chin, airing his privates and leaving him nowhere to put his arms. Furious, he turned a bland expression to the princess, who had the gall to laugh!

"Nobly done, sir," she managed between melodious giggles.

Her laughter was in keeping with her carefully constructed façade of feminine virtue, but completely out of character with the manipulative viper he knew her to be. Disgusted, he forced his expression to remain calm.

Curran had no patience with women who tried to be icons of womanly virtue. Nor did he like the fashionable image of feminine beauty Diedre personified with her small pointed chin, bowed lips, high forehead, flat facial structure, and slightly protruding eyes. He preferred women whose strong spirits lit fire in their eyes. Women who were honest and lived life fully.

"Do get up," the princess urged. "You shall have my chair, and I shall take another."

They rose as one, Curran's anger tempered by grudging admiration. How skillfully she had manipulated him, humbling him only to rescue his pride by humbling herself even more. He'd have to remember that.

"Sit, sir. Sit. You've earned the privilege." She indicated her own empty chair as she went to fetch another.

Curran did as she asked, but not without trepidation. If someone were to see him thus . . . No sooner was he settled in the throne than the princess drew a light, armless chair next to his outstretched legs and sat down facing him, close enough to touch his chin. Too close.

Instinctively, he crossed his legs at the ankles and leaned away from her. It had been a long time since anyone, man or woman, had dared to crowd him thus.

The princess looked deep into his eyes. "Few warriors posses that kind of self-control," she said with admiration. "Most would have blustered the air blue or stormed out rather than place themselves in such a laughable position."

"So it was a test," he observed. "I wondered."

She searched his face, making him even more uneasy, prompting him to stare back in challenge. This close, she could not so easily conceal the intelligence behind her placid expression. Nor the ambition.

Or was she simply allowing him to see, and if so, why?

Curran was certain he'd hidden the questions that were going through his mind, but he must have betrayed something.

"Ah." Her gray-green eyes narrowed. "I see you are every bit as clever as I hoped. That pleases me."

Why was she paying him such attention now, months after he'd arrived? "I am your highness's to command."

"I rather doubt that," she said without rancor. "But you have proven useful."

Curran decided to respond to such frankness in kind. "So it was you who hired me, not Drust."

Instantly, her features congealed. "You may be clever, sir," she clipped out, her quiet tone as hard as the dark stone sea cliffs on which the fortress stood. "But you could use a lesson in discretion."

"I am a warrior, madam, not a statesman," he countered flatly. "Why have you summoned me here?"

It pleased him to see a flash of anger in her eyes, but no sooner had she betrayed herself than she reverted to her prim, wifely demeanor. "I suppose allowances must be made," she murmured in a condescending tone. "A man such as you, no breeding, no proper manners."

"Aye, your highness." Curran allowed himself a satisfied smile. "A man such as I." He sobered. "Who asks you yet again, why have you summoned me here?"

Her gaze lowered to her handwork. "It's no secret that we have hostages within the fortress, and no secret who they are," she said calmly. "It's also common knowledge that their brothers have offered a compelling reward for any man who can free them."

Curran froze. How had she found out? And how much did she know?

As always when he was cornered, time seemed to slow. The princess lifted her gaze to meet his, her expression as flat as a painted Madonna's. "Naturally, my lord husband is most concerned. He has asked me to question you."

She knew! He could see it in her eyes.

But why confront him here, alone, with no witnesses? It made no sense.

The familiar coldness of battle-haze tingled through him, slowing his breathing, magnifying every sound, every movement around him.

"I can't imagine why he involved me, a mere woman," she continued in her girlish voice, "but as always, I am my husband's to command."

In any other circumstance, Curran would have appreciated the deft irony with which she'd turned his own words back at him, but he was too preoccupied readying himself to fight or flee.

"So I have summoned you privately to enlist your services in finding this spy among us." She blinked up at him. "You will be compensated, of course. Lord Drust has recently taken lands and cattle near Nigg. For your help in this, he bids me offer them to you. As his knight and vassal." She granted him a simper of a smile. "Your sword, of course, will no longer be your own to sell, but Lord Drust considers it a fair bargain. I think it most generous, myself."

Drust, indeed!

Now Curran understood, and all too well.

The offer was a bribe, a most impressive one: abandon his efforts to free the hostages in exchange for lands, cattle, rank . . . and Drust's—or more accurately, Diedre's—foot upon his neck. It was not the slavery of his childhood, but it was slavery, nonetheless. The very thought of it made him shake with outrage. He'd sacrificed everything for his freedom: his family, his honor, his very soul. And she had the nerve to think he would become one of Drust's creatures!

Yet he had little choice but to accept, even though he only did it for show. He would not live to see the morrow if he didn't.

This unexpected change might even work to his advantage. "A most generous offer—one no sane man would refuse." Deliberately, he eased back into the soft furs. A few key concessions were needed before he agreed. "There might be more than one spy, you know. I have my suspicions."

"Mmmmm." Diedre's expression remained bland, but he knew he'd surprised her. She'd heard nothing of another conspirator because there wasn't one. He'd planted the notion to divert further suspicion.

"If there is another," the princess said as casually as if she were discussing the weather, "Lord Drust would expect you to eliminate them. A reasonable request, don't you think, considering the richness of your reward."

The woman was clever, changing the terms for her own benefit after the agreement had been made, but Curran was in no position to argue, and they both knew it.

"I would need free access throughout the fortress," he countered, "even to the prisoners themselves. I could pose as their rescuer, perhaps learn something from them."

Her features hardened. "Doubtless, you will be most convincing in such a role." She arched a skeptical eyebrow and considered. Then she rose, bringing Curran to his feet.

Diedre lifted one of the silver necklaces that disappeared into her neckline and removed it, exposing the sturdy iron key that had been hanging concealed beneath her bliaut. She proffered it. "This opens the dungeon."

The princess fluttered her stubby eyelashes. "Don't worry. I have others."

Curran took the key, surprised to find it so warm. He hadn't thought the cold-blooded princess capable of such heat.

He draped the chain over his own head and dropped the key behind his black tunic. "And my freedom within the fortress?"

"The order shall be given," she said demurely. "You will be careful, of course. Such subterfuges are fraught with danger. Why, one false step, and your life could be forfeit—" She snapped her delicate fingers. "—this quickly."

Curran understood perfectly. "There shall be no false steps."

"Let us hope not." She reclaimed her seat on the throne. "You are dismissed."

Curran bowed, then pivoted and left.

The quest had turned deadly, for the hunter had now become prey.

chapter five

Bera had almost finished spinning the scarlet wool when she felt a prickling at the back of her neck. She paused. "Osann?"

Silence.

Of course it wasn't Osann. The child was quiet, but Bera always heard her coming.

Resuming her work, she felt the prickle again. Probably just the bothersome proof of someone's evil thoughts of her. But instinct prompted her to turn and face the closed door.

What she saw drove the air from her lungs and set her heart alurch.

The Dark Warrior, here inside her chamber, staring at her with lethal intensity!

How in blazes had he managed to get in without alerting her? She'd heard nothing!

More important, why had he come?

He'd met with the princess, probably just come from her chamber. Was he here now on Diedre's orders?

He made no move, just stood there watching, his lean, dangerous presence crowding her small stone cubicle unbearably, his steady breath clouding the frigid air between them. Bera recognized that watching, waiting stillness; she went there herself when preparing to strike.

Did he mean to kill her?

No. If that were true, she'd be dead already.

Then why was he here?

Years of training transformed her initial shock into deadly survival reflex. Her senses sharpened to brittle clarity; she swiftly evaluated her opponent. He was dressed for court, not combat. Yet though he appeared unarmed, Bera knew better. Her gaze darted from the soft black suede of his boots to the telltale impression of a hidden lashing across a powerful thigh, to the wide black leather girdle that spanned his narrow hips. Oh aye, he was armed, but so was she.

Her hand retracted smoothly through the slit in her cloak and found one of her three concealed daggers.

She silently cursed the knave for sneaking up on her, and doubly cursed herself for letting him.

Was he trying to rattle her? He'd already done that by opening her door, slipping inside, and closing it behind him without betraying his presence.

It occurred to her that he might be a *taisch*, a fetch instead of flesh, and a shiver of foreboding chased down her arms, but she did not falter.

Flesh or spirit, it made no matter. Whatever he wanted, he wouldn't get it.

The hungry warmth of battle-lust brought her to her feet. "Get out," she said, her voice low with warning.

She was certain she detected an incongruous flicker of amusement in his steady blue eyes.

Let him think he had the upper hand, she told herself. He'd find out otherwise soon enough.

Smooth and silent as a ghost, he closed the distance between them, all the while keeping his empty hands in plain sight. He halted so close she could smell the scent of smoke and sea salt in his immaculate black tunic and golden hair, mingled with the unmistakable smell of a man.

He was flesh and bone, all right. She could feel his heat even stronger than the waning coals in her brazier.

Bera had never been so close to a man who was not her brother. His nearness tempered the fear she hid, sending an intoxicating thrill from her secret parts to her whole body. Disconcerted though she was by that, she did not back away, for his closeness made it easier to kill him with one well-aimed stab.

Unflinching, she looked up into his cold blue eyes. "What do you want?"

"To see what you hide beneath that hood," he responded in a tone that made her wonder what he would do to her once he'd seen.

She remembered the arrogant way he had cupped her sex. He'd already handled her like a whore. Had he come here now to make her one?

She glared at him with scorn. Let him try to ravish her! He would die for it.

Aye, her practical self warned. *You can kill him, but what then? How will you dispose of the body? Such a big body, and an important one. He'll be missed immediately. And if you're discovered . . . A weaver for a warrior? Drust won't see that as a fair exchange. Cloak or no cloak, it'll be into the cauldron with you, and—*

The inner voice silenced abruptly when her uninvited guest shoved back her hood and caught hold of her shoulders so he could subject her to a cynical inspection.

She hadn't realized how dependent she'd become on seeing the world without being seen until he stripped away the hood, exposing her. He had done it on purpose to get the upper hand, yet she managed to hide the sudden vulnerability she felt.

But the flash of disappointment in his eyes when he

first looked on her face . . . That, she would not easily forget.

Bera knew she was far from beautiful, but with that one look, the arrogant intruder had landed a stinging blow to her woman's heart.

"You mongrel," she spat out even as she brought her dagger up hard against the flesh just below his breast-bone. "How dare you violate my privacy and gawk at me as if I were some slave-girl?"

He froze, his hands spread in midair on either side of her head. "Nice move. I scarcely felt that coming."

"You never felt it coming at all," she said smoothly.

His answering smile conceded nothing.

"I told you to get out," she repeated.

His only response was to lean harder into her dagger. She felt the elegant fabric of his tunic rip, then his bliaut, then the unmistakable resistance of bare flesh against the razor-sharp tip. That too gave way as he forced the cold metal just below the surface of his skin.

Clearly, he did not think her capable of thrusting the dagger home.

Her pulse pounded even heavier at the insult, but she turned the outrage into ice. "Don't make me kill you," she threatened.

"You won't. Not here. Not now." He addressed her as an equal, though his tone was smug. "It would raise too many questions, draw too much attention."

"No one would ever know," she said smoothly. "You would simply disappear." She wouldn't mind killing him—not just for his violation of her chamber, her privacy, and her person, but for his obvious disappointment when he'd seen her face.

The trouble was, he was right. She didn't want to kill him. Not here. Not now. Bera had neither the time nor the inclination to cover a killing in broad daylight.

She simply wanted him to leave. "Back away slowly, and you may leave with your life."

For the first time, his handsome face showed signs of animation. "You're a bold, stubborn little thing, aren't you?" He was enjoying their dangerous dance, she could tell.

"You're not leaving," she stated flatly, wondering again what he really wanted of her.

She had dreamed of this Dark Warrior, for even old maids had yearnings and could dream. But in her dreams whenever she had gotten close to him—reached out to touch and be touched—the handsome warrior had become diffuse, as insubstantial as fog.

He was anything but insubstantial now. She could smell his man's scent filling her nostrils, feel the solid substance of his hardened body against her blade, experience the heat and tension of the space he occupied.

But why was he here?

"Have we reached an impasse?" she asked archly.

No sooner were the words out of her mouth, than she felt a sharp prick of cold metal in her ear.

"*Now* we've reached an impasse," he murmured with grim amusement.

At the edge of her vision, she could just make out his hand holding the slender dagger he'd inserted into her ear.

His sleeve! Of course. She should never have let his hands so close.

"One false move," he said quietly, "and we're both dead. Is that what you want?"

"That depends." He might be bluffing, but she wasn't. "What do *you* want? Why did you come here, really? The truth, or we both die."

His smile broadened, exposing white, even teeth. "I told you. I wanted to see what you were hiding beneath that hood."

"You've seen me," she shot back. "Yet you're still here."

The Dark Warrior said nothing, only stared at her with that maddening, superior expression that dismissed her as both warrior and woman.

To her horror, she heard herself speak aloud the defensive question that formed in her mind. "You have seen me, then. What think you of the woman you uncovered?" Where did *that* come from?

His frank gaze darted from feature to feature. "An unremarkable face—"

Unremarkable! Bera bristled, yet she managed to cloak the outrage that threatened to erase ten years of training.

"—yet oddly ageless." He kept his own expression as blank as hers, but it was the eyes that could not lie, so she watched his closely while he inspected her. "I see a few creases at the eyes, but the jawline is firm . . ." His pupils dilated when he scanned her neck. "The skin tight, sun-stained as a man's, neither poxed nor scarred nor marked with wohl."

He flicked past her eyes. "Dark eyes, brown or black."

They're brown! she railed in silence.

A brief circuit dismissed her hair. "Dark hair drawn back severely." He leveled his gaze to hers. "That is what I see."

"Now tell me why." None of the rest mattered, only that.

"Why what?"

"Why was it so important to see my face?" Bera asked coldly. "And don't pretend it was idle curiosity. I've watched you; there's nothing idle about you."

He shrugged. "You kept it hidden. Hidden things are dangerous. Secrets are dangerous."

If only he knew how dangerous. "And what is *your* secret?" she countered.

His cynical smile was hardly reassuring. "I am made of secrets. Without them, I would not exist."

An elegant answer.

"Have you other plans for this day?" he asked with more than a hint of sarcasm, "or do you intend to remain as we are until one of us wilts?" He cocked a golden eyebrow. "It won't be me."

He had a point. Already, her hand was numb from holding her dagger at the ready.

Blast. Why hadn't he accepted her offer to let him leave? Her neck was getting stiff from trying not to move her head, and the muscles in her arm were beginning to tremble with fatigue.

She would not serve her brothers by killing or by dying this day. How could she get him to stand down?

She thought of her brothers and the way they resolved such confrontations.

Of course. What she needed was a compromise or some simple, pride-saving gesture. The man towering over her seemed an unlikely candidate for compromise, so she opted for a pride-saving gesture.

Not that her own pride couldn't use a little saving.

She wracked her brain for endless seconds before an inspiration struck her. "I propose a bargain." She cocked her own half-smile. "You got what you wanted; you've seen my face. Grant me the answer to a simple question, and honor will be satisfied. For now, at least."

"Hmmm." He freshened his grip on his dagger, considering.

Bera understood his hesitation. "I'll even tell you the question."

That caught his interest. "Tell it, then."

"I would know your name."

His face betrayed surprise . . . and suspicion, but she

could see him wavering. "That's not a question."

"A request, then. Just your name," she urged. "The one your mother called you." She saw a flicker at the mention of his mother and was encouraged.

"A bold little thing indeed. I'll give you that." He said it with an interesting mixture of annoyance and admiration. "And fearless."

"Not fearless," Bera confessed. "Fear is useful. It sharpens my senses and gives me strength. But I'm not afraid of you," she said and meant it.

The silence between them lengthened, intensifying her awareness of just how tall and strong and close he was.

Perhaps she *should* be afraid of him.

"Curran," he said tightly at long last. "My name is Curran."

She felt his dagger ease from her ear and gratefully retracted hers. Both of them took a step backward, weapons still in hand.

"Curran." She tried the name and liked the sound of it.

He glowered at her. "Know it, but say it not."

"Curran," she promptly repeated, as much to please herself as to bother him.

"By all the pitch in all the oceans," he growled. "Already, I regret myself. I had my dagger in your ear—"

"While *my* dagger was poised to strike your heart," she reminded him.

"You were at the disadvantage."

"Hah." She'd endured enough of his arrogance. "So I let you think, but—"

Both of them said at exactly the same time: "I could easily have disarmed you."

A beat of surprised silence followed, then Bera burst out laughing. How absurd, both of them, pecking away at each other like two old roosters.

The Dark Warrior—Curran—glared at her, then slid his dagger back up his sleeve. He turned to storm out just as Osann opened the door.

The poor child took one look at him and slid to the floor in boneless terror.

Bera rushed past him. "Osann, child!" She scooped the frightened little girl into her arms and carried her to the pallet, where she sat, cuddling her close. Fear had sucked what little warmth there was from her frail arms and legs, so Bera tucked a warm blanket around her. "Here, now. The Weaver is here. No one's going to hurt you." She scowled up at the Dark Warrior, only to find an inquisitive gleam in his eye.

"And who is this?" he asked.

Bera's heart sank. She'd reacted on instinct to protect Osann, but in showing her affection for the little girl, she had placed the child in grave peril. Would the Dark Warrior use the child to get to her?

But she could not undo what had already been done. The beer was out of the bucket, and it would do no good to second-guess herself.

As always when she'd made a mistake, Bera went on the offensive. "Big, brave warrior," she accused. "You frightened the life from her."

He studied them both with odd intensity. "Who is she?"

"She's mine," Bera answered fiercely, rubbing Osann's arms through the blanket. At the anger in her voice, Osann tensed.

"No, she's not."

Bera didn't like the speculative way he said it. Not wanting to further upset the child, though, she forced herself to speak conversationally. "And how would you know?"

"I've watched you since you came. There was no child." His eyes narrowed. "I can find the truth easily enough. Do you want me asking questions about her, bringing up your name?"

Insufferable man. He went straight for the soft spot. "The child *is* mine, in a way." Bera crossed her arms protectively over Osann. "She had no one, so I took her in."

Abruptly, the curiosity in his demeanor hardened, along with his voice. "As a slave?"

"As a *child*," she shot back. "A cold, hungry child in need of love and protection." She bent her lips to Osann's ear and murmured, "You're safe now. I'm here."

As swiftly as it had shown itself, his anger disappeared. He looked from Bera to Osann and back. "You care for her," he said, puzzled.

"Aye. I care for her." His reaction baffled Bera. She'd expected him to gloat that he'd found a weakness, a way to manipulate her. But instead, he seemed genuinely surprised. "What matter is that to you?"

Curran looked at her as if seeing her for the first time. "It matters much." To her amazement, he extended his hand toward Osann's back, his expression asking permission to touch.

At Bera's nod of consent, he stroked the little girl's back with surprising tenderness.

Osann flinched as if she'd been struck at first, but when the large, callused hand did her no harm, she subsided into tense stillness.

"It's all right, child," Bera soothed. "No one will ever hurt you again, if I can help it."

To her amazement, Curran added his own assurance to hers. "Fear not. No harm will come to her from me."

From the conviction in his voice, Bera could almost believe it.

He exhaled heavily. "You surprise me, Weaver, and it's been a long time since I was surprised by anything."

"Any*one*," she corrected, offended yet again.

He rose beside them, but made no move to leave.

"Curran?" The name made him seem less threatening somehow.

At the sound of it, though, he went rigid. "What?"

"Get out," she said without inflection.

He actually chuckled. Without a word, he turned and left.

The warmth of his brief laughter strangely lifted her spirits as she considered what had just transpired . . . or more accurately, what had *not* transpired.

Once she was sure he had gone, Bera gave Osann a squeeze. "Are you all right now?"

The little girl nodded. She remained curled close for a few moments longer, then eased to her feet.

Bera knew she would do the child no favor by catering to her fears, so she put her to work. She reached up and retrieved two bunches of precious dyestuffs from their peg on the rafters. "These berries could use a night of heat before I crush them. And the herbs." She handed them to Osann. "Take them to the forge-house, my brave one, and hang them there, but not too close to the fire pits." She patted Osann's thin shoulder. "Tomorrow morning, I'll send you to fetch them. Then I'll show you how to make wonderful colors from them. Would you like that?"

Osann's face lit with an eager smile. "Aye, mistress." In the resilient way of children, she seemed to have gotten over her fright and set about her task without hesitation.

Alone once more, Bera returned to her spinning, humming brightly.

She still didn't know what had happened here or why, but never again would the maddening, mysterious golden warrior be the Dark Warrior to her. From now on, he was simply Curran.

Unless she had to kill him, of course.

chapter six

Midmorning of the next day, Bera was positioning the last vertical thread on the loom when a wild-eyed, panting Osann burst into her chamber, then raced over to grab Bera's arm. She tugged with surprising strength. "Hurry, mistress! Lord Drust . . . he's summoned everyone to the Great Well. We must make haste."

A warning chill raced up Bera's spine.

"Child, you're shaking!" Bera covered the little girl's cold, rough hand with her own warm ones. For the moment, her concern for Osann overrode her alarm. "We'll go, I promise, but for now, come to Bera." She met with only halfhearted resistance as she drew the panting child into her lap. "Calm yourself. Take a deep breath . . . That's it. Now tell Bera what's happened."

"An execution," Osann gasped out. "I was bringing the herbs from the storehouse like you told me to, but it started to snow, and the wind was so cold . . ." Tears welled in her hazel eyes. "I thought the Great Hall was empty, so I cut through the back. I almost made it, but then Lord Drust started shouting and stamping about and breaking things and throwing people—"

"People?" This *was* serious.

"People," Osann confirmed, her tight little voice getting higher with every word. "And he was yelling and yelling, and I was so scared, and everyone was running—"

"You're safe now," Bera said even as her thoughts turned to her brothers. *Dear God, don't let it have to do with them.* "What was Lord Drust saying?"

Osann clung to her like a drowning kitten grasping a branch in a torrent. "He ordered the slaves to fetch the great cauldron and bring everyone, everyone, to the Great Well. And then he looked right at me." Her frail little body shuddered. " 'What are *you* doing here?' he shouted. His face . . . I thought he would kill me, then and there."

"I dropped the herbs," she wailed, burrowing into Bera's shoulder. "I'm sorry, so sorry." Her muffled voice cut straight to Bera's heart, but the child did not weep. So young, yet all her tears already had been spent. "You can beat me for it, but please not now. I deserve it, but please not now." She pulled back and looked up at Bera with pleading eyes.

Only a stone would not be moved by that anguished little face.

"It's all right, sweeting." One day Osann would know that she was safe with Bera, but a lifetime of abuse and distrust was not so easily forgotten. "Rest easy. I shall not punish you." She forced a reassuring smile and stroked Osann's hair. "Did Lord Drust say who was to be executed, and why?"

"I'm sorry, truly I am, but I can't remember who." Osann looked away, clearly ashamed to have failed Bera again so soon after dropping the herbs. "I don't think he said a name."

"It's all right. Perhaps he said why, though, gave a reason . . ."

"Maybe. I'm not sure."

Bera hid her growing anxiety. "Close your eyes and think back. You're in the Great Hall, and suddenly you hear Lord Drust. Tell me what he's saying."

Eyes squeezed shut, Osann strained to remember, then her face eased. "He said it was dultery. Not in his own household, he shouted. Didn't care *who* it was, they would die for it." She frowned, her eyes opening. "Then he said something about cook-hold. I didn't know what that meant, but his face was so red, I thought he might explode."

Cook-hold?

Cuckold!

Mother Earth! Had he found out about Evan and his wife?

Suddenly the room seemed too bright, everything too faraway.

"There's to be an execution. Now," Osann whispered, her words atremble with awe and terror. "And we all have to watch. Lord Drust said so."

Adultery. Cuckold. Execution.

Bera sat rigid. What could she do? There was no time, no time.

Osann wrestled from her embrace. "We must go, mistress. Lord Drust will punish us if we're late. I know he will."

"You go ahead," Bera instructed. What little preparations she could make, she would. "I'll be along. I must do something here first."

"Please, mistress," the little girl begged, "don't make me go by myself."

What had she been thinking, sending the child to an execution alone? "Wait outside, and let no one enter. If they insist, tell them I'm on the chamber pot."

She closed the door behind Osann, then threw off what she was wearing and changed into her slave clothes, this time buckling on her sturdy leather girdle and sliding her sword discreetly behind its left side. She lashed a dagger inside her thigh, then secreted two others within easy reach. Then she shoved her tunic and bliaut into her bag and secured its drawstrings to her girdle. Her cloak—the garment that had become her security— covered everything. When she walked out into the hall, she was ready.

"Hurry, mistress," Osann pleaded when she joined her in the corridor. "Everyone else has gone."

"Not everyone." Bera pointed to the princess's door as they approached it. "Both her highness's guards are still there, so she must be as well." No sooner were the words out of her mouth, though, than two burly warriors exited the chamber, followed by a grim, defiant princess in a magnificent cloak of winter fox. Two more warriors hastened her progress none too gently from behind.

Was *Diedre* the one to be executed for adultery? She looked as if she were marching to her death.

That meant Evan . . .

Bera's knees went weak, but somehow she managed to keep walking. *You're jumping to conclusions,* her practical self chided. *It might not be what you think. Wait and see.* In a deliberate effort to calm her wild conjectures, she directed her attention back to Osann. "Stay close to me, little one," she instructed softly. "With luck, everyone will be so busy looking at the princess, they won't notice us. We'll take the back way to the well."

She followed the grim procession out into the icy wind and snow, then hastened for the shortcut to the well. When they reached the crest of the earthen swale, she looked down and saw the crowd gathered below in front of a huge silvered cauldron and a platform bearing Drust on his throne beside an empty chair for Diedre. Behind him, the greatest of his warlords stood armed and ready.

"Hurry, Osann. We must be in place before the princess reaches the gathering."

As she had hoped, everyone had turned to watch the royal "escort." Bera hustled Osann to the edge of the shivering crowd and found a discreet spot to watch from atop a grindstone. Pulling Osann up after her, she scanned the ominous gathering.

The huge silvered cauldron stood like some great, upended bell supported by impressive timbers, its lip against the hastily erected platform. Icy puddles on the ground beneath indicated it had been filled.

Death by drowning. The very thought of it made Bera shudder. A shameful, ignominious way to die.

Rumor had it that all executions, even royal ones, were carried out in the eerie subterranean chamber of the Great Well, but for some reason, this one was not.

In shocked silence, warriors, peasants, slaves, and nobles alike cleared a path for the princess and her guards. Diedre mounted the platform with great dignity, but her rigid face was still as pale as the furs that surrounded it.

Swathed in dark wolfskins, Lord Drust did not look at his wife. He sat hunched forward on his throne, his meaty hands gripping and twisting at the carved armrests in anger—or was it anticipation? Princess Diedre settled to her chair beside him and stared out over the crowd as if they weren't there. Her gloved hands lowered the fur hood that hugged her face, revealing a huge purple bruise on her left cheek.

The sight of that bruise sent a fresh tingle of alarm through Bera. It boded ill indeed that Drust or his men had touched Diedre, much less struck her. Did it mean he'd caught her in some unforgivable crime—like cuckolding him with a handsome prisoner?

If so, Evan would be the first to drown, but his royal lover would soon follow.

Bera couldn't let him die that way. Drowning was the one death a warrior feared—the one death *she* feared, so deeply that nightmares of drowning haunted her sleep. A cold hand closed inside the pit of her belly.

She couldn't let Evan die that way.

Bera looked again to the grim tableau. Rescue was hopeless with so many of Drust's men standing at the ready, but she could try, at least, to spare her brother the shame of drowning with his legs flailing helplessly in the air. She'd run him through herself if she had to, or die trying.

Brilliant, she thought. *And what happens then? Evan dies anyway; eight of your brothers are still held captive; and the rest of the family has lost its only bartering currency—you! Not to mention Osann. How long will she last without you?*

She couldn't let herself think about that.

Tense murmurs rippled through the gathered witnesses as Drust's coarse sons and their even coarser wives and children moved to the fore, their beady eyes bright as vultures' eager for a fresh carcass.

A blast of wind drove Osann closer against her cloak. Sheltering the child with her warm sleeves, Bera peered anxiously at the warriors gathered on either side of the platform, but saw no sign of her brothers.

Or the Dark Warrior.

She scanned again but did not find him. Why wasn't Curran here? For some reason, his absence seemed another bad omen.

Abruptly, the uneasy murmurs of the crowd fell silent when Lord Drust stood. He looked up to the prison tower and bellowed, "Bring the accused before us for punishment."

The guards at the rampart relayed the call. "Bring the accused for punishment!"

All eyes looked up to the stumbling, cloaked figure who staggered between two guards and was all but dragged down the stairway and across the greensward.

Too short to be Evan—or was that only wishful thinking?

Her heart pounding, Bera watched the condemned roughly handed up to the platform, then shoved at Drust's feet.

"Remove the cloak," Drust roared. "Let all see this evil in our midst."

Three chieftains pulled the condemned aright to do their master's bidding. For a split second, Bera felt her breath and heart suspend. But when the cloak was torn away, she saw that the condemned was Princess Alma. She'd been tortured, and was clad in a blood-spattered chainse, her matted hair covering her face.

Not Evan, thank God!

Relief made her so lightheaded she wavered where she stood.

Two strong, black-gloved hands gripped her upper arms to steady her from behind, and Bera's terror was renewed. Instantly, she shifted her sword forward to escape detection, then drew Osann to the front to shield her.

"Drust's own daughter, Princess Alma," Curran murmured close beside her hood.

She'd wondered where he was, but the *last* thing she needed was Curran breathing down her neck and holding her upper arms as if she were his prisoner. She twisted violently against his grasp, but he easily held her fast.

Furious, she hissed, "Is this always the way you make your presence known to a woman, by sneaking up and grabbing her?"

"Stay quiet," he murmured. "Don't call attention to yourself."

Up on the platform, a heated argument had broken out between Drust, his anguished wife, and the priest.

Bera eased Osann to the edge of the grindstone, then tried to crouch to the little girl's level. When Curran realized what she was doing, he promptly let go of her arms, but she could tell from Osann's anxious glances that he remained behind her.

"It's all right, Osann," she said, hoping it was true. "He won't hurt us." Bera gave her a lingering hug, then drew back. "It's far too cold out here for you." She pointed to a low stone building nearby. "So I want you to creep over to that doorway, out of the wind, and stay there until this ugly business is settled. Then go straight back to our chamber and wait for me. Understand?"

Osann nodded, but her expression remained uncertain. She pointed at the storage building. "Stand over there," she dutifully repeated, "and afterwards, go straight back to our chamber to wait."

"Perfect. Now go."

To Bera's amazement, Osann aimed a baleful scowl up at the Dark Warrior before hopping down from the grindstone and scampering away.

That simple expression of loyalty strengthened Bera and calmed the warring forces deep within her. She turned to face Curran. "If anything happens to me," she said quietly, "please see that someone looks after Osann. She could never survive without a protector."

"You're an odd one, Weaver." As usual, his guarded expression betrayed little of his feelings, but she thought she saw a hint of respect in the way he looked at her. "What makes you think I would concern myself with a slave-child?"

"I don't know," she said honestly. "But somehow, I feel you would."

A sharp cry brought her attention back to the platform, where Diedre was being forcibly restrained in her chair, begging mercy for her daughter.

Curran stayed close but made no further move to lay hold of Bera. "Do you know what's going on?"

"Only what you just told me," she answered truthfully. "I do not engage in gossip. It is dangerous, and people invariably expect something for the things they tell."

Up on the platform, the anguished priest stood wringing his hands as Lord Drust sat sulking, deliberately ignoring his poor, wretched daughter and his wife's desperate pleas for clemency.

Now that Bera no longer had to worry about Evan, the full import of this unholy proceeding came home to her.

"Nine months ago," Curran murmured close to her ear, "Lord Drust gave his only daughter to wed his half-brother, Morfran." He paused. "I think he did it to spite his wife for loving the girl so much more than she did their sons, who looked and acted like Drust." His words were quiet but brittle as flint and just as sharp. "This morning before dawn, Princess Alma delivered Morfran's firstborn—a hideous, malformed monster of a babe with parts both male and female. It breathed but thrice from the gaping hole in its face before it died. The priest took one look at it and fainted dead away." He paused.

When he spoke again, his voice resonated disgust. "Morfran was abed with his wench when they brought him the news. The craven coward promptly accused his wife of mating with the devil, thereby removing himself from any shame or responsibility. Drust went along with his brother's groundless accusations."

So that was why the cauldron instead of the well. Alma was still bleeding from childbirth.

Bera had known that Drust resented his only daughter because she alone, of all his children, had a place in Diedre's heart. But to allow this travesty, simply out of jealousy or resentment . . . the cruel injustice of it made her insides roil.

"Her mother tried to intervene," Curran said evenly,

"but Drust struck her unconscious and ordered her kept to her room by force."

Bera stared straight ahead. Until now, she had never thought of Diedre as the slightest bit maternal, but the dragon princess before them was all mother, fiercely trying to protect her child. Her cheeks wet with tears, Diedre struggled in vain against the burly men who held her. The shifting wind brought the sound of her pleas to Bera at the back of the gathering. "Mercy, my lord husband," she begged. "Mercy. She is your daughter, too, the bearer of our royal bloodline. Spare her, I beg you. She is innocent. Spare her."

Drust turned away in smug satisfaction. "There can be no mercy when the law of God and man is broken," he thundered over the crowd. "She has confessed. Let justice be done."

At the hands of Drust's infamous torturers, anyone would confess to anything.

The only sounds confirming Drust's verdict came from his sons, who watched in triumph as their sister's hands were bound behind her in preparation for her execution.

When Princess Alma was led to the edge of the cauldron, her mother stopped fighting. Diedre could not embrace the daughter she loved, but she offered the only comfort she could with tender looks and murmured words of devotion. Bera could not bear to look. She closed her eyes and heard Princess Alma speak.

"Nothing," the condemned woman wailed. "As God is my witness, I have done nothing to deserve this! I am innocent!" Alma had been betrayed by her own husband and her father, the very men who were supposed to protect her. "I am innocent, I tell you! Inno—"

Her words were cut short by the sound of a splash. Bera leaned hard against Curran, grateful for his strong, protective presence. At first, there were no sounds of struggle, but after long seconds that seemed like days, there was more splashing, until at last, all was still.

Only then did Bera feel the tears that had escaped her.

She heard Princess Diedre lift up a keening wail that raised the hairs on her head and arms.

"Justice has been served!" Drust bellowed. "You are dismissed."

The crowd began to disperse with a rumble of subdued chatter.

" 'Tis the husband who should be drowned," Bera whispered hoarsely through the sound of a mother's grief. "Or that bastard of a father of hers."

"Aye," Curran confirmed.

Bera turned away from the horror and looked up to find him gazing at the grim scene, his features unreadable. Only his eyes betrayed the bitterness with which he spoke. "And there are those who say that God is just."

"The sins of the fathers shall be visited upon the sons unto the fourth generation," she quoted dully. The Dragon Princess's sins had borne bitter fruit—not for herself, but for her daughter. How brutally ironic, that Diedre, guilty of adultery, was forced to watch her innocent daughter shamed and executed for that very offense. "Perhaps the daughter has suffered for the sins of her mother this day."

She felt Curran tense. "What could you know of that?" he demanded. "And how?"

She'd said too much. Suddenly weighted by what she'd seen, where she was, what she must yet do, she scarcely had the strength to stand. "Pure conjecture," she said wearily.

Endless minutes ticked by before more splashing signaled removal of the body.

Princess Diedre's wail of grief cut short. "Get your

filthy hands off her," she screeched. "Give her to me! I'm her mother! Give her to me."

Curran was glad The Weaver had turned away from the pitiful scene on the platform, but he had no intention of letting her comment about the "sins of the mother" drop. She knew something about Princess Diedre's dalliance with the hostage. He was certain of it.

Pressure would get him nowhere, though. She was stubborn, this one; yesterday had proved it.

Who was she, really? he wondered. Why was she here?

She was wary of him, yet she had not escaped when the execution was over. Curran deliberately moved in close to her left side. She pulled away abruptly, but not before he felt her hidden sword against his leg.

"Interesting," he mused aloud now that the rest of the crowd was safely out of earshot, "and dangerous."

"None of your business," she snapped, her shoulders squaring.

Curran suppressed a smile. Something had prompted her to take such a risk. What had she feared might happen here? "A dagger might be overlooked," he said quietly, "but a concealed sword in a public assembly . . . That's grounds for summary execution."

"We've witnessed one execution today," she retorted. "Would you make it two?" Too stubborn to retreat even in the face of such perilous innuendo, she stood her ground beside him.

Curran knew that game well: Whoever moved first, lost.

He didn't usually indulge in games, but he had actually begun to enjoy his dangerous dance with The Weaver. Feisty little thing, she was, but her size would be her undoing in the end. A swift, clever opponent with a longer reach—someone like him—could easily run her through.

For some strange reason, though, he hoped he wouldn't be the one to kill her. Damned if he knew why, but she'd gotten under his skin from that first meeting in the cookhouse.

He watched her now as she pretended to ignore him. What was it about her that drew him?

Maybe it was because she was so different. She had not resorted to feminine wiles like the other women whose paths he'd crossed. Not that he would have been tempted if she had. She was plain as peat, and he preferred softer, simpler partners when he needed to relieve his male urges. Yet when he remembered the feel of her taut buttocks against his loins, his manhood leapt.

For all her warrior's ways, she was still, after all, a woman, and he was a man. But his attraction went deeper than that. Perhaps he was drawn to the uneasy balance of coiled energy and tenuous restraint she radiated from beneath her mystic cloak. Whatever the cause, she fascinated him.

A woman with a sword, skilled as any warrior and arrogant enough for two. A woman who would risk execution to bear concealed arms at this shameful exhibition.

Curran tried to fit the pieces together. Arrogant. Clever. A skilled warrior. Too well spoken to be a mere weaver.

A ridiculously improbable idea struck him—improbable, but not impossible.

Could it be?

The pieces fit. She'd arrived at about the right time and managed to garner free run of the fortress. Most telling of all, she knew about Diedre's adulterous trysts with the hostage.

Curran peered at the hooded "Weaver" with razor sharpness. Could *this* be the notorious Princess Bera, the fearsome hag with horns instead of breasts? The woman he was risking all to win?

Princess Bera, here, literally right under his nose?

If so, the irony was too delicious.

But if she was . . .

Curran's amusement evaporated. Not only must he free her brothers and make good their escape, he would have to bring her along and keep her safe in the process.

He must find her out, and soon. "I bid you good evening, *Weaver*." He bowed, surrendering the field—for the moment. "Until we meet again."

She clasped her hands inside her deep sleeves and nodded. "Not too soon, I hope."

"Sooner than you might imagine," he answered.

Tonight, if all went well.

chapter seven

"What happens when somebody dies?" Osann asked on the way back from supper.

After what they'd seen this day, Bera understood why the child would be curious about death, but she felt ill-prepared to answer. "The priests tell us that the good go to heaven and the wicked burn in hell," she ventured as she opened the door to the stone fortress, then followed Osann inside. "But the stories of our people say that all of us pass over into the Otherworld when we die."

"I've heard all about hell," Osann confided as she held Bera's hand and led the way up the narrow stairs. "When I die, that's where I want to go,"

Her calm assurance startled Bera as much as what she'd said. "Why in the world would you want to go there?"

"To find my mama." She glanced back at Bera. "Lynet the cook said that's where she went."

"But hell . . ."

"Fire and brimstone," Osann recited in singsong, jumping the stairs with both little feet. "Torment without end. No water, no succor, no God, no friend." She dropped back close beside Bera. "Doesn't matter. I want to be with my mama."

So she knew of hell's torments, but loved her mother

too much to care. The depth of her devotion resurrected the ghosts of Bera's own long-buried sorrow. She swung the child up astride her hip as they passed the guardroom below the princess's chamber.

Now that Osann had been deloused, bathed, and dressed in warm shoes and decent clothes, she smelled sweet as honey.

"Pay no attention to Lynet the cook," Bera told her, "or anyone else who says your mama went to hell." She prayed she could offer Osann comfort that no one had been able to offer her. "How could they know? Have they been to hell and seen for themselves? No." Not yet, anyway.

"But . . .." Osann's small face crumpled. "Then where *is* my mama?"

"Watching over you." Bera had never been one to dwell on matters of faith, but this one thing she believed with all her heart. "Loving you. Waiting for the day when you will be together again."

"Oh." Osann looked up at her with absolute trust. "Is she watching me now?"

"Yes." Bera smiled. "Just as my mama is watching over me."

Osann relaxed against her. "Missy," she used her endearing nickname for Bera, a shortened form of mistress, "do you think they know each other, your mama and mine?"

"Probably." Did they?

It was the sort of thing Bera didn't usually think about. She'd spent the last twelve years living in the moment, dodging the specters of the past and never looking forward beyond the next, most pressing challenge. But to think that their mothers were together somewhere, watching over them both . . .

"I think so, too." Osann yawned. "Maybe that's why we're together."

"Maybe it is." The idea appealed to Bera more than she would have imagined.

On the landing just ahead, two grim, unfamiliar warriors stood in the flickering torchlight at the princess's door. Drust's men, not Diedre's.

Bera eased Osann to her feet in the protection of her shadow. There was no need for words of warning, for in Bera's long life and Osann's brief one, danger was as much a part of existence as breathing.

Without a sound, the little girl all but disappeared into the folds of the cloak, matching her steps to Bera's.

Bera didn't think the guards had seen Osann, but they had certainly noticed *her*. Both men tightened their grips on their swords and followed her progress with hawk's eyes.

Blast. If these were permanent replacements for the princess's regular guards, she was back where she'd started weeks ago. From the look of them, the two warriors were not the type to be lulled into complacency about her presence, not matter how frequently they saw her.

That complicated matters, but she would manage anyway. She had to.

She and Osann glided past as unobtrusively as possible. When they were safely back in their chamber, Bera stirred the peat in the brazier, then added a goodly chunk to take the edge off the cold and darkness.

Osann made straight for the pallet they shared. As soon as she had settled beneath the blankets, she resumed their conversation as if they'd never been interrupted. "This Otherworld . . . what's that like?"

Bera thought it bizarre that today's execution had transformed this once-silent child into a chatter-pate, but she was grateful Osann had finally begun to share her thoughts, whatever the cause. Suppressing a yawn, she did her best to answer. "The Otherworld is like ours, some say," she answered, undressing.

"Which do you believe in," Osann asked sleepily, "heaven and hell, or the Otherworld?"

"I don't know," Bera said frankly. "No one's ever come back to tell me which is real." She reached under the blankets and gave Osann's ribs a quick tickle. "Especially not Lynet the cook."

Osann actually giggled, and in the joyous, molten sound, Bera was reminded of her brothers' children . . . before the Vikings had come and their fathers had been taken hostage.

A tug of longing pulled within her chest. Would she ever play with her nieces and nephews again? Would she ever see home, sleep in her own bed?

Bera shoved the questions—and the hurt—back into the dark abyss from which they'd come and busied herself arranging four wooly sheepskins atop the blankets.

"Come to bed, Missy." Osann curled toward the wall on her side in anticipation.

Bera hesitated. Osann had grown dependent on her protective presence to fall asleep, snuggling close every night. And truth be told, Bera did not mind. It was as close to being a mother as she would probably ever come. Yet tired as she was tonight, she feared that if she lay down, even for a little while, she'd sleep the night away.

She'd failed to visit her brothers last night for that very reason. That must not happen tonight. The day's events had made warning Evan even more urgent. She could not let another night pass without telling him that he must avoid the princess at all costs.

"Are you coming?" A piteous little voice wafted from beneath the blankets. "It's lonesome without you. And *cold*."

"Aye. I'm coming," she said against her better judgment. But just until Osann fell asleep.

Bera had taken the waif as a body slave, but somewhere along the way, she had ended up caring for Osann instead of the other way round. "I'm coming." She slipped beneath the covers and drew the little girl into the curve of her body. Immediately, they both relaxed.

"Wouldn't it be wonderful if Otherworld was like this, all warm and cuddly?" Osann murmured, half asleep already.

"Yes, it would." Bera stroked her hair. "Yes, it would."

Mmmmm. It was summer, and she was little again, safe in her mother's arms on a sunlit hill, listening to her mother's voice recite the stories of their generations while the cattle grazed below. She was safe and whole and happy in a time before everything turned evil.

Bera drank in the sweet, familiar scent of her mother's skin and reveled in the comfort of her embrace. Yet no matter how real this smelled and felt and sounded, a huge and hidden sadness told her this could not be real. Her mother was dead—long dead—and nothing was safe anymore.

Afraid that if she looked up into her mother's beloved face she would find it smashed and ruined from her father's blows, Bera burrowed deeper and prayed the illusion would go on forever.

But as she'd feared, her mother's voice fell silent and she pulled away. Bera was suddenly alone. "Mama!" she cried across the empty landscape. "Come back! Mama!"

"She's dead," Evan's voice said from behind her in the dream. "We need to talk."

No longer a child, Bera spun around to find him bound as if for execution. "We need to talk," he repeated woodenly.

Evan!

She shot aright, panting, wide awake and blinking tears from her eyes.

What time was it? How long had she slept?

Beside her Osann murmured insensibly, then burrowed deeper under the covers and settled to steady, even breathing.

Sucking in the cold air to stimulate her wits, Bera crept from the pallet, then groped her way to the food and clothing she had hidden. Shivering, she changed into her slave clothes, armed herself, then donned her cloak and eased into the hallway. Step by cautious step, she made her way toward Princess Diedre's room and the stairs beyond.

Bera had no idea what the new guards would do when they saw her skulking about in the middle of the night, but she had to take the chance.

Please, let them be asleep.

They weren't. But neither of them challenged her. It was eerie going by their dark, glistening stares, but once she was safely past, she met no one else as she stole down to the Great Hall and the stairs, then hid her cloak and hastened to the rear door.

The cold outside fairly stole her breath, yet she was glad for it. On a night like this, only a blaze or an enemy attack would pry anyone, even a warrior, from his bed.

She made it to the tower without crossing paths with any of the sentries. Once inside, she crept past the sleeping guard without incident, then descended to the dungeon door. There she braced one foot on one side wall and the other on the wall opposite, then repeated her arduous, spiderlike climb to the ventilation slot high above the door. Panting from effort when she reached it, she wriggled her head and shoulders into the narrow slit. The stench from her brothers' cell struck her like a body blow, leaving her gagging. How in heaven, hell, or the Otherworld could her brothers endure such foulness?

"Psst. It's me." By sheer force of will, she choked back the nausea. "Here's your food." She dropped the bag and heard it caught. "There's not as much as last time. My little slave-girl is so thin, I—"

"It's all right, Bera," Airell whispered. "We still have plenty from last night."

Last night!

She quaked to think how close she had come to bumping into her rival. That was the last thing she needed. She covered her anxiety by saying, "I'm glad you have enough food."

"You must tell me what's happened." It was Evan who spoke, his voice urgent. "The guard said the princess was executed." His tense pause revealed as much as the strain of raw fear in his whisper. "Please . . . I must know."

Not *we* must know, but *I* must know.

Bera put the pieces together and for the first time in her life, felt ashamed of her brother. Evan was no longer using the dragon princess—if he ever had. It was Diedre who had her hooks in him, not the other way round.

Appalled, she considered telling him it was Diedre, not Alma, who'd been executed for adultery, but honor kept her from the lie. "It was Princess Alma," she said at last. "Her husband accused her of consorting with the devil because she gave birth to a malformed child."

Far below, speculative whispers circulated among her brothers.

"Was it true, then?" Kegan asked in horror. "Do you think she really gave herself to the devil?"

Were all men superstitious blockheads, even her own brothers?

"I'll tell you what I think." Bera directed the choler she felt for Evan to Kegan. "I think she was innocent, and her coward of a husband threw his wife into the cauldron to save his male pride!"

"You *would* think as much," Roy muttered.

"Shut up, all of you." True to his status as thane of Pitlanric, Angus took charge. "We're wastin' time." The whispers ceased, but tension remained, thick as peat smoke.

Angus was right. They were wasting precious time. "Evan," she blurted out, "you must not see the princess again." She took a leveling breath, and her stomach lurched afresh at the stink. "Drust had his own daughter shamed and executed on the mere accusation of adultery. If he finds out about you and his wife, he'll have you both killed. Do not go to her."

"I'm a prisoner," her brother argued. "What choice have I if Diedre sends for me? None."

Diedre! So it was Diedre *now.*

"Tell her you're sick," Bera retorted. "Tell her anything, but don't go to her chamber."

"If I tell her I'm sick, she'll send a litter and have me carried to her." He was torn—she could hear it in his voice—but the dragon princess's talons were in deep. He *wanted* to go back.

Not for the first time, she pitied her brother, yet his weakness put them all at risk. "Go if you must, then," she conceded, "but keep your cock between your own legs." Her bluntness sent her brothers into startled silence, but Bera was past caring. "Ballocks and Banshis, Evan, try to think with your head instead of your prong. Bedding her has gained you nothing." She did her best to calm her whisper. "Put a stop to it, any way you can. Don't kiss her, don't embrace her, don't take her hand, don't even get near her, or you'll both end up in the cauldron. Hell, you'll *all* end up in the cauldron."

"She's right, Evan," Airell murmured, "and you know it."

The others kept silent.

After a brief, anguished pause, Evan addressed her in a tight whisper. "I'll do what I can, but you've got to get us out of here."

"Soon," she promised. "I've set up a diversion and figured out a way to get us horses. And I've almost enough herbs to drug the guards. It won't be long— erk!"

Two powerful hands snatched her from her perch, sending a jolt of pure panic through her as she was jerked back and immobilized against a rock-hard torso. She heard a muffled commotion from the cell. Her bothers probably thought she'd been caught, and rightly so. Palming her dagger, Bera inhaled sharply, and her panic promptly evaporated. Even over the stink from the dungeon, one whiff was all she needed to identify the familiar scent of her attacker.

Curran.

Was *he* the one who'd been visiting her brothers? Or had he simply followed her here, and if so, why?

Quick as an eel, he stripped the dagger from her hand.

Blast!

Bera went limp, hoping the unexpected lack of resistance would cause him to falter, but it didn't. His arm only tightened across her waist, making it hard to breathe.

He levered her upper body back up hard against his own and put a dagger to her throat. "Do exactly as I say, or die here and now," he whispered into her cap-covered ear.

Bera didn't believe for a second that he would kill her. Men like Curran were never coy about such matters. Yet the fact that she was still alive meant he must need her that way. The question was, why?

"Did you hear me?" he said, his breath warm against her ear.

Bera nodded. Her mind churned for ways to escape even as she noted the contrast between her own hammering heartbeats and Curran's powerful, measured pulse. It couldn't be easy, holding her in midair while braced between the walls, yet he showed no sign of strain. Bera told herself it was because his long legs enabled a much more stable perch than her short ones had, but she knew the truth: Here was a man she might not be able to beat.

"Hold on," he whispered. "I'm taking you down now."

Again, she nodded, eager to find out what he wanted of her.

Smooth and silent as a great cat, he brought them down.

He must not be working for Drust—in this, at least—or he'd simply have raised an alarm. Could he be working for his own ends?

Or for Diedre?

That was a daunting prospect. If Curran and Diedre were in league with each other, that meant Bera was caught up in a far more treacherous game than she had reckoned.

The moment their feet touched the floor, Curran grasped her wrists, pinning them wide against the dungeon's armored door as he pressed her against its metal surface.

Bera was surprised to feel the pressure of a formidable erection hard against her hindparts and wondered what it signified. Did he mean to ravish her?

That she could believe.

"Who are you," he asked in that deep, velvet whisper, "and what business have you with the wretched souls beyond this door?"

"I bring them food," she cracked out, "at my master's order."

Oddly, he didn't ask who her master was. Instead, he let out a brief, derisive breath and proceeded to search her in a fashion that was anything but brisk.

His hand was warm and dry against her flesh as he caressed the inside of her thigh, then moved upward to linger atop the dagger hidden there. Bera's breath caught in her throat.

What was he doing, and why?

Deftly, he removed the dagger, but did not retract his hand. Instead, he stroked higher, deliberately parting the folds of her womanhood. She gasped. With exquisite pressure and deliberation, he slid the edge of his hand against her, sending a jolt straight through her, sharp and hot and hungry as a scream.

Against her will, a shudder rippled through her. Was this how the princess had snared her brother Evan?

The question jarred her like a bucketful of icy water, bringing her back to her senses.

She was up against a master. Good as he was, Curran had surely recognized her as The Weaver by her scent. "Take the dagger and get your hands off me," she grated out.

He slid the weapon from its thong, but did not take his hand away. "Not until I've finished." He explored her legs with maddening slowness, then moved to her boots, finding both of the small blades hidden there. "That's better."

She had only one tiny dagger left, but Bera knew he'd never think to look within the tightly coiled braids at her nape, so she did not despair.

He stepped back. Through the rough fabric of her clothes, he felt her buttocks and up her sides the way a blind man would savor a naked wench.

"Do you always search people this way?" she hissed, afraid her body would again betray her.

"Only you," he murmured. He spun her around and

leaned hard against her, pressing his thick leather girdle into her waist and the unmistakable bulge beneath it into her belly.

"Get off me," she warned.

He obliged with a dry chuckle, but he wasn't finished with her yet. All business now, he roughly searched her breasts and belly before retreating.

Dimly revealed by the distant torchlight, his body was a stark silhouette that blocked her from escape. She heard a rustle of fabric, then saw him loft a half-laden pouch through the ventilation slot high above them.

He bent close, crowding her. "Follow me. I have to meet someone. Then we'll talk." Grasping her shoulders, he pushed her ahead of him toward the stairs and the sleeping guard. "And you *will* talk."

"With whom?" Bera glanced back at the barely visible features of his rugged face. "Princess Diedre?" If so, all was lost.

Her question prompted a flash of white teeth. "Nay." His grin disappeared as quickly as it had come. "With me." He nudged her forward. "Make haste. We've a lot of ground to cover."

Where was he taking her, and why?

Bera decided to play along—for the time being, anyway. She needed answers, and this seemed the best way to get them.

She could always escape if she needed to. Or kill him.

chapter eight

Curran was good, all right. He guided her swiftly past the sleeping guard and through the hallway beyond.

As soon as they reached the tower's anteroom, he drew her aside and bound her wrists behind her with expert speed and skill. Bera did her best to keep some slack in the bindings, but he knew what he was doing and tightened the narrow leather thong until it dug into her skin. "Do not try to escape." He led her, tethered to him like a hound on a leash, out the door into the stinging wind, then prodded her ahead of him. After that, the tip of his dagger—or hers, blast him—did all the talking for him.

Though she was certain he had no intention of actually stabbing her, she didn't want to push her luck. She did want to find out what he was up to; she didn't like being tied—or the way he was handling her. The answers that had seemed so important to her only moments before now didn't seem worth the risk of accompanying him to his secret rendezvous. Bera reconsidered and decided that when a chance came to escape, she would take it.

Curran gave her no opening as he urged her toward the upper rampart. She wondered again where he was going and who he was meeting and what plans he had for her. And how long it would take them to get there. He was warmly cloaked, but her threadbare slave disguise offered scant protection from the wind. Already, her face and hands and feet were numb. Nevertheless, she primed herself to act at the first opportunity.

She glanced up to the cloudy sky and wished the Tempest Mother would do something, anything, to aid her. She sensed no storm, but offered up a hasty prayer for help anyway. *Mighty God, all the force of wind and rain are yours to direct. The Tempest Mother is but your messenger, I know, but I beg you, loose her now with driving rain or snow to hide our passage. Give me a chance, at least, to escape. Help me now, and I vow I'll go back to confession.* Her practical inner self prodded her to add, *As soon as we get back to Pitlanric.*

Nothing came forth from the clouds.

It occurred to her that she might have offended the God of Abraham, Isaac, and Jacob with that last bit. *Well, I can't very well go to confession here! Only a fool would trust Diedre's priest.*

Still no storm or snow, so she reconciled herself to getting out of this on her own.

She needed little urging to keep up the pace as they hugged the eastern side of the citadel; it helped stave off the cold. But when they stepped from behind the upper ramparts, both of them were lashed by stinging sea-spray from the crashing waves below.

Perfect. Now she was half frozen and *wet*—hardly any condition to take on a man like Curran.

But it wasn't long before he provided her the opportunity she'd been waiting for. As soon as they reached the bottom of the upper rampart, he pulled her into the shadows and leaned out for a look at the entrance to the Great Well halfway across the greensward. Bera leaned out right behind him.

There was no guard at the top of the sunken stairwell,

only an eerie glow punctuated by fitful sparks from below. The sentry must have taken shelter from the wind.

Surely Curran did not mean to take her *there*!

There was something wicked about the well. She had
felt it when she'd investigated the cavernous structure
weeks ago in search of her brothers. Bera didn't care
how many souls had been baptized here, those damp
stone walls had seen too many executions to be anything
but evil.

Yet it wasn't the evil that frightened her—she had
faced that oft enough, as oft and as resolutely as she'd
faced death. What frightened her was that the dank and
eerie cavern was a drowning place. A great, pagan
drowning place.

Drowning: *That* she feared.

The memory of Princess Alma's execution sent a bitter twist of terror through her gut.

Curran turned back to her, producing another stout
thong from beneath his cloak. "Sit." His dagger backed
up the command, so she plopped down onto the soggy
turf with squish.

Ick. Now her arse would be frozen, along with her
hands and feet.

"Don't try anything," he warned, making short work
of tying her ankles. "Stay. I'll be back."

Sit. Stay. Like a *dog*.

Well, he'd picked the wrong dog to bait. This one
would bite!

Bera went to work on her bindings even as she
watched his cloaked silhouette turn, then stride toward
the Great Well with all the confidence of a man sent by
Drust himself.

Frantically, she twisted her wrists and clawed at the
bindings with numbed fingers. Cold as she was, she
scarcely felt the leather cutting into her flesh, but soon

the thongs were slick with blood. She didn't mind; that made it easier.

Concentrate, she told herself even as she saw Curran approach the stairwell. Keep working. Don't think. Just feel the bindings, take advantage of the slightest slack.

She watched him pause at the top of the stairwell. Illuminated by the subterranean glow, his powerful stature and swirling cloak made him look like a true lord of darkness returning to his domain. As he descended below the turf, a shiver quaked through her.

There wasn't much time. He'd make short work of the guard.

She felt the bindings begin to give. One more twist, and . . .

The same moment she broke free, the stairwell went ominously dark.

Quickly, quickly. He'll be back any minute.

Bera knew she could outrun him, if only her legs were free. The small dagger hidden in her bun would make short work of the thongs, but getting it free would take longer than untying, so she made do with her frozen, bloody fingers. She had just gained her feet and launched herself toward escape when a slate-hard slab of man flattened her onto the turf.

"You vex me, woman," Curran rumbled through the ringing in her ears. "I told you not to try anything."

Bera would have cursed him good and proper, but she didn't have her breath. A strangled "Get . . . off . . . me," was all she could manage.

He obliged, only to snatch her to her feet and shove her toward the well.

The freezing wind whistling in her ears, Bera did her best to focus on her adversary, not where he was taking her. When they reached the stone stairs, she looked down and saw the overturned brazier and a few scattered lumps of peat still glowing faintly, but no guard.

Curran urged her forward. "Mind your steps." As they passed through the embers, he drew his sword, speared a smoldering chunk of peat, then held it forth to light their way—if light was a word to be used for such a feeble illumination.

When they reached the gaping black rectangle that led into the well, Bera balked. She didn't fear him, but she did fear drowning. Facing the black maw of the well, her confidence faltered. Maybe he did mean to kill her. Damned if she'd let him make her nightmares come true without a fight. Better to take a blade than to drown in the bottomless black waters of the well.

Curran nudged her forward. "Move on."

"Nay." Twisting around, she glared into the shadowed nothingness of his hooded face. "I say you're a coward, for only a coward would act as you have. If you had one shred of honor, you'd give me back my dagger and fight it out, here and now."

"Very dramatic." His condescending tone made her even angrier. "But I have other matters to attend to at the moment, and other plans for you after that."

"What plans?" she challenged.

"You'll see." So quickly she scarcely had time to flinch, he enveloped her in an iron embrace. "Can you swim?" he whispered ominously.

"Like a fish!" she snapped, determined not to let him see her fear.

She could always tell him who she was. That little bit of information would turn things around, especially if he was, in fact, the one who had come to free her brothers. She was the prize, so he could not harm her.

A gust of wind blew down the faint sound of the second watch-call from the upper ward.

"Make haste. It's time." He spun her round and shoved her through the doorway onto the stone platform that edged the still, black square of the well.

Bera was grateful for the feeble glow at the end of Curran's sword. The place would be a blind man's hell without it. Hewn from solid bedrock, the walls and ceiling acted with the surface of the water to magnify the slightest sound a hundredfold.

"Why have you brought me here?" She said it softly, but her voice echoed like a herdsman's call.

"I told you; I'm meeting someone," he said almost casually. "And unless you wish to bear responsibility for the death of one of Lord Drust's favorites—" He aimed the glowing ember toward a pedestal in the corner. "You'll get behind that pedestal and stay there without making a sound." Curran swirled his dark cloak from his shoulders and tossed it to her. "Cover up with that. If you're smart, you'll stay quiet."

The shoulders were still warm from his body, so she gratefully wrapped the cloak around her. Unfortunately, he took advantage of the opportunity to put the dagger just below her ribs again. That game was beginning to wear on her.

He urged her to the pedestal and stood there until she was safely tucked away.

Bera went along, but only to lull him into a false sense of security. She was a princess and a warrior. He would rue the day he had ordered her about like a bondwoman.

"Remember. Not a sound." He flicked his sword and sailed the ember into the well, plunging them into absolute darkness.

Just like in her drowning dreams.

Suddenly she felt as if she'd been nailed up in her own coffin. She went clammy, her hands shaking as she distracted herself by loosing the tight coil of tiny braids that hid her smallest dagger. Once she had it free, she shook out the braids, then sat alert to the sounds of the cavern. Fortunately, her eyes had adjusted enough for her to see Curran's silhouette just inside the doorway.

Again, she wondered who was meeting him and why.

Bera wasn't sure how much time had passed when the sound of footsteps echoed from the stone stairs and a cloaked figure paused in the doorway. "Sssst! Are you there?"

A woman's voice!

Bera hadn't expected that. Who was she?

"I am here." Curran's reply echoed in the darkness.

Startled, the figure jumped back into clear silhouette against the open doorway. The visitor couldn't see Curran, but Bera knew that as long as the woman remained in the doorway, he could see her just as Bera could.

"Have you got them?" he asked.

"Here." The woman proffered a sack that clinked of metal. "All of them, as promised."

Malisande? Bera couldn't be sure.

The woman clutched the sack close as her echo died to eerie stillness. "And my payment?"

Curran's arm appeared in the doorway, a small purse dangling from his fingers. "Hand me the keys, and I'll release your payment."

Keys! Keys to what?

The woman hesitated, then warily extended the sack toward his hand.

Keeping her eyes on the figure in the doorway, Bera took advantage of the distraction to ease silently from behind the pedestal. Her first careful step, though, made a grating sound that echoed all the way across the cavern.

"What was that?" the woman demanded. Without waiting for an answer, she snatched the purse from Curran. "You want the keys?" she said. "Well, here they are." She hurled the sack of keys into the center of the well, where it landed with hardly a splash. Then she pivoted and sprinted away.

Curran leapt after her, but took only two steps before he stopped, remembering Bera, no doubt.

Meanwhile, Bera dropped his cloak and managed to cover several yards, almost reaching the doorway before Curran's shoulders spanned the opening. "You might as well tell me where you are," he said, his voice thickened by anger. "I'll find you anyway."

She held her breath and froze. He'd find her, all right—when she jumped him and put her dagger to his eye.

Luck was with her. Only half a pace away, he took a step toward the well and turned his back to her. Bera launched herself at his head, climbed him like a tree, and wrapped herself around him just as she'd done with Angus.

But Curran was neither as thick-witted nor as sluggish as Angus. She never got a stable grip on him. Before she could bring her dagger to his eye, he twisted free of her, grabbed her arm and leg, and heaved her sprawling over the water.

She had time for only an instant of chagrin before she slapped, spread-eagled on her back, to the surface and sank.

The icy water was so cold it stole her breath and all but stopped her heart. Every muscle in her body locked in rigid spasm. She couldn't move, couldn't even think.

It was happening, just like in her nightmares. Unable to move, she sank into the bottomless blackness.

Strangely, she felt no need to breathe—just an unexplainable sense of detachment and mild surprise that this would be her end.

She wanted to move, tried to swim, but her body refused to obey. She knew what to do and willed it to happen, but nothing worked. Even her mind seemed slow. It took great effort to form her thoughts, but in what she believed to be her last moments, she directed the most hideous curse she could come up with onto the well and the man who had done this to her. Then she prayed that her body would rot and poison every soul at Burghead—all but her brothers and Osann.

That was when her hindside hit the bottom of the well—and something lumpy.

Could it be? She hadn't sunk for long . . . or had she? Her mind was so fuddled she didn't even know which way was up anymore.

Sleepy, so sleepy.

Fight it! her inner voice yelled. *Don't give up! You'll die.*

She tried again to move, but felt as if she was locked in a solid block of ice.

So sleepy.

Just as she decided this was a battle she could not win, she heard a muffled splash, then sloshing that got louder and louder until the water around her swirled with sound and motion, and she was jerked back up into the world of the living.

"Cursed woman." Curran's voice was tight with fear as he pounded her back. "Were you *trying* to drown?"

She'd show *him* who was cursed, as soon as she could move again!

He peeled her dagger from her frozen fingers, tossed her unceremoniously over his shoulder, then paused, bent down, and came up with what sounded like the keys. "A lot of good these will do me if you die on me," he muttered as he labored toward the platform.

Aha, she thought idly, bumping against him with his every step. She'd been right; he wanted her alive, not dead.

Completely numb now, she felt like a distant observer instead of a drowning victim. Her bobbing, upside down view was more than a little confusing, but she finally realized she was seeing the dim image of Curran's wool-covered buttocks and the water splashing against his thighs.

"Like a fish," he grumbled. "Hah."

She wanted to say, "Nobody can swim in water that cold!" but when she tried, she ended up coughing her lungs out.

"That's it." He gave her backside a hefty smack. "Cough it out." She'd barely begun to gain control of her breathing when he laid her with surprising gentleness on the platform. "Fool woman." Panting from exertion, he hoisted himself from the water and sat beside her to empty his boots. "Like as not we'll both come down with the ague, and then who will help your brothers?"

It took a moment for his words to sink in, but when they did, Bera snapped instantly from her dazed confusion. "... *your brothers!*" Propelled by fury, she shot aright, glared at the dark shape of his mighty head, then launched her fist as hard as her frozen arm allowed toward where she hoped his face would be.

At long last, she caught him unawares. Her knuckles met flesh and bone with satisfying force.

"Ack!" Curran caught her wrist in an iron grip and held it immobile. "Why, you ungrateful little savage!"

"You knew who I was!" Her accusation echoed off the walls and ceiling like the chiming of a great bell, but Bera didn't care. Molten outrage thawed her heart and sent white-hot needles scorching through her frozen limbs. She struggled to her feet and he rose with her. "You knew I was a princess, yet twice you've handled me like a whore! I'll kill you for that, if it's the last thing I do."

Curran released her wrist but remained wary. "I think you'll change your mind about that," he said with a definite note of grim amusement.

Bera's fingers curled to claws. Did he *dare* to mock her? She grabbed a shock of his hair and twisted. "How did you know who I was?" she demanded. "Who told you?"

"No one told me." He didn't flinch. "I figured it out for myself."

Cursed man. He couldn't possibly be telling the truth. She'd covered her tracks too well. Someone had to have told him, but who?

Diedre?

The thought sent her stomach plummeting.

If Diedre knew the truth, Bera was a pawn in a far more dangerous game than Curran's.

She let go of his hair. "And who have *you* told?"

"Ah, Bera." He said her name as if he already had the right. "I'm disappointed that you would even ask such a thing. Why would I tell anyone who you really are?"

"For gain," she fairly spat. "You're a mercenary; you have no honor, only greed, so you sell yourself to the highest bidder. It's no secret that Diedre has great treasure."

"If treasure were what I wanted, that might be true," he conceded, "but it's not what I want. I came back to Burghead on a quest, and I mean to finish it." He hefted the keys, then tucked them securely behind his girdle. "Now behave—at least until I free your brothers."

Behave! Bera saw red. *No one* told her to behave! "Until *you* free them?" she railed, shivering as she tried to wring the water from her clothes. "Why do you think I came here, you lowborn son of a mongrel? *I* shall be the one to free them."

"No you won't," he said as smoothly as ice on stone. "*I* will. And you, my scheming, sharp-tongued princess, are my prize, God help me."

"Never," she snarled.

"*Now.*" He said with a grim confidence that brought her up short. He squared with her. "Help me, and this time tomorrow night, you, your brothers, and I will all be safely on our way back to Pitlanric. Refuse, and I'll have no choice but to knock you senseless and drug you until it's all over. Either way, I win."

Pig farts and witches' breath! He had her boxed into a corner. Unwilling to admit it yet, Bera rubbed her fist and hoped his eye hurt as bad as her knuckles.

"I should think you'd be grateful, actually," he had the gall to add, "that I am willing to share the credit for a deed I planned."

"I have a plan," she countered through chattering teeth. "One that will be ready in only a week. We need no help from you."

"A week?" He let out a humorless chuckle. "That would be too late. Drust knows about Evan. That's why he had poor Alma drowned, to punish his wife."

"Nay." Bera didn't want to believe it, but the memory of her own father's face, crazed with lust and drink, reminded her that fathers were capable of the most heinous cruelty. "You just made that up," she argued without conviction. "Even Drust wouldn' stoop so low as to have his own daughter killed jus' for spite." Why was her tongue so thick? She could scarcely form the words. "Not 'is own daughter."

"I speak the truth," Curran said quietly. "Our Princess Diedre made a mighty thane of Drust, but now he chafes beneath her thumb and would have her dead. Your brother provided a perfect excuse." He groped for his cloak and found it. "The Beast has ordered all nine of your brothers executed four days hence in front of Diedre—after they've been tortured and publicly confess their adulterous trysts with her."

Tortured! Executed!

If he was telling the truth . . . but how could she know? Bera would have wept but for the numbing cold that seemed to have seeped into her bones. At least she had stopped shivering. If only she could sleep . . .

As if he sensed she was nearing the end of herself, Curran wrapped his cloak around her and chafed her through it. "The choice is yours. Marry me now and help me, or wake up on the way back to Pitlanric with a hell of a headache and marry me anyway." ·

A derisive snort escaped her. "Marry you? *Now?*"

"Aye. For your sake, now."

"Whadda you mean, for *my* sake?" she demanded, vaguely astonished that she sounded like a drunkard in his cups.

"As I said, I have no intention of letting you go until this is over. Just this moment, though, you're in real danger of freezing," he calmly explained. "I know of a safe hiding place, but we dare not light a fire there. That leaves only one way I can think of to get dry and warm each other up. For your sake, I would do it as your husband."

"My husband!" Whatever ideas of rutting he might have, she would make quick work of them. A naked man was a vulnerable man. She would only pretend to go along. Once she was warm, she would take care of her "husband."

"Decide," he said with ominous intensity.

Bera hesitated only briefly. "There are terms."

"Name them."

She jabbed a frozen finger at his chest. "Strike me, and I'll kill you."

"Agreed." His ready reply held a note of amusement that made her wonder if he really meant it, but she was serious enough for both of them.

"Force me," she went on with another jab, "an' I'll kill you."

"Reasonable enough." He waited.

Pig farts and witches' breath! Why couldn't she think straight? "There's something else," she muttered, "but hang me if I can remember. Oh yes!" She jabbed him a third time. "Touch one of my nieces or my brothers' wives—"

"And you'll kill me," he finished for her. "I'm getting a pretty good picture of how you plan to handle things."

"Aye," she mumbled, "an' dohn' you forget it!"

"Is that it?" he asked.

Some distant, rational part of her raised a frantic alarm at what she was about to do, but Bera ignored it. The truth was, she wanted to sleep with this golden warrior almost as much as she wanted to sleep, period.

"Very well. I marry you." She could always deny the marriage later. No one would take a hireling's word over hers.

"And I marry you," he responded. " 'Tis done, then."

He paused. "And don't get any ideas about denying it later. With or without your help, I will free your brothers, so you will be honor-bound to truly be my wife."

She'd just see about that! "My poor sainted mother mus' be rollin' in her grave, God rest her soul," she grumbled as he led her toward the doorway and the whistling wind beyond.

"Well, unless you want to join her, I suggest you step lively so we can get you out of those wet clothes and warm you up." He pulled off her cap and raised the hood of his cloak over her wet hair.

Warm up, indeed, Bera fumed. She would warm him up, all right.

chapter nine

Outside in the wind Bera willed her steps to match Curran's, but by the time they crossed the greensward, she was shambling, fuddle-headed as a quail.

"Come on, sleepyhead." Curran actually sounded worried. "Let's get you out of this wind." His arm tightened across her shoulders as he guided her past the building where Osann had waited during the execution. Beyond it, a smaller one leaned snugly against the wall of the lower rampart. Curran drew her into the doorway.

Bera heard him fumble with the keys. "What'r ya doin'?"

"What does it sound like I'm doing?" he asked in typical male fashion. "I'm getting the keys."

"S'this yer wunnerful hidin' place?" It looked like an ancient sheepcote to her.

"Don't talk, Bera."

"I'll talk if I blasted well please," she retorted. "An' if you dohn' like it, dohn' lissen."

"Your speech is slurred," he said tightly, trying another key. "You've stopped trembling. If I don't get you inside and warmed up soon, it will be too late."

Bera leaned against the door and laid her head back on the weathered wood. "No ball-snippin', blunderheaded well is gonna freeze *me* to death."

He tried another key, and this time, the lock tumbled, whereupon Bera's weight promptly sent the door wide open, leaving her in a heap on the hay-strewn peat floor.

At last. She could go to sleep. Closing her eyes to the sweet scent of summer grass mingled with the musty undertone of good dry peat, she barely heard him lock the door behind them.

Curran removed the key, hoping there was still time to keep Bera from freezing. He groped through the darkness until he found her still, cold form.

If she died . . .

She couldn't die. He wouldn't let her. She was his one chance to escape his rootless, relentless existence. His one chance to live a decent life; to fight for honor instead of gain; to sire children whose bloodline would command respect.

"Up, woman." All but frozen himself, he laid hold to her and lugged her to the haypile. Feeling for a spot to lay her, he discovered that they were not the first who had slept here. Just above knee-level, someone had shaped a bed in the dried grass.

He pulled his cloak from her, spread it across the hay, then laid Bera atop it, leaving room for himself. It wasn't easy undressing her; his hands were shaking badly. He knew his own chills did not matter, because his torso had gone only halfway into the well. But Bera's smaller body had been immersed completely in the icy water, and her symptoms were cause for concern. He had seen men freeze to death before and recognized the danger signs.

More concerned with her condition than with what he was uncovering, he stripped her boots and leggins from her, then wrestled off her sodden tunic. She wore nothing underneath, a fact that surprised him. He'd have thought a princess—even one disguised as a slave—would have warm underwear, at least.

Chafing her arms and legs, he found them cold as a corpse's. Alarmed, he laid his ear between her breasts and was relieved to hear a heartbeat—slow and faint, but steady.

There was still time.

He hastened to strip away his own clothes and wring the moisture from the damp wool. Then he laid them atop Bera and piled her well with hay. But he knew that wouldn't be enough. He'd have to share what little warmth he had with her, or she might never wake again.

Shivering almost uncontrollably, he slid onto the cloak and drew her into the shelter of his torso. A loud gasp escaped him when her icy buttocks came into contact with his manhood, sending his balls halfway to his waist.

This was going to take a *lot* of chafing . . . and some tall thinking.

Make that *hard* thinking, he corrected dryly.

Fighting off the urge to go to sleep himself, he worked his legs against hers and briskly rubbed her arms and body. Slowly but surely, she warmed from cold to cool. He wasn't certain how long he kept it up before his own body started to respond, but once it did, his skin awakened to the feel of the woman curled against him: the smooth curve of her taut buttocks against his cock; the firm resilience of her muscular arms and legs; the youthful roundness of her breasts.

He slid his palms down her ribs and abdomen, then threaded his fingers into the springy curls at the apex of her legs, seeking the sweet, moist softness hidden there. Sure enough, he found her sex warm and wet to the touch. And touch her he did, his own desire growing with every texture, every secret fold.

His bride. Curran could scarce believe it. He had actually married a princess, and she was his to take. He wondered if her lovemaking would be as savage as the rest of her. The prospect sent an exquisite shudder through his nether parts and spawned, unbidden, the vivid image of his storm goddess.

That fantasy was all it took. A ravenous jolt of lust sent his heart straight into his cock. "Bera," he said hoarsely, his voice ragged with wanting. "Wake up, Bera." When she didn't respond, his fingers probed deeper, testing her and finding her maidenhead intact.

"Damn."

His cock twitched in anticipation of piercing that veil of virginity, but his brain held him in check. Even he had scruples. He couldn't take her while she was insensible.

That left nothing but to wake her up, yet he had to be gentle. Their earlier confrontation had convinced him not to underestimate this savage princess in his arms. She'd probably try to kill him if he woke her rudely, and even in her weakened state, Bera was capable of doing some damage. She'd come close to besting him twice. If she was to accept him as a lover, he'd have to woo her back to consciousness.

He found the nubbin that could excite even a virgin to lust and rolled it between his fingers, then flicked it gently back and forth. Just as he felt it begin to enlarge and stiffen, Bera gave a long, satisfied moan and arched against his touch.

"Bera," he tried again.

"Mmmm," she answered, still only half conscious. " 'Sa wunnerful dream."

"It's not a dream, Bera. It's your wedding night, and I'm your husband."

Bera stretched, enjoying the illusion. Of course it was a dream. She had dreamed of Curran before.

But this was a better dream than before. Warmer— warm as a smooth river stone fresh from the embers. This dream had textures, smells. She was enveloped, embraced. Muscles moved against her body. Crisp hair tickled her skin. The firm, hot resistance of an erection nestled against her buttocks.

Bera shuddered with pleasure, her inward parts contracting.

Not a dream, her mind and body told her. Curran. Her husband.

But she would never marry a man so lowly. Not that he wouldn't make someone a good husband. He was, after all, a superb warrior, and handsome in a Viking sort of way.

She snuggled closer to the firm, warm flesh beside her, clinging to the dream and denying the truth her mind had told her. Bera kept her eyes closed, convinced that if she opened them, her dream lover would disappear. She turned in his arms and wrapped her leg across his strong male thighs. His muscles flexed beneath her.

She smoothed her hand over the planes and textures of his naked body.

So this was what a man felt like, smelled like.

It was good, better than her lonely imaginings had ever conceived.

His large, gentle hand slid back down to her sex, where his fingers parted the folds and rubbed some magic place, setting off another golden explosion of desire.

Curran.

Real. This was real, and she liked it.

"Whatever that is you're doing," she said raggedly, "please don't stop. It's the best thing I've ever felt." Her own hand, hungry for the feel of him, stroked lower, coming into contact with the exquisitely smooth tip of his erection.

It leapt at her touch, causing an answering paroxysm deep inside her.

Fascinated, she followed the urging of her desire and

threaded her fingers into the curls that nestled at its base, cupped his weighty balls in her hand, then stroked the length of his shaft.

Her intimate exploration made him gasp, then go rigid, his manhood pressed hard to her touch.

Amazing, how such an unimpressive cluster of flesh could swell to such proud proportion.

Back home she had hidden in the rafters and watched the churls' May revels, so she knew what cocks were for. But she seriously doubted one so large could fit inside of her. Her woman's place contracted at the thought of trying.

Perhaps she ought to check its size again.

It was smooth, yet not. Firm, yet resilient to her touch. She closed her fingers around the shaft and slid back up to the tip.

Curran gasped. "Sweet lord, woman." He hesitated, as if trying to hold back, then rolled atop her, his legs parting hers, his erection poised. Savage now, he sought her mouth and kissed her, hot and hard and demanding, his body pressed insistently to hers.

Curran's hunger raised her own, and Bera joined the fierce and tender war of flesh in earnest now. She broke the kiss, digging her nails into his back and drawing him even closer. "My body is hungry for your cock," she said raggedly. "Put it inside me, now."

Curran almost spilled his seed. Bera spoke and made love like a wild woman, and he was past ready to take her. But she was a virgin. "There will be pain this first time," he croaked out, pulling back in an effort to slow his own responses, but her hand closed around him, setting the darkness alive with sparks.

"It's so big," she said, her voice husky. "Will it fit?"

"It will fit." Shaking, not from hunger now but from desire held in check, he eased the tip inside her and met with the sweet resistance of her maidenhead.

Bera writhed against him. "Such precious torture cannot be endured."

He wanted to be gentle this first time, but Bera would have nothing of gentleness. She dug her nails into his shoulders and impaled herself with a shriek. It was a cry of triumph, not of pain.

She was hot and tight and wet, and it took all his concentration not to spend himself then and there. Slowly, he retracted to the brink, then slid deep, savoring every sensation.

"More." Bera dug her claws into his buttocks and drew him harder, faster, until both of them were panting with every thrust, flesh slapping flesh.

Curran couldn't hold back any longer. He spilled his seed, but he kept the pace until she straightened her legs and arched against him with a rending cry of satisfaction.

Instantly, she went limp, the muscles inside her fluttering. When he tried to pull away, she held him back. "Stay. I want to feel you inside me."

Was she always this frank? He hoped so. "It does go down, you know."

"Mmmm." She tightened around him, and he answered with a throb. When Nature took its course, he rolled onto his back and drew her close beside him.

To his surprise, she sought his member and caressed it. "Hmmm. Sticky."

"It seals our marriage," he quipped.

She stretched like a cat against him, then snuggled closer to his warmth. "Being married might not be so bad after all," she said sleepily. "Not if we can do this on a regular basis."

"Indeed." The idea appealed to Curran more than he cared to admit. Perhaps it was her fierceness, or her courage and determination, or her frankness—maybe all of those—but she had managed to touch him in a way that no woman ever had before.

"And how often will we be mating?" she inquired without the slightest hint of modesty. "Every night?"

Curran couldn't help it; he let out a rolling chuckle. "If you wish."

"Oh, I wish," she said frankly.

Smiling in the darkness, he risked a little frankness of his own. "You surprise me, Bera. I've always heard that highborn ladies have little enthusiasm for the baser appetites of life."

"Hmph! I should think our Princess Diedre would have disabused you of *that* ridiculous notion."

"A point well taken." Curran allowed himself to wonder what life with Bera would be like. Difficult, no doubt, but never dull.

She lay still for so long, he thought she had fallen asleep. Then she said with more than a hint of defensiveness, "I am old, you know."

Age. Even wild women were obsessed with it. "How old?" he asked with mock severity.

After a pause, she blurted out, "Twenty-six."

He was genuinely surprised. He ran his hand down her side. She didn't look that old, and she certainly didn't act it—probably because she had yet to endure the rigors of childbirth.

She was not soft and pliable like the other unmarried noblewomen he had seen, but Bera's spark and fitness combined to give the illusion of youth, despite her advanced years.

"So you see," she said tightly, "I cannot give you children."

Curran felt a sinking sensation in his gut. No children? That meant no future, no one to carry on his name. "Have you ceased your courses, then?" he asked, his voice harsher than he intended.

"Nay," she answered to his vast relief. "But the midwife says my womb must surely have shriveled up by now."

Children were the only immortality a man could count on, and Curran wanted them. He hadn't realized how much until just now. "Has the midwife examined you?"

"She has not!" Bera huffed. "I would not let someone like that look at me, much less touch me."

"Then you do not know that you can't have children." Not that it mattered. She was a princess and the marriage had been consummated.

"So if you wish to be free of me," she said softly, "I will understand."

Curran tensed. He did not want to think that this was a deliberate ploy to be shed of him, but his self-protective instincts would not let him see it otherwise. All the warm feelings he had started to have for Bera suddenly went cold. "Think you for one moment that I would give up my reward for any reason, even that? Nay, lady. You are bound to me in the eyes of God and man, and I am your lord. All you have is mine."

His harsh words struck Bera like a mace. Was that all she was to him? A prize that bought him what he could not win for himself: a respectable place among his betters?

Stung, she recoiled and sat up. Already, the darkness had softened. She must hurry if she was to make it back into the citadel unseen. "Where are my clothes?"

Without a word, Curran reached beyond her and drew the cold, damp raiments down. Bera snatched them, shivering at the thought of putting them on so soon after she had finally begun to get warm. But pride kept her from gasping when she did. As soon as she was dressed, she crawled across Curran, relishing every ice-cold contact of her clothes on his bare skin.

Served him right, the evil, calculating son of a sow. "Where are my shoes?"

"On the ground just beside us," he said with deceptive quietness.

She pulled them on, then stomped to the door. It was locked, and he had the key. The last thing she wanted to do was ask him for anything. He was probably lying there laughing at her. "The key," she said imperiously without looking back. "I would leave."

She heard him rise and felt him approach from behind. When he reached around to place the key on the lock, she felt his cloak brush against her back.

"Don't forget," he reminded her. "Tonight must be the night. I plan to free your brothers just before the first watch. Can you provide a diversion?"

"Aye." Bera put her wounded pride on hold. He trusted her to help in the escape, at least. "A fire?"

"As long as it's a big one, something that will draw everyone away from the stables and the gates."

"It will be." Why did he have to stand so close, crowding her? "I know how to create a diversion."

"If I didn't think you could, I would not have asked." His voice softened as he reached for his leggins. "We are on the same side, you know."

He was right. The escape was all that mattered. "I have sleeping potions enough for four men," she volunteered. "Do you need them?"

"Potions? Nay." Curran drew up his sodden leggins without so much as a flinch. "That's a woman's weapon, not a warrior's." He stood. Even in the darkness, the sight of him was enough to send a disconcerting shard of lust through Bera. "Better an honest kill." He shrugged into his tunic, then sat to pull on his wet boots. "Drug a man, and he wakes to ride against you. And ride against us Drust's men will."

Bera was not a child that he should speak to her so.

"My brothers and I can take care of any who follow."

"Like they took care of themselves when they came here?" he asked without a shred of tact.

"That was treachery," she shot back.

"And what else would they expect from Drust?"

"Take care, *husband*," Bera warned in deadly earnest. "We may say what we will of each other, but my brothers and I brook no criticism from outsiders. Do I make myself clear?"

Curran stood and donned his cloak. "You forget one thing, *wife*: I am not an outsider any longer. You made me part of the family, and as such, I'll speak the truth as I see fit."

Bera resisted the urge to slap his arrogant face. "You have much to learn, sir, about being a part of a proper family."

"And you," he said, unlocking the door, "have much to learn, ma'am, about being a proper wife."

chapter ten

Bera felt as if she had just closed her eyes when a knock sounded at her door.

She forced one eye open and saw the gray light of dawn.

Dawn? Not yet!

The knocking resumed—urgent, persistent.

She tried to get up, but after last night's ordeal, she felt several heartbeats behind reality.

The knocking didn't go away.

Not good, this early. Definitely not good, but she was too tired to worry why. It took what little sensibility she had left to ready herself for whatever might be waiting on the other side of that door.

Easing Osann aside, she sat up, scrubbed her face with her hands in an effort to stir her blood, then rose, donned her cloak, and went to see who it was.

Surely it wouldn't be Curran. He had better sense than to come here.

She opened the door to find Diedre's lady Malisande, her eyes red and swollen. "My lady would have you come at once, Weaver."

Why would the princess send for her? Bera could think of no reason that boded well. Something about this didn't smell right. "I have not yet dressed or broken my fast," Bera equivocated. "Pray, grant me a little time to—"

"You are dressed well enough." Malisande took rough hold of Bera's arm. "And there is food and drink aplenty in her highness's chamber. My instructions were to bring you at once—" Her voice broke. "—and that, at least, I can do."

Bera understood Malisande's frustration, but she did not relish the idea of going into Diedre's lair unarmed. Curran had all her daggers. She considered breaking free and making some excuse so she could get her sword.

Malisande, though, had no intention of letting go of Bera. "Not another word. You have been summoned. Obey, or I shall call for the guards." Without waiting for a response, she all but dragged Bera toward the royal chamber.

This definitely did not bode well.

Bera looked back through the doorway and saw Osann peeking in fear from under the covers. "It's all right, Osann," she called over her shoulder. "I shall be back soon, with food. Lots of it."

Then, rather than allow Malisande to pull her along like a disobedient churl on her way to a whipping, she quickened her pace and took the lead. To her chagrin, Malisande did not let go, even when they passed the hawk-eyed guards and entered the sumptuous chamber that had become Diedre's prison.

The princess's chair was drawn close to the fire, like an old woman's. She sat huddled in furs, her face haggard.

Bera felt true pity for the woman, which made no sense, for Diedre was her enemy and still capable of wreaking havoc. But remembering Alma's execution . . . Diedre's sins had indeed borne bitter fruit, and her worst sin had not been adultery, but her determination to gain power in a man's world. The cruelest punishments seemed reserved for that.

Bera wondered how long it would be before *she* suffered *her* punishment for living free as a warrior all these years. A harsh reckoning would come; it always did for women like her and Diedre.

Perhaps it had come already.

Malisande drew Bera to the hearth and at last let go of her. "I have brought The Weaver, your highness."

"Leave us." Diedre's voice, like the rest of her, seemed to have aged a decade in a day. Tragedy had stripped away her mask of matronly propriety, revealing the anguished, bitter woman underneath.

She waited until her maid had gone to turn and look at Bera. "Remove your cloak. I would see you."

Unwilling to expose herself, Bera bowed low. "I humbly beg your highness's pardon, but I am wearing only my chainse underneath. Your highness's summons came so early, I had no time to dress properly."

Diedre's eyes narrowed. "My grief has not made a fool of me, nor has it left me in any mood to tolerate such insolence. I gave you a direct order. Do it." She spoke like a woman who had nothing left to lose, and anyone who had nothing to lose was dangerous—especially a woman.

Deciding that this was a battle better left unfought, Bera removed her cloak and folded it across her arm.

"That's better." Diedre motioned to the low chair facing her on the hearth. "Sit you. There are things of which we must speak, before . . ." She did not finish.

Bera tensed, interpreting the unfinished comment as confirmation that Diedre must have discovered what Drust had in store for her.

The dragon princess fixed her with a piercing gaze. "How have you managed it?" she asked obliquely.

Taken aback, Bera frowned. "Managed what, your highness?"

"Avoiding marriage all these years."

Did she know who Bera really was? Bera looked into her eyes and saw she did.

But how? Struggling to cover her alarm and the frantic questions that went through her mind, she realized someone must have betrayed her.

Diedre was staring at her, expecting an answer, so she decided that the safest course was the truth—a little of it, anyway. "I have not escaped marriage, your highness," she confessed, already regretting what she'd done last night.

Well, not quite *all* of what she'd done, she amended at a stab of remembered passion.

"You're *not* an old maid?" Diedre was openly skeptical. "I had heard otherwise." Even in her grief and imprisonment, the dragon princess still played her perverse games with the lives of those about her. And a dangerous game it was.

Bera shivered, feeling vulnerable and exposed without her cloak.

So Diedre had discovered who she was. Bera knew her every word must be carefully chosen, but her mind was clogged with questions, making it difficult to concentrate.

Had Curran betrayed her, come straight from their mating to report who she was to the princess? Had he been playing both sides all along?

She wouldn't put it past him.

Another possibility left her even sicker.

Evan. Surely *he* could not have betrayed her identity.

Or could he? Remembering his anguish when he thought it was Diedre who'd been executed, Bera had to wonder.

Was there no honor among men at all?

If either Curran or Evan was in league with the princess, what would that mean for the planned escape?

Shaken, she made what she hoped was a safe response to Diedre's comment. "In the end, all women—even the highest-born of princesses—are at the mercy of men, no matter what we do."

" 'Tis true." Diedre's eyes glazed as she stared into the smoking peat fire. "When a princess weds," she said bitterly, "she weds beneath her, for it is through her, and her alone, that the blood of kings is bestowed. And I—" She shuddered. "I was bartered to Drust, shackled for life to The Beast."

Bera had been bartered, too, by the brothers she loved and trusted—still loved, in spite of everything. But she alone bore responsibility for giving herself away to an outcast, a man without honor.

"Once we take them into our beds and our bodies," Diedre continued, "they become lord over us, controlling not only our lives, but also the lands we brought them and the children we bear them." Unconsciously, she rubbed her abdomen as if her empty womb ached for the daughter she had lost. "That's the cruelest irony of all, and numbness is our only refuge."

"Your highness has suffered worst of all, methinks," Bera said with real sympathy.

Diedre looked at her in anger. "Waste no pity on me. I shall welcome death when it comes, for it will bring an end to feeling."

"That's the cost for caring," Bera said as much for herself as Diedre. "The pain that always follows."

She had cared last night, had exposed herself to Curran, openly expressing both her pleasure in their joining and her fear that she could not give him children. And what had Curran done in response? He'd struck her to the core, concerned only with the lands and status their marriage brought him. "Is there any man in this world worth caring for?" she asked. "Any man worth saving?"

Diedre regarded her sharply, then her expression sagged. "For me, there is one. Like me, he is chained to one he hates." She stared again into the fire. "I should hate him worst of all, because he made me remember what it's like to have a heart and hope. How I wish he hadn't."

Clearly, she was speaking of Evan.

"Do you want him punished for that?" Bera dared to ask. She had no reason to expect an honest answer, yet now that they were speaking as the equals they were, she hoped for one. "Would you have him die, for *that*?"

Diedre met her questioning gaze with one of her own, then sighed in resignation. "No. I should, but the heart is a foolish thing. I would have him live, so the memory—or the illusion—of love might live on with him."

So she did love Evan! The revelation was as poignant as it was surprising. Or was this just another ploy in the dragon princess's elaborate game?

Bera's instincts told her that Diedre had spoken true. She chose her next words carefully. "There might be a way for all to survive this."

Diedre's expression sharpened. "Well done. You do not disappoint me." She actually smiled, but Bera saw no joy in the expression, only grim satisfaction. Diedre leaned closer and lowered her voice. "No man can accuse, who is not there to do so."

Did she know of the escape plan, or was she merely suggesting one?

Either implication was troubling enough.

The time for games was over. "Perhaps I could be of service, then," Bera said softly, "to rid your highness's household of strangers."

Diedre nodded. " 'Tis why you came, is it not?"

Bera felt her throat tighten, her heartbeat quicken in

alarm, but she remained outwardly calm. "Your help might make it easier."

"Look outside my door," Diedre retorted. "I cannot even help myself. Drust has left me with nothing, not even my keys."

Her keys. Bera wondered fleetingly if the keys Curran had obtained might not in fact be Diedre's. But they couldn't have been. Drust would have turned the fortress inside out until he found them.

"I shall do what I can on my own," Bera conceded. "But first, I must eat and sleep." She glanced pointedly at the tempting spread of food on the princess's table.

"Take it," Diedre volunteered. "And the wine. I'll have Malisande bring it to your chamber." She arched an elegant eyebrow. "You would be well advised to stay out of sight, at least until dark. No one close to me is safe. Drust is out of control, drunk with wine and rage." She eased down into her chair. "What little influence I have left, I shall use to see that no one enters your chamber."

Bera stood. "Then I beg your leave."

Diedre rose with her. "There is one more thing you must know," she added. "Your household harbors a traitor, one more than willing to see you and your family destroyed. I do not know if Drust is also paying—"

The door burst open and two of Drust's chieftains stormed in.

Feeling as if she'd been caught naked, Bera turned away from them and hastily donned her cloak.

"Lord Drust has sent us," a gruff voice declared.

As soon as she was safely covered, she turned and recognized Murdoc, Drust's second-in-command. A terrified Malisande lurked just inside the door.

Bera's heart lurched. What did this signify? Had Drust changed his plan, moved the executions up? Were her brothers being tortured even now?

"Lord Drust has sent us to escort your highness to him," Murdoc said with the same convincing deference he always used with his princess. "If your highness will please." The amenities were only rhetorical, as all present knew. A summons by Drust was an order, not a suggestion.

Like one already dead, Diedre rose and glided toward the door.

Bera wanted to call out after her, but she knew Diedre would never reveal the name of the traitor before witnesses. She might never have the chance to reveal it.

Malisande fell in behind her mistress at the doorway, but Murdoc eased her aside. "She'll be back," he promised. Judging from his tone, he believed it, yet Bera knew better than to count on such assurances. Who could say what Drust would do?

Diedre showed no fear. "Malisande, see that The Weaver is well fed," she said without looking back. "And that she is allowed to work in her chamber undisturbed." Then, calm and aloof, she went to meet the husband who hated her as much as she hated him.

"Thank you, your highness," Bera called after her, wondering what new calamity this day would bring.

True to Diedre's command, Malisande delivered the food, making no secret of her disdain for such "waste." "Her Highness has given orders that you are to work undisturbed for the rest of the day," she said in parting. "So see that you work."

When she was gone, Bera ate a hearty meal and insisted that Osann do the same. Next, she enlisted the child's help to braid and arrange her long auburn hair for battle. Then she changed into her boots, bliaut, and tunic. That done, she drew her sword from its hiding place.

Osann's eyes went big as trenchers.

Bera was surprised. She had thought Osann would have long since found the weapon. She held it down where Osann could see it better. "This was made specially for me. I brought it with me from my home, Pitlanric," Bera explained to her.

Osann stared at the sword in awe.

"Would you like to touch it?" Bera asked.

"Nay." Fear flickered in her eyes. "My hand would fall off."

"Who told you such a thing?"

"All the servants say so," she said breathlessly. "If a slave ever touches a weapon, his hand will fall off. Or worse."

"That's nonsense," Bera said. "I touch weapons all the time, and as you can see, I still have all my parts."

Osann was not convinced. "But you are not a slave."

"When we get to Pitlanric, I'll show you." Bera laid the sword within easy reach.

"Are we going to Pitlanric?" Osann asked, her tiny, heart-shaped face betraying a mix of emotions.

"Aye." Bera drew her close and gave her a hug. "God willing," she whispered, "tonight we will see the last of this place."

Osann tucked her chin, skeptical. "You're going to *steal* me?" she whispered.

"That I am." Bera gave her ribs a tickle. "And I shall not let them take you back. Ever. I shall use my special sword to protect you always."

Releasing the little girl, Bera nodded to the large loom. "I will need my bobbins when we get back to Pitlanric, so that I can teach you all my secrets. Then you'll be able to weave yourself a magic cloak, just as fine as mine."

Osann burst into a dimpled smile. "I would like to be a weaver, just like you." Immediately, she began to remove Bera's special bobbins from the large loom.

Bera didn't mind seeing her start on the sun cloak taken apart. It had served its purpose, and she'd never intended to finish it.

She dismantled the portable loom that had taken her three years to perfect, then she gathered the pieces and tied them into a tidy bundle.

When everything was ready to pack, she drew out the two sacks she'd brought with her from Pitlanric. The heavier one held her princess necklace sewn into a secret pocket in the bottom. Sitting on the pallet with one of her hooks, she set about loosing it.

Live or die, she would do what must be done this night, but as a princess, not a slave.

Osann watched in tense silence. Bera didn't hear a peep out of her until the last stitch holding the massive silver chain gave way and she drew it out into the light.

Osann gasped aloud. "Did you steal it? They'll kill you if they find you—"

"Nay, child. I did not steal it," Bera assured her. "I was born to it, as was my mother before me, and her mother before her." She laid it into Osann's lap, along with its polishing cloth. "Polish this well," she said confidentially, "for I mean to wear it when we leave this place tonight."

Osann held the necklace as if it were made of glass and gently began to rub away the weeks of tarnish.

Bera packed the small loom and bobbins. Once that was done, she stowed the remainder of the food in the other sack. She looked through the yarns she had so carefully made and decided to take the most precious, the scarlet, filling what little space was left. She stuffed as much as she could into the tops of the bags, then tied the two sacks together.

Only one more thing to do. She tucked the keys Curran had given her into the pocket of her tunic, then added her wicks and flints and sat back to wait.

She was ready.

Now, if only Curran would do what he had promised . . .

Was she being a fool to think he would?

What choice do you have? her practical self asked. *Everything Diedre said confirmed his story.*

Blinking heavily, she ordered her mind to quit such useless questions and concentrate on doing her part. The rest was in God's hands.

And Curran's.

Of course, she hadn't noticed *God* doing anything to free her brothers on His own.

A huge yawn interrupted the irreverent thought.

You're rambling! she scolded herself. *Stop insulting the Lord God Almighty and get some sleep!*

Under other circumstances, she would have sat up waiting, going over the plans in her mind, imagining possible complications and the responses she might make. But Bera had reached the end of herself. She had to sleep, even if only for a few hours.

"That's enough, Osann." Her hand stilled Osann's polishing. "Put it on me."

Reverently, the little girl draped the glowing chain around her neck and fastened the clasps. It felt right, and Bera hoped the sensation was a good omen. Her cloak and hood would hide the chain when they left, but for now, Bera risked wearing it in the open.

She drew Osann to the pallet and sat beside her. "I have one more task for you, the most important task you have ever done."

"I will do it," Osann said with touching determination. "Your highness has only to name the task."

Strange, how odd Bera's proper title sounded after only a few weeks without it.

"I must rest now," she explained, her eyes half-lidded with fatigue, "but I cannot sleep long past sundown. I'm counting on you to wake me as soon as it's dark, no matter how difficult that might be." She pointed to the laver. "Splash me with water, if you must, even pinch me, but wake me as soon as it's dark."

Osann pulled away, visibly terrified to use such methods on her mistress—especially now that she knew Bera was a princess. Diedre had ordered slaves killed for much less.

"I am depending on you, Osann," Bera confided, so weary that she bordered on tears herself. "I *must* get some sleep, but I dare not close my eyes unless I know you will wake me in time. Everything depends upon it."

Osann chewed her lip, obviously torn between her loyalty for Bera and the bitter lessons of her life. In the end, loyalty won out. "I shall do it," she said. "Rest easy, your highness. I shall wake you in time."

"I know you will." Bera drew the little girl close for another big hug, but released her sadly when she felt Osann stiffen. Already, her rank had come between them. "Keep watch while I sleep."

"Yes, your highness."

Sad that she would never again be "Missy" to her little girl, Bera went to sleep.

A cold drop of water splashed her eye, then another, but it wasn't Bera getting wet, not really. Just a dream of wetness.

"Mistress!" a distant child's voice summoned. "It is time."

More drops, almost a splash. Still, only a dream.

"Please, your highness. Wake up," the voice pleaded, a little closer now, but still distant. "Everything depends upon it. Wake up."

Everything depends upon it. There was something about that—

A sharp pain at the base of her fingernail jarred her.

Pain. Definitely not a dream.

She heard a moan. Her own?

"May God forgive me," the anguished little voice was closer still. "You told me to do what I must, your highness. Please don't kill me for it."

Agony erupted from the base of Bera's left middle fingernail.

"The devil!" she cried aloud, eliciting a frightened shush from her attacker. She woke sitting up, shaking her throbbing finger. "Where in blue blazes did you learn to do *that*?"

"From Henda the scullery maid." Osann's answer was thready with tears. "She does it to me whenever no one else is looking." She sniffed loudly. "I'm so sorry I hurt you, your highness, but nothing else worked, and you told me to do what I must."

Please don't kill me for it.

Poor lamb. Learning that Bera was a princess had probably erased whatever fragile trust had grown between them. Bera resolved then and there to free the child—if both of them were still alive this time the morrow.

"There, there." Still shaking her injured finger, she circled Osann's shoulders with her other arm and gave her a brief hug. "You've done well."

She inhaled deeply as she rose, glad for the cold air to clear her head. "We'll leave together," she whispered, donning her cloak. She located Osann in the darkness, then found the sacks and laid them over the little girl's shoulder, balancing the weight as evenly as she could. "Take these. Once we're outside, make your way to the stables without being seen, then hide away there." She grinned in the darkness. "I know you can do it. You're a master at disappearing."

"Aye, your highness." She thought she heard a smile in Osann's reply.

"I will join you at the stable later." Bera slid her sword into place, then closed her cloak. "Stay hidden until I come, no matter what alarms you hear."

"Aye, your highness." Osann moved in close, but not as close as before.

"There will be many men with me when I come," Bera explained, "men who smell very bad. They are my brothers. If anything happens to me, obey them as you would me."

"Aye, your highness," Osann said calmly. "But nothing bad will happen to you."

"Your mouth to God's ear," Bera muttered. "Remember," she said as she raised her hood. "If he stinks, you can trust him."

Strained though it was, Osann's giggle was music to her ears.

She took a deep breath and summoned up the image of Drust as he watched his daughter's execution. Then she imagined herself standing beside him with her sword raised to strike.

A welcome rush of battle-lust cleared the lingering cobwebs from her mind and erased the weary aches of her body.

This night, more than her brothers would be avenged.

"Come. It is time." She opened the door and led Osann to meet their destiny.

chapter eleven

Bera had her worries about what Drust might have done this day, but she had to trust that Curran would have contacted her if anything significant had changed.

It wasn't easy, trusting Curran, but then again, it couldn't be easy for him to trust her, either. Their alliance was every bit as forced and unsettled as their marriage. Still, in the absence of any word to the contrary, she had little choice but to move forward with their plan.

There could be no turning back.

This time the morrow, she would be dead or on her way back to Pitlanric with her brothers. No other options existed.

She had to believe her brothers were alive and that Curran would bring them to the stable as he'd promised. Believing made it possible for her to do what must be done.

From the moment she shepherded Osann into the hallway for what she devoutly hoped was the last time, she did her best to focus on victory, not her fears. Moving down the hallway, she conjured up the image of all of them—she and Osann, her brothers, and even Curran—galloping unopposed through the main gate to freedom while the granary burned in the distance behind them.

The vision came easily—a good omen.

Bera drew Osann close into the folds of her cloak as they approached Diedre's chamber, where the two warriors stood again on guard. So Murdoc had kept his word and brought the princess back. But in what condition?

A tiny shudder coursed up Bera's back at the thought of what Drust might have done to his wife. Shaking it off, she forced her steps to a judicious pace as she sheltered Osann past the waiting warriors.

Lord, You can make a way where there is no way, she prayed as she went. *Confound our enemies. Help us safe to freedom, and I will take my place among The Wives without complaint.*

Had she promised that before?

This time, I mean it, God. Truly.

Instead of the peace that signaled God's acceptance, she felt a pang of conscience. She'd made so many vows to God, only to break them, that she could hardly blame Him for not believing her this time.

But this time she truly did mean it. To convince Him of her sincerity, she added a grudging, *I'll even be a proper wife to Curran. I swear it on my honor as a warrior and a princess.*

If that didn't convince Him, nothing would.

Satisfied, she hastened Osann through the Great Hall, into the service warren, then down a narrow corridor to the servants' entrance.

"Halt." An unfamiliar sentry armed with a stave stood and blocked their path.

Blast. Of all times for the regular guard to be off duty. Bera had counted on his being there, sound asleep as usual.

"I am her highness's weaver," she said calmly, glad that Osann had drawn up close behind her, out of sight. "On her highness's business."

"Hmmt. Her highness, is it?" The replacement eyed

her with disdain. "And what sort of business would that be in the middle of the night, I'd like to know."

Bera's voice hardened. "If you think I would share her highness's private concerns with the likes of you, think again. Now step aside."

Perhaps under the circumstances it had been a mistake to invoke Diedre. Bera eased her arm out of the sleeve and laid hold to her sword beneath her cloak. She'd rather not kill the man, for someone might find his body, even if she hid it, and raise an alarm.

The sentry wavered. "Nobody told me anything about business such as this."

"By all means, then, send a page to the princess for confirmation," Bera said with regal sarcasm. "Those of us who serve her work deep into the night, every night, but her highness retires early. Have her wakened, though. She will not disavow me, but I am certain she'll be most eager to know who had her roused in the middle of the night."

The aging warrior pulled at his lower lip, then thought better of himself. He scowled at her, but moved aside. "Very well, then. Pass."

Head high, she moved past him. Like the shadow from a flame, Osann stuck close, altering her position so the guard never even saw her.

So far, Bera's prayer was working.

She shoved open the armored door and hustled Osann outside. As soon as they were across the threshold, she stepped aside and let the strong sea gale slam the heavy door shut behind them.

Standing in the wind-scoured common, Bera could almost feel the portents swirling around them, hanging heavy in the lowering clouds. She and her brothers would dance the blade this night and win or lose at destiny's decree. The dire peril of what must now be set in motion stirred her blood and fortified her warrior's heart.

It wasn't as cold outside as it had been the night before, but even though her bones still ached from last night's escapade, she was glad for the wind. It would fan the flames, making it easier to set the granary ablaze. As long as it didn't rain.

Once they were safely beyond the torchlit entry, Bera looked up at the clouds and smelled the air. No rain, not for a while anyway. And it didn't feel like snow. Perhaps the Tempest Mother hadn't turned against her after all.

The upper ward was deserted as it had been the night before, every door and window tightly shuttered. Just to be safe, though, she kept to the shadows until it was time for her and Osann to go their separate ways.

At the seaward corner of the citadel, Bera stopped and squatted to Osann's level. "Remember—'"

"I remember," Osann interrupted with uncharacteristic assertiveness. "Go to the stable and hide. You and your stinky brothers will come."

Bera grinned, then sobered. "Or just my stinky brothers."

"No," Osann would hear none of that. "*You* and your stinky brothers will come for me, and then we will all be free."

She said it with such conviction, Bera could almost believe it. The woman in her wanted to cradle Osann in her arms to comfort and draw comfort, but the warrior in her had been loosed, so she gave the little girl's hindside an affectionate swat instead. "Off with you now, and may God keep you."

She watched until Osann melted into the darkness in the general direction of the stables. Then she set out toward the warriors' lodgings, anxious to begin.

Moving swiftly, she drew her sword and kissed its blade for luck. She could almost hear Airell saying, "Just do the job and live to tell it."

The watchman would be starting his rounds any time

now. When she reached the lodging, she waited in the shadows. Long minutes passed before a lone figure pushed aside the skins over the doorway and stepped out onto the wind. After a spate of huffing and puffing and stamping his feet, he drew his sword, took one of the torches mounted beside the door, then set out for the first station of his rounds.

Bera raced for the granary. Approaching it from behind, she kept to the base of the circular stone building until she saw the lone guard. He was huddled deep in his furs by a brazier at the doorway, his cudgel propped against the wall.

Quiet as a spring snowfall, she crept up on his leeward side. She made it to within a yard of him without being heard, then stopped. Carefully, she took a firm grip near the end of her blade with her right hand, then picked up a pebble with her left and tossed it past him to the door. When he rose and turned to investigate, she whacked him atop the head with the pommel of her sword much as she'd whacked Tundarr that day so many months ago.

The impact produced a satisfying bonk.

Fool. He hadn't even picked up his cudgel.

Like Tundarr, he staggered, but did not topple—just stood there, slightly acant, his cudgel still propped by the wall.

Blast! Some people didn't know when to fall down. Now she'd have to run him through.

She flipped her sword-grip back into her hand and positioned for a death-thrust, but hesitated.

Bera had never flinched from an honest kill in a fair fight, but there was no honor in skewering an unarmed enemy from behind. It would make an unlucky beginning for this night's work.

He hadn't even tried to defend himself.

She decided to give him a poke with her blade before she finished him.

That was all it took. He toppled like a storm-struck oak.

Bera gave his pate another tap for good measure, tied him with his own furs, then dragged him to a spot behind an adjacent building where she hoped no one would find him until they were long gone.

Blast, but she was out of shape after all these weeks of inactivity. Huffing and puffing, she hastened back to use the key Curran had given her.

The key worked perfectly. She hurried inside and made straight for the bales of sweet summer grass piled to one side. In a matter of minutes, she had strewn great heaps of grass around the mound of precious grain. Then she gathered a fat sheaf of hay, struck her flints, fanned the embers to a flame, and used the makeshift torch to ignite the dried grass.

Between the exertion of hiding the guard and the heat of the fire, she was actually warm for the first time in two days.

Bera exited, closed the door, locked it, and sprinted for the stables.

She looked back only once and was gratified to see smoke pouring from the thatch and orange flames licking at the eaves.

She had just reached the stables when the first alarm went out.

"Fire! Fire!" The one cry guaranteed to empty every building in the compound and the village beyond.

Deep in the dungeon, Curran heard the alarm, too. When he did, the knot of tension in his chest eased, but only slightly. They weren't out of the woods yet.

By the flickering light of the torch he'd taken from the guard's station, he put the massive key into the lock and turned. The mechanism screeched like the Banshi, but Curran didn't have to worry about alerting the guard. He lay dead on the floor beside him, just as Curran had found him. Poisoned, no doubt.

It took both hands and a lot of muscle to open the door. When he did, the stench almost knocked him over. Inside, a circle of filthy men crowded forward, one cleaner than the rest, and nine pairs of suspicious eyes blinked at him with suspicion from haggard, unshaven faces.

"Can you walk?" he asked.

"Who wants to know?" a short, dark-haired one demanded.

"I'm Curran, Bera's husband, come to get you out of this cursed place." Ignoring their sudden collective intake of breath, he picked up the dead guard and thrust the body forward. "Here. Hide him as best you can."

Nine pairs of arms reached out. The first few who got hold of the body whisked it away.

"We haven't much time," Curran told them, anxious to be on their way. "Can you walk?"

"Aye. We're fit enough," said the tallest, whose intense blue eyes contrasted sharply with his graying black hair. He was gaunt, but still formidable. "Have you any weapons?"

"Only my own and these." He handed out the daggers he'd taken from Bera.

"Hey," one of them challenged. "These look like Bera's."

The tall one stepped forward. "Nobody takes Bera's daggers from her, not if she's livin'." He glared at Curran, the dagger poised. "What have you done with our sister?"

"I told you. I married her." Curran stood his ground. "She's waiting for us now at the stables," he said, hoping it was true. "She was the one who set fire to the granary to draw everyone away from the horses. With luck, we'll meet no opposition." He motioned them forward. "Unless you'd rather stay here, we must be off to the stables."

The men exchanged wary glances, then shuffled forward, still unsteady on their legs. Curran knew the feeling; he'd spent his time in the well of sorrows. So he also knew that they would regain their strides quick enough.

He scanned the ragtag procession. The nine moved as one, helping each other up the stairs. "Are any ill or injured?"

The tall one turned. Or was it the same one? "Nay. We're well enough to ride." He nudged the thickset blond beside him. "Orrin here is deaf, but he does just fine with us."

"Right, then." Curran doused the torch in the overflowing offal bucket, then closed and locked the door. That done, he worked his way to the head of the stairs and took the lead.

They were moving slow, but not so slow they wouldn't make it. "Brace yourselves," he warned when he reached the entry. "The wind's up outside."

"I'd be willin' to freeze my pecker for a breath of fresh air," one of them rumbled, setting loose a ragged chorus of coughs and chuckles.

"Wait here," he cautioned. "I'll make sure no one's about." Sword drawn, he shoved the door open against the gale and slipped outside. Just as he had hoped, everyone seemed occupied with saving the granary. At the far side of the ward, he saw warriors, slaves, and servants alike working fast and furious to pass buckets from the well in the lower ward to the fire.

Curran fought the door back open and braced himself against it. "Hurry. The stables are to the left, beyond the citadel. Keep to the shadows." As soon as they were out, he caught up with the first in line and led the way.

Within a matter of yards, they were all walking at a decent pace.

"So," the tallest murmured. "You're Curran."

"Aye." This was no time for small talk, but Curran humored his brother-by-law. "And you?"

"Angus. I'm the oldest." He indicated another tall one. "That's my twin brother Airell."

Identical twins.

Curran just nodded. It would take some getting used to, being around these brothers who were so accustomed to living and talking as a group. Yet already, he envied the way they protected each other.

Picking up the pace, he urged them faster toward the stable. . . . and escape.

By the time the alarm reached its peak, Bera had made it to the stable where the finest of the warhorses were kept. Already, grooms, stableboys, and horsemen were scrambling out into the night, buckets in hand, leaving the skittish horses to fend for themselves.

She waited until all had grown still, then eased inside, sword drawn and ready. Disturbed by the alarm, the warhorses stamped and pulled at their tethers, but she saw no sign that anyone had stayed behind to tend them.

Stall by stall, she made certain—all twenty-two stalls and twenty horses. She covered every square foot, including the loft, without finding anyone—including Osann.

Worried that some ill might have befallen the child, she leaned down from the loft and checked again to make sure the stable was empty before descending the ladder. She climbed down. When she reached the bottom, she turned to find someone standing right behind her.

Years of training brought her sword high, ready to

strike, but the split second before she acted, her conscious mind intervened.

Osann. It was Osann, and she'd almost struck her down.

"Blessed saints, child!" she whispered. Heart pounding, she lowered her weapon. "You scared the life out of me. Where *were* you?"

"You said to hide," Osann reminded her. "So I hid." She looked around. "Where are your stinky brothers?"

"They're coming." Bera drew her into an empty stall to wait. "Soon. They'll be here soon." They had to be. There would be no other chances, and she would not leave without them.

Long minutes passed before Osann stood up and smiled. "I smell them," she said in that sweet little-girl voice. "They're here."

Bera held her back and cautiously looked out to see. She smelled nothing but the familiar odors of hay and horseshite, and heard nothing but the stamp of shifting hooves, distant shouts, and the whistle of the wind.

Then she picked it up—a faint whiff of the dungeon. They *were* here. Excited yet still on edge, she drew Osann beside the stable doors and waited, her sword at the ready, just in case.

A black-cloaked figure came through first.

Curran. Bera recognized the fabric of his cloak even before she saw the telltale set of his shoulders. When he turned and saw her sword poised, he stiffened much as she had upon finding Osann. He did a better job of covering his surprise than she had, though. His only comment was a sarcastic, "Save your strength for the enemy."

Whatever retort she might have made was instantly forgotten when Angus came through the door. Bera fell on him and hugged him soundly, oblivious to the stink. He was so thin.

He pushed her to arm's length. "Nice coat."

Behind him came Roy, then Airell, then Kegan and Orrin, followed by Becan, Donall and Fidach, and last, Evan.

Thanks be to God, they were all upright and looked well enough, considering their ordeal. She would have hugged them every one, but there wasn't time. Already, they were bridling the horses that would take them to freedom.

"There are more than enough horses," she said to Angus, "but I don't think we should leave any behind. Will it slow us down too much to take them all?"

"Nay." He addressed his brothers. "Make sure we leave none behind, lads." Then he turned back to Bera and saw Osann peeking from the folds of her cloak. "What the devil is that?"

Bera swung the child up astride her hip. "She's mine, you great lummox. Now quit wasting time and find a horse." She pointed to the dappled gelding in the first stall. "We'll take this one."

It took only moments to bridle it, loose its tether, and hoist Osann—sacks and all—to its withers. Bera mounted by taking hold of a rope that hung from the rafters and swinging herself astride the horse's wide, muscular back.

To her dismay, it caused a sharp stab of pain in her most intimate parts, which she did her best to ignore.

"Have you ever ridden a horse before?" she asked, turning the little girl around and pulling her close the way a churl held her babe in the fields.

Osann shook her head, then nestled it between Bera's breasts, her thin arms tight around Bera's ribs and her legs wrapped around her hips.

"That's all right," Bera reassured her. "You just hold onto me and let me worry about staying on the horse."

Osann nodded again.

Bera urged the gelding from its stall and found her brothers mounted and waiting to leave. Only Curran remained afoot, standing ready to open the doors beside his magnificent black stallion, ready and loaded with all his gear. Each of her brothers held the tether to at least one more horse, and several of them had armed themselves with pitchforks and staves.

Angus nodded to her. "Lead the way. We'll take care of the horses. You look after the child."

"Here. My sword." As she rode to the fore, she lifted her weapon to toss it to him, but she thought better of it when Angus raised a huge, impressive blade of his own.

"Thanks for offering your toothpick, Little Bit, but I won't be needing it." Angus grinned like his old self. "Curran gave me one of his."

Petty though it was, she couldn't help resenting the fact that Curran, not she, had been the cause of that smile. Had this stranger of a husband already filled the place she'd fought so hard to earn among her brothers?

Angus looked to Curran. "Ready?"

Without a word, Curran swung the door open. Bera launched her horse past him without looking back, remembering her vision of riding safely through the stockade. She took the most direct route to the main gate. What they would find there, she did not know.

Behind her, the thunder of hooves sounded like an army.

Almost there. They were almost free.

chapter twelve

———

Diedre heard the cries of "Fire! Fire!" and rose from her chair, still half-dazed from staring, empty, into the embers for hours.

Fire, somewhere in the compound. She should go to supervise the—

Wait. She couldn't go anywhere. And there was something else . . .

Fire.

Of course. A glimmer in the back of her mind ignited. Bera.

For the first time in days, Diedre actually smiled, but there was no warmth in it.

A blaze made an excellent diversion. She hadn't doubted for a moment that Bera would do her part. And the Dark Warrior—he had the keys Malisande had risked her life to steal from Drust.

The thought of Bera and the arrogant mercenary working together on Evan's escape gave Diedre her second, and equally mirthless, smile. Two heads on the hound, those two were, but they would see to it that Evan and his brothers went free.

She stirred the embers, then threw on another chunk of charcoal and subsided into her chair. Cold, so cold.

Would she ever be warm again? She drew her fur cloak up around her.

Pity, that a woman of Bera's rank and courage had ended up forced to marry such a scoundrel as the Dark Warrior, but Evan's safety—and Diedre's own—had been her first concern.

Why should Bera be any different, anyway? Princesses were born to marry for the good of their families and bear children. Given the choice of a small-minded, coarse-featured nobleman like Drust or a handsome, arrogant commoner like the Dark Warrior, Diedre would choose the latter. At least Bera's children would be brave and comely—not coarse and small-minded like Diedre's. All except Alma.

The thought of her daughter loosed a crushing pulse of grief. Her only consolation was that death had freed Alma from Drust and his depraved half brother.

Diedre wished, as she often had in these past few horrendous days, that she could follow her daughter in death. But that would be too easy. She had to stay alive to make Drust suffer for what he'd done.

Malisande's distinctive knock interrupted her bitter reverie.

"Enter."

Silent and unobtrusive as ever, Malisande entered the room they had shared for the past eleven years. She was breathing hard, her face ruddy from the cold and the considerable distances she had just covered.

"Is everything taken care of?" Diedre asked, knowing it had been. Malisande had never failed her yet, but Diedre no more trusted the woman than she would trust a wolf for a pet.

"Aye." Her expression smug, Malisande curtsied deeply like a penitent expecting a blessing.

She would get no blessing from Diedre, not now, not ever, for Malisande was no penitent. She fed on treachery and loved to poison, especially when her victims were men.

"No surprises? No problems?"

"Nay." Malisande rose. "All was accomplished just as your highness wished."

That meant the dungeon master and the sentries at the gate were dead.

Men. They never could resist a cup of warm mead on a cold night,

"The calls of 'fire' went up just as the last sentry fell," Malisande volunteered. "No one will find them until the blaze is out."

"And where is the fire?" Not that Diedre cared.

"The granary, your highness."

Three days ago, any threat to their precious foodstuffs would have sent Diedre into a frenzy. Now she hoped it all burned, every kernel.

"You may retire."

"May I help your highness prepare for bed?" her servant asked.

"Nay." Diedre stared into the glowing coals. "I prefer to sit up." To think about Evan escaping this accursed place, and about the look on Drust's face when he found his precious hostages gone.

For the third time since Alma's death, Diedre smiled again.

Curran kept watch at the rear, but indications were that no one had even seen them leave. Behind them, the flames from the granary had risen so high they lit the entire fortress. Up ahead, Bera and Angus had reached the gatehouse at the upper stockade. To Curran's amazement, the gates were open and they rode through unopposed.

Riding like a spirit loosed from the pits of hell, Bera led them without hesitation through the maze of ditches

and into the village beyond, her hood blown back and
the silvered images of her moon cloak visible even in
the darkness. She must have studied and memorized the
most direct escape route, but even so, Curran was deeply
impressed by the fearless way she navigated the perilous
course. Despite the child clinging to her, she rode in
perfect harmony with her mount, so attuned to its rhythm
and stride that she and the horse moved as one. Curran
had never seen a mere mortal ride as she did—only his
storm goddess.

And these brothers . . . They, too, rode full-out, fol-
lowing their sister and each other with absolute trust and
skill. A single mistake at the fore would have brought
down all behind, but they swiftly reached the edge of
the village and the flat expanse beyond.

Only one more obstacle—the last stockade across the
neck of the peninsula.

If they met opposition at the stockade, he and his
sword would be needed up front. Curran swung wide
and urged his stallion forward until he rode abreast of
Bera and Angus at the fore.

Another brother rode up beside Bera and shouted,
"Give me your sword! You cannot fight carrying a
child!"

For the first time since they'd ridden out, Bera hesitated, but not for long. She tossed her sword to her
brother, then dropped back into the pack.

A princess who did not let her pride stand in the way
of common sense! Curran was even more impressed
with this woman he had married.

They did meet opposition at the stockade. As he bore
down on the gates, Curran counted six—no, seven—
guards positioned in front of them.

From the corner of his vision, he saw a lone rider
bolt toward the village. Two of the brothers tossed the

reins of their extra mounts to two others, then peeled away to intercept the messenger.

The guards put up an acceptable fight, but they were no match for mounted warriors—even starved ones armed with only staves and pitchforks. Angus and Curran took care of the three with swords, and the others easily brought down the remaining four.

By the time they were done, the two who had intercepted the messenger had returned leading yet another horse and were helping Bera open the barred gate.

At last, the doors swung open, and the ragtag warriors poured through it to freedom.

Curran looked back at the promontory and saw that the flames had died down, leaving the citadel and surrounding buildings washed in a soft reddish glow.

It wouldn't be long, though, before Drust discovered the escape and rallied his men to follow. There were other horses to be had, of course, but not enough to mount Murdoc and all his men, and it would take some time to collect them from the outer barns.

Curran estimated they would have an hour's lead, at best.

Not much of a lead.

Bera made straight for the sandy shoreline where the surf would cover their tracks. The brothers followed in perfect order like the well-trained company of warriors they were.

They managed to cover at least ten miles before the horses started to flag. When they reached a stream leading to the beach, Bera turned up it and slowed to a trot. Only when they were deep in the forest did she stop and dismount beside the brook.

One by one, the brothers joined the gathering, too winded to speak as they tied their horses, then collapsed into a stinking heap on the bed of leaves.

Did they always keep so close? Curran wondered. Or

had they simply grown accustomed to it in the dungeon, to stay warm?

More than a little winded himself, he sank to the base of an oak and leaned back against it to rest. The only sounds were the wind whistling through the bare branches above them and the dried leaves rustling on the forest floor.

Curran watched Bera open the sack, whisper to the slave-girl, then share the chore of distributing food and drink to her panting brothers.

One by one, she fed and hugged them all. Watching her exchange looks and touches with her brothers, Curran felt more like an outsider than he ever had in his life.

This was her family, not his. He'd been foolish to hope it might be otherwise. But they seemed to be good men—brave, accomplished warriors, men he would not be ashamed to fight beside. He could be grateful for that, at least. He had married a princess and freed her brothers, sealing the match. Why wish for more, when that was good enough?

But Curran had always wished for more. It had driven him to leave his family behind in slavery, never to see them again. That was his curse, to wish for more when he already had what others thought was good enough.

The silent slave-girl Osann brought him a large chunk of bread, but Curran took only a little, mindful of the gaunt faces and bony hands before him. The brothers needed it more than he did.

He noticed that Bera took no food herself, but sat beyond her brothers and coaxed the child into her lap so she could feed the waif.

"Twenty miles, and we'll reach the mouth of the firth." After the silence, Angus's voice sounded far too loud. "We'll change mounts there and ride like hell for Caithness." He looked to Curran. "Agreed?"

It was a small gesture of respect, but a significant one. Curran decided that this was as good a time as any to reveal the rest of his plan. "In the forest beyond the next bay, I have hidden three stout wooden boats." He could feel the crackle of interest from the brothers even before he heard their murmurs of speculation. "We can cross the firth and put in at Nigg or Golspie. Even if Drust should see us, he'll never be able to catch us by land."

"I'd rather row than ride," one of them declared. "After three months in that hell-hole, my balls have forgotten how to get along with a horse."

Amid a chorus of commiserating chuckles, another spoke up. "But what about the horses? We could sure use 'em back home, especially since Drust stole ours."

"Aye. They're worth a king's ransom," another agreed. " 'Twould be a sin to leave 'em behind."

Curran had no intention of leaving his horse behind. He'd row Voltan in a boat by himself, if he had to.

"Kegan and I will take the horses overland," a strong voice volunteered.

Curran saw Bera's head snap up and wondered why.

"It's a risk," Angus said. "Drust will be after you."

"We've stolen from Drust before and gotten away with it," the brother boasted. "Anyway, Angus, we all know how badly Kegan and I fare with boats. Not that pukin' our guts out could make us smell any worse than . . ." The rest was lost in a tide of halfhearted pommels and groans.

"It's agreed, then?" Angus asked.

This was something new, a leader who asked his men's opinions. Curran wasn't sure he liked it.

"I don't want 'em in the boat with *me*, I can tell you."

"Me, either."

"Evan and Kegan are the fittest of us all. If they want to do it, I say, let 'em."

"All right, then," Angus ruled. "Evan and Kegan will follow with the horses."

The arrangement didn't seem to set well with Bera. She shot a worried look at the brother who had volunteered.

It was easy to tell that none of the brothers wanted to split up, but Curran could see why they were willing to risk it. And he admired the two who'd offered. Someone had said their names, but damned if he could remember.

Would he live long enough to know them by their voices as well as their names, he wondered?

Would they live long enough?

After a contemplative silence, Angus turned to Curran and spoke again. "Before we go, I do have a question for you, Curran."

Here it came. Curran braced himself. "And what would that be?"

"How come you're sittin' way over there, and your bride is way over here?"

It wasn't the question Curran had expected.

Bera spoke up before he could frame a response. "That is my fault." She rose and turned to Curran. "Pray forgive me, my lord husband. I was so concerned with feeding my brothers that I have neglected you sorely." Was that *Bera*, his Bera? He'd have thought she'd rather choke to death than utter such words! Yet to Curran's amazement—and her brothers', judging from their stunned expressions—she had indeed spoken them.

All eyes watched as she drew the child to his side and sat, the picture of a proper wife.

Curran stared at her in disbelief. Who was this woman? Certainly not the ferocious, savvy fighter he had married. Not that he minded being treated with deference and honor. He just couldn't figure out why she would suddenly change her attitude so completely.

Confounded, he decided to switch the conversation to the question he had expected Angus to ask. Might as well get it over with up front. He addressed the chieftain without amenities. "Your question took me by surprise. I had expected you, as chieftain, to ask about my lineage and my profession."

"Hah!" Angus's laugh was resonant and full. "I already know all I need to know of you, sir." He held up one finger. "First, you rescued us and brought us to freedom." He held up another. "Next, you rode and fought for us as a great warrior." He patted Curran's ceremonial sword. "Not to mention the fact that you shared this fine blade with me, a total stranger." He held up a third finger. "And last, but by no means least, may God have mercy on your soul, you somehow managed to get our little sister to marry you!"

At that, the brothers burst into hoots and jibes and all manner of ribald comments.

Curran was glad it was dark so they couldn't see the humiliating flush that warmed his neck and face. He had expected Bera's family to ridicule him, not her. It rankled to hear them make fun of their sister, especially after what she had risked for them. He silenced them with an emphatic, "It was not I who freed you, but Bera and I together. Without her, we would still be fighting our way out of Burghead."

This time it was Bera's turn to be amazed. In the chastened silence that followed, she looked at him as if she'd never seen him before. "Thank you," she murmured. "My lord husband honors me."

Suddenly awkward, Curran brushed away the dead leaves that had blown into his lap. "My lady wife brings honor to herself."

Apparently, Bera was no more accustomed to receiving compliments than he was to giving them, for she rose, dazed, and backed away toward the horses. "Come,

Osann." She held out her hand for the child. "It's almost time to go. We must make ready."

Another round of merciless teasing erupted from the brothers.

"Hoo, would you look at that, now? Little Bit has gone into retreat at last!"

"What have you done with my sister, and who is this you've brought here in her place?"

"What's the matter, Bera? Found a man at last you cannot master?"

"By Mother Earth and all the winds at sea! She's actin' like a *woman!*"

"Enough!" Angus stood and bellowed. "Shut it! They can probably hear you loud-mouthed half-wits all the way back in Burghead! Now up with you, and to horse. We've boats to find."

For the tenth time in as many minutes, Bera wondered where in blazes those accursed boats were.

After their brief respite, Curran had taken the lead and set a relentless pace, a pace she wasn't certain she could keep up much longer. She would have slowed already, were it not for the brothers who followed behind her. If they could manage to keep going in their weakened condition, so could she.

She'd done her best to find a comfortable position on the gelding, but her body ached from Osann's weight, and her hindside hurt almost as much as the swollen, tender folds between her legs.

In an effort to distract herself from pain and fatigue, Bera directed her concentration to the magnificent steed and equally magnificent rider ahead of her. Perhaps it was Curran's masculine compulsion to subdue the stallion he rode, but he—like most men—rode in constant tension with his mount. She could teach him a thing or two about riding, once they were safely home.

Still, he cut an impressive figure, his black cloak flapping like the wings of some mythic creature sprung from darkness.

Recalling the homage he had paid her, she felt herself flush, and a surprising twinge of desire momentarily displaced the pain between her legs. She wondered now, as she had then, why he had been so determined to share the credit with her.

Bera would have liked to think his praise was genuine, but her strong sense of skepticism wouldn't let her. Could the deference she had paid him prompted him to return the favor, perchance? Or was his a calculated gesture designed to win over her bothers—and her?

The possibility stung her woman's pride, but she supposed she should be grateful he was trying to get along. And regardless of Curran's motive, she had to admit she liked being treated with honor.

It occurred to her that perhaps this arrogant commoner she had married might like being treated with honor himself.

Hard as it was to swallow, that was probably her wifely obligation, though precious few of The Wives exhibited such deference to their husbands.

A nudge of conscience prompted her to pray. *You kept your part of the bargain, God—so far, at least. I'll keep mine.*

Up ahead Curran slowed to read the distant hills and the features of the woods. Then he made for the woods and motioned them to follow.

At last! It had to be the boats.

"Just a little longer," she murmured to Osann, "and we'll all get in our magic boats and let the ocean rock you safe to sleep."

Osann nodded, burrowing closer. The last few hours had to have been brutally uncomfortable for the child, but true to her nature, she hadn't uttered a single complaint, just soaked Bera's chest with her silent tears.

To Bera's relief, Curran led them straight to the boats he'd turned over and covered with leaves and branches in a narrow ditch.

He dismounted and walked gingerly to uncover the means for their escape.

It heartened Bera to see that even the Dark Warrior himself got saddlesore. She slid from her horse, then wrapped Osann in her cloak and settled her a safe distance from the horses. "Wait here. I won't be long." Her brothers were clearly exhausted, but with all the horses, it shouldn't be too difficult to drag the boats into the water.

She did her best to conceal her own discomfort as she walked over to help Curran and Airell remove the remaining branches while the others righted the first boat, revealing its high stern and prow.

Viking!

"Are they all Viking?" she asked Curran, incredulous. "How in blue blazes did you come by boats such as these?" She blurted the question impulsively, fully expecting to be ignored. Her brothers were always ignoring her questions. Why should Curran be any different?

"Don't ask the man, Bera," Airell teased, knowing her penchant for argument, "unless you're willin' to accept his answer."

Curran shot him an odd look, then turned to Bera and said, "They're all Viking. I took them from a raiding party."

"Three ships? You?" Roy said derisively. "Vikings don't give up their ships." He may not have meant to challenge Curran's story, but he had, and a tense silence gripped the gathering. It was a blood offense to question any warrior's truthfulness—especially in the presence of others. Roy's tongue had landed him neck-deep in trouble, as usual.

Curran straightened to stare at Roy for endless seconds.

Bera wished she'd never asked the question in the first place. Her fool brother had no idea whom he'd just insulted. "Who cares how he got them?" she snapped. "Be grateful they're here. Now shut your trap, Roy, and heave."

Curran's face betrayed his anger—not at Roy, but at Bera for attempting to save him from her brother.

In a flash, Curran grabbed her at the waist and snatched her up under his arm. "Pray forgive my lady wife, brother Roy," he said with infuriating calm. "She seems to hold a grievously exalted idea of her own abilities and a woefully deficient appreciation of mine."

Instantly, the tension was broken. Her brothers roared, but Bera was outraged. "Why you pompous, arrogant fugitive from a pigsty!" She did her best to kick and strike Curran, but succeeded only in twisting herself into an impossibly awkward and painful position. "Give me back my dagger, you lowborn son of an ass," she demanded, flailing away, "Fight me like a man! I'll show you grievous! Let me go, you weasel-faced barn rat!"

"Let you go?" Curran cocked his head at a grinning Angus, and at his nod, let her go. Straight into the boat tethered to the horses. Through her brothers' laughter, she heard the slap of hands on horseflesh, and was tossed off-balance when the boat shuddered, then bumped along the ground toward the firth. She rolled around in the bottom like so much ballast.

By the time she managed to right herself and stand, they had reached the strip of sandy beach. Angus and Airell, identical grins on their faces, looked back from leading the horses. "You've chosen well, Bera."

"Aye," Airell confirmed. "We like him."

"You would!" she shot back, hurt that her brothers

had so quickly sided with Curran against her.

"You'd like him, too," Airell advised, "if you could just manage to behave yourself for more than twenty minutes."

"Behave myself?" That did it. What little self-control she had left snapped. "I might have promised God to be a wife to that . . . that son of a jackass, but I never said anything about behaving myself, so don't hold your breath!"

Angus turned to his twin. "Promised God?"

"Oooooo. A vow to God," Airell responded with exaggerated awe. "This *is* serious."

Hell's bells! Bera couldn't believe she'd told them about her vow. They'd never let her forget it now.

And neither will God, she reminded herself. *Take care, Bera. We're not at Pitlanric yet.*

Oh, shut up!

"I only married him for you," she said heatedly as she clambered out of the boat. "All of you."

"For us." The twins only laughed harder. "She married him for *us*."

Deep down inside, Bera had hoped that freeing her brothers would make them accept her as one of them, but clearly it hadn't. They'd change their tune when they learned what she and Curran had saved them from, though.

Buoyed by righteous anger, she stomped back toward the forest to collect Osann, her parting thought that vow or no vow, she would *not* "behave herself."

chapter thirteen

It was midday. Blessedly, the wind had shifted, blowing them northeast toward Golspie, but the shores of Caithness looked as far away to Bera as they had at dawn. And the two other boats were barely visible in the distance ahead.

She and Orrin and Roy and Curran had rowed just as long as the others, but were miles behind, thanks to Curran's stallion.

Curran had gloves, but the rest of them had resorted to using the crimson yarn to cushion their hands from the oars. It only helped a little, but the color hid the blood.

The steed was well behaved, at least. It hadn't stirred since Curran had settled it into the bottom of the boat, and its hulking presence had kept Osann warm as she slept curled against its flank. But Bera still couldn't fathom why Curran had insisted on bringing the animal with them.

Everyone else had entrusted the rest of the horses to Kegan and Evan. Why hadn't Curran?

In spite of her efforts to transform her resentment into icy strength, Bera grew angrier and more resentful about the stallion's presence with every stroke of the oars.

Curran had that effect on her. Ever since he'd caught

her in the dungeon, her self-control seemed to have deserted her entirely.

Numb with fatigue, she looked over her shoulder, past the stallion to the bow of the boat where Roy and Orrin rowed. Their gaunt faces were flushed, their necks corded; they strained with every stroke. Yet they hadn't complained. And they hadn't so much as blinked when Curran had put the stallion aboard. None of her brothers had.

"It's very selfish, you know," she said to Curran's back.

"What?" He huffed it out as if he scarcely had breath enough for even that single word.

"Bringing this horse." She was winded, too. "It wasn't fair to the others." She stroked her oars. "Roy and Orrin were exhausted when they came aboard." Stroke. "Pulling all this weight—"

"I haven't heard *them* complaining," he panted out. "Nobody asked them to row with us, anyway."

"No one had to," she shot back, offended. "We're a family." Stroke. "We look out for each other." Stroke. "Where help is needed—" Stroke. "—help is given."

Curran said nothing. His silence made her wonder if he even had the means to understand. Not that she expected him to. A man with no honor, no ties, no loyalties to anyone but himself . . . How could he begin to understand the bond of blood and trust that united her family?

Behind her, the stallion snorted and shivered, and she heard a noise from the bow of the boat. She turned to see that Orrin had tumbled from his seat, insensible.

Bera shipped her oars, then grabbed the provisions and clambered past the stallion. When she reached Orrin, Roy nodded in gratitude but never missed a stroke. "I did my best to get him to take a rest." A wan smile momentarily softened the strain on his face. "But when

I poked him, the stubborn blockhead wouldn't look at me."

Orrin always did that when he didn't like what they were trying to tell him. He made use of his deafness to block them out by closing his eyes or looking the other way. Even a cat could take lessons in ignoring from her deaf brother.

Bera checked him over. He stank to high heaven, but his breathing was good. Suppressing a gag, she shifted him into her lap. "He'll be all right." She rooted out the wineskin, then pulled open Orrin's bottom lip and dripped wine against his gums.

He didn't open his eyes, but he did swallow.

"That's it," she coaxed, though she knew he couldn't hear her. It took several swallows before he began to come around. When he opened his eyes, she made the face that never failed to win a smile from him.

"Nou!" He grinned and patted her arm with blistered, scarlet-bound hands.

"No, *you*," she answered as she always did, laying her finger to the tip of his nose. She drew some bread and cheese from the provisions and put a bit of crust into his mouth. Then she flicked her index finger to her lips in the signal for "eat."

Orrin struggled to get up, but she shook her head in denial and easily restrained him. She laid her yarn-wrapped palm to the side of her face and tipped her head in the gesture for "rest." But instead of lying back, her exhausted brother grabbed her hand and exposed the bloody yarn and oozing blisters on her palm.

"Neh," he said in the thick, guttural speech of the deaf. "Eh mih oo ih."

Nay. Let me do it.

Bera responded by grabbing his wrist and prying back his fingers to reveal the similar state of his own hand. Then she raised her finger and circled it, indicating all in the boat, and smacked her fist into her aching palm.

We all do it.

Slamming his eyes shut, Orrin clamped his lips into a stubborn line.

This called for extreme measures. Bera grabbed his pale, scraggly beard and twisted with all her might.

His eyes shot open. "Aaagh!"

That got his attention.

She repeated the signs for "eat" and "rest," then shoved him aside none too gently to show she meant business, and climbed back to her seat.

When Orrin sat up, Roy abandoned his oars only long enough to make the signs himself, then shake a fist in mock threat at his brother.

Outnumbered, Orrin gave in and settled next to the stallion to rest and eat.

"From now on," Curran said over his shoulder from the stern, "every five hundred strokes, one of us will take a break." He looked past Bera to Roy. "Agreed?"

"Agreed," Roy answered.

"Agreed," Bera chimed in, fully aware that Curran hadn't been asking for her approval, only her brother's.

Her husband had a lot to learn about being part of a family.

But then again, as Curran had reminded her, she had a lot to learn about being a proper wife.

Taking shifts helped. Whenever they weren't rowing, Bera and Roy and Orrin navigated. As the day wore on, they moved in closer to the northern shore of the firth. So when darkness fell, leaving the shoreline illuminated only by the faint night-glow that filtered through the clouds, they were able to make out where they were.

It seemed to Bera that they should have reached Golspie by now, but she did her best not to think about how much farther they had to row.

Instead, she "thought herself past it," as she always

did when suffering through an ordeal. Soon it will be over, she told herself. This will all be behind us. We'll be safely back at home—Evan and Kegan, too.

She imagined bathing in the great stone tub of the washhouse, with all The Wives bringing kettles of hot water and passing food and wine. Then she fantasized about putting on a clean, warm chainse and crawling into bed to sleep for at least three days.

Not alone, her practical self intruded. *Your bed is Curran's now. And he'll probably want to—*

Nay! Surely not! Bera winced just thinking about it. If there was any justice in the world, Curran would be no more interested in mating than she was. Not right away.

Roy was on watch, so it was he who spotted the others. "I see them." He pointed to the rugged shoreline. "Half a mile ahead, between those two rocky outcroppings. A strip of sand . . ."

Orrin followed Bera and Curran's lead and shipped his oars to stand and look. Even Osann crept from her snug spot and peeked over the side. Sure enough, on the secluded strand ahead two boats rocked in the surf.

And no sign of Drust's riders on the hills beyond, thank God.

"Look, Osann," Bera said. "We're almost there."

"Last one to his oars is a lemming!" Roy challenged as he scrambled for his place.

Her energy renewed, Bera pulled hard and fast with the others until at last they heard the welcome crunch of sand against the keel. Her waiting brothers pulled the boat ashore, then clamored to help them out.

Airell lifted Osann over the side and directed her to Becan's care. Then he turned and reached up to Bera. She could see that his hands were swollen, but not raw. "We were beginning to get worried," he said as he helped her down. "We feared the stallion might have gotten skittish and spilled you all into the firth."

Determined not to utter one word of complaint about the stallion, Bera followed Airell toward the cleft in the rocks where Becan and Osann were waiting. Not one word about the horse, she told herself. It was over; they'd made it. Any mention of the hardship would be weak and unworthy.

"That cursed horse didn't spill us," she heard herself say, "but he damned near killed us, rowing that huge-arsed hunk of horseflesh twenty miles across the firth."

She gasped in horror. Shite. How had *that* gotten out?

"More like thirty miles, actually, but the wind was with us." Airell grinned and gave her a good-natured elbow to the ribs. "You did well, Little Bit. Most men twice your size couldn't have managed what you did in the last night and day."

"Roy and Orrin did," she said, tears escaping unbidden. "Orrin rowed till he fainted, and Roy's hands are even worse than mine." Dear heaven, she sounded like Roy, blathering on. She wanted to stop, but she couldn't. It just came pouring out. "And both of them so thin and weak from the dungeon. It wasn't fair to make them do it. It wasn't fair." Abruptly, the tears stopped and she stared stupidly at the raw, bleeding flesh in her palms. "And now, God only knows how any of us could manage in a fight." Her voice had gone flat. "I couldn't even hold a dagger, much less a sword."

Why couldn't she move her feet? And what was that strange feeling in her chest, like the fizz of a wave at the edge of the surf?

Airell guided her to the sheltered cleft in the rock. "We've had hours to rest while we waited. Now it's your turn. Lie here while we make ready to travel."

"Just for a little while." Bera lay back. After twenty miles on horseback and another thirty rowing, the coarse sand felt like the finest bed she'd ever lain upon.

Seven miles to Pitlanric. Just seven more miles, and she'd be home.

What then? her practical self asked. *What will you do when Drust comes calling?*

Bera couldn't think about that—*wouldn't* think about that.

First, she would rest.

Then she would walk, all the way home.

She'd think about Drust when she was home.

"Come on, Little Bit," a familiar voice chided. "Time to go."

But she'd just closed her eyes . . .

Gentle hands lifted her and set her to her feet.

She swayed, cold and stiff and aching, then opened her eyes to find Becan steadying her. Sweet, wiry Becan, who loved to dance and hated to fight and sang like an angel. "How long was I asleep?"

"Not long enough, I'll marry," he answered, dry as ever.

Truer words were never said, but just knowing how close they were to home made her eager to leave, despite the agony of every step.

Don't think about the pain, she told herself. Think about home.

Home. It seemed a lifetime since she'd fled Pitlanric, desperate to escape its hardship and monotony, fired with dreams of saving her brothers. Now she wanted nothing more than to go home and stay there—Moina, Fenella, The Wives, and all.

She might even kiss Moina on the mouth when she got there, just to see the expression on her face!

A small arm circled her hips and Bera looked down to find her reliable little shadow. "Come, little one," she said, starting up. "Home is just a short walk away." She would have given Osann a reassuring pat, but her hands were curled in spasm like claws.

The three of them set out behind Angus, Roy, and Orrin. Fidach and Airell brought up the rear.

Someone was missing, she realized with a start. Bera scanned the procession and realized who it was. "Where's Donall?"

"I'd have thought you'd ask about your husband," Becan said. "Have you forgotten him so soon?"

Bera's embarrassment was tempered by a dreadful sinking sensation. Where was Curran?

She looked to the beach and saw that the boats were gone. Her sinking sensation yawned into a frightening chasm. "I'm in no mood for jokes, Becan," she snapped. "Where's Curran?"

"Calm yourself," he said, taken aback. "He and Donall rode ahead for help. And horses."

It shocked Bera how relieved she was to know her husband hadn't left her.

Was she losing her mind? The man was a commoner, a rogue. She hardly knew him. Why should she care if he left them . . . her?

And why in blazes had she felt as if someone had ripped her lungs out when she'd thought he had? It made no sense. No sense at all.

"You're awfully quiet," Becan said. Like Airell, he always could see through her. But neither he nor Airell used their ability to her disadvantage, for which she loved them both dearly.

"I was just thinking about home," she lied. "Lavena will be so glad to see you. She's been frantic since we learned what happened."

"Lavena." Becan said his wife's name like a prayer. How he adored his shy, round little woman. "The children," he added, almost if he was afraid to ask. "Are they . . . is everyone—"

"They were fine when I left, all of them," she hastened to reassure him.

"Thanks be to God." His steps moved a little livelier.

If anything bad had happened since she'd left, they would all find out soon enough. For the moment, Bera concentrated on the grand reunion they would have.

Like the hiss of an asp on her pillow in the deep of night, though, Diedre's voice slithered into her thoughts. *There is a traitor in your midst.*

"What's wrong," Becan asked her. "You suddenly went stiff."

"Nothing," she lied again. "Just a cramp."

Bera shoved Diedre's warning into the box of things she must deal with later—the Viking raids, the threat of war with Drust, the vow she'd made and now must keep—and closed the lid, tight.

Deliberately, she spoke of happier things. "I wonder if Lyonesse has had her baby yet?" she asked. "It should have been time."

"I didn't even know she was expecting," Becan said, his voice brightening.

"Lyonesse didn't tell us until after you all had left," she said. "Roy may not even know, and he's her husband."

"He'd have said something to us in the dungeon if he did," Becan said. "That's how we passed the time, sharing stories of home, wondering what was happening back at Pitlanric." He smiled, eager for news of home. "Tell me what happened after we left Pitlanric. Every detail."

Bera had always detested The Wives' endless small talk, but suddenly she realized what a treasure it was to share the everyday details of their lives. "Little Mina broke her arm, but Lavena helped Peigi set it, and it healed true." She thought back to how things had been before she'd left. "Orrin's twins had the ague, but they both survived. And Melva has another one on the way, of course."

"Of course." Becan chuckled. "You'd think with all his wenches, Kegan would give his poor wife a rest. I swear, I've never seen the woman without a babe at her breast."

Bera's heart tugged, but she covered it with a light-hearted, "The man's insatiable. But Melva doesn't care about the wenches, not as long as Kegan keeps the garden growing at home. She just loves having babies." Bera might love it, too, if only she had the chance.

"Aye, but as soon as they're weaned," her brother said without rancor, "it's off to the nurses with 'em, and don't come back until they're old enough to work."

They shared a chuckle, then continued to pass the weary way with talk of home.

The sky had just begun to lighten when they saw the riders and horses heading their way from the direction of Pitlanric, Curran's unmistakable silhouette at the fore. In spite of herself, Bera's heart swelled at the sight of him. He could have remained to rest at Pitlanric, but he'd come back for them. He'd come back for her.

"Thanks be to God," she said. Even with rescue in sight, her legs kept their plodding pace as if they had a will of their own.

"Thanks be to God," Osann mimicked, her first words since they'd set out.

Poor little lamb. With her two steps to their one, the trek had been twice as far for her. "Look, Osann. Curran has come for us."

Sure enough, he rode straight for them, and when he dismounted and came for her, Bera stared at him like one in a trance. The toll of their ordeal seemed only to have made him more handsome, deepening his eyes from blue to the cobalt of a winter's twilight sky.

Curran nodded to Becan. "I thank you for watching

over my lady wife." His voice was hoarse with fatigue, but his arms were strong when he scooped her up to carry her to Voltan.

"Osann!" Bera looked down and saw Osann take Becan's hand without a qualm.

"Don't worry, Bera," she said in a firm but weary little voice. "I'll be fine with your stinky brother."

Becan laughed out loud, but Curran frowned.

"It's a long story," Bera said. "I'll tell you on the way back home."

"Home," he repeated, a flicker of expression crossing his haggard features. It was not concern or fear or even relief. Bera wondered what feelings he was trying so hard to hide.

Curran lifted her into the saddle, then mounted and settled behind her with his arms close on either side. "Home," he said again, and this time Bera recognized the emotion in his voice.

It was hope.

chapter fourteen

Curran noted that Bera asked him only once to hurry as they neared Pitlanric, but when he deliberately lagged behind the others, she said nothing more.

A perceptive woman, this wife of his, and intelligent.

Curran wasn't certain how he felt about that. The truth was, he wasn't certain how he felt about anything from this moment forward. He hadn't let himself think that far, and now, here he was. Husband to a princess with a huge and boisterous family.

For the last nineteen years, he had lived his life from task to task, surviving the best way he knew how. Now he realized that that was all he knew: survival. He knew nothing at all about living.

But these men did. He'd seen it in the way they helped each other and fought to make it home. Watching them enter Pitlanric ahead of him, he saw it in the strength they drew from the familiar sights and sounds around them. He heard it in the way they called to their wives and gathered their children. He sensed it in the invisible connection that linked them all to this place and each other.

And it frightened him, left him uncertain.

Could Bera sense that, he wondered?

He looked down to see her plain, sturdy face bathed in quiet tears.

His heart twisted. Did she weep for the joy of her family made whole again, or in grief for what that had cost her?

Curran suspected it was both.

He nodded toward a lone woman standing apart, watching the others. "Who is that?"

Bera wiped her tears, swallowed heavily, then spoke. "Fenella. Evan's wife."

"And Evan is . . ."

"Bringing the horses with Kegan. They'll be along soon." She said it with such conviction, he could almost believe that they would escape Drust.

When he and Donall had ridden in last night, there had been no time to get his bearings. Curran had stayed in the background while Donall and his three youngest brothers rallied the fortress and prepared to bring the others back. He'd spoken only to ask that he and his horse be fed so he could go back for the others.

The three had eyed him keenly while Donall told of their escape, but they'd been too polite or too preoccupied to press Curran with questions.

Curran had noted one thing, though. They'd approved of his determination to go back for Bera himself.

He had thought it a good beginning. But now, surrounded by tumult, he wasn't so sure. Would he ever be a part of this, really? Did he want to?

As they rode through the compound, a lame woman spotted Bera and called out to her, but everyone else only eyed them with interest or suspicion before going back to their own reunions.

Was it his imagination, or did the women look at Bera with almost as much reservation as they looked at him?

He would discover soon enough.

Curran scanned the fortress around him. It stood

proudly atop a great swale, surrounded by miles of rolling moors and pastures. Within its well-tended stockades, a stone tower presided over a single, large stone
building surrounded by an orderly collection of gardens,
paths, pens, and tidy thatched houses situated around a
picturesque little tarn.

And in between those structures, people—so many of
them. Children racing about in excitement; slaves hur-
rying with food and blankets; wives calling directions
and doing their best to bring order in chaos. All of them
with one thing in common, at least: a keen interest in
Curran, the stranger in their midst.

So much noise and confusion. So much life.

His life, now.

"Where do we go?" he asked Bera.

She pointed to the stone building by the tower.
"There. My chamber—" She faltered. "*Our* chamber ad-
joins the Great Hall."

The contrast between her lofty accommodations and
the homey cottages of her brothers brought home the
privilege of Bera's status. Curran wasn't at all certain he
wanted to be set apart from the others in such a way,
but he suddenly felt so weary he could scarcely keep his
head up. He led Voltan to the door and halted numbly
as servants swarmed up to help them dismount. "See that
he's well-rubbed," he said to the churl who took the
reins.

Curran turned to help Bera down, and she slid easily
into his arms. The blood-soaked yarn around her hands
had dried and stiffened in the cold. His own gloves had
done the same, but Curran only cared about one thing.
"I hope there's a bed in there."

"Aye, there is. A grand one," Bera said wryly. "And
a chamber pot."

"A grand one?" he retorted.

"It needs to be," she said with a weary smile. "I'm about to explode."

The woman was honest; he'd give her that.

"Curran! Bera!" With mock severity, Boyd rushed from the Great Hall and enveloped his sister in a bearlike embrace. "I'd thrash you here and now if I wasn't so glad to see you."

"As if you could thrash me," she shot back without rancor. She landed an affectionate blow to his shoulder, then broke the embrace. "Any sign of Drust or his men?"

"Nay. We sent lookouts when Donall and Curran arrived. There's been no word yet." He looked up to the rapidly thickening clouds that roiled overhead. "There's a storm coming. Perchance it will send Drust back to Burghead." He looked sidelong at Curran, clearly ill at ease discussing such matters in front of a stranger. "If anything happens, I'll let you know."

Seeing how this brother spoke with Bera warrior to warrior, as he would to any of his brothers, Curran realized why he had sensed no connection between Bera and the women of Pitlanric. She had no place among the women, only among her brothers.

What that would mean for him, he could only guess.

"We'll sleep with our swords at the ready," Bera said wearily as she limped toward her chamber.

"Rest well," Boyd called after her. He turned to Curran, a wicked grin on his face. "You'll need your sword to sleep with that one." He sobered, glancing after his sister with affection—and regret. "It's our fault she knows nothing of women's ways. When our mother . . . died, we trained her as one of us." He looked back to Curran. "As her brother, I would ask a boon. Be patient with her in her . . . conjugal obligations. She has endured much, and may have difficulty . . ." He shifted uneasily, and Curran wondered what past abuses Bera might have endured. "Just be patient with her, I pray."

At a complete loss for a response, Curran bowed briefly to his brother-by-law, then followed his wife into their chamber.

The room was of humble proportion, but he was pleased to see it had an enormous bed—a bed that Bera was now taking up completely, sound asleep across it, fully dressed and cloaked, her sword in her hand.

Apparently, not going to bed armed was one of those women's things she hadn't learned. That, and leaving room for her husband on the mattress.

Curran couldn't help but smile. Why in blazes was she holding her sword? Had she expected him to attack her?

Hell, after what he'd just been through, he couldn't attack a kitten! And all he wanted was sleep.

He threw off his cloak, then disarmed his wife and pulled her into position on the left side of the bed, covering her in furs before he stripped to the skin and joined her. As always when he slept, he slid his sword lengthwise just under the mattress within easy reach. Only then did he allow himself to rest.

His last thought as he burrowed naked between the furs was that he'd never slept in a featherbed before. It felt as warm and soft as a fat woman's belly.

The next thing he knew, he was simmering up from the sleep of the dead. And he had the oddest feeling—

He opened his eyes to find himself surrounded by strangers, all of them staring at him!

On reflex, Curran snatched up his blade and rolled out of bed, ready to fight, reducing the herd of onlookers to shrieking terror.

Short. Not warriors. Children!

Stiff as a corpse popping up in its coffin, Bera sat up abruptly on the far side of the bed wearing only her chainse. "What?" she shouted, her braids askew and her face creased from sleep. "What?"

Everyone froze, including Curran.

"What the hell were all these children doing in here?" he bellowed.

Bera blinked from the children, to Curran, then back to the children. Her eyes cleared, and when they did, a spark of humor brightened them. "They're my nieces and nephews," she said, curling her lips in a vain effort to keep from smiling. "It seems they're here for a look at Aunt Bera's new husband."

Her gaze—along with everyone else's—dropped to the formidable erection that stuck out like a pothook between his legs. "And you've given them quite a good look indeed."

What kind of place *was* this?

"Out!" Curran shouted, determined not to show his embarrassment. When he saw real fear in some of the children's eyes, he realized he was brandishing his sword. At children!

Irate, he cast the blade to the bed, then pointed to the open door. "I said out! Now!"

Laughing and shrieking, the children retreated in a most disorderly fashion, leaving the door wide open behind them as they scattered through the Great Hall beyond.

He strode to the door for an emphatic, "And stay out!" then closed it with a slam on a bevy of startled workers who stood staring at him from the Great Hall.

Bera flopped back to the bed. "I'll speak to the children later," she said, anything but penitent. "It won't happen again."

"See that it doesn't." Shivering, Curran relieved himself in the chamber pot. When he'd finished, he turned to find Bera watching in curious amazement.

"Does a man have no privacy in this place?" he grumbled, feeling self-conscious for the first time in memory.

He'd lived often among warriors, but even they were polite enough to ignore basic bodily necessities.

"Sorry." She didn't look sorry. "I didn't mean to embarrass you." Still, she did not take her eyes from his manhood. "It's just that I've never seen a man do that . . . I mean, my brothers always made me turn away whenever . . ." She colored violently. "This isn't coming out right."

"Perhaps it shouldn't come out at all," he retorted. Curran shivered, his erection flagging. The fire had long since gone out and the room was cold. Where was his tunic? He spotted it on the floor beyond the bed.

"You're cold." Bera patted the furs beside her. "Come back to bed, and I'll see about something to eat."

Curran needed little encouragement. He was back under the furs in a flash.

Moving like an old woman, Bera eased her legs over the side of the bed, then hobbled to the table and brought back a tray of cheese, cold beans, bread, and beer that must have been left there the night before.

It couldn't have been easy for her to carry the tray, for her scarlet-bound hands were curled like claws, but she made no complaint.

Her poor hands . . . Curran contented himself that now that she was married, Bera would no longer have to do a man's work. She could concentrate on her weaving instead of fighting—lay down her sword and join the world of women she'd been denied.

Deep in the featherbed, his bare skin stroked by furs, he decided he might just like being cared for by a wife.

He stretched, and the heaviness of his muscles told him he'd been asleep for a long time. His stomach growled so loud Bera raised her eyebrows and smiled as she set the tray in the center of the bed.

"I could eat an ox." He yawned, then leaned over to retrieve his tunic from the floor beside the bed. It was cold going on, but soon it warmed to his skin.

Pushing the sleeves up, he sat aright and helped himself to a chunk of cheese. "What time is it?"

"Better yet, what day is it?" Completely unselfconscious, Bera sat cross-legged on the bed opposite Curran and used a chunk of dark bread to dip up some beans. She savored the rich, satisfying mouthful. "Mmmm. Ula's beans. They're even good cold." She followed it with a swig of beer, then wiped her mouth on the sleeve of her chainse.

Hardly the manners of a princess. But then, Bera was not like any princess Curran had ever met, and he had met many.

"Who's Ula?" he asked, dipping his own crust into the bowl.

"Boyd's wife."

The beans were good, as was the bread. "And Boyd is . . . ?"

"Tenth. We spoke with him last night."

Curran was terrible with names. He'd never get the brothers straight, much less their hoard of wives and children.

So much to learn. He was on uncertain ground here and didn't like the feeling. He took another chunk of bread and cheese.

As if she had read his mind, Bera cocked a wry half-smile. "Don't worry," she assured him as she ate. "I'll help you with my brothers' names. You'll learn them easily enough when we're all back in training. As for The Wives . . ." Her expression told him there was no love lost there. "Well, you'll learn them, too, in time." She dipped another crust with gusto. "Assuming Drust doesn't wipe us all out first."

"He'll come," Curran said matter-of-factly.

"Aye," she said with equal fatalism. "But, God willing, not right away. The weather has turned to our advantage."

Curran paused. "How so?"

"It's snowing outside. Hard."

"How can you tell?" The snug chamber's windows were high and covered with parchment.

She stilled and closed her eyes. "From the sound."

Curran had never spent long enough in any one place to master such subtleties. It appealed to him to think that someday he, too, would know the sounds of Pitlanric as well as she.

He brought the conversation back to a sticking point. "You mentioned training—all of us in training."

"Aye." Bera looked at her damaged hands and sighed. "It will take some time before I can hold a sword again, but Lavena makes a salve that heals wounds with amazing speed." She tried to close her fingers, but couldn't. "Two weeks, three at the most, and I'll be able to—"

"We are married, Bera," Curran interrupted, compelled to straighten this out.

"Aye." She faced him squarely, the look in her eyes anything but submissive. "Married we are."

Remembering her brother's plea for patience, Curran did his best to be diplomatic. "It's no business of mine why your brothers chose to train with you," he said. "You were their responsibility, and that was their decision to make. But now that we are married, that responsibility is mine. I see no need for you to live as a warrior any longer. I shall be your protector now."

"Is that so?" Bera sat very straight, her features rigid, but her voice resonated with anger. "And who will protect me from my protector?"

She has endured much.

His bride leveled a killing look on him. "I will continue to train with my brothers, and I will continue to fight beside them. When you married me, you gained the privilege of training and fighting as one of us. But that does not give you the right to keep me from the field of honor."

"And what about our unborn children?" Curran countered. "Would you endanger them?"

She dismissed the idea with a snort. "I told you. There will be no children."

"And I told you," he answered, beginning to weary of her high-handed manner, "that there is no reason to think there won't be children."

"Well, that remains to be seen, then, doesn't it?" She flounced from the bed and began gathering the discarded clothes she had thrown off in the night.

When a knock sounded at the door, she straightened with a haughty, "Enter."

Angus opened the door and ducked the lintel to come inside. Beyond him, the activity in the Great Hall stopped for a heartbeat as everyone craned to see past him, then resumed working.

Curran would know those intense, worried blue eyes anywhere, but he wouldn't have recognized anything else. Clean, warmly swathed in rich plaid, his beard trimmed and his graying hair tamed by tidy braids from the temples, Angus was a new man. "Curran." He nodded in acknowledgment.

"Angus."

Bera shrugged on her cloak and hurried to embrace her brother. "Come in, come in."

Angus hugged her, then faced his sister squarely, his eyes searching hers. "Are you all right?"

"Aye," she answered, succinct as ever.

Angus scanned the room, then called through the open doorway, "We need a fire in here, and some warm mead for the newlyweds."

"I'd get up," Curran volunteered, "but—"

"Ach, man. Stay where you are." Angus granted him

a tired grin. "You've earned a rest, along with our gratitude."

Four silent slaves—or were they slaves? Curran
couldn't tell—hastened in bearing charcoal and kindling
and food and drink. No one spoke until the four had left
and closed the door behind them, a fact that Curran
noted.

"Any word of Drust?" Bera asked her brother.

"Boyd sent the lads out as soon as he learned we were
on our way. They went as far as Nigg. No sign of Drust.
But they did spot Evan and Kegan. We're expectin'
them any time now."

"So soon?" Bera asked.

"Soon?" Angus surveyed his sister's disheveled state
with a chuckle. "It's been two days and half another!"
He grinned, erasing years from his haggard face. "The
Wives have been badgerin' me since yesterday to send
somebody in here to check on you. Moina was convinced you'd killed each other." He shot Curran a knowing wink. "That wife of mine wore me down, but I
wouldn't give her the satisfaction of comin' herself. So
I sent the children, just to make certain you were both
still breathin'."

"So you sent them," Bera said with an impish smile.
"I feared they'd come on their own."

Angus turned to Curran. "Quite a lesson in anatomy
you gave them, brother. And the workers in the hall.
Everybody's talkin' about it."

Curran did his best to reserve judgment, but he wasn't
at all sure he would ever get used to the intimate details
of his life—and his body—being common fodder for
Bera's huge, nosy family.

"I thank you for not sending Moina, at least," Bera
said. Obviously, she held no affection for Angus's wife.
"But Curran and I would appreciate some privacy."

"Then you shall have it." Angus rose. "At least until

Kegan and Evan are safely back. Then we will celebrate—your marriage and our return."

"And Drust?" Curran asked.

Angus sighed. "He'll come when he comes, and we'll watch until he does. But for now, a feast is in order."

Bera followed her brother to the door and held it open for him. As before, curious faces turned their way, but Bera seemed not to notice. "We need to talk," she said quietly to her brother.

Nodding, Angus shot Curran an uneasy glance. "Later. I'll send for you."

"Thank you." She closed the door, and they were alone again.

As alone as two people could be among more than a hundred others who watched their every move.

She picked up the goblets of warm mead and carried them to the bed, their spicy vapors wafting in her wake. "Let's stay in bed for a while longer," she suggested as she handed one to him, burrowing her feet under the furs. "I'm not quite ready to face what's waiting on the other side of that door."

Curran touched the rim of his goblet to hers. "Nor I."

The sweet, warm liquid went down fast and easy. When both of the goblets were empty, he drew her into the shelter of his arm. "But I am ready for what is waiting in this bed."

Bera stiffened, yet she did not pull away. "If it's all the same to you, I really don't think I can . . . I mean, all that riding after weeks away from my horse, and then, well—"

"You're sore," he said. He was sore, too.

"Aye." She relaxed a little.

"Then we'll just play a bit."

"Play?" There was skepticism in her voice, but curiosity, too.

"Mmm-hmm." It was the only kind of play Curran

knew. His palm grazed the fine fabric that covered her breast and brushed the nipple instantly erect.

"Ah," she said, her eyes closed in pleasure. "That's nice."

He smoothed across the other breast, then gently explored the contours of her body through her chainse. Her breathing shifted with his touch until her reservation melted into expectation.

"I like this play," she murmured.

Curran stroked up her leg, pushing the hem of her chainse higher and higher until he found her sex, where the lightest brush of his fingers sent a shudder through her.

To his surprise, she mirrored his motions, stroking up his leg and brushing his manhood beneath his tunic.

"If you do that," he warned, "I might not be content with play."

"And if you do that," she said huskily, "I might not, either."

Curran chuckled. "As you wish, your highness."

Bera arched against his touch. "I wish."

"They've returned, your highness," Malisande whispered into Diedre's ear.

Diedre stitched away as usual, though she doubted she would ever need this particular battle plan. She had devised it for the conquest of Pitlanric. Now she hoped they would never go there. Yet something inside of her compelled her to finish it, as she'd always been compelled to finish things.

"Any prisoners?" she asked, knowing there wouldn't be, in any event.

"Nay."

"And the horses?"

"They had no extra horses," Malisande said.

Diedre was pleased. Evan had escaped, then. And the

loss of Drust's mounts would rankle her husband almost as much as the loss of his prisoners—and Diedre's accusers.

She was safe. For the moment, at least.

Diedre pressed her elbow against the pocket that held her poisoned dagger and took comfort from its presence. Safe.

Now all that was left to do was to finish things with Drust before he finished her.

chapter fifteen

Just after midday, Bera knocked on the door to the tower room.

"Come in," Angus said absently.

She found him with Airell and Boyd reviewing scattered sheets of parchment at the room's only table. Bera recognized the lines and cross-markings of inventories in their native script of Ogam.

All three of her brothers looked up, and seeing them side by side, she was saddened to note the toll the past few months had taken. Angus and Airell's legendary bulk was but a memory, and worry had snuffed the mischief out of Boyd. He looked old. They all did.

"Bera," Boyd acknowledged. Without further comment, he and Airell left the two of them alone.

Angus motioned for her to take a seat. "Things were bad when we left. They haven't gotten any better." He offered her a strained smile.

"The horses will help," she said.

"Aye. A bit." He exhaled heavily. "But I did not ask you here to speak of that." He cocked his head and really looked at her, his dark brows drawn together in concern. "How are you really? I know what you told me before, but he was there."

"His name is Curran," she heard herself say.

"Aye. Curran." Angus shifted, suddenly awkward. "I had hoped that one of us would have a chance to talk with you before you married. I'm told that mothers usually do this sort of thing."

But their mother was twelve years dead, her passing only a brutal memory.

Bera appreciated what Angus was trying to do. Part of her wanted to tell him it was not necessary, yet the greater part was curious to see what he would say. It was selfish of her, but she let him go on.

"I considered asking one of the women to speak with you," he continued, "but somehow, that didn't seem right." Angus looked away. "None of them could understand. They weren't there that night. They don't know what he did to you."

"It's all right, Angus. Truly." It couldn't have been easy for him to speak of that night. None of them ever had. "That is in the past, long buried. It does not affect the way I feel about . . . my . . . conjugal responsibilities."

She could tell from his expression that he didn't believe her.

How could she put it? Even she had *some* modesty. "Being with Curran . . ." Blast. She had no skill for indirectness. "Oh, ballocks and Banshis. What's the point of being delicate?" She looked at her brother and said flat-out, "The marriage has been consummated. It was fine."

More than fine, her body reminded her with a brief contraction that made her blush like a maiden. "I meant it when I said I'm all right."

She felt the blush deepen and feared that he would never let her live it down.

But instead of teasing her, he peered at her as if she had turned into someone else. "And this union, you accept it?"

"I have accepted it," she said stoically, bracing her elbows on the chair arms and steepling her fingers.

"Can you trust him, though?" he asked. "Perhaps not right away, but later, if he proves himself? Will you ever be able to trust him?"

"If he proves himself trustworthy, why wouldn't I?" she asked, wondering what had prompted this.

"Because we only taught you to protect yourself," he said. Angus sighed. "I've often wondered if our father's brutality, what he did to you and Mother, would keep you from trusting a husband. But I didn't know what do about it, and I didn't want to bring up such a painful subject. None of us could bear to talk about it. So we didn't. We let you go on fighting, working to protect yourself."

"I never thought of things that way," she said honestly. "Who could say? Maybe that was behind my obsession with besting you all," she admitted. Maybe it was behind her determination to remain a warrior.

The possibility merited some thought.

Angus broke the awkward silence. "About your marriage—there's one thing I do not understand," he ventured. "Curran says you married him before he freed us. Is this true?"

"Aye."

"But why?" he asked, puzzled. "Boyd says you were so opposed to it."

Why? She'd asked herself the same question a hundred times. "At the time, there seemed to be good reason." She frowned, uncomfortable with excuses, yet uncertain of the truth herself. "I could claim duress, but that would not be fair to Curran. He gave me the choice, and I made it."

She offered Angus a wan smile. "Maybe I thought we wouldn't survive, so it wouldn't matter. Maybe I was so cold I couldn't think at all." Remembering the cold and darkness of the well, she shivered. "Maybe I wanted to do it," she confessed. "Whatever the reason, I did it."

Angus nodded.

"Curran is my husband." That much was true. Inescapable. "What do you think of him?"

"It matters not what any of us think of him," he said frankly. "He is our brother, one of us."

"You might not say that if you knew who he really is," she ventured.

"Bera." Angus leaned forward in irritation. "I know you think I'm a blockhead—you say so often enough—but even a blockhead would recognize the Dark Warrior. It wasn't difficult, considering his stature, his skill, his black shield and dark clothes, and that horse of his." Angus subsided into his chair. "Of course we know who he is."

"And that does not matter?" Clearly, it didn't.

Bera didn't know whether to be relieved or insulted. Curran was, after all, little better than a churl.

"It cannot matter," Angus said. "He freed us. He is your husband. That's it, then." He leaned back. "Frankly, his reputation is worth its weight in gold. I, for one, am glad to have him on our side."

"I see." Too much was changing too fast. Bera felt as if her brothers had already replaced her with the stranger she had married. Wounded, she shifted the conversation to her real reason for coming. "There is something else we must discuss. We have a problem, Angus, a serious one."

He glanced to the inventories scratched out on neat lines in Ogam. "You mean *another* problem."

"There is a traitor in our midst," she informed him. "Someone working for Drust."

Angus stilled. "What do you know, and how do you know it?"

"Princess Diedre told me."

He snorted. "The woman whose treachery made hostages of us? And you believed her?" He shook his head. "I had thought you too clever for such an obvious ruse."

"And what if it's not a ruse?" she challenged. "What if she was telling the truth? I think she was."

"And who is this traitor among us, then?"

"Someone close, within our midst." As she said it, she realized how very unconvincing this all sounded. But she had to make him see. "I do not know the name. The princess was taken away before she could tell me."

"Taken away?" Angus was understandably skeptical. He rose to pace the narrow strip behind the table. "How very convenient—for her."

"I know she wasn't lying."

"And why in heaven and earth would she tell you something like that?" He waved his long, bony arms.

"She had her reasons," Bera told him.

Angus waited for her to enumerate those reasons.

How could she make him understand without betraying her loyalty to Evan? "I have no proof, but I know she spoke the truth. This warning was a gift. We must make use of it."

"And who would such a gift serve?" he challenged. "Bad enough that we face an enemy of Drust's strength. Now you would have us suspicious of each other?"

"But if it's true," she argued, "think what that would mean. One traitor inside our defenses could open us all to the enemy, reveal where we hide the children and the food. Even where we hide the cattle. That is all it would take. One."

Suddenly bleak, Angus threw himself back into his chair. "Assuming this is true, how would you suggest we go about finding such a traitor?"

That was the problem. "There is no way. Not until it's too late."

Both of them knew she spoke rightly.

"Any ideas who it might be?" he asked.

"Not one of the brothers," she said emphatically, despite a tiny niggle of suspicion born of Evan's love for Diedre. "A slave?" she guessed. "One of The Wives. My husband . . ."

"Not Curran," he said with conviction.

"You seem awfully sure of that." Bera wished she could be so certain.

"It would make no sense," Angus explained. "Drust had us where he wanted us. If Curran were in league with him, why would he help us escape?"

"You're right." It surprised Bera how relieved that made her, but then the sickening weight of distrust returned. "Unless he is in league with Diedre."

"Why would Diedre want us to escape?" he countered.

Bera knew why, but she could not bring herself to betray Evan's weakness. "Why, indeed?"

Angus rubbed his hands over his face. "Shite. This is a nasty business."

He turned to stare unseeing through the narrow window, then shook off his melancholy. "Kegan and Evan are safely back, so we've scheduled the feast for tonight." He rose and crossed to take her arm. "The women have great bride-plans for you this afternoon, I hear."

"Lavena talked me into it," she grumbled.

"Marriage has always been your destiny, Bera," her brother reminded her. "Can you not enjoy it now? You are a bride, a woman, a princess of the realm."

"I am a warrior, Angus," she said, suddenly feeling old and hard and somehow betrayed. "You made me the warrior I am, all of you. It took twelve long years. Do you think I could become something else overnight?"

She shook her head. "I cannot. I am still your sister.

Still a warrior. Yet now I have no place among you. How can I be happy about that?"

"Other wives have found cause for happiness," he told her gently. "I can only hope that you will, too."

"We can both hope for that." She gave her brother a brief hug, then began her descent into the kingdom of The Wives.

"Ooch! Stop that!" Bera didn't know why she'd let Lavena talk her into this. She felt like she was being picked to pieces.

The Wives swarmed over her like ants, four of them studiously—and painfully—undoing the tight, tiny braids Osann had worked so hard to plait back in Burghead. Moina and Fenella, of course, were the most enthusiastic at tugging her hair. Of the others, five were busy measuring her and altering one of Fenella's castoff gowns, and three were putting together a bride-crown of dried herbs and flowers. There was barely room for all of them in the chamber adjoining the kitchens, but at least it was warm.

Bera's only comfort was that Curran was being subjected to similar torture at the hands of her brothers somewhere in the compound.

"Lift your arm," Melva instructed. When Bera did, Melva stretched a measuring cord from her armpit to her ankle. "We'll have to take off five at the hem."

Bera didn't miss the criticism implicit in the arch of Fenella's flawless brow.

"You can scrub me and fluff me and stuff me into that dress of Fenella's," she said defensively, "but I'll still look like a mudwump trying to be a rose."

The cattier of The Wives thought that was particularly funny, but neither Lavena nor Ula nor Melva nor Olwyn nor Lyonesse laughed.

"Bera, you do not look like a mudwump," Lavena

protested, rubbing her special salve into the wounds she had soaked and cleaned in Bera's palms. "How's that?"

Bera only winced a little when she flexed her hands. "Better. Much better."

"Good. I'll bandage them after you've bathed."

At last, the tugging on her hair ceased. "I've been dying to get my hands on that hair of yours for years," Moina declared.

"Who would have imagined there'd be so much of it?" Fenella said. "We might just be able to come up with something almost pretty."

"Bring on the tub!" Moina shouted to any and all. "And the water!"

"I've been married for days," Bera grumbled. "So I don't really see the point of this."

"Did you think you could escape us so easily?" Lyonesse teased. "Oh, no. Even our ferocious Bera must submit to the rituals of a bride. To ignore them would bring bad fortune."

Bera sighed. "I suppose we've had enough bad fortune already."

"Exactly."

The tub arrived, and Bera was relieved to see that at least one bucket in three of the water that went in was hot from the kettles. When the water reached two feet deep, Moina nodded to her. "All right. Off with your chainse and into the tub."

"Nay." Bera clung to her undergarment. "I shall not stand naked to be handled by the lot of you!"

Moina shot a pointed look to Lavena, who said, "It is tradition, Bera. We must wash you, head to toe." She motioned to the waiting women. "It was the same for all of us."

"You're lucky," Lyonesse chimed in. "At least you know us. When I came to marry Roy, I knew no one. But I submitted. It is tradition."

"We all did," gentle, buxom Melva added.

This, from her allies among The Wives!

Bera looked to the twelve faces gathered round her and realized that in this matter, at least, the women were united.

It was a turning point, and Bera knew it. If she refused, she would never be accepted among The Wives. She wasn't sure she would be anyway, but at least she recognized the ritual as the ceremony of passing it was.

"Oh, all right." She snatched off her chainse and stomped into the tub. "Wash me, then," she said, delicious chills running up her legs from the warm water.

No one moved. Cloths and buckets in hand, they all stood staring at her body in shock.

Bera looked down at her reddened, swollen inner thighs and the many bruises on her body. "Well, what did you expect?" she challenged, proud of every mark. Then she realized what they were thinking. "Curran didn't do this to me. Well, he did some of it, but only because I attacked him." Blast! The more she said, the worse it sounded.

She took a deep, leveling breath, then motioned to the bruises on her body. "I got these bruises freeing your husbands." She pointed to her reddened thighs. "And this is what happens when you ride thirty miles after being out of the saddle for more than a month." She glared at them. "If you're finished staring, get on with it. It's cold, standing here."

"Oh, Bera." Soft-hearted Lavena burst into tears. "I never realized . . . We never even thought about . . ."

Chastened, Bera sat down in the tub. The warm water stung her thighs and swollen buttocks, but it felt wonderful everywhere else. "Stop crying, Lavena. It's not your fault." She looked to Fenella, the only one who seemed to have recovered her wits. "Pig farts and witches' breath! Get on with it!"

Fenella smiled and promptly poured the contents of the bucket she was holding over Bera's head.

It was cold, of course.

Four hours later, Bera paced anxiously in her room. She had heard everyone coming in, the scraping of benches and calls of greeting and animated conversations, and she'd smelled the mouth-watering aromas of fresh beef and onions and bread and spiced wine. Everything must be ready.

Why hadn't Angus come for her?

And why was she so nervous? It wasn't as if she and Curran hadn't seen each other before.

She felt a small hand on her arm. "You look so beautiful, your highness," Osann repeated for at least the fifth time.

"And so do you," she replied on cue. Bera gave Osann a hug and straightened the folds of the warm length of plaid that wrapped the child's sturdy new clothes. Already the dark circles under Osann's eyes had faded.

Boyd had offered to bring her up with his own girls, but Osann had been adamant. She wanted to be with Bera.

Bera sat, careful of her hair. It felt so odd, all that hair tumbling down her back.

The women had told her not to bind it up before she went to bed, but Bera was convinced she'd strangle herself in her sleep if she didn't. And how was she supposed to get the tangles out the next morning?

At last, the knock sounded at the door.

She rose, her stomach aflutter. "Enter."

Angus stepped inside, resplendent in his furs, ceremonial brooch, and silver coronet. When he saw her, a flicker of memory softened his features. "I never realized how much like Mother you look." He touched her auburn waves. "She was lovely once, and you remind me of her then."

Bera's only memory of their mother was of a thin, harried woman, old before her time. Yet from the wonder in her brother's face, she knew that had not always been so. "Thank you."

Angus smiled. "Ready?"

"Let's get this over with," she answered, laying her hand atop his.

Bera had faced armed enemies with less trepidation than she felt walking out into the Great Hall. As she had feared, all eyes were on her as Angus led her toward the head table where Curran was waiting. But it was so good to see everyone together again that she almost didn't mind. The families filled the Great Hall: mothers, fathers, older children, babies, and nurses. Even Father Maclin and his wife were present. Not a place at the board was empty.

Bera looked to the head table and saw Curran, an expression of guarded wonder on his face as he watched her coming closer.

It almost, but not quite, erased the memory of his disappointment that first time he'd seen her.

As always, Curran's presence dominated the table at which he sat, but tonight, he looked especially handsome. His golden hair glowed clean and healthy in the torchlight, and his immaculate black clothes stood in sharp contrast to her brothers' colorful, bulky plaids.

Elegant. That was the word that described him.

And dangerous.

Oddly flustered by the intensity of his gaze, she directed her attention elsewhere.

One by one, she sought her brothers' faces and found them looking back with pride. Only Evan looked strained, but Fenella preened beside him as usual. Everyone else seemed genuinely happy. Such moments were rare indeed.

Becan began to sing a bride-song, and the more musical of the family joined in with lute and pipes and timbrel and voice.

This hall had seen so many wedding feasts. How many times had she watched this same processional for her brothers' wives? Heard the same bride-song? And in all those times, she had never wished to be the bride. Yet here she was.

So why did she feel as if she were an observer—set apart, watching, instead of experiencing the moment?

She looked to Curran and had the notion that he, too, felt somehow removed. They had that in common, at least. They were both misfits.

Angus led her to Curran's side, where he transferred her hand to Curran's, thereby granting his official blessing to their union. Then he turned to address the assembly. When he raised his hands, the music and singing halted. "Princes of Caledon, brave warriors, fair ladies, and honored guests," he announced loudly, quelling the speculative murmurs of her kinfolk. "Pray with us as we give thanks to a merciful God for His deliverance from evil, His blessings on this union, and His bountiful provision." He nodded to the priest. "Father."

Carried away by the exalted occasion, Father Maclin prayed on at such length that his wife finally whacked him on the thigh and whispered loudly for him to end it before the food got cold. He did, and the feast began in earnest.

Amid a roar of conversation and laughter, servants, slaves, and several of the older children hastened forth with food and drink, the likes of which Bera hadn't seen since the raid. Part of her felt guilty to be the cause of such reckless extravagance, but then she remembered that the celebration was as much for her brothers' safe return as for her marriage.

Airell passed the platter of roasted beef to Curran. "There is a tradition among our people," he said with a gleam of mischief. "To insure good fortune, a bride and groom at their wedding feast have a solemn obligation to speak only the truth to each other. A single lie could curse their union forever. So be careful what you ask each other," he said with a wink. "And be doubly careful what you answer." With that, he turned back to his own celebration.

Bera would happily have strangled her brother for bringing up that particular bit of lore.

"Is this true?" Curran asked, a disturbing spark of interest in his blue eyes.

"Aye," she said uneasily, worried what he might ask her next. "It is a custom of our people."

"Do you believe in such things?"

Bera shrugged. "My brothers and I have had enough bad fortune already. I would not want to ask for more."

Angus passed her a platter of boiled turnips and onions, and all around them the usual tales of wedding mishaps got louder and bawdier.

Curran considered Bera's response, then peered into her face. "Do you think of our marriage as part of that bad fortune?" He cocked his head. "Remember the curse when you answer."

She framed her answer carefully. "I thought so at first," she answered honestly. "But I am finding that there are compensations."

"Such as?" The man was shameless.

Airell chose that moment to turn their way. "The man asked you a question, Bera. Better tell him the truth." Blessedly, he went right back to regaling his poor wife Gitta with the same off-color stories he told at every wedding feast.

Curran was not one to be distracted by interruptions. "You were about to tell me the compensations of being my wife," he reminded her.

Bera wasn't about to feed his arrogance by telling him how handsome he was, so she groped for something else to say. "You're an excellent warrior, fit and strong. That will benefit the family," she said truthfully. "You do not talk too much or drink too much, as far as I can tell." She thought further. "You bring a superior steed and good weapons to the union."

"And?" He was enjoying this entirely too much, the knave.

She decided to teach him a lesson by being honest indeed. "I like the way you touch me when we're naked," she said distinctly. "And I've especially enjoyed your cock."

As it happened, conversations all around them hit a fateful lull at just that moment, so everyone within ten feet heard her.

In the heartbeat of silence that followed, Bera wished the floor would open up and swallow her. Then the hall erupted into riotous laughter.

Perfect.

At one of the lower tables, she spied a nephew pointing to Curran and holding a parsnip to his crotch in imitation of their new uncle's unexpected introduction to family life.

"Ballocks and Banshis!" she muttered under her breath.

She fully expected Curran to be livid with anger, but when she finally dared look at him, she was amazed to see him laughing. Not pretending to laugh. He was really laughing. And then he stood up and took several bows, to the further delight of her family.

Just like that, he was one of them, part of the celebration—no longer a stranger in their midst.

Bera observed the transformation as if she were in a bubble watching from afar, and a sick throb of jealousy pulsed through her. He had managed so quickly something that still eluded her.

She hoped this embarrassing incident would put an end to Curran's questions, but when everyone had settled back down, he asked her another. "How do you do it?"

"Do what?" she asked as a servant refilled their glasses with the best wine.

He scanned the laughing, jesting crowd. "Stay alone, in the midst of all these people."

"I'm not alone," she protested, believing her denial until she said it, then recognizing it for the lie it was. "I've never been alone. This is my family."

Their voices filled the hall, echoing off the stone walls and floors. And the heat of their bodies warmed the place to a cozy, comfortable temperature. She heard the sound of Becan's voice, rich and full as he sang a ballad of love.

"And yet, you are alone," Curran said.

How had he known that?

"I am a part of this." She motioned to the crowded hall. "Think of what it takes for all of us to survive. We all have our place. From the time a child can walk until his dotage, every soul takes his part in the life of Pitlanric."

"And your part?" Curran asked.

Bera closed her eyes briefly. For the past twelve years, she had turned her back on her true obligation—to marry and perpetuate her lineage—but she could deny it no longer. "I have trained to protect my people, fought for them, hunted and fished to put food on their tables, worked the herds."

"Nothing with the women?" Curran asked.

"I weave," she said defensively.

"Your work is magical," he said, "and I know it is

important to you, or you wouldn't have risked bringing your equipment back with you from Burghead."

"It took me three years to make that portable loom and those bobbins," she informed him. "I wasn't about to leave them behind."

Angus passed her a trencher of fresh rolls, sweet butter, and boiled eggs. Bera helped herself, then held the platter for Curran.

He dipped a roll in butter, then took a hearty bite. "Mmmm. Good."

"They're made with honey," she said, passing the tray to Airell.

Again, Curran reverted to the topic they'd been discussing before the interruption. "So. You weave. But weaving is a solitary task. A woman's work, but not among the women."

Seeing her irritation, he took another sip of wine, then shifted the subject. "Was it hard, being the only daughter?"

"It was what it was," she answered candidly. "I knew nothing else."

He looked to the servants shuttling food from the cook-fires. "Tell me about your slaves."

An odd request. Though his questions seemed random, Bera knew there was nothing random about this man she'd married. "There aren't many, not even a dozen," she disclosed. "My brothers have no taste for conquest. They stay busy enough with Pitlanric."

Across the room, Cusantin's wife Graine shrieked with laughter, then huddled back with her sister, Lynet, who was married to Connal. Two sisters married to twins. Bera still thought Angus had made a mistake with that arrangement.

Curran followed the sound and shook his head. "Can they tell their husbands apart?" he asked. "I certainly can't."

"I have it on good authority that Connal and Cusantin have switched places for days, with their wives none the wiser," she confided. "But knowing Graine and Lynet, I suspect they knew all along and did it so they could compare notes."

"A frightening prospect," Curran said with a grin.

"My brothers have no one to blame but themselves."

Curran scanned the gathering. "Your brothers seem like good men," he observed. "What sort of man was your father? Do you remember him?"

Bera stiffened. Had someone told him something? Surely her brothers would not have dared.

"Your father," Curran prompted.

Bera had known this would come up sooner or later. She had hoped it would be later. It was an ill omen at her wedding feast, yet she was loath to lie. "He was a man," she said. "I was fourteen when he died." She offered nothing more, only a silent prayer that the dead would stay buried where they belonged.

Bera realized that she could turn the tables. "What about you, your family?"

Curran's features congealed. "I had a family once."

Suddenly the noise and motion all around them seemed to recede into the background.

When he volunteered nothing further, she asked, "Mother? Father? Sisters and brothers?"

Curran glanced down into his cup. "Mother. Father. Three sisters. Two brothers."

"And?" She studied the elegant hands that held the silver wedding goblet. "What happened to them?"

He looked askance at her, as if she were a threat. "What do you mean?"

"You said you had a family *once*," she explained. "What happened to them?"

Pain, long buried, etched Curran's face. He dragged deep at his wine before replying. "I don't know."

Surely he couldn't be serious. "If you don't want to talk about it, just say so."

"I don't want to talk about," he said evenly, "but you asked me a question, and I answered it honestly. I don't know what happened to my family."

"How can that be?" Bera could scarcely imagine such a thing.

"I went away. When I came back, they were gone."

"All of them?"

"All."

Bera looked to her brothers and their families, trying to think what it would be like to come home to Pitlanric and find everyone gone. "It must be terrible, not knowing what happened to them."

His guard went up. "Life goes on."

She had made him sad, and Bera regretted that, especially after seeing him laugh. "Perhaps the past is best left buried for both of us."

"Aye," her husband agreed.

Angus stood up beside them, his cup raised. "Princes of Caledon, brave warriors, fair ladies, and honored guests, here's to the bride and groom, Princess Bera, and her consort, Curran, now brother to us all!"

All stood, their cups lifted high. "Princess Bera and her consort, Curran, now brother to us all!"

Bera looked at this man whom fate had used to force her to her rightful destiny. "You have a family now," she told him. "More than you bargained for, I'll marry."

He nodded. "As are you."

chapter sixteen

One week later at Burghead

"Your highness." Murdoc bowed to Diedre, clearly uneasy at having been summoned.

It pleased her to see him so. Nervous men betrayed more than they ever imagined. Let him wonder why she'd waited until now to send for him.

She granted him only a brief glance before turning her eyes back to the embroidery she was stitching as a memorial for Alma. "I thank you for coming so quickly." Never mind that it had been days since Malisande had brought her news of Drust's return and his illness. Diedre knew she would remain a pariah as long as Drust lived. "Please, sit." She nodded to the empty chair opposite her.

Without comment, he perched uneasily on the edge of the seat.

"May I offer you something to drink? Some wine? Or perhaps mead, on a rainy day such as this one."

"A touch of wine would be most welcome."

After Malisande had poured, Diedre dismissed her. "Attend me outside. See that Lord Murdoc and I are not disturbed."

Once they were alone, she waited a good little while

to speak further, giving Murdoc time to stew. She had done some very large favors for Murdoc in the past. Now it was time to see if he would be willing to repay those favors. "Word has reached me that my lord husband was seized with the ague when the storm turned him back from Pitlanric," she said with convincing wifely concern, as if she had just heard of her husband's illness. "Naturally, I am most anxious to inquire about his health."

"Naturally." The strain of the past few days was clearly etched on Murdoc's face, but he betrayed nothing else. "He is very ill. A lesser man would have died. Lord Drust has been in and out of delirium since we brought him back to Burghead. I do not know how long he can go on this way."

"My lord husband always manages to survive," she said with more than a touch of irony. "So. What of his prisoners?"

Murdoc shifted. "We could not overtake them. The storm . . ."

"Of course," Diedre consoled. "The storm." She knew better, thanks to Malisande. Storm or no storm, Evan and his brothers—and Bera—had been too clever for them.

Good for Bera! A pity, though, that she was yoked to that mercenary, but at least he was handsome. Perhaps Bera would take some pleasure from him.

Diedre returned to the matter at hand. "And my horses?"

"When Lord Drust first fell ill in the field," Murdoc explained, "I offered to take our warriors on to Pitlanric to recover the horses, but he would hear nothing of it. He was determined to lead us himself, and still is."

Diedre smiled in earnest. For once, she approved her husband's stubbornness. Every day of delay gave Evan and his brothers time to grow stronger and prepare for the attack. The thought of Drust's killing Evan . . .

She shuddered inwardly, fighting to quell the fear that came with caring and vainly wishing she could hate Evan for making her feel.

Why did she care what happened at Pitlanric? She and Evan would never see each other again. Their illicit love had been a sadistic jest of fate, nothing more. A joke that had broken her heart almost a brutally as losing Alma had.

"Ah," she said to Murdoc, "then you will not ride for Pitlanric until Lord Drust rides with you."

"It is my lord's command," he clipped out, his posture and expression betraying his frustration at such an order.

Now that she had put Murdoc firmly in his place, Diedre decided to reveal her true reason for summoning him. "Yesterday, we received an urgent message from Kenneth MacAlpin at Scone." She extracted the message from her sewing bag and handed it to him. "Since my lord husband was so ill, I took the liberty of reading it." She had always read Drust's messages for him. Many in Burghead could read and write Ogam, but only she and Murdock knew Latin.

She watched the chieftain struggle to translate the lengthy message.

Of all Drust's chieftains, Murdoc was the only one with a mind worth reckoning. He was strong, cunning, and intelligent—a valuable combination in an ally, but dangerous in an opponent. That was why she had made certain to keep him in her debt.

But would he take her side over Drust's?

When he was done, he laid the missive aside with a thoughtful sigh. "Caledon and Dalraida," he mused, "united under MacAlpin—the son of a Caledonian princess and a Dalraidan king."

"What think you of this, Murdoc?"

"A better question might be," he said shrewdly, "what think *you* of this, your highness?"

It was no secret she had been grooming Drust, positioning him for a try at the throne of Caledon. But since Alma—

"I think it a most fortuitous development indeed," she said, happily anticipating Drust's rage when he learned a Dalraidan would dare to make himself sovereign over the seven kings and the subkings of Caledon.

Drust would be livid. If MacAlpin succeeded in uniting Caledon and Dalraida, he would destroy The Beast's chance to win the throne of Caledon. Diedre knew how much her husband wanted that throne; she had planted the hunger in him long ago and nurtured it for years. Now that hunger would be an instrument of her revenge.

She retrieved the document and read over it once again. Would Murdoc take the bait, realize what a secret alliance with MacAlpin could do for him and his chieftains? If he did betray Drust and ally himself with MacAlpin, would he become too powerful to control?

Before Evan, she had loved the game of plots and intrigues. She'd fed on manipulating the greed and appetites in the men around her. But now the game had ceased to be a game. Grim and hollow, it had become a war of survival instead.

She proffered the message to Murdoc. "MacAlpin offers his protection to all who swear allegiance to him."

"Aye. But most of the northern tribes will fight," he said with absolute conviction.

"Most?" She lifted her chin to peer at him. "Some will not?"

"Some *may* not," he corrected. "Our hostages from Pitlanric, for example."

Evan, the man she loved, and Bera, the only woman she had ever thought of as her equal. "They're in no shape to wage a war," she said mildly, covering her true feelings, "with us or anyone else."

If Pitlanric sided with MacAlpin, would MacAlpin protect them from her husband? *Could* MacAlpin protect them from Drust?

"And what of us?" she asked Murdoc, her voice harsher than she had intended. "If the choice was yours to make, would you fight?"

There were no secrets from her in Burghead; she knew of Murdoc's discontent. But could she count on him to help her?

"It is not my choice to make, your highness, but my lord's." Murdoc was no fool.

"And if he sought your advice?"

"I might advise him to consider peace, consolidate his power in the northern regions under MacAlpin."

"As would I." For the first time in her life, she longed for peace instead of power. Let MacAlpin play the game of greed and power. She had lost her taste for it. "But alas, Lord Drust no longer heeds my counsel."

"Nor mine, your highness," Murdoc added. "He will fight. The only question is when."

"And where." Diedre handed him the message. "Pray, take this to my lord husband, along with my heartfelt prayers for his recovery." She leveled her gaze to his. "I would be most grateful to know his reactions. And any plans he makes."

Murdoc considered, then nodded his assent.

He would help her, and she would help MacAlpin.

Eight weeks after the escape, at Pitlanric

Buffeted by a moist gust of March wind, Curran reached the top of the ladder with yet another bundle of thatch. "This is the last of what we brought."

Airell glanced up from the patch he was working on just above him. "That should do it."

When Curran leaned over to hand him the bundle, the ladder started to slide sideways on the rain-slick thatch. His stomach lurched. "Catch!" He tossed the bundle to Airell, then grabbed at the roof to keep the ladder—and himself—from falling.

To spare Curran's pride, Airell kept right on working until everything was under control, just as all the other brothers had done when Curran had made mistakes. One by one, they'd worked beside him, invited him into their homes, and introduced him to their families. For eight weeks, the brothers had been initiating Curran into the unfamiliar tasks of maintaining the fortress. So far, he had tried his hand at forging iron, mucking stalls, wood-working, repairing walls, weaving fences, digging drains, delivering calves, mending the stockades, grinding grain, and now, patching the thatch on Airell's house. Whenever Curran went awry—as he often did—the brothers invariably pretended not to notice.

"How do you keep from slipping on this stuff?" Curran said when he and the ladder were back in place. Bera had to be embarrassed to have such an inept husband.

"It comes with experience," Airell reassured him. "You'll learn."

Curran had learned a lot in these past two months. The thing that had affected him most, though, was seeing how everyone at Pitlanric worked together to survive. The brothers were all so different—some easier to like than others—yet each accepted his place in the order of the fortress without question.

Where Curran's place would be, he could only guess.

Even among the women and children, responsibility took precedence over pride or personalities. Curran watched as he went about his own chores, and he came to see the subtle, reassuring rhythm of their lives. Work was the common thread that bound them all together. It overrode dispositions, conflicts, jealousies, and all the other inevitable human frailties.

Lately, the only place that didn't feel out of place to Curran was the bed he and Bera shared. There, he was truly at home.

Yet he envied the way everyone here seemed to know what was needed and expected, and he looked forward to the time when he would know it, too.

If they had the time.

Drust would not forget them, or his horses. Why he had delayed this long, Curran couldn't imagine. All he knew was that he was grateful for the time.

"There." Airell tapped the last of the thatch into the tight blond patch. "That should do it." He nodded down to Curran. "Climb down and hold the ladder."

Curran did.

When Airell joined him on the ground, the older man put his arm around Curran's shoulders. "Well done. You'll be a thatcher in no time."

"If watching is as good as doing," Curran quipped, "then perhaps I will."

"It's a beginning." Airell clapped his shoulder, then motioned him inside. "Come. See my house."

After seeing this one, Curran would have been to all the brothers' houses but Angus's.

Airell pulled open the door. "Gitta! We'll be wantin' something hot!"

Curran followed him into the spacious cottage. As with all the brothers' houses, he marveled at how primitive these thatched dwellings were in comparison to his and Bera's chamber. Yet no one seemed to mind but him. He looked over the cozy interior, where the usual wide ledges of dried peat hugged the side walls. Draped with furs and wool, the platforms served as beds, chairs, or tables as needed. There was a long table with benches at the center of the cozy room, though, and that was where Airell sat.

Gitta wore a sour expression when she looked up from her cook-fire at the far end of the room. Curran bristled, but then he remembered that Gitta almost always wore a sour expression. He thanked the fates that he didn't have to live with *that*. Bera had a temper, but at least she wasn't sour.

"It's about time you fixed that hole in the roof," Airell's wife grumbled as she stirred a kettle of something savory. "God knows what fell in the food till that was done." She lifted a wooden bowl and ladled it full, then carried it to Curran. "Here." She smacked the bowl onto the table.

Curran peered into the bowl, doing his best to hide his reservations. While she served her husband, he searched for whatever "God knows what" might have fallen into the soup. Unfortunately, everything in the bowl looked like "God knows what," so he gave up and put courtesy before queasiness. He took a mouthful and was pleasantly surprised to find it very tasty. "Good soup, Gitta. Very good."

She actually smiled, her happy expression transforming her into a lovely woman indeed. Airell regarded his wife with open tenderness, and Curran saw the bond of concern that anchored their marriage. Wondering what sadness had made Gitta's smiles so rare, he resolved to do his best to coax one from her whenever he had the chance.

All it had taken this time was a few words of praise.

That was another thing Curran had learned—the power of praise. Bera's brothers used it liberally, as did she.

"So," he asked his brother-by-law. "What task is next for us?"

"More work on the stockade," Airell answered.

"Boyd and Fidach have been at it since morning. I told them we'd help as soon as we finished here."

Curran nodded. "I am yours to command, my brother," he said with a smile.

It still amazed him how much work these men were doing so soon after their imprisonment. They were truly a hardy lot. And The Wives. Most of the women, Bera included, worked prodigiously and without complaint.

"And when it gets dark," Airell said with good humor, "we'll sup and go to bed, then start all over again in the morning."

Curran didn't mind. Not yet, anyway. Perhaps he would someday, when the routine became familiar enough to lose its challenge. But for now, he was well content to spend his days working alongside The Brothers and his nights snuggled with Bera in their warm featherbed.

He was content.

It was a new feeling for him, one he liked.

Bera was lost in thought at her loom when Osann hurried into the weaving house. "Your highness," she called. "A messenger has just arrived."

No cause for alarm, Bera told herself, but her heart quickened its pace. "Where is he?"

"At the Great Hall," Osann replied. "He's very dirty," she added. "Lady Lavena said he'd ridden all the way from Scone."

Scone? King's business.

Bera laid aside the shuttle and stood. "I'm off to the Great Hall, then. Find my lord husband and ask him to join us at the tower room." She thought back to her waking conversation with Curran. "I think he's working on Lord Airell's roof. Bid them both come at once."

The message would be dire, for only a dire matter justified sending a rider from the capital.

After a rainy morning, the sun shone outside for the first time in three weeks, warming the wards of Pitlanric with the promise of spring. Under other circumstances, she would have lingered in crossing the turf, but Bera made straight for the Great Hall.

She wasn't the only one who had hurried to see the messenger. By the time she got there, she had to work her way through a crowd of curious children to get inside, where many of the adults had already gathered.

The air within the Great Hall was thick with tension, but only Angus spoke, asking the filthy, travel-worn messenger, "And you're sure you saw no one on your way to Nigg and Cadboll?"

"No one," the messenger said between gulps of beer and hungry bites of bread. "No sign of smoke. No fresh tracks. And the settlements were closed up tight. They would not even let me in, but sent someone out to collect the message."

Little wonder. All of eastern Caithness stood ready for an attack from Drust.

Angus nodded to Moina. "See he's taken care of."

Bera followed his gaze as he peered at the gathering. Everyone was there but Curran and Airell. Angus turned to the two brothers closest to where he was standing. "Boyd and Roy, post the lads on lookout, then join us. The rest of us will meet in the tower." Striding for the door, he shot a warning glance at an agitated cluster of The Wives—Graine, Peigi, Olwyn, and Lynet. Resident alarmists, the four were voicing wild predictions of catastrophe and doom loud enough for even the children to hear. "Stop carrying on and go back to your work!" Angus ordered them. "You're frightening the children!"

They scattered with a mixture of nervous laughter and sullen retorts.

Bera had turned to follow the men when Fenella

oozed up close beside her. "And where do you think you're going, my sister?"

"That, Fenella," Bera replied with as much civility as she could manage, "is none of your concern."

"Ah, but it is." Fenella took her arm. "You are one of us now. It's foolish to pretend otherwise."

"I am married," Bera acknowledged. "But that does not make me one of you." She pulled free of her cloying sister-by-law. "I am still princess, and Pitlanric is still mine. So I shall continue to sit in council with my brothers."

"You may have helped your brothers escape Burghead and sealed me to this place in the process," Fenella hissed, "but you sealed yourself as well. You are one of us."

"I'm the same as I ever was," Bera retorted, wondering what she'd meant by "sealed me to this place."

A flash of hateful triumph hardened Fenella's flawless features. "Say what you will, it doesn't change the truth. And the truth is, you're chattel, just like the rest of us. Royal chattel, perhaps, but chattel nonetheless. Your precious brothers traded you for their freedom. To a *mercenary*, a man without honor or family. A man—"

Whatever she was going to say was cut short by a flint-hard, "Your brothers are waiting for you, Bera." From out of nowhere, Curran stepped to Bera's side, glaring at Fenella with icy menace.

Fenella went rigid, and for a moment, Bera thought the woman was actually going to faint. Being Fenella, she didn't, of course. She merely closed her mouth, turned, and retreated.

"Glory be to God!" Bera exclaimed. To say that she was thrilled would have been an understatement. In front of the children and everyone, she threw her arms around Curran's neck and kissed him hard on the lips. "Thank you! Thank you!" She wanted to reward him with the wonderful news only she knew, but decided to wait until they were alone together.

"Bera!" Curran colored violently. Mingled with his surprise and embarrassment, though, she was certain she detected at least a hint of pride at her public display of affection.

She stepped back, straightened her cloak, then took his arm and headed for the tower. "You saved me from The Wives," she said quietly. "No one has ever done that. Ever."

Curran frowned slightly the way he always did when he didn't understand something. He must have been wondering why she would need protection from her own family. "She was insulting you. And me."

"Fenella always insults me," she confessed. "But this was the first time anyone has ever come to my defense."

"I told you, Bera," he said in all seriousness, "you have a protector now."

"I thought you were speaking of your sword when you said that to me." Bera looked at her husband and a new understanding dawned inside her. "It never occurred to me that you might protect me from my family." Too deeply moved to trust herself, she glanced away. "I am grateful for that, Curran. I pray you would continue."

She *was* grateful, and for the first time, chastened when it came to Curran's pride. He had defended hers with Fenella, but what had Bera done to defend his pride with the rest of the family? She'd simply ignored Moina and Fenella's endless snide remarks about Curran. And when Graine and Lynet had whispered about Curran and Bera behind their hands, she'd done nothing to discipline them. Bera realized she'd done nothing to protect her husband's pride.

She would from now on.

Curran followed her up the stairs. Halfway to the tower room, she halted and turned to him. "I have a question," she said. "Did my brothers really send you for me just now, or did you only say that to get Fenella's goat?"

Curran studied her with that serious look of his, then answered simply, "*I* wanted you there. It's where you belong."

Unexpected tears welled into her eyes. She took a deep, leveling breath, then lifted her head and proceeded. For the first time in her life, she went into council with her brothers feeling that she had an ally.

How her brothers would react to having Curran there, she would not venture to guess. They were the last to come, and the brothers looked up as one when they entered, but not in disapproval.

Angus nodded to Curran. "We welcome our brother Curran to this solemn council."

Curran seated Bera, then addressed the brothers before taking a seat himself. "Before I sit as one of you, I would ask your indulgence."

Bera sensed her brothers tighten.

What was Curran doing?

She saw him reach for his dagger and froze. When a blade was drawn among warriors, blood must be spilled, and all the brothers went for their own weapons the moment he unsheathed his.

But before anyone could retaliate, Curran swiftly cut a thin red line across his wrist, then laid the blade to the table, his bleeding wrist raised before him. "I pledge my blood, my sword, my body, and my soul, to defend the honor and welfare of my lady wife. And her brother princes, and the family that has now become my own."

His gaze met Bera's, and something powerful passed between them. Her heart swelled. She wanted so much for this to be the man Curran truly was. She could be proud of that man, proud to be his wife.

Curran's gesture had been a noble one, albeit a dangerous one, but it had a profound effect on the gathering. Instantly, approval replaced the tension.

In a show of faith, Bera picked up Curran's dagger and cut a shallow gash along her own wrist, then rose to mix her blood with his.

A man could make his own honor, and she prayed that Curran was making his.

In solemn progression, her brothers rose and did as she had done. Not another word was spoken until all had settled back down into their seats.

Angus opened the sealed message, and cursed. "It's in Latin." He handed it to Evan, the only one among them who had been able to master the language.

Evan pored over it at length, a pained expression on his face, then finally shoved it to the center of the table. "It's from Kenneth MacAlpin. He claims rightful crown to Caledon and Dalraida."

An explosion of questions erupted from the brothers.

A unified nation, Bera mused. It wasn't the first time she had heard of such a thing, but it was the first time she knew of that any king had actually tried to unite the two nations. The idea appealed to her, especially now. At last, she had a compelling reason to think of the future.

Curran sat silent while the brothers kept up their roar of conjecture.

"Shut it!" Angus bellowed. "Everyone will have his chance, but one at a time."

"Who is this Kenneth MacAlpin?" Fidach demanded as the others quieted. Fidach never merely asked; he always demanded.

"The document says he is the lawful son of a marriage between Alpin, a king of Dalraida, and his wife, Princess Tagreth of Caledon. It also says he defeated the Vikings in Dalraida two years ago and has ruled there ever since."

"His mother a princess?" Becan commented. "That would give him the right to try for the throne of Caledon."

"To try," Angus said.

Evan looked at the document and shook his head. "My Latin is rusty. I'd like for Father Maclin to go over this with me, but the main points are clear enough. MacAlpin pledges his support for all thanes who will accept his sovereignty."

"And what will he want in return?" Boyd asked. "Does it say?"

"Ach," Airell interjected. "What is says means nothing, even if he names a price. What is wanted is always more than what is asked."

Evan studied the closely spaced writing. "Unity. Peace among the tribes. 'A reasonable tribute.' "

"*His* idea of reasonable," Connor put in. "Which will doubtless be far more than ours."

Bera listened, assessing everything against the good of Pitlanric. Beside her, Curran watched and listened, too.

The questions and discussion went on for more than an hour before everyone had a chance to settle back and digest the implications of MacAlpin's message.

After a prolonged, thoughtful silence, Evan spoke up. "Curran, have you traveled to Dalraida?"

All eyes shifted to the newest member of the family council.

"Aye," he answered.

Angus leaned forward. "Do you know of this MacAlpin?"

"Aye."

Evan laughed. "If you keep askin' him yes and no questions, we'll be at this all night." He turned to Curran. "Tell us what you know of the man."

The tight set of Curran's jaw was the only betrayal

of his discomfort at being the center of attention. Yet he hesitated only briefly before beginning to speak. "I fought with him against the Vikings. He is a great warrior—skilled and daring. Ruthless when he needs to be, but not a brute. He told us then that neither Dalraida nor Caledon would ever be free of Viking harassment as long as we remained divided, fighting against each other." He ran a hand through his golden mane. "It seems he has decided to undertake that unification."

"What sort of man is he?" Angus asked.

"I watched him closely with his thanes and allies, and I was impressed," Curran answered. "Those who know him respect him deeply. I never spoke with him personally, but I sat in council with him many times. In all my travels, I have yet to see as wise a man, or one who inspires such loyalty from so many."

"And those who oppose him?" Airell asked.

"He crushes," Curran replied succinctly.

"Could he do it?" This, from Roy. "Caledon is three times the size of Dalraida. Many will choose to fight. Could he quell such opposition?"

Curran nodded. "He's the only man I've ever seen who could."

"The question is," Fidach said, "will he succeed?"

"Nothing is certain," Evan countered. "If it is his destiny, he will prevail."

"What think you of his chances?" Angus asked Curran.

"Evan's right; nothing is certain," Curran responded. "Yet some men shape their own destinies, and I think MacAlpin is one of those men."

Another thoughtful silence stilled the room.

When the quiet had gone on long enough, Angus ended it with, "We haven't heard from Bera." They all looked to her in genuine expectation. "Tell us what you think."

As always, Bera was gratified that her brothers valued her counsel, but she needed more information before she committed to an opinion. She turned to Curran and asked, "What of Drust? Will he fight?"

"Drust wants Caledon for himself," Curran responded. "He'd be loath to accept anyone as overlord, much less a Dalraidan."

It was the answer she had expected. "Then this could be a real opportunity for us—to be rid of Drust *and* the raiders from the Orkneys." She looked from brother to brother. "You went to Drust in peace, seeking an alliance. You took that risk, and he broke every law of hospitality, every code of honor, and betrayed you— drugged you at his own table and took you prisoner." She pointed to the message. "This king has come to us, a king who would stand with us against Drust, and against the Vikings. I think we should consider it."

"So do I," Angus said. "Let us meet again midmorning tomorrow, after we've had some time to think this over. In the meantime, I think it best to double our watches."

Bera agreed, as did all present. They were unanimous in that one thing, at least.

Curran's voice was all but lost in a chorus of "aye's." "Drust will come here first," he said without raising his voice.

The brothers halted abruptly.

"He'll come here first," he repeated. "I know him. Unless MacAlpin is already halfway to Burghead, Drust will attack us, then deal with MacAlpin."

Angus frowned. "You seem very sure."

Bera wondered how he could be so certain, too, but Curran had worked at Burghead for months. He had grounds to know their enemy.

"I am sure." Curran clasped his hands in front of him. "We took twenty of his finest warhorses, enough to mount a tenth of his army. Drust will need those horses to fight MacAlpin. And he'll want to strike us while we're still weakened from his treachery—before MacAlpin gets far enough north to help us." He exhaled heavily. "Frankly, I'm surprised he hasn't done it before now."

So was Bera. Everything Curran said made perfect sense to her.

"We all expected Drust to attack us sooner," Evan agreed. "Something must have happened, but what?"

"There are ways to find out," Curran ventured.

Bera's heart skipped. Surely, he didn't intend to—

"What do you mean?" Angus asked.

"I could go back to Burghead, enter the fortress in secret." He didn't look at Bera.

Leave? Go back to Burghead? Without thinking, she slid her hand to her belly. No one spoke, yet she could read the subtle signs of suspicion on her brothers' faces.

At last, Curran looked at her, but his face was blank, closed. The Dark Warrior, not Curran her husband.

"Why should you be the one?" she asked, her own suspicions roused by the ache she felt at the way he'd shut her out.

"I was merely volunteering," he shot back. "I have much experience with stealth. I am fit. I know the fortress like the palm of my own hand—every defense, every weakness, all the schedules and rotations."

Inarguable points, all. Yet something in Bera recoiled at the idea of his leaving, going back to Drust . . . and Diedre.

Leaving her, with his child inside her.

She should have told him days ago, when she'd first found out. Now, she couldn't. He sat beside her, but the distance might as well have been a mile.

"We never send a man alone on a mission," Angus declared.

"Then send someone with me," Curran suggested. His golden brows drew together in concern. "I do not blame you for being suspicious of my offer." He scanned the brothers. "You do not know me well, and I have yet to prove myself. Send me, and you will have your proof."

"You freed us," Airell said. "That is proof enough."

"It's not enough, and we all know it," Curran said calmly. "Let me go to Burghead."

"I'll go with him," Evan said.

Evan!

Why would Evan want to go back, unless it was to see the princess?

Bad enough, that Curran should go. But if he went with Evan, the potential for disaster was staggering.

She hadn't thought this could get any worse, but Evan's offer complicated things impossibly. The brothers knew of Evan's trysts with Diedre, but only Bera knew he was besotted with the woman. Yet several of the others seemed almost as taken aback by Evan's offer as she. Perhaps they suspected the truth after all.

The whole, horrible mess left her feeling sick.

"This business about Burghead is a separate issue entirely." Angus scowled down at the table for several seconds before facing the assembly. "I think it best we reach a decision on MacAlpin's offer first. Once that is done and the messenger is on his way, we can discuss sending someone to Burghead. Agreed?"

One by one, all nodded.

Bera should have told Angus about Evan and Diedre when they first discussed the traitor. Now at least she would have a chance to rectify the matter.

But she could not tell Curran about the baby. Not until this was resolved.

A baby. It still didn't seem real to her. To be granted such a gift now, when everything was in turmoil . . .

Irony had always been one of Bera's favorite things, but she did not like living it.

If Curran stayed at Pitlanric, she would tell him about the baby. If he went back to Burghead . . . she might not get the chance to tell him, ever.

"Very well, then," Angus concluded, ending her reverie. "We'll meet back here tomorrow at midmorning to come to a consensus about MacAlpin."

As they all filed out, Bera's practical self intruded. *Well, that was a quick turnaround. On the way in, you were vowing to uphold your husband's honor. On the way out, you already suspect him of duplicity, perhaps even adultery. You even suspected your own brother!*

With good reason, she countered internally. How could she do otherwise? The welfare of Pitlanric was at stake.

He knows you suspect him, her practical self argued. *He may seem invulnerable, but you know better. And you, most of all, have the power to wound him. Take care.*

Bera would, but she had to take care of Pitlanric first. It was her duty.

chapter seventeen

Three days later, Curran lay awake in their bed long after the house had gone quiet and Bera had fallen asleep. Ever since he had offered to go to Burghead, she had seemed withdrawn. She was keeping something from him, something important. Much as he hated to admit it, he was deeply troubled by his wife's lack of trust.

They were still new to each other, he rationalized. Perhaps trust would come with time. But he sensed something deep in Bera that held her back, and he wondered what it was.

"Can't sleep?" she murmured, nuzzling against him.

Expecting her to drift off again, he said nothing, but his silence had the opposite effect.

She raised up slightly to stroke the hair at his temples. "Tell me."

How could he? She was most of the reason he'd lain awake.

Bera sat up beside him. "Tell me."

Part of him wanted to, but the greater part—schooled by years of secrecy—warned against it.

"I'm not going to leave you alone until you tell me," she declared, and Curran knew she meant it. "It's not the alliance with MacAlpin, is it?"

"Nay," he managed. "I was all for it. You know that."

Along with Angus, they had spent two days convincing the rest of the council. Together.

"Ah. So it's Burghead," she reasoned. "We offended you, didn't we?" She peered at him in the darkness. "I offended you."

She'd read his mind, and not for the first time, either. How did she do that? It was disconcerting, being married to someone who had the ability to worm into his private thoughts.

"Curran, our reservations were not meant to cast a slur on your honor," she explained, but her patronizing tone stung his pride.

"Of course they did," he responded tightly. "From the moment I made the offer, I was suspect."

"Can you blame us?" At least she hadn't tried to deny it. "Try to see it from our side. You were working for Drust before you freed us—"

"I was working for myself," he interrupted. "Drust had hired me to train his men. At least, I thought it was he who had hired me. I didn't find out Princess Diedre was behind it until just before the escape."

He paused to get a grip on his anger before continuing. "I'd been at Burghead for months before your brothers were taken hostage. The whole thing sickened me. I wanted out, but I knew better than to antagonize a man like Drust. So when he needed someone to take an important message to Scone, I volunteered, planning never to go back." He was surprised how good it felt to explain things to Bera, but he couldn't help wishing he'd had the chance to explain to the council. "It was in Scone that I learned of your brothers' offer, and everything—the circumstances, the timing, my connections with Drust—fell into place. I saw that destiny had provided the perfect means for me to free the hostages and win a royal wife."

He felt Bera stiffen and regretted his bluntness. She

was more than just a prize to him, but he didn't know how to tell her. "It was a worthy quest, with a worthy reward. That's the truth, all of it." He rolled away and settled with his back to her. "I am your husband. You could choose to believe me, to support me with your brothers."

Bera was anything but apologetic. "What about Diedre?" She whacked his shoulder. "You've admitted that she was behind your being at Burghead. Do you deny that you were working for her directly?"

Curran rolled back over to face her. How in blazes could she have known about that? "Where did you get such an idea?"

"The same place I get all my ideas," she snapped. "Well?"

He hadn't told her because he hadn't thought it relevant, but now he saw that it mattered very much to Bera. "Several weeks after you came, she summoned me to her chamber." Thinking back, he remembered that Bera had been there. "You were leaving as I arrived, as a matter of fact."

"Aye. Go on."

"She told me someone had been bringing food to the prisoners and might be working to free them. It was obvious she knew I was the one, but Diedre is far too clever to do away with an adversary when she could turn him into an ally." His already wounded pride boiled up inside him when he thought of what had happened next. "Because I was a mercenary, she assumed I would sell myself to the highest bidder. So she offered me lands of my own and cattle if I would stop whoever was trying to help your brothers."

"And you agreed?" It was more an indictment than a question.

"Of course I agreed," he retorted. "What choice did I have?" He exhaled heavily, wanting to convince her, yet resenting the need to do so. "That didn't mean I was working for her. I merely wanted her to think I was."

"I see." Clearly, she didn't.

"What about you?" he countered. "You seemed to have been awfully thick with her highness."

Bera hesitated.

"I was honest with you," he challenged. "Would you not grant me the same?" That convinced her, as he'd known it would.

"At first," she said, "I stuck close to Diedre so I could learn what was going on," she said. "And I learned very quickly that Diedre was the one who really ran things at Burghead. But I also saw Drust turn on her."

"And?"

"What he did to Alma . . ." She eased closer, unconsciously stroking his temple the way she often did when they talked before falling asleep, and he took comfort from her touch. "It changed Diedre, turned her against him completely."

"And what did all that have to do with you?" He was aware that Bera had taken Alma's death hard, but he had no clue as to why.

"She let me know that she had discovered who I really was."

Curran didn't trust his ears. "She what?"

"She knew who I was. And she wanted my brothers to escape."

He couldn't believe it. "How did she know who you were?"

Bera studied him in silence before she answered. "Diedre is the cleverest person I have ever met," she said. "Still, it didn't seem possible that she had figured it out on her own." He sensed the tension heightening between them and wondered why. "But then I found out you knew. So I assumed that either she had told you, or you had told her."

No wonder she was suspicious of his offer to go back to Burghead! "Did it not occur to you that if I wanted to marry you, I would be the last person to betray you to a woman like Diedre?"

"Aye, but there's that 'if.' "

He could hardly blame her for doubting him back then. Yet this was two months later. Obviously, he hadn't made the progress he'd hoped to with Bera. "So when I offered to go back, you thought it was to meet with Diedre."

"I did not know about the bounty she had offered, but I couldn't help wondering what else she might have promised you."

Was that a note of jealousy he heard in her voice? If so, he was baffled. Why would Bera be jealous of Diedre? Then it dawned on him what his wife suspected him of besides treachery. She was afraid the princess had gotten her hooks into him the same way she'd gotten them into Evan!

Where in blazes had Bera gotten a preposterous notion like that one? Curran bristled, but then thought better of confronting her. She was jealous. That meant she cared.

"And it didn't help that Evan was the one who volunteered to go with me," he mused aloud.

"No," she admitted, relaxing. "After his . . . trysts with Diedre, his eagerness to go back there was . . . worrisome."

Again, he had the strong feeling she was holding something back. Something about Evan and Diedre.

"I know about Evan and Diedre," he said softly, pulling her closer.

"Everyone knows he slept with her, and why, but—"

"I know he was besotted with her. It's not that hard to see." He sighed, stroking her upper arm. "Your brothers probably know it, too, but they're too loyal to say anything. Just as you were."

He asked another question that had been troubling him. "So why did the council agree to send us?"

"We didn't all agree," she reminded him.

True. Bera had been against it to the last. It had taken the entire day to reach a decision, with minor arguments raised instead of the real issues of trust, but in the end, Angus had added his tie-breaking vote to the six in favor. "Why did seven vote in favor, really?" Curran asked.

Bera sighed, the vinegar gone out of her. "I can only guess."

"You know your brothers," he prodded. "Tell me why."

"Because we need to know what is happening with Drust. Because they wanted to give you both a chance to prove yourselves, to put an end to suspicion." Shivering, she snuggled back down into the furs. "Suspicion is a corrosive thing. Already it has eaten away at the trust that unites our family."

And whatever trust might have grown between the two of them.

"And you?" Curran drew her to his side, wishing he could protect her from all of this. "How do you feel about the council's decision?"

"I am afraid," she whispered hoarsely.

He stroked the smooth curve of her back. "Of what?"

"That you or Evan might betray us." She said it calmly despite the warm tears that wet his shoulder, and Curran went still, shocked to hear her say it, yet glad she had trusted him with the truth. "But most of all, that you might not come back."

He hadn't expected that. "I will come back. And I won't betray you, or the family."

She nodded, but he knew the fear was still inside her.

Wanting to reassure her, he pulled her close to kiss her gently on the eyes, then the lips, but she stiffened in his embrace.

Stung by her rejection, he asked her sadly, "How many times will I have to prove myself to you, Bera? Will I ever win your trust?"

After a long silence, she said, "You're assuming I have trust to give any man as a husband."

"Are you saying you don't?" he asked, wondering what terrible thing had wounded her so that she couldn't even trust her own husband.

"I'm saying I do not know." Another honest answer, but a troubling one.

"Why?"

"There are things that happened long ago." She shuddered, and a chill of foreboding coursed through Curran. "Some day we will speak of them, but not tonight." He felt her hand slide down his torso to stroke his cock seductively. Her touch set off a jolt of desire that brought his manhood instantly to life. "Tonight," she murmured, "I want you to hold me and make love to me until I cannot think."

"Until neither of us can think," he said, his own hands searching out the places that set her lust aflame.

He raised up beside her and drew the covers back, exposing the lean elegance of her naked body. Wordlessly, she opened her legs to him, inviting him to claim the space between. Hastened by a stab of lust, he knelt there, his hands exploring the now-familiar textures of her ribs, her breasts, her thighs.

Her eyes darkened at his touch, and she answered with her own searching hands, stroking the corded muscles of his thighs, then drawing his head down to her breasts. She gasped and arched against him when he suckled her nipples erect. Then she sought his manhood, stroking, flicking, teasing at its tip.

"You're mine," he told her raggedly as he drove himself inside her.

She met him thrust for thrust, her nails digging into his buttocks as she drew him deeper. "And you are mine." She said it fiercely, claiming more than just his body. "Mine, and no one else's."

It was a savage mounting, harsh and territorial. But for the first time, it was not enough. Curran brought her to release and found his own, but his soul was still left wanting. He needed more. He needed her respect, her trust. Her heart.

Panting, he collapsed beside her and held her close, astounded by the realization that somewhere along the way, he had lost his own heart to the woman in his arms.

Bera could not bring herself to see Curran and Evan off. Everyone else would be there watching, and she was afraid she might somehow betray the desperate plan she had decided upon deep in the night.

She'd stayed in bed this morning while Curran packed the few things he was taking, then kissed him farewell and watched him leave their chamber.

When the door had closed behind him, she'd risen from her bed and bade Osann help her tuck her hair into a smooth, tight bun at the base of her neck.

Osann remained silent until they were done. Then Bera unlocked her wedding chest and began to draw out what she planned to take. "Your highness is leaving?" the little girl asked with more than a hint of alarm. "Where are we going?"

"Not you, my sweeting," Bera told her as gently as she could. "Only I. I'm going to Burghead."

"Burghead?" Osann grasped her hand in terror. "Please, Missy," she begged, reverting to their old familiarity. "Don't go there. They'll kill you, and I'll never see you again." She started to cry. "Please don't go. I love you."

Bera sat on the edge of her bed and drew Osann into her lap. "It's all right. Nothing bad will happen to me. Lord Curran and Lord Evan and I will keep each other safe. I may not even go to the fortress. I'll just wait somewhere nearby until Lord Curran finds out what's afoot." She stroked Osann's fine, silky hair. "But I have to be with him. I can have no peace unless I go."

"I can have no peace unless you stay." Osann wept into her shoulder.

Guilt and sadness weighed heavy in Bera's chest, but she had no choice. She had to know the truth about Curran's involvement with Diedre, not just for Pitlanric's sake, but for hers and the baby's.

Was this how Curran had felt when she asked him not to go? she wondered. It was a miserable feeling.

Osann's sobs gradually subsided. Sniffling, she looked up at Bera through narrowed lids. "Why didn't you leave with Lord Curran?"

Bera shrugged. She was no good at lying. Looking into that small, concerned face, she didn't want to. "It's very important that I go along, but men can be so stubborn sometimes. They'd never give permission. So I'll just have to follow them in secret until it's too late for them to send me back. Then I'll show myself and ask forgiveness."

A small smile claimed Osann's mouth. "That's wicked." Clearly, she approved.

Bera grinned. "Aye, but it works." She sobered. "But it must remain our secret. No one else can know I've gone until at least noon tomorrow."

Osann's expression fell again. "But they'll see you're missing long before then."

"Not if I tell them I wish to rest without being disturbed for the remainder of the day. Tomorrow morning, you can tell anyone who inquires that I am resting still. Try to delay discovery as long as possible past midday, but do not worry if they find out sooner. Just do the best you can." She eased Osann from her lap and went to her desk. After hastily scratching out an explanation in Ogam, she folded and sealed the parchment, addressing it to Angus. "There." She doubted her brothers would come after her, for she was no longer the prize. In their eyes, she was Curran's problem now.

She carried the note to Osann and tucked it into her tunic. "Hide this until tomorrow, as late as you can manage. Then give it to Lord Angus. He will not punish you for obeying my express orders."

Osann accepted it with a troubled look. So Bera gave her a warm hug of reassurance before rising. "Come. Help me pack."

Together, they filled a stout woolen bag with the few things she would need for her journey. A bedroll concealing her weapons and second bag full of food and wine would complete her requirements for the journey. This time, she would escape Pitlanric well armed and supplied, mounted on Tundarr.

Curran and Evan had been gone for more than an hour by the time she'd collected everything, sent Osann to hide the bundles in Tundarr's stall, and told several of The Wives and servants that she wished to spend the rest of the day in her room undisturbed.

Bera got as far as the weaving house on her way to the stables before she crossed paths with anyone. Airell spied her and altered his route to intercept her.

"You seem awfully solemn," he observed. "Still worried about Curran and Evan?"

"Aye," she admitted. The memory of Osann's tears prompted her to say, "But there's something else."

"And what would that be?"

"It's silly. There's no reason for me to worry, but I

can't help wondering what would happen to Osann if anything should happen to me."

Airell studied her, puzzled. "Angus said you had asked that we bring her up like any of our own children. We all agreed to do so."

"Aye. But I worry who would take her. Lavena's children are grown, so she has no need of more. Ula's got enough of her own to worry about. Lyonesse is good-hearted, but I think her temper would frighten Osann half to death. And Olwyn has her hands full with Orrin and their boys."

"Why worry about that now, all of a sudden?" he asked, his eyes narrowing. "What's going on, Bera?"

Bera feared she'd made a mistake in bringing it up. "Nothing. Everything. Never mind." She picked up her skirts and headed for the weaving house, but Airell held her arm.

"If anything should happen to you," he said, "all of us will watch over Osann and make sure she is well loved."

Bera looked into his eyes and saw sympathy—for her and for Osann. "I just want her to have a mother who will love her as I do, no matter what happens."

"She will. You have my oath on it."

They parted ways. Bera went to the weaving house and waited for long minutes until she felt safe heading back to the stables.

It wasn't easy saddling Tundarr by herself, but at last she managed it. Tying her substantial bundles to the back of the saddle took only a little while, then she was ready. Now, if only she could get away clean.

She walked Tundarr behind the service buildings, then kept to the base of the stockade until she came to the gatehouse, where she mounted.

Luckily, fourteen-year-old Parrus, one of Becan's

lads, was on duty. "Hello, Auntie," he called down to her.

"Raise the gate, Parrus. It's a beautiful day, and I'm crazy for a good, long ride."

Parrus frowned, eyeing the bundles on her saddle.

"I packed a lunch and a brought a blanket so I could eat in comfort in the sunshine."

"Well . . ." Parrus scratched his puny beginnings of a beard. "I don't know." Of all times for him to be difficult.

"I know they told you none of the women should be allowed outside the compound," she said. "But then, I've never been one of the women, have I?" She grinned up at him.

"Nay. You haven't." Unconvinced, he rubbed his finger back and forth along his cheek.

"Oh, come on, Parrus," she urged, smiling. "Remember that time I helped you sneak back inside the morning after the fair? And the time that keg of malt spirits disappeared, I never told anybody I had seen you—"

"All right, all right." Parrus scanned the compound, then quickly cranked up the heavy wooden gate.

"Thank you," she called once she was on the other side. "I'll never forget this."

"Please do," Parrus called after her as she rode away. "I have already."

Curran and Evan's hoofprints were easy to follow in the soft earth track that led to Nigg. They'd been moving at a steady pace, but it wouldn't be hard to catch up with them. Bera would wait until they were beyond the mouth of the firth to make her presence known, though. By then, it would be too late to send her back.

Stretching out on the long, sloping road to Nigg and Cadboll, she settled to enjoy her ride and did not let herself think of what would happen at home when they found her gone.

*   *,   *

Curran spread his bedding close to the fire and lay down to get some welcome sleep. He needed it after staying up so late talking to Bera.

Strange, how accustomed he'd become to having her close beside him when he slept. He missed her already.

"How did you find a place like this?" Evan asked him, peering up at the vault of the small cave that hid them from prying eyes.

"A man from Nigg told me about it, many years ago." Curran drew up the thick plaid blanket Bera had woven, and remembered the storm goddess he'd seen after camping here last summer. "I camped here last summer, on my way to Burghead."

Evan tucked his chin. "This is hardly on the way to Burghead."

In times past, such a contradictory statement would have earned Evan an immediate challenge to arms. But Curran had come to recognize the brothers' minor contentions for what they were—a constant game of opposition, argument, and good-natured torment that took the place of more serious confrontations. "This is on the way," he said calmly, "if you're coming from the northwest coast."

"There's nothing on the northwest coast," Evan parried.

"There were Vikings," Curran informed him. "At least, until I got there."

"More Vikings," Evan said, then yawned. "Do you think we'll ever be rid of them?"

"We will if MacAlpin succeeds in uniting all the tribes."

"And what will happen then?"

What would happen then? He thought of Bera and wondered if what she'd said about not being able to have children was true. If it was, they could adopt some, perhaps even rescue some from slavery, as Bera had rescued Osann. "We might have peace," he said quietly. "Time to raise our children, grow our food, tend our herds."

The fire was dying now, and only the glow of embers lit the cave.

"You sound as though you would like that," Evan said sleepily.

"I would." Curran closed his eyes and wished for Bera warm beside him. "It is a dream I've had."

"A warrior like you?" Evan sounded unconvinced. "Would you not miss the thrill of combat, the chance to prove yourself the greatest warrior in all of Caledon?"

"Such a life is empty, lonely," Curran confessed. "Death waits for you around every corner, over every horizon, behind every wall." He sighed. "I'd rather learn of living."

"What about Drust?"

"One last dance with death," Curran said as he turned over to go to sleep.

Half a mile ahead in a sheltering copse of larches, Bera lay snugly bundled in furs, her stomach full with good cheese and hearty bread. It had taken some time to find a discreet place to sleep, especially since it was already dark by the time Curran and Evan had disappeared into their cave. But the trees provided adequate cover, so she could rest easy.

Tomorrow, she would set out ahead of the men, riding off the trail and dropping back only when they stopped to camp. By then, they would be beyond Dingwall, and she could safely join them.

She fell asleep smiling, imagining the expression on their faces when she joined them at their campfire.

chapter eighteen

Curran and Evan's masculine arrogance worked in Bera's favor. Not once during the day that followed had they given any indication that they suspected someone was watching them.

Men were so predictable.

She knew her husband and brother were confident she'd stay safely locked away at Pitlanric. It probably hadn't even occurred to them that she might follow.

Bera waited until Evan and Curran had set up camp and gotten a fire going before she rode through the cleft in the rocks that led to their hiding place.

Recognizing Tundarr's and Bera's scents, neither of their horses gave warning of her approach. So the sound of her steed's hooves on the rocky ground caught Curran and Evan by surprise. She heard them scrambling, and they were waiting with swords in hand when she emerged from the darkness.

"Bera!" Curran snarled through curled lips.

Evan reacted with a split second of shock, followed by, "Shite, Bera. You've gone too far this time!" When she only smiled at him, he let out a familiar sigh of grudging acceptance.

Curran's whole body bunched with anger and frustration. "Of all the hollow-pated, goose-brained, mud-sucking, idiot things to do—"

"And it's good to see you, too, my lord husband," she said with only a smidgen of sarcasm.

Actually, they had taken it better than she'd expected.

"Blast!" Curran slammed his sword to his bedding, then dropped down beside the weapon, scowling. "All right," he demanded. "Let's hear it."

Evan looked at them both with an expression that said he wished he were anywhere but in the middle of this. Cranking his mouth down at one side, he let out a long breath, then sat at the farthest corner of his bedding.

"I came to be with you," she said, untying the roll of fur behind her saddle.

"That is obvious," Curran clipped out. "The question is, why?"

Bera kicked the scattering of pebbles from a flat spot beside him, then spread her blanket of furs. That done, she descended to sit as gracefully as she could. "I could not think for worrying about the two of you. So I had to come. It's that simple."

"No it's not," Curran fairly growled. "We are perfectly capable of taking care of ourselves, Bera. I need no wife to watch over me!"

Where in blazes had he gotten a turned-around idea like that? "I didn't think you did," she retorted, "though I should imagine you would be grateful for another sword." She aimed her most regal glare at him. "I came to be with you."

"To be with us," Curran said to Evan, and both of them rolled their eyes.

Men were such children! As a wife, she resented Curran's attitude. As a warrior, she would not tolerate it. Her sword was an asset to any mission. But men did have their pride.

"If you do not wish me to go all the way to Burghead," she offered as a compromise, "I won't. I can find a safe place to wait for you, as long as it's not too far from you."

"You're not going anywhere with us," Curran said in precise tones. "First thing tomorrow, you are going back to Pitlanric, and that's that."

Knowing her antagonism for any ultimatum, Evan pursed his lips and winced.

It wasn't easy, but Bera kept a tight rein on her temper. Curran still had a lot to learn about her. She looked her husband in the eye and stated, "I am not going back, and you cannot make me."

"Cannot?" Curran roared, his fair skin reddening. He launched to his feet. "We'll see who cannot."

So he meant to subdue her by force! Well, Bera had other plans.

Outrage set her blood to humming with desperate energy. Arming herself with a dagger in each hand, she rolled to her feet and struck a stance for combat. "I knew it would happen eventually, that you'd try to bully me, just like my father. You're all alike."

He halted, taken aback by her words, but she glared into his cold blue eyes. "Come on. Try it. I'm not helpless like my mother. I can fight back. I may not be able to stop you, but I'll sure as hell hurt you." She adjusted her grip on the daggers.

Curran looked to Evan in consternation. "Does she always overreact this way when someone tells her what to do?"

Evan grinned. "Only if she doesn't want to do it."

If there was anything she hated more than being given an ultimatum, it was being spoken about instead of to, as if she were a slave or a small child. "Do not talk about me as if I hadn't the wit to speak for myself!" she warned.

"How do you deal with this?" Curran asked Evan.

"Not too well," Evan said, sheepish. "At first, we tried fighting it out like she wanted, but that always ended up with somebody about to be killed—usually one of us." He shrugged. "It was never about anything important enough to die for. We didn't want to kill her, just make her behave."

"Behave?" Bera saw red. Her brother had used the one word guaranteed to send her over the edge. "I decide how I'll behave. No one tells me to behave."

"See what I mean?" Evan shook his head. "I keep forgetting not to use that word." He looked askance to Curran. "Not a good idea to use that word with Bera. Ever."

"Women." Curran regarded her as if she were a lunatic, and a harmless one at that.

"Aye, women," Evan agreed. "Everything's always life or death. They just don't get it."

Bera circled closer, disappointed, miserable, and furious all at once. She had come here to find the truth, but the truth Curran had shown her was a bitter one. She would teach him not to threaten her with force again, if it was the last thing she ever did. She would not be a willing victim to any man, especially a husband.

"I do believe she means business," Curran said to her brother, seeing the look in her eye. "What do we do now?"

Evan's eyebrows shot up. "I think this is between you and my sister."

"I've had enough of this sideways speaking," she interjected. "Talk to me, not about me, or you'll live to regret it."

"I've already lived to regret it," Curran grumbled, but at least he said it to her.

"Oh, hell." He turned his back on her. "This solves nothing." Leaving her standing there like a fool, daggers drawn, he lay down on his bedding in a huff.

"And what do you think you're doing?" she demanded.

Curran rolled himself into his blanket, then settled with his back to her. "I'm going to sleep."

"This isn't finished yet," she protested. And this wasn't the way things were supposed to play out.

"It's finished as far as I'm concerned." He hunkered down to go to sleep.

Bera looked to Evan and found he'd done the same. The cowards! They'd quit in the middle of the confrontation.

She exhaled heavily and dropped her daggers to her sides.

"You might want to get some sleep, Bera. Burghead is a hard ride away."

So she *had* won!

Triumphant, she lay down and rolled into her furs. It wasn't until she was almost asleep that she realized he hadn't even tried to strike her.

Had she misjudged him? Overreacted, as he'd said?

Bera resolved to find out. If she was wrong, she would make it up to him. But the frightened fourteen-year-old she had once been told her she wasn't wrong.

Galloping toward Burghead the next morning, Curran was glad to reach a long, level stretch of land. But instead of taking advantage of the flat terrain to spread out, Bera galloped up beside him and shouted, "You could ride easier and faster if you would go with your horse instead of fighting him."

Still smarting from their confrontation the night before, Curran glared at her. "Thank you for the suggestion," he said with sarcasm. "But I've managed well enough so far doing it my way."

Evan laughed. "She knows what she's talking about, brother. We all resisted at first, but one by one, she wore us down. And what she taught us worked."

If the brothers had done it . . . "So you think you could teach me, eh?" he asked her, his dark mood lightening just a bit. He saw her face brighten, and some of his lingering resentment eased.

"Aye." Her smile was strong and warm as summer sun. "Close your eyes and feel Voltan's natural rhythm. Relax, and learn the feel of his gait."

"Close my eyes?" Curran shook his head. "Only an idiot would close his eyes at a full gallop."

"Trust your mount," she chided. "He knows what he's doing. If you trust him, he will respect you for it."

"He's a horse," he retorted. "Horses can be trained to obey, but they cannot learn respect."

"You're wrong, Curran. Watch this." She angled away from him, then loosened her reins and secured them to her saddle, giving Tundarr his head. Abandoning the stirrups, she hopped lithely into the saddle and stood, her arms out to the sides for balance.

"Blessed Mother!" Curran's heart went to his throat. "Evan, how can I stop her?"

"You can't," Evan answered, grinning. "So you might as well enjoy it. Watch. She knows what she's doing."

"Are you watching?" Bera called, her eyes straight ahead.

"Aye, I'm watching," he shouted in anger. The woman was foolhardy, no two ways about it.

"All right, then," she said, appropriating his favorite phrase.

Curran watched in anxious admiration as she relaxed her stance, then closed her eyes and tilted her head up to the spring sun.

In a flash, he remembered another rider galloping the same way, her eyes closed and face upturned to the rain, her unbound auburn hair plastered to her tight, muscular, naked body.

Bera's body!

Bera's princess chain at her neck.

Bera's mighty stallion galloping beneath her.

Bera was his storm goddess, the one he had fantasized about while making love to her!

The irony of it struck him giddy, and he exploded into laughter.

Bera was his storm goddess! He'd had her all along, and didn't know it.

At the sound of his hilarity, she slipped back astride Tundarr and caught up her reins. She rode in closer, her puzzled expression more than a little defensive. "What's so funny?" she demanded.

Evan seemed eager to know, too, but he had the good manners not to ask.

Curran wiped the tears from his eyes and let out a heavy, cleansing breath. He couldn't remember laughing that hard. Well, that once at their wedding feast. And Bera had been the cause of that, too.

No one else had ever been able to make him laugh. It was a gift, this penchant his wife had, a precious gift that set him free.

And he had married a goddess.

"I'm sorry," he told her. "I did not mean to give offense. Seeing you that way just made me remember something else. The joke's on me, not you."

Bera remained skeptical. "Then by all means share it," she said icily.

"I will not," he declared, grinning like an ass eating briars as he threw her own words back at her. "And you can't make me."

"Then you shall have no peace until you do," she snapped. "Even if it takes the rest of the way to Burghead."

*   *   *

They never made it to Burghead. Just after they reached the Culbin Forest, Curran raised his hand and halted.

All three of them heard it: the distant sound of an advancing army.

Curran pointed to the south, away from the noise, and they moved swiftly to hide their horses out of harm's way. Then they stole back on foot to see what was happening.

"MacAlpin?" Bera whispered hopefully from behind a great oak.

Curran's watchful expression was grim.. "Or Drust."

They waited in agonizing suspense until at last, through the trees, they saw Drust at the head of the procession.

Bera closed her eyes and cursed inwardly. She had so hoped it would be MacAlpin.

When she felt Evan lurch beside her, she opened her eyes and followed his line of vision to see Diedre just beyond her husband, connected to him by a silver chain and manacles. Her mouth was gagged, and little wonder why. The woman's serpent tongue was as dangerous as any dagger.

So Drust had had enough of his royal wife at last.

Bera couldn't help feeling sorry for Diedre—and for Evan.

She leaned close to Curran to whisper, "How far do you think they'll go before they camp?"

"Drust's men are hardened," he whispered back. "They may not stop to rest. Once they've all gotten past, we'll follow them." He turned to Evan. "Pitlanric must be warned. Will you ride?"

His eyes still glued to Diedre, Evan shook his head in stubborn denial. "I cannot leave her."

Curran glanced to the princess, then back at Evan in disappointment. He turned to Bera and whispered, "Can you convince him? I fear it won't go well with any of us if he stays."

"I could no more convince him to go than you could convince me last night," she whispered back. "I fear he is bewitched."

"Then will you ride back to warn them?" he asked her.

Bera's heart sank. She was the logical one to go. But Evan's refusal had only deepened her suspicions of him, and she still felt compelled to stay with Curran.

"They seem in no hurry. Give me until nightfall," she proposed. "If they show no signs of stopping, I will ride ahead and warn them at home."

When he looked skeptical, she tried logic. "It's not as if Pitlanric is unprepared. Drust's army moves slowly, so I'll get home at least three hours ahead of them. That's plenty of time for the family to hide the children and food in our underground vault outside the stockade. And get the cattle and horses to the sea caves, then seal up the settlement."

"I can see you've thought this out." Suspicion darkened his blue gaze. "But why do you want to stay here?"

"If the army does camp tonight, and I think they will," she told him, "we just might have a chance take Drust prisoner. And Diedre."

"You think that will make any difference?" Curran shook his head. "Murdoc would be delighted for the chance to take Drust's place. He's been working toward that end for years."

"Then we'll seize him, too," she suggested. "Or kill him."

Evan had to have heard them, but he gave no sign of it.

She could see that Curran was considering the idea, though. "Three for three," he mused in a thoughtful whisper.

After a prolonged silence, his expression cleared. He took her face into his hands and planted a big kiss on her lips, taking her completely by surprise. "Bera," he murmured, "I never thought I'd say this, but I'm glad you came along."

The setting sun had scarcely touched the western hills when Drust's army stopped to camp in the basin where the Ness flowed into the mouth of the firth.

Watching from the crest of a hill overhead, Curran said to Bera, "You were right." He rolled onto his back and gazed into the twilight sky. "Now all we have to do is find them, take them, and get away with it."

"Easy as stepping in a hole," Evan said dryly.

By unspoken agreement, Curran took charge of the planning, with Bera contributing some impressive strategies. All three of them made careful note of where Drust's and Diedre's tents were pitched. Oddly—but to their great advantage—Diedre's tent was at the outer edge of camp on the opposite side from Drust's. The supply wagons were grouped at the center. Beyond that, the horses were tied, saddled and ready for any emergency.

As the moonless dark fell, he and Evan and Bera memorized the deployment. Then as they waited for the camp to settle, they reviewed their course of action over and over until all three of them knew every step. Curran challenged them with possible complications and solutions, but Bera was the only one who responded. Evan listened in morose silence. Again, Bera's perceptions and strategies were brilliant. Again, Curran marveled at this warrior woman he had married.

Below them in the camp, Drust noisily entertained his chieftains in his brightly lit tent. At the campfires all around it, warriors and foot soldiers diced, drank, or slept. No one, aside from the two bored guards at the entrance to Diedre's tent, seemed interested at all in her. The area around her tent was deserted.

Curran waited until most of the two hundred men had rolled into their bedding, then he led the way down the hill and across the marshy ground on foot. As planned, he and Evan made short work of the two perimeter sentries posted nearest Diedre's tent. After donning the sentries' clothing and hiding the bodies, he waited until he was certain all was well, then signaled Bera to come forward.

He and Evan held her between them as if she were a prisoner, and took her straight to Diedre's tent.

Both guards tensed when they saw them coming, but Curran maintained an air of bored irritation.

"Who goes there?" one of the two guards asked.

Cleverly, Bera dropped her head. "Another prisoner," Curran said with the rough accents of a northern warrior. "Lord Drust thought she could cool her heels with her highness."

The guard hesitated, then relaxed. "The master's rough on women."

They were the last words he would ever utter.

Close enough to attack, Evan and Curran moved swiftly and silently to dispatch the guards. While Bera slipped inside, they rolled the bodies to the far side of the tent, stripped them of their plaids and weapons, then stashed them under the edge of the canvas where no one would find them till morning.

A single lamp was the only illumination within, but it gave enough light for Bera to see Diedre lying on a featherbed at the far end of the fur-strewn floor of the tent.

"Who is there?" Diedre asked, sitting up. Bera heard the clink of the manacles and chain.

She stepped forward, praying this wasn't a trap. "It is I."

"You?" For once, it seemed she'd succeeded in surprising Diedre. "But how? Why?"

Bera moved in close, her dagger drawn. Only a fool would let down her guard in Diedre's presence, manacles or no manacles. "To stop the attack." She drew a silken sash from a pile of Diedre's clothes.

"Taking me will do nothing to stop the attack," Diedre argued, her voice low. "The only reason Drust hasn't already killed me is that he wants me alive to see him destroy Pitlanric. He wants me to watch as he tortures and kills Evan."

A tingle of foreboding spread cold and eerie throughout Bera's body. *Evan, Evan, why did you insist on coming?*

Had destiny conspired to seal her brother's doom?

Bera dared not show her fear to Diedre. "I must gag you," she said, moving behind Diedre to slip the silken sash over her mouth. Diedre gave no indication that she would resist, but when Bera laid her dagger at the far end of Diedre's pallet so she could tie the gag, her prisoner rolled over in a flash, striking Bera's head with one of the manacles as she went for the dagger.

Bera saw stars, yet managed to twist away from Diedre and lunge for the dagger herself.

Curran and Evan must have heard the commotion, because the two of them burst in and swiftly moved to stop Diedre.

Bera pulled away, her hand on her abdomen in a gesture of protection. Now that she was in such desperate danger, the baby seemed real to her indeed.

It wasn't Evan and Curran's efforts that subdued the princess. Diedre caught a glimpse of Evan's face and froze.

Even in the frail lamplight, Bera could see the war of emotions in his face as he gazed into his lover's eyes.

"No," Diedre moaned. "It can't be you. You can't be

here. He knows about us. He means to torture you and kill you." Anguish distorted her Madonna features. "You must leave now, while there's still time."

"I cannot leave," he said harshly. "Not until we've taken Drust—and Murdoc. I cannot let them destroy Pitlanric."

"Ah," she said, her own voice hardening. "Protecting your dear wife Fenella?"

"Protecting my family," he corrected. Evan's eyes narrowed. "How did you know my wife's name? I never told you."

"I overheard my husband discussing her," she said. "She had sent word that she was willing to betray you all, but her price was high: three hundred pieces of silver."

Fenella! She was the traitor! Relief and consternation fought for control of Bera's emotions.

"Fenella?" Evan looked as if someone had just run him through. Bera knew no love was lost between him and his wife, but the shame of such a betrayal had to be devastating.

Thinking back, she remembered what Fenella had said the night of the first council. *You may have helped your brothers escape Burghead and sealed me to this place in the process . . .*

So that was what she'd meant. She'd betrayed the brothers to Drust in hopes of being free of Evan—and Pitlanric.

And now she was waiting back at Pitlanric to betray them again.

The pain of that knowledge was tempered, though, by the realization that neither Evan nor Curran was the traitor.

Bera should have known, should have trusted her husband and her brother.

"You might have told me," Evan said to Diedre in a cracked whisper.

"What good would that have done while you were hostage?" Diedre asked, miserable. "It would only have hurt you, and you'd been hurt enough, especially by me." She covered her face with her hands. "I tried to tell Bera, but Murdoc dragged me away before I could say the name."

"It's true, Evan," Bera confirmed. "She did try to tell me. And I fear she's telling the truth about Fenella. It all fits. Fenella said something to me after we returned." She hated this, hated it. "It all fits."

"One of us needs to go back straightaway and make sure she doesn't do any further damage," Curran said.

When he saw Bera and Evan exchange pointed glances, Curran bent to whisper in Bera's ear. "What will happen to Fenella when we bring this accusation?"

"Our punishment for treachery is terrible," Bera whispered back. "I've seen it only once, and it went on for days. Traitors are stripped naked, whipped, then tortured in front of those they betrayed. Only when death is eminent are they drowned and their bodies cast to the dogs."

"You needn't whisper," Evan said in a low voice that shook with suppressed emotion. "I know what you're talking about. And I know she is guilty." He closed his eyes in agony. "Let me be the one to go," he choked out. "But not until we've gotten Drust."

Bera looked to Curran, but he was the one who confronted Evan with what they both were thinking. "I fear your hatred, Evan. It makes a man do crazy things."

"I will not fail you," her brother said in deadly earnest. "And I will not go until we have Drust."

Diedre's eyes narrowed. "Send *her*." She looked to Bera. "She has no business being here in the first place.

Bera may not care about her child, but I am not willing to bear the guilt if something happens."

Stunned, Bera pulled away from Diedre. How could she have known about the baby? Was she a witch?

"What child?" Curran demanded, cold fury in his eyes.

"The child she's carrying," Diedre replied smugly. "Yours."

Grabbing Bera's upper arms, he faced her, his fair skin mottled by rage. "Is this true?"

"I haven't known that long myself." Why had he had to find out from Diedre? "I was going to tell you, but then you volunteered to come here." Would he believe her? "I was afraid that you might be the traitor, afraid of what might have passed between you and Diedre. So I had to come. I had to know the truth."

"Well, you know it now. But at what risk?"

She could see her suspicions of him wounded Curran to the core. The pain in his eyes made her want to melt away into nothingness. There was anger there, too—anger that she had endangered their child.

"You must go," he ordered, pointing to the tent flap. "Immediately."

"Curran, I can't." She tried to engage his reason. "We planned this through for me to wait here with Diedre, then leave with you and our hostages."

"We'll take you out of camp, then come back for Drust and Murdoc."

"And leave me alone to fend for myself? That's not rational, Curran, and you know it," she argued. "Assuming Diedre doesn't escape and raise an alarm—"

"I would not!" Diedre interrupted with a vehement whisper. "I would never do anything to endanger Evan." No one was foolish enough to pay her any mind.

"If I did go, and you capture Drust and Murdoc as we planned," Bera continued to Curran, "pray, tell me how you mean to get the three of them safely out of camp."

That was the real snag, and no denying it. Unless all three were in their control, the attack could go on.

"With three of us, we can hold a dagger to each of their throats," she reminded them. "But with only two of you, you'll never manage it."

"She's right." Evan's tone was grim. "Weighing the risks, I'd say we'll all be safer if we stick to the plan."

That meant leaving Bera with Diedre while they lured Murdoc away from the chieftains and took him prisoner. Then they would bring him back here and send word to Drust that Murdoc wanted to see him privately in Diedre's tent. Once all three hostages were in their control, they would be able to demand horses and safely flee the camp.

Curran was obviously torn to the point of agony, but after consideration, he grudgingly agreed. "All right. We'll go as planned." He glared at Bera. "But only if you swear you will not place yourself—and my child—at unnecessary risk."

Bera shared the anguish he showed. "I swear it, with a solemn oath to God," she vowed.

"Ah, we can rest easy now," Evan said caustically, all too aware of the many such vows she'd broken.

Shamed, Bera made no reply. Instead, she assured God that this was one vow she meant to keep.

She watched as Curran and Evan bound Diedre, gagged her, then laid her back on the featherbed and covered her with furs. By shifting a few chests and boxes, they fashioned a place for Bera to hide, then they left.

Bera waited, clammy with fear for her husband and brother, as well as for the success of their desperate mission.

Diedre lay quiet for a while, then flopped onto her back with a huff.

"How did you know about the child?" Bera asked quietly, moving close to Diedre's head.

"I 'ust knew," Diedre managed around the gag.

Bera pulled the silken binding down enough for her to speak, but was ready to push it back into place should Diedre try to cry out.

"It's true," her hostage murmured. "I can sense such things."

"So now you're a seer, as well as a temptress and a manipulator." Bera shot her a skeptical glance. "You'll pardon me if I do not believe you."

"Believe what you will," Diedre shot back, "but I can see it in the roundness of your face."

"Why did you tell my husband?" Bera demanded.

"He had a right to know."

He did have a right to know, and Bera deeply regretted that Diedre had been the one to tell him. She should have told him as soon as she knew, but suspicion had poisoned her, as it had poisoned all who'd come into contact with the dragon princess.

The bitter taste of remorse in her mouth, Bera said, "I am not some gullible goose-brain, Diedre. Why did you tell him, really?"

Diedre arched an eyebrow. "We're alike, you know."

"No we're not." The idea was not as abhorrent as she would have thought, though.

"Yes we are," Diedre said. "We're two women trying to make our way in a world of men, both of us forced into marriages with mates who are beneath us."

A clever tactic, trying to distract her, but Bera didn't take the bait. She knew better than to discuss personal matters with an adversary as clever as Diedre. And she'd learned from Curran how to counter such a ploy. "You have not answered my question. Why did you tell Curran about the baby? What could you possibly have hoped to achieve?"

Diedre sighed. "It is always good strategy to divide one's opponents, get them arguing among themselves." A slight smile curved her lips. "It almost worked. I was almost rid of one of you."

"Do you *want* them to fail?" Bera could not understand Diedre's thinking. "If Drust plans to kill you, I should think you'd want to have him captured."

"I *want* him dead," she answered evenly.

"And if he were," Bera asked her, "what then?" They had already broken the warrior's code in killing two sentries by stealth. Why not Drust?

"I have not allowed myself to think beyond that happy prospect," Diedre said.

"Would you still attack Pitlanric?"

"You stole twenty of my horses," Diedre accused.

"And you stole my brothers' mounts, nine of them," Bera said calmly. And drugged them when they came to your table in peace, she thought, but did not say.

If there was only some a way to make peace. Bera wracked her brain, then had an idea. "My brothers suffered greatly as your prisoners, not to mention the work they lost. Some compensation seems fair for that. What if we returned eight of your horses? Would that settle the debt?"

"Ah, we *are* alike." Diedre smiled in earnest, then sobered. "Eleven," she countered.

"Ten," Bera offered.

Diedre hesitated only briefly. "Done."

"Agreed. So you would call off the attack, then?" Bera knew Diedre's promise wasn't worth the breath she used to make it, but she took some small comfort from the exchange.

"Aye. I would call off the attack. And agree to the alliance you seek."

As if her agreement would do any good. Drust was still alive, and they had yet to take him and Murdoc and escape.

The very moment she thought Murdoc's name, Evan and Curran thrust him through the tent flap.

Bera repositioned Diedre's gag, then rose to help the others.

Curran held Murdoc's distinctive helmet beneath his arm. "Any problems?" he asked her.

"None," she answered, weak with relief to see him safe. "We talked. I'll tell you about it later."

Evan said nothing, and Bera knew better than to speak to him. She had never seen her brother so grim. Yet he remained in perfect control, his blade tight against Murdoc's throat just below the jawbone.

Curran pressed his dagger hard against Murdoc's back, angling the blade up from the base of the ribcage for a lethal strike.

"All right," he said low and deadly into Murdoc's ear. "Here's how things are going to go if you want to stay alive. I'm going to push you into the doorway. I want you to stand there and call for a messenger, then stop him before he gets too close. Tell him you need to see Drust here immediately, alone, to discuss an important new development." He nudged the tip of his dagger, causing Murdoc to wince. "Obey, and you'll live to command your men again. Try anything, and I'll kill you, then take your clothes and do the job myself." He cocked a golden eyebrow. "After all those months working together," he said in a startlingly accurate imitation of Murdoc's voice, "I think I could pass as you."

Bera was shocked at this unexpected skill. She would never have thought of Curran as a mimic, but he demonstrated an impressive talent for it.

What other impressive talents did he hide?

The veins bulged at Murdoc's temples, but eventually

he agreed. "I'll do it." Any fool could see from the tension in his body, though, that he wasn't ready to give up yet.

"Be careful." Bera took hold of Curran's arm. "I don't trust him."

"Neither do I," he responded. "But a dagger to the back has a way of encouraging cooperation."

She tightened her grip, peering into Curran's eyes by the dim illumination of the lamp's single flame. "Would you do it? Stab him in the back?" Bera knew the answer. Curran had never been bound by the warrior's code. Why should she expect him to be now?

"With as little hesitation as he would stab me," he said with an edge of iron, the same iron reflected in his eyes. "I do not make idle threats, Bera. What I say I will do, I do."

She realized it was foolish to expect the Dark Warrior to adopt her brothers' code of ethics simply because he'd married her—as foolish as it was for her family to expect Bera to become one of The Wives overnight, simply because she'd taken a husband.

"I'll shield the lamp," she offered, "so no one can see you behind him."

She was frightened—especially for her unborn child—but years of training kept her cold and calculating, alert for any challenge. She watched her brother and Curran position Murdoc at the entrance.

As luck would have it, a foot soldier walked behind the wagons to urinate only a dozen yards away.

"You there," Murdoc called out, his voice hoarse. "I need a messenger. Come here."

"Not too close," Curran reminded him from behind.

"That's close enough," Murdoc said. "Find Lord Drust immediately. Tell him I must see him here at once. There has been an urgent development, something I must discuss with him here, in private." Curran jabbed him, so he added, "Fail, and I'll cut off your balls my-self."

"Aye, sir." The soldier must have noticed that the guards were gone, for she heard him ask, "Would you like me to have them send someone to stand sentry? Lord Drust was most insistent that her highness be—"

"Think you that I cannot guard her well enough?" Murdoc lashed out with genuine outrage. "Stop wasting time and repeat the message to me." It was a standard request when the message was an important one. After the soldier did so, he nodded. "Off with you, then. As I said, this is most urgent."

Evan peeked past the tent flap. Long seconds passed, then he pulled Murdoc back inside. "He's gone." He looked to Curran. "Everything is working just as we planned it."

Both Curran and Bera hastily made the sign against the hex that came from speaking such arrogance.

Curran nodded to her brother. "Help me tie Murdoc's feet and get his clothes. Then we'll bind his hands again and gag him." He tugged at Murdoc's plaid. "We'll hide him and the princess behind those chests."

"Put them together?" Evan was more than dubious. "Do you think that's wise?"

"Easier to keep watch over them." Curran removed the sentry's plaid and began to cut it, then pull long strips for binding. "This should tie him up tight."

The weaver in Bera cringed at the sound of the fabric ripping, but she picked up the other plaid they'd taken from the guards and began ripping it into bindings, too. Drust was a powerful man. It would take a lot of woolen bindings to hold him down.

Curran cocked his head toward Bera's hiding place. "We'll tie him up tight. Once that's done, Evan, take a couple of those boxes to the front and crouch behind them. I'll pretend to be Murdoc and sit with my back to

Drust. I want him well inside the tent before we strike."
He looked at Bera. "You get under the covers and pretend to be Diedre."

There was no denying the brilliance of his plan.

"And then?" she asked.

"Then we wait for The Beast to step into our trap."

Bera ached with fear that Curran would place himself
in such a dangerous, vulnerable position. Instinctively,
she smoothed her hand across her abdomen and said a
prayer for his protection and their unborn child's. "Let's
hope we can subdue Drust without rousing half the
camp."

"He'll come," Curran said with quiet conviction as
he draped Murdoc's plaid, bunching the fabric about him
to simulate the stockier man's girth. Donning Murdoc's
helmet, he shifted to a shorter posture. The transformation was eerily convincing. "We'll take The Beast," he
said with Murdoc's voice. "We have to, or we're all
dead."

Bera nodded, knowing full well what was at stake:
not just their lives, but the lives of everyone back at
Pitlanric.

chapter nineteen

Curran knew from experience that something had to go wrong.

Even with Murdoc's helmet on, he heard the sound of Drust's approach. The Beast's heavy footfalls and grumbling grew louder and louder until there was a swish of the tent flap as he strode through.

"Murdoc!" the thane bellowed as he stomped toward Curran. "Where the hell are the guards? And what's so cursed important that you drag me away from my chieftains when we're planning an attack?"

Curran stood to Murdoc's height and turned to see his adversary, but even with the helmet on, he took care to keep his face in shadow. Beyond Drust, he saw Evan rise and step into the clear.

Then it happened: The messenger came through the tent flap! Seeing Evan, the man drew his sword and dagger.

"Behind you!" Curran ground out.

Thinking the warning was meant for him, Drust armed himself and pivoted to see Evan grappling with the messenger.

Curran shoved his sword to Drust's back, planning to immobilize him as he had Murdoc, but his blade met with firm resistance. Body armor! In the split second it took him to bring his dagger into play, Drust turned and did his best to skewer him.

Like a she-wolf come from nowhere, Bera threw back the covers and launched herself at Drust's head, climbing him as she'd once tried to climb Curran.

Fortunately, Drust was slower than he. Bera had her dagger to his throat before he could make a move. "Call him off," she snarled into Drust's hairy ear. When he hesitated, she bit down on his ear, hard. "I said, call him off!"

"Hold!" Drust fairly screamed. Blood poured from his ear, and Bera spat as if she'd tasted poison. But she kept her blade hard to his throat.

The soldier hesitated, then thought better of it, but the opening was all Evan needed to bring down the pommel of his sword with a dull thud on the man's skull.

The soldier's eyes rolled back and he sank to the ground.

Curran turned to relieve Drust of his weapons as Evan did the same for their unexpected intruder. That done, he and Evan removed Drust's body armor, then set about tying his hands and feet while Bera kept one dagger to his throat and another to his eye.

"That was foolhardy," Curran chided her as he and Evan fought Drust's rigid resistance to bind him. "You swore to me that you wouldn't—"

"It worked, didn't it?" she retorted, unchastened. "We're fine."

Her oblique reference to the baby did little to reassure him.

As soon as he had Drust's hands safely tied, Curran sat on the warlord's massive hip to catch his breath. Evan joined him, panting from tying Drust's ankles. The Beast had lived up to his name, struggling to the last, even with a dagger to his throat.

Bera snatched up the few remaining strips of wool. "I'll bind and gag the intruder."

Much as he hated to admit it, Curran was glad she was with them. Her argument had been correct. They couldn't have managed without her. Though that rankled—and he was still angry with her for putting their child at risk—he couldn't help being proud of her.

"What now?" Evan asked Curran.

"Help me with the others."

It didn't surprise him that Evan made straight for Diedre and not Murdoc. Evan helped her gently to her feet, and she leaned against him like a weak and sickly child. "This gag is too tight," he announced. "She can hardly breathe. I'm going to remove it."

Curran didn't like the sound of that, or the reason behind it. "I wouldn't do that if I were you."

"Well, you're not me, though, are you?" He peeled the silken fabric down until it cleared her chin, then kissed her, hard and hungry. Diedre returned his kiss with equal ardor.

Curran was grateful that Drust couldn't see them. He might just break his bindings and go for Evan. Just to be safe, though, he stuffed two bits of plaid into Drust's ears, then blindfolded the thane. Now Drust could neither see, hear, nor speak.

Curran stood. Bera had been awfully quiet. He looked for her and saw that she had turned away, ashamed of her brother, no doubt.

Evan laid his cheek to Diedre's and held her as if he never meant to let her go. "We need horses and safe passage out of camp," he told her. "Who should we approach with our demands?"

Diedre stiffened. She pulled back, alarm on her haggard features. "Approach no one. Drust has given orders that if he should be taken hostage, his men are to attack, immediately and without reservation—even at risk of his life."

"Don't believe her," Curran warned. "She's using you, just like she uses everyone."

"I love Evan," Diedre protested. "I would gladly lay down my life for him." When she saw that Curran was unconvinced, she said, "I'd get the horses for you myself, but I cannot. Everyone knows I am a prisoner, and why."

Curran stared into the single flame, uncertain what to do next. He knew of no such order, but Drust might well have issued it after the escape. If Diedre was telling the truth . . .

The huge knot inside his chest tightened. Had they come so close, only to lose in the end? He thought of Bera and his unborn child and Pitlanric and the life he'd come to love. So much to lose.

Too much to lose. There had to be a way to win; he just had to find it.

"How many guards on the horses?" he asked the princess.

"Usually only two," Diedre answered. "But I can't be sure. Drust may have doubled or even tripled the guards since you stole so many of our steeds. I have no way of knowing anymore."

Suddenly the tent's sides billowed with a snap, and everyone but Drust jumped.

Several tense, watchful seconds passed before Evan broke the silence. "Just the wind."

"Why can't we walk them out on foot," Bera suggested, "then ride double back to Pitlanric?"

"Too slow." This from Evan. "They'd easily overtake us."

"Evan's right," Diedre confirmed.

Curran was just thinking that Drust had been entirely too quiet when the warlord rolled to his feet with a muffled roar and snatched off his blindfold as he slit the bindings at his ankles with a tiny dagger they had missed.

Bera jumped back, but not quickly enough. Drust's long arm reached out and he grabbed her tunic, jerking her hard against him. His huge hand easily stripped her dagger from her and put it to her throat.

Curran froze, not wanting to provoke Drust any further. His heart turned over in his chest at the sight of the blade against Bera's throat, but he knew he had to talk Drust down. It was Bera's only chance.

At the edge of his vision, he caught a glimpse of Diedre struggling briefly with Evan. She came up with Evan's sword and dagger, which she used to cut herself free. Too shocked to respond, Evan just stood there.

"I can play at this game, too," Drust rumbled. Curran saw Bera wince at the rank odor of his breath.

Careful, he told himself. Ease him down. Try to shift his attention away from Bera. Drust wouldn't hesitate to cut Bera's throat, and Curran knew it.

"Don't do it," Diedre warned her husband. Evan's sword in her left hand, she held the blade of his dagger in her right, ready to throw. Moving clear of Curran, she eased closer to Drust. "Let her go."

Drust's laugh was the grunt of a beast. "Ah, my loving wife," he sneered. "The fact that you wish me to spare this annoying little flea just makes killing her more enjoyable."

"My wife is only a woman," Curran said in as offhand a manner as he could manage with his heart pounding like thunder.

Bera looked to him with a mixture of trust and desperation. "Think of our people, Curran," she rasped from beneath Drust's blade. "Do what you must to save Pitlanric, even if it means my death."

"So dramatic." Curran waved a hand in dismissal of

what she'd said. "What honor is there for you in killing her? Fight me, warrior to warrior," he challenged, praying that Drust's infamous pride would convince him to take the bait. "Let fate decide who's the better man. Let her go. She's only a woman."

"Only a woman?" Bera exclaimed with fire in her eyes.

The infamous pride he'd succeeded in stirring wasn't Drust's.

Blast. Would Bera never learn when to shut up? Curran wanted Drust's attention on him, not her.

"Hold your tongue, wife," he said mildly. "This is warrior's business." He looked to Drust. "What's the matter? I should think you'd be glad for a chance to best a man of my reputation. Or does that frighten you?" He shook his head. "I had thought you made of sterner stuff."

"Hah!" Drust's beady little eyes glistened with malice. "I will fight the infamous Dark Warrior, and I will win. As soon as I've—"

The motion of his dagger on Bera's neck was slight, but Curran saw the blood blooming from the cut Drust made. "Bera! No!" He hurled himself at The Beast. Halfway there, a dagger sailed past him and struck Drust dead in the eye, penetrating to the crosspiece.

Diedre.

Curran lunged for Bera and pulled her from the lifeless arms of her attacker. Drust fell back, but Curran saw only the shock on Bera's face, and the blood. He could smell it, see it washing over her throat from the dark gash below her jawbone.

Bera looked up at him with stunned disbelief. "He cut my throat. The bastard cut my throat."

She could talk, at least. That meant Drust hadn't severed her windpipe.

Evan and Diedre rushed to their side.

"Let me see." Diedre gingerly examined the wound, then wet a strip of plaid and laid it snugly across the cut. "Try to keep still. The cold water will help stop the bleeding. The cut isn't deep. You'll be all right."

"Thank God." Curran sagged with relief.

Diedre looked at him with open scorn, then addressed Bera in tight whisper. "We can kill Murdoc, too, and blame it all on him." She pointed to Curran. "My chieftains will execute him, and then we'll both be free."

"Are you mad?" Bera shot back, appalled.

"You were forced to marry this . . . hireling," Diedre said, "just as I was forced to marry Drust. I am offering you a chance at freedom. Say the word, and you will be a widow."

Bera's hands tightened on Curran's sleeves. "He's my husband. I love him!"

Curran looked down at her in amazement. "You what?"

"I love you." Why hadn't she realized it before? It was so simple.

She did love him. Knowing it, the pain at her throat dimmed, and something profound within her settled warmly into place, like a long-lost child at last finding her way home.

Despite the desperate danger they were in, Bera marveled. "I love you," she repeated in wonder, gazing into Curran's astounded expression. Had anyone ever truly loved him before?

"She does love him, Diedre," Evan affirmed. "Bera is no good at deception. If she says she loves him, she does."

Diedre recoiled as if she'd been confronted by the spirit of the Banshi. "But why? He is far beneath her."

Bera felt Curran stiffen.

"Curran is not beneath her," Evan said with conviction. "Honor isn't born into a person; it is created from within. Curran may not be of noble blood, but he has a noble heart, and I am proud to call him brother." His voice hardened. "Bera and I both would gladly die to protect him. Or kill."

"Is that a threat?" Diedre asked, her voice resonant with warning.

"Merely a statement of fact," Evan answered.

Troubled, Diedre rose, then crossed to Drust's body. She took his weapons first, then removed a key he was wearing on a chain around his neck.

"Here," Evan offered. "Let me help you with that." Using the key, he unlocked the manacles.

"Keep them," Diedre instructed as she rid herself of the shackles. "They're silver. Very valuable." She tossed Bera's dagger to her.

Evan frowned. "Forget the silver." He threw the manacles onto her bedding, then took hold of Diedre's shoulders and gazed on her with sadness. "Drust is dead. This is your chance to turn away from scheming and manipulations." He searched her face. "Can you do that? Are you capable of changing? Answer me from your heart."

"I want to." Diedre threw her arms around Evan and drew him close. "What a blessing it would be simply to live my life—to stop worrying who might be working against me every minute of the day." She closed her eyes. "You cannot begin to know what a burden it's been, never trusting anyone, never having the luxury of taking anything at face value." She let out a shuddering sigh. "It has made a prison of my own skin, and I would gladly turn away from that."

"Then help us escape." Evan held her close. "If we can get you and Murdoc out of here, there can be peace between our people."

Bera witnessed a startling transformation in Diedre. The peace that Evan spoke of invaded the once-cynical princess, changing her posture, her expression, her eyes.

The harsh lines beside her mouth softened, making her look years younger. No longer was she the dragon princess.

"I'll help you," Diedre declared. "Trust me, Evan. Let me atone for at least a little of the grief I've caused you and your family. Give me a chance to prove myself."

"Do it, Evan," Curran surprised Bera by saying. "Even she deserves a chance to redeem herself."

Evan turned to Curran. "You would risk our lives by trusting her?"

"You and your family gave me a chance to prove myself." Curran looked into Bera's face, his own suffused with hope. "And so did you, my ferocious wife, in spite of your suspicions that I might be a traitor."

He cared for her. She could see it in his face, hear it in the tender way he spoke to her. Tears of joy blurred Bera's vision. "Then I shall trust her, but only as far as a one-legged man can jump."

"That's not very far," Curran observed, "but it's a start." He gave her a squeeze, then looked up to Evan. "First, we must get three horses. Once we have them, we need to bring them to this side of the camp, then smuggle Murdoc and Diedre safely back to our own mounts."

"But if we leave Drust's body behind," Bera felt compelled to say, "won't they suspect that Diedre and Murdoc killed him, then fled?"

"You have a point," Evan agreed. Protective of Diedre, he would not put her at such risk. "We cannot leave him here."

"Then we'll take his body with us," Curran said.

Another strong gust of wind struck the tent like the breath of some great night-beast.

"I have pen and parchment," Diedre offered. "I could leave behind a note in Ogam." She thought a moment, then continued. "I could say that we've learned Mac-

Alpin is on his way to subdue Burghead, so the three of us have gone to Pitlanric to negotiate a settlement. And I'll order the army to turn back immediately to prepare to defend Burghead."

"Diedre," Evan warned when he saw her lapse into her old ways.

Curran interrupted before Evan voiced any further objections. "An excellent strategy, Diedre. Will the chieftains believe it and do as ordered?"

Diedre nodded, her face hard. "They will. There's bad blood between Drust and MacAlpin, and all of them know it. Our warriors will be anxious to protect their families."

"All right, then." Curran turned his attention to Bera. "Do you feel well enough to stay here and watch over Murdoc while the three of us we go for the horses?"

"Aye." Her neck was still bleeding, but only slightly. "I'll be fine. Go on." While Evan and Curran carried Murdoc to Diedre's bed and covered him, Bera struggled to her feet, ignoring the lightheadedness that came with her rapid shift in position.

Curran started for the door, but halted halfway there. He came back to take Bera into his arms and kiss her. "I love you, too," he whispered in her ear.

Bera held onto him until he pulled away.

"We'll be back." He left the tent with Evan and Diedre close behind him.

Diedre made good on her promise. Two hours later, they were safely on their way back to Pitlanric. When they stopped to water the horses, Evan approached Bera and Curran. "I must ride ahead." His shoulders were stooped, as if all the stones of Burghead were piled upon them. "There are things I must do."

"Take Bera with you," Curran said. "Diedre and I can handle Murdoc."

The request took Bera by surprise. Upon consideration, though, she understood. Curran didn't want Evan
to face Fenella's betrayal alone. Much as she hated to
leave her husband, she understood the compassion behind his request. "Good idea. I'll go back with Evan so
all will be ready when you arrive."

"There's no need of that," Evan argued. "Stay with
the others. I'll make sure everything is ready for you."

"I want to go with you," Bera said. "Please, brother.
Let me stand beside you when—"

"Very well," he snapped. "Come if you wish. But I
don't want to talk about it."

They both knew what he did not wish to talk about.
"Agreed," she said. "We shall not speak of anything unless you want to."

Poor Evan. Bera's heart broke for him, but no one
could make this any easier, not even she.

Bera could scarcely move by the time they crested the
last hill and saw Pitlanric. They had ridden hard, and
with every mile that passed, Evan had grown more grim.

"Thank God," she said as they started on the last leg
to home.

"God?" Evan murmured, looking like a man on his
way to his own execution. "You think God has any part
of what they'll do to Fenella?"

"It is a just punishment for so great a crime, and God
is just," she reminded her brother. "He does not wink at
sin."

"My sin is as great as hers. Fenella is my wife, yet I
have never loved her. And I gave my heart to another,
a woman who was married to someone else—an enemy!
Is that treason any less because I'm a man?"

"It's not the same, Evan." Bera searched for the
words she needed. "True, adultery is a great sin, a sin
against your wife and your own body—and Drust and

Diedre. But Fenella betrayed us all. She would gladly have led us to the slaughter, our whole tribe."

"Let him who is without sin cast the first stone," Evan quoted.

"If it were up to me, I would handle this differently. But our brothers . . ." Bera sighed, her mind fogged by fatigue. "Once they find out what she did—and we must tell them; they have a right to know—they will demand that tradition be followed. Fenella betrayed them to a beast, threatened their families, Evan, their children."

He looked up at Pitlanric. "I am her husband. What needs to be done, I will do." He slowed his pace as if he dreaded reaching the gates and the inevitable confrontation beyond.

"Evan, don't." Bera had never seen him so filled with hatred. "Can you live with yourself if you harm her?"

"I could not live with myself if I did stood idle while they torture her," he ground out. "I, who am as guilty as she. What I do will be a mercy."

"Evan—"

He turned on her like a wild beast. "Do not interfere, Bera! And say nothing to the others. I'm her husband. I shall be the one to tell them, but not until she is beyond their reach. I owe her that much."

"I have to tell the others, Ev. But I'll ask them to respect your privacy. If they're willing, we'll wait until you give the word to deal with Fenella."

They rode on in strained silence until she could bear the tension no longer. "After the years of misery she's subjected you to, I should think you would not be inclined to mercy."

"You'd think wrong, then." Evan stared toward Pitlanric in the distance. "She was devastated when she found out she was barren. I told her it didn't matter, that I would not cast her out. But I think that made her hate me even more." He looked to Bera. "Imagine being barren in a tribe like ours. Everywhere she turned, there were children and wives great with child. Little wonder she was bitter."

"Believe it or not," Bera said quietly, "I do understand. For years, I've been convinced that I had missed my chance to have children."

"I could see how much you loved the babies," Evan confided.

"But I did not betray our family because I couldn't have a baby," she said. "And neither did Fenella. She betrayed us all because she hates us."

"You've always been stronger than Fenella," he countered. "She's so alone. I think if she had been able to bear a child, even one, things would have been different."

"Aye, they'd be different." Bera said, regretting the anger in her voice. "Fenella would be a selfish, vain, deceitful traitor with a *child*."

"Does it matter anymore?" he asked, his tone as weary as the rest of him looked. "She did what she did, and death will be her punishment."

"Give her a chance to explain herself," she surprised herself by saying. "Diedre might be lying, you know."

"She's not lying," Evan retorted, emphatic.

The next was difficult, but it had to be said. "Do you believe Diedre because she's telling the truth?" she asked. "Or because it will free you to marry her, now that Drust is dead?"

Her questions hit home. Evan turned on Bera, his words angry and resentful. "You're a hard woman, Bera. Too hard."

"I did not say it to be hard. I said it because I love you too much to let you do this without at least considering that Diedre might be using you, just as she's used everyone else."

"She loves me, and I love her," he said, but it lacked

conviction. "It has to be real. She wouldn't use me."

"All I ask is that you think long and hard about it before you do anything to Fenella."

"All right. I will." He closed his eyes, suddenly looking like an old man.

Bera brought Tundarr close and reached over to clasp her brother's arm. "I'm so sorry about all this, Evan."

His eyes filled with tears, and he looked away in silence.

By the time they reached Pitlanric, the gate was open and the entire tribe was waiting for them on the greensward with shouts of welcome.

Bera did her best to hide her concern as the family thronged around them and helped her down from Tundarr. Immediately, she was besieged with questions. "I went because I wanted to be with my husband," she told a scowling Airell. "Curran's fine," she assured Lavena. "He's coming later, with quite a surprise."

"What's wrong with Evan?" Angus asked her. "I've never seen him look so . . . bleak."

"We need to talk about that. Can the council assemble?"

"Don't you want to eat first?" Angus asked. "And get some rest?"

Bera looked to Evan and saw that he was ignoring his brothers' questions. "No. It can't wait."

Angus followed her line of vision and saw Evan pull Moina aside. "I do not see my wife," he asked Moina. "Where is she?"

"I told her you were coming," Moina responded, criticism implicit in her tone and expression. "Yet she would not stir from your house. She says she has a headache."

Evan lifted his hand and spoke above the welcoming chatter. "Pray, excuse me, all. I am overweary and would visit with my wife alone."

Bera watched him go with a heavy heart.

Justice and mercy were in her brother's hands.

She only wished that Curran were safely home to stand beside her in the tempest that was sure to follow.

She held onto Angus's arm. "Assemble the council. There is much to tell, and unless I tell it quickly, I fear I'll fall asleep before I finish."

She would tell them everything—about what happened with Drust, Diedre's "conversion" and her allegations about Fenella . . . everything. Then she would lay her weary bones in bed and wait for Curran.

He would come. She willed it so.

chapter twenty

Curran had suspected that once Drust was dead, Diedre would drop her Madonna ruse, and he was right.

She'd been both imperious and relentless in demanding that they make all haste to Pitlanric. He'd been mightily tempted to gag her again, but before she left, Bera had asked him not to, so he endured Diedre's arrogance.

Bera. He sent up a brief but heartfelt prayer that by now she and Evan had reached Pitlanric safely.

He'd been riding for twelve hours, stopping only to water and rest their horses.

Evan was doubtless the reason behind Diedre's determination to reach Pitlanric. If so, the matter must be dealt with before they got there. "Why are you pressing so hard?" he asked for the twentieth time. "We're almost there."

For the twentieth time, Diedre pretended she hadn't heard him.

"You said Drust's men will return to Burghead," Curran shouted over the noise of galloping hooves. Conversation wasn't easy at the speed they were riding. "Are you afraid they'll go after us instead?"

"Nay," she shouted hoarsely, worn down by his persistence. "Without Drust or Murdoc, they will go back to Burghead."

"Then why are you pushing so hard?" he asked. "It's obvious you're just as weary and saddlesore as the rest of us."

From one of the two mounts tethered behind Curran, Murdoc grunted in agreement, his bound hands gripping the high crest at the front of his saddle.

"I *am* exhausted," the princess said. "And sore." Her eyes welled with tears, but she fought them back. "But none of that matters. I must be with Evan. Fenella . . . he will need me to comfort him in such a trial."

Curran marveled that lust could blind such an intelligent woman to the obvious. "Evan might want your comfort," he shouted to her, "but when we get to Pitlanric, he will *need* you to keep your distance."

The truth was ugly, but Diedre had to hear it. Curran only hoped she truly cared for Evan and wouldn't use what he was about to say to destroy Evan—and the unity of the family. "The best thing you can do for Evan would be to avoid him. His brothers know Evan bedded you, but they only suspect that you've bewitched him. You'll do the man no favors by confirming their fears. They'd never trust him again."

Curran hardened himself to the anguish she showed. Evan was his brother now. He had to protect Evan, even from his own lustful folly.

"Why would they condemn him?" she shouted back at him. "Is it such a crime to love someone?"

"To love an enemy, yes. Think!" Curran urged. "Fenella will be tortured and executed based on your accusation alone. How would it look for Evan if you betray the illicit love the two of you share?" He used the term "love" advisedly.

"Blessed Mother," she moaned, deflated. "I had not thought of it that way. You're right." She eased her mount to a gentler pace, and Curran gratefully slowed to match her progress, as did the tethered horses bearing Drust's body and Murdoc.

"You promised Evan you would try to turn from your old ways," he reminded her. "This is your chance to prove that. For his sake, stay away from him, at least until this whole sordid mess has settled down."

Diedre's feminine pride reared its stubborn head. "What if he won't let me stay away? If I do not come to Evan, he will come to me."

"He's been thinking with his cock, that's for sure," Curran observed. He glared at her in challenge. "So don't tell him what you're doing, or why. Remain aloof. Treat him the same as you treat the other brothers. Ask Ula or Olwyn or Lavena to attend you at all times, so he cannot see you alone."

"Ula, Olwyn, or Lavena," she repeated.

"Aye. They will not take offense at such a request, but the others might."

Diedre slumped, reining her mount back to a walk. Again, he eased to her pace. "I will do as you suggest," she said wearily, "but only for Evan, not because you said I must."

Curran remembered Diedre's saying that she and Bera were alike, and in this, at least, he had to agree. These princesses would not be commanded by their own husbands or anyone else's. "We're not far from home," he consoled her. "At the rate we've been going, we may only be a few hours behind Evan and Bera."

Home. Bera. Curran felt a surge of longing to be back in their bed, holding each other. Holding his storm goddess. Talking through the fateful events of the past few days.

Before their marriage, he'd avoided speaking to anyone for fear he might betray some tiny thing that would end up causing his death. But now, he was eager to hear

Bera's perspective on what had happened, and to share his own.

Safe. Their bed had become a safe place, a refuge in life's raging uncertainties—a place to love and be loved.

Thinking of it, he felt as if some part of him, deep inside, had laid down its sword at last.

If only he could get Bera to do the same.

"They're coming!"

Bera heard the shout and forced herself to sit up, her body still weary but warmed from a dream of making love with Curran.

As her mind began to clear, she smiled as she remembered the council meeting and the surprise that would be waiting for Curran upon his return.

Osann hastened to the side of the bed. "Let me help your highness with her hair." She smiled broadly, triggering adorable dimples in her cheeks. "I know her highness will want to look her best for Lord Curran's return."

Yawning, Bera drew her into a hug. "When we are in chamber," she reminded Osann, "her highness would prefer to be Missy."

Osann hugged her back. "Sorry. I've gotten so used to—"

"No need to be sorry," Bera interrupted affectionately. "I'll just keep reminding you." She yawned again, loud and long.

Osann stilled. "Everyone says that Princess Diedre will be with Lord Curran," she said in a shaky whisper. "Is that true?"

"Aye." Bera sighed, holding Osann tighter.

"Will she take me back to Burghead?"

"Never," Bera murmured fiercely. "I'll never let her take you back." She held Osann out and looked her in the eye. "Princess Diedre is our prisoner. She cannot take you back. And even if she were not a prisoner, I would not let her."

"Good." Osann smiled up at her with absolute trust. Then she wriggled free to fetch Bera's combs and brushes. "We must hurry. Lord Curran will want to see you there when he comes through the gate."

"Oh, he will, will he?" Bera teased, standing to her feet. Every muscle in her body ached, but especially her legs. "And how do you know that?"

"Because he loves you," the little girl said with the wisdom of innocence. She drew up a stool and Bera descended gingerly so that Osann could brush out and dress her hair. "He loves you, he loves you," Osann sang as she worked.

"Did Lord Curran tell you that?" Bera asked. It was enough that he had told her, but she was curious.

"Nay, silly," Osann answered. "It's plain to see, the way he looks at you when he thinks no one is watching."

A tear escaped before Bera could stop it.

"Oh, Missy. I did not mean to make you sad." Osann stopped brushing and looked to her with worry. "I thought you'd be glad to know it."

"I am glad to know it," Bera reassured her, smiling through the tears that overflowed. "These are tears of joy, not sorrow."

"Oh, good." Osann handed her a linen napkin. "Joy or not, though, you must stop crying, my Missy. You're making your eyes all red, and how will that look to Lord Curran?"

Bera chuckled, mopping her eyes. She'd created a monster by allowing Osann such familiarity, but she didn't care. The child could boss her till the heath sprouted roses; Bera would obey only when it suited her to do so.

Osann finished brushing out her hair, then wove a small braid from each temple and joined them at the back with a ribbon. "There. You look like a bride. Now you must hurry and dress."

After a hasty change into her best bliaut and tunic, Bera donned her most beautiful plaid and walked briskly to the ward, her heart pounding with excitement. Her husband was coming home.

Beyond the stockade, Curran looked ahead as they approached the gatehouse and felt an odd sensation. He'd been a stranger when last he'd come here, but this time he was coming home, to Bera and their family. The depth of emotion that prompted surprised him.

Diedre straightened her dusty clothes and did her best to look regal.

For Evan's sake, and the family's, Curran prayed she would keep her word and do as she'd promised.

They rode through the gatehouse and saw that the entire family had gathered to welcome them atop the greensward. It was a most subdued reunion, though. The brothers stood at the fore, backed up by pointing, whispering wives and children. But the only one Curran saw was Bera.

She stood quietly beside her brothers, her eyes on him alone, and her face luminous. She looked more than a princess; she looked a queen. Her auburn hair glowed with fire in the sun, and the wind molded her bliaut and tunic against her taut body. But the thing he noticed most was the joy that lit her face.

He stared at her in wonder. Once, he had thought her plain. Now he saw the beauty that shone from within: her courage, her strength, and the love she bore him. He was humbled—and deeply grateful—that destiny had linked his life to hers.

When he stopped his mount, she came close and reached up to touch his arm. "What? No greeting for your wife?" she asked, only half-teasing.

"Hello, wife." What peace he felt, gazing into her face. Curran eased an aching leg over the saddle and slid to ground. Oblivious to the dust of the last thirty miles, he put his arms around her and drew her close. "Saints, but it feels good to hold you," he murmured.

"It feels good to me, too, but being in bed will feel even better. I could sleep for days."

He closed his eyes and nodded. "And I."

"Greetings, your highness," he heard Angus say. Curran looked beside them and saw that all the brothers had formed a tight arc facing Diedre. The rest of the family looked on, exchanging mumbled conjectures about Diedre, Drust's body, and the chieftain still bound and gagged in the saddle. "On behalf of my family," Angus said to her with a strong note of irony, "allow me to welcome you to Pitlanric."

Diedre remained aloof, but her gaze darted through the crowd. Curran did the same and realized that Evan wasn't there.

Nor was Fenella.

Their absence sent a thread of foreboding through him. But even that could not erase the sense of peace he felt with Bera in his arms. He kissed her long and hard and hungrily, and she all but melted.

Since Diedre seemed to have no intention of dismounting, Angus turned to Curran and landed a friendly clout on his back. "Welcome home, brother. I can see you missed your wife."

Curran pulled himself from Bera's lips. Forcing his attention to less intimate matters, he bowed to Angus, but kept his arm around Bera's shoulders. "It would be advisable to see that Murdoc is well treated," he said confidentially. "We may need him later."

Angus nodded. "I agree." He motioned Connal and Cusantin forward, then instructed the younger twins to see their prisoner safely and comfortably settled.

While Angus was busy with that, Curran glanced up at Diedre, who remained mounted, probably to underscore her superior rank. When Angus returned, Curran told him quietly, "Keep the princess under heavy guard, preferably in a room with no windows." He looked at her again askance. "It's dangerous to leave her alone, even for a second. Do you think Ula or Lavena or Olwyn could attend her? Two would be best, I think."

"She's already made that request," Angus revealed. He met Curran's gaze with respect. "Judging from her restraint, I reasoned that you had spoken to her about . . . things."

So Angus knew, too.

He gripped Curran's forearm. "Thank you, Curran, for doing that. And for all the rest. I'm grateful, and so is the family." His voice thickened with emotion. "I am proud to call you brother."

That alone was enough to make Curran's heart swell, but Angus wasn't finished yet.

"Witness!" Angus shouted, turning all eyes to him as he removed the silver band that was his crown and held it up. "The new thane of Pitlanric!" He placed the circlet on Curran, who stood speechless in amazement.

Surely the others would take grievous offense at such a—

"Hail, Curran, Thane of Pitlanric!" the brothers shouted as one, their expressions confirming Angus's actions. The children cheered, and most of The Wives applauded, Gitta the loudest. Only Moina held back, no doubt resentful that her husband had been displaced.

"You've earned it, Curran," Bera said with pride. "From this day, we honor you as thane. And I honor you as husband."

Tears of joy stung the back of Curran's eyes. His princess honored him. His goddess. His wife.

And his family. No longer Bera's family, but his.

But Curran's moment of triumph was not to last. The celebration halted abruptly when Diedre looked beyond the crowd and let out a blood-curdling scream.

Everyone turned. A chilling silence fell as the crowd stepped back to clear a path for Evan, who strode forward with a bloody sword in his hand.

Curran tightened his grip on Bera's shoulders.

"Dear God," she breathed out. "What's he done?"

Curran knew, and he regarded Evan with sympathy and respect.

Evan advanced to him and knelt, his face downcast as he offered up his bloody sword. "The traitor has been executed. Fenella is dead."

Moina shrieked, and a harsh tide of whispers erupted.

Two deeply held traditions had been breached this day, putting Curran's leadership to a critical test. Daunted, he took the bloodied sword from Evan's hands. "Evan, we had no trial—"

"There was no need." Evan looked up at him in bitter resignation. "When I confronted her, she confessed, threw it in my face."

Bera groaned and drew back, but Curran was relieved.

In his first act as thane, he raised the bloody sword high, silencing the crowd with, "Hear ye all!" The murmurs faded. "Upon the condemnation of her own willing confession, the traitor Fenella has been executed by her lord and husband, Evan, who in his mercy spared his lady wife from torture and humiliation."

He handed Evan back his sword and helped him to his feet beside him. "I commend my brother's clemency and wisdom in this matter." Curran glared at the crowd. "Any who disapprove Lord Evan's actions are hereby commanded to bring their complaints to me, and me alone."

All the brothers nodded in grave agreement, even Orrin.

"Those who ignore this order," Curran said firmly, "will be gagged for a month, publicly and privately, with no exceptions. Is that understood?"

That should take care of Moina.

A chorus of startled "Ayes" came from the crowd, but it was the brothers who shouted their agreement most heartily.

Evan grasped Curran's arm. "I . . . don't know how to thank—"

"It is I who owe you thanks, my brother," Curran said with conviction, loud enough for everyone to hear. "You have spared the family a great ordeal and set an admirable example of mercy. I meant it when I said you are to be commended." He clapped his hand on Evan's upper arm, his voice dropping. "Rest now. We'll take care of . . . everything."

"Do not throw her to the dogs," Evan asked. "I don't think I could bear to see her body torn to bits."

Angus stepped in. "I'll bury her." He enveloped his brother in a bear hug, then parted gruffly. "Airell and I will set things to rights at your house straightaway. Then you can return to rest. We'll send a slave to care for you."

"Nay," Bera interjected. She looked to Curran. "With my lord's permission, I would see Evan home and settled."

"Of course," Curran was quick to say.

Bera sought her brother's assent. "Evan?"

"You always understand me," he said with weary gratitude. "Aye."

Bera circled Evan's waist with a gentle arm. "I need a drink. How about you?" When he nodded, she addressed Angus. "I'll bring him home in a quarter-hour. Will that give you enough time?"

"Aye. We'll take her out onto the heath and bury her where no one can find her." ·

Bera looked with longing to Curran. "Rest, husband. I shall attend you in our chamber shortly."

Much as he yearned to bring her to their bed and lie beside her, Curran was glad she had taken compassion on her brother.

"Wake me if I've gone to sleep," he called after her as she guided Evan toward the kitchens.

Curran turned to the lingering crowd. "You are dismissed. Let this be a day of mourning for the treachery that existed in our midst."

As the family began to disperse, Curran turned to deal with the princess and found her gazing after Evan, her face rigid. He reached up to help her dismount. "Your highness." Diedre had become his problem now that he was thane.

Crumbling at last, Diedre slid into his arms a broken woman.

"This is the cost of your games, Diedre," he murmured into her ear before he handed her over to Roy and Orrin. "Don't try any tricks here at Pitlanric. I may be thane, but no code of honor will keep me from cutting your throat if you cause my family any further trouble. Is that understood?"

Diedre jerked free of him. "Understood," she said with a flash of royal temper. "You may be thane, but such a lowly office does not give you the right to call me by my Christian name. Never dare to do so again. Is *that* understood?"

Curran granted her a brief bow. "Understood." He couldn't help admiring Diedre's spirit. Even in defeat, she kept her pride.

But she was no match for his Bera. Now *there* was a princess.

Curran watched as Roy and Orrin led Diedre away,

then he plodded toward his bed. Soon. Bera would be in his arms soon.

Bera returned to find her husband sound asleep. He never even stirred as she undressed him, then dragged and rolled him to his side of the bed and covered him with a clean linen sheet and blanket of furs.

Almost cross-eyed with fatigue, Bera found her crock of dried rose petals and handed them to Osann. "Go to the kitchens to warm some clear spring water and steep these in it, then bring the bowl to me."

Osann bowed and exited.

While Bera was waiting, she stripped to her chainse and relieved herself, then ate some bread and cheese. Evan had been like a ghost, but she'd managed to get some hot bread and spirit into him before she took him home and made sure he went to bed. With luck, he would sleep for days.

Just as Curran was sleeping now.

Her husband lay so still, she got worried and went over to put her ear to his chest. Slow and powerful, his great heart beat a steady rhythm.

When Osann knocked softly, Bera opened the door and took the steaming, aromatic bowl of water. "Thank you. I'll send for you when I need you next. There is a place for you with Lord Boyd's girls."

Osann's face brightened. As always, she enjoyed staying with Boyd's family. "God give you good rest, Missy," she whispered, then scampered off to be with Boyd's little girls.

Bera elbowed the door closed and carried the steaming bowl to the small table next to Curran's side of the bed. Gently and methodically, she wiped him clean with the warm rose water and dried him, but he didn't stir, not even when she washed his cock. It woke up, but couldn't wake the rest of him.

Disappointed, she rolled him over and washed his hindside from his neck to his toes. Still nothing. Bera covered him warmly and gave up.

Resigned, she carried the bowl of now-cool water to her side of the bed. After removing her chainse, she washed and dried herself. Then she set the bowl aside and crawled under the covers with her husband. Snuggling against him, she thought about all that had happened and felt so proud. Curran was more than just a man she loved; he was a great man she admired—a husband she trusted with all her heart at last.

Not like her father. Curran would be different, a man their children could love and be proud of.

Their children. Bera placed her hand over her belly and finally let herself rejoice at the miracle inside her. She fell asleep wishing that it would be a girl.

Somewhere in the night, she dreamed it was summer. The roses were blooming all around her, scenting the warm air with their fragrance. And Curran was loving her, stroking her . . .

Bera opened her eyes and found herself in bed at Pitlanric, but the warmth and delicious feel of Curran's hands on her body were real.

"I woke up," he said in the darkness, kneeling between her outspread legs, his hands stroking down her naked torso.

He bent forward and teased her nipples with his teeth. Then he suckled her while his hand explored her hidden folds and found the magic nubbin, sending exquisite agonies through her body with every touch.

"Stand up, my storm goddess," he demanded hoarsely. "Let me worship you."

"I am no goddess," she said, but did as he asked.

"Yes, you are." He nuzzled her sex with his mouth, his hands stroking her hindparts in gentle torture.

Bera gasped and gripped his thick golden hair near the scalp.

"I saw you riding naked last summer," he murmured, his breath warm on her bare skin. "I thought you were a storm goddess. I wanted you then, more than any woman I had ever seen."

"That was you?" She remembered the dark stranger who had frightened her so. Of course.

Her passion aflame, she urged him to his feet and grasped the pulsing smoothness of his member. "I think I like being a goddess," she said huskily. "Worship me." She tightened her fingers against its firm resistance. "Worship me with this."

Curran grabbed her buttocks and lifted her to his hips, stabbing his ready cock into her hot, hungry sex.

Bera gripped his upper arms and leaned back. Savoring each slow, deliberate thrust until she could bear it no longer, then urging him to a faster pace with the pressure of her legs.

The bed protested with loud creaks, so Curran knelt, but did not lay her down. Knees spread wide on the mattress, he balanced her against him. His head thrown back, he pumped into her faster and harder, releasing a primal groan with every thrust.

Bera dug her short nails into the corded muscles of his upper arms and met him eagerly until her passion exploded in satisfaction. Seconds behind her, Curran let out a sated growl.

At that exact moment, the bed fell apart, sending the mattress—with them on it—to the floor in a clatter of collapsing bedframe. They tumbled into a heap on the mattress.

Bera shrieked, then burst out laughing. She extracted herself from the tangle of arms and legs and flopped back onto the featherbed. "We broke the bed!" she said inanely between peals of laughter that were matched by Curran's.

"Aye," Curran gasped out. "Broke it good and proper."

His laughter stopped abruptly, and he scooped her into his arms. "You don't think it hurt the baby, do you?"

"No. No. The baby's fine." Bera stroked the sides of his beloved face. "We're both fine."

He relaxed into the featherbed, taking her with him. Fortunately, the collapse had deposited the mattress level on the floor, with no broken pieces beneath.

"Pooh on the bed." Bera nuzzled his chest and settled contentedly into his embrace. "We'll be fine on the floor. I don't want to get up and try to put the frame back together."

"Neither do I." Curran drew the covers up around them, then pulled her to his side. "I want to talk."

A man who wanted to talk. Now *there* was a miracle! "About what?"

"About my past," he said quietly.

"I want to hear, Curran," she said, deeply moved by the significance of the gift he was about to give her. "Your secrets are safe with me."

"I appreciate that." He kissed the top of her head. She sensed a tension in his hesitation, and when he spoke, she understood why. "I was born a slave, Bera."

"And?" Bera didn't have to pretend it didn't matter; to her surprise, it didn't.

"You married a slave," he said grimly.

She tightened her embrace, mindful of his pride yet desperate to ease the shame he must be feeling. "I married *you*. That's all that matters, the man you are. Not where you came from or what you might have done before God sent you to me."

"You mean that, don't you?" he said in amazement.

"With all my heart, Curran," she assured him. "And with all my trust."

"Your trust?" He reared up in the darkness to look at her. "I thought you said you had no trust to give a husband. That I was just like your father—"

Bera placed her finger to his lips to silence him. "I was wrong about that. Wrong about a lot of things."

Curran flopped back down beside her. He stared into the darkness. "But what has changed? That was only two nights ago."

"A lot has happened in that short time. You know that." She searched for the right words. "Somehow, I finally understood the truth, what really matters. Maybe it was the danger, realizing how terrible it would be if anything happened to you. Maybe it was your courage, and the honor with which you acquitted yourself."

"Honor?" Curran let out a harsh chuckle. "I broke almost every rule of your precious warrior's code."

"And so did every warrior who opposed us," Bera was quick to say. "You did what was right, Curran, what was necessary." How could she make him understand? "I had a long talk with my brothers when Evan and I came home. I told them everything you'd done for us, and for me. It was their unanimous decision to make you thane." She smoothed her palm across the fine golden hairs of his forearm. "I was born to my rank, beloved. You attained yours by trial of honor. So yours is greater, in my eyes and in the eyes of my brothers." She curled tighter against him. "I am proud to love you. Proud to be your wife."

Curran lay in silence, stroking her in gentle rhythm. When at last he spoke, his voice was thick with emotion. "I pray God gives me the strength and wisdom to be worthy of such trust."

"He will."

Curran had shared his secret shame. Now it was her

turn. Bera braced herself to resurrect the ghosts—and the guilt—of ten years past. "There is something you must know about me." She groped for a way to say it, then decided to put it plain. "I killed my father."

Curran's breathing halted. After a pause that seemed like aeons, he said, "Knowing you, I assume there were extenuating circumstances. Do you want to tell me about it?"

"Aye." She took a deep breath. "My father was an evil man. He drank too much and constantly beat and insulted my mother, flaunting his wenches to her face. At fourteen, I was still unmarried. My mother had tried for several years to convince my father to arrange a match, but he did not want to part with my dowry, and I did not press the matter. Seeing the way he treated our mother, I feared what sort of man he would choose for me.

"He'd been drinking that night and was in a nastier mood than usual." As always when she even thought about that night, the demons did their best to surround her. But this time, warm in Curran's arms, she knew she was safe. They couldn't touch her. "I didn't bring his spirits quickly enough, so when I handed him a new flagon, he smashed the side of my face with the empty one, cursing me."

A shiver of remembered dread ripple through her. "I screamed, and Mother came running from the hallway. She shouted for the servants to fetch my brothers, then she ran to help me. When she tried to come between us, he hurled her aside and kicked me full in the ribs. Broke four of them." Remembering the pain, she took a deep breath. "Mother was screaming at him and trying to stop him, but he was crazed. He kept hitting me and kicking me, so she grabbed a poker and struck him on the head."

She could see it, hear it, smell it—the blood and the sour smell of rage and decay from her father.

"It didn't stop him, but it drew him away from me. I was all but insensible by then. He snatched the poker from my mother's hand and started hitting her and hitting her. Her face . . ." Bera buried her face into Curran's shoulder.

"I never should have cried out in the first place. He wouldn't have killed her if—"

"He would have killed you, and maybe your mother, too," Curran said with resonant assurance. "Men like him are killers, Bera. You did nothing wrong. It's not your fault. It's his."

Bera realized she was crying but was helpless to stop. "I tried to stop him. I jumped on his arm and bit him and kicked, anything to stop him from hitting her, but he hurled me aside. By then, Angus had come running. He rushed in and saw what was happening." Remembering the shame and rage in her brother's face, she felt the blood curdling in her veins. "He saw my face, and the blood on my clothes, and Father killing Mother. He did his best to save her, but Father was like a wild animal. He hurled Angus aside as if he were a child, and kept on hitting her. Blood was everywhere. Pounding at her face, her skull—"

Blessedly, Curran interrupted with firm but gentle words. "Don't think about that. Get past it. Tell me what happened next."

"Angus stabbed my father. Twice, in the back, to the hilt. Then he just stood there, the dagger in his hand." A dreadful numbness overtook her, but she fought to keep talking. "Finally, Father stopped hitting Mother. The poker was still in his hand. He turned and looked at Angus with such surprise. Then he toppled to the floor on his back. He was still alive. The sounds he made . . ."

"That's over now," Curran soothed. "Tell me what happened next."

Bera shivered. "My brothers . . . they had come, and

they saw everything. Airell went to Angus and took the dagger . . ." She was cold, and so sleepy, an unnatural sleepiness, stealing into her bones.

Curran shook her gently. "Don't leave me now, Bera," he said with real fear in his voice. "Stay with me. Tell me what happened next."

"Airell took the dagger. Never said anything, just looked at me and all the others. His eyes . . ." She shuddered again. "He stood over Father and stabbed him in the chest. Then he rose and held out the dagger. Orrin came next. Then Evan and Becan and Roy. Then Boyd and Donall."

She closed her eyes with a sigh. "Then Kegan and Fidach. Connal and Cusantin were the youngest. They went last. But it wasn't over. Not until I had added mine. I did not cover my wounds, or the blood on my skin and clothes. I took the knife and knelt down beside my father and stabbed him, and stabbed him, and stabbed him." Her fist beat out the deadly motion on Curran's chest.

There. She'd said it, and the world had not shattered.

His hand covered hers, stilling it. "Oh, Bera." She heard the anguish in his voice. "My dear one." He rocked her gently, as if she were a child.

"We never spoke of it again," she murmured. "They buried Father in unholy ground somewhere on the heath, just like they're burying Fenella. We put Mother in holy ground by the chapel. The day after her funeral, my brothers took me into training so no man could ever do to me what our father had done."

"Now I understand," Curran said, still rocking her. "Everything. And I love you, Bera, more than ever. You're safe now; you have me. You can lay down your sword at last."

It was the last thing she heard before drifting into oblivion.

*   *   *

Curran leaned close to his wife and murmured for the hundredth time, "Come back to me, Bera. I love you. Don't leave us. I need you. The baby needs you."

Curran laid his forehead to her motionless arm and fought the tears of remorse that stung the backs of his eyes. He cursed himself yet again for encouraging the confession that had led to her stupor.

He did not feel her move, but when she stroked his hair, he said a prayer of gratitude to God and looked up to see her frowning, her face still pale as parchment.

"What's wrong, Curran?" she asked him. "What's happened?"

He sat on the side of the bed and drew her into his arms. "I thought you had left me."

She held him weakly, but she held him. "How long have I been asleep?" she asked. "I feel as if I've come back from the dead."

"You have, I think." Curran kissed her eyes, her cheeks, her nose, her chin. "You've been insensible for three whole days. I was frantic."

"Well, I'm up now." She stretched, yawning hugely, so he eased her back against her pillows. "Mmmm." Her stomach growled so loud it all but echoed. "I'm thirsty. And hungry."

"Little wonder." He handed her the wine and cheese that had been brought for him. "Drink and eat. You'll feel stronger."

Curran marveled at her resilience. He didn't know where she'd been or what had brought her back, but she'd come back in a hurry.

"What's happened to Murdoc and Diedre?" she asked, her eyes alive again.

"The council met and decided to take them, along with Drust's body, to MacAlpin and let him arbitrate a settlement."

Bera nodded in approval, her eyes narrowed. "That's brilliant. I never would have thought of it." She cocked her head at Curran. "It was your idea, wasn't it?"

It pleased him that she'd known. "Aye. We'd already agreed to an alliance with MacAlpin. It seemed only fair that we lay this in his lap." He broke off a bit of cheese and ate it. "He's a wise and just man. I trust him to decide well."

Bera wiggled her hindside and winced. "Poor Diedre. Back in the saddle for all that way. I don't want to get anywhere near a horse for at least a month." She laid her hand to her abdomen and smiled. "Make that seven months."

"Does this mean you'll give up training?" Curran asked.

"Who will go along with the hostages to MacAlpin?" Bera deflected.

"Fidach, Angus, Roy, and Becan. They've already left. It took a day to build a coffin for Drust and mend the wagon to haul it, so they couldn't leave until yesterday."

She stilled. "Are you worried that they'll get there safely?"

Curran shook his head. "Worry would be a waste of time. I trust your brothers. And I trust that God will watch over them. He's certainly been watching over us."

"Aye, that He has." She paused, pensive. "I remember what we talked about before I fell asleep," she said softly.

Curran's stomach tightened.

She looked into his eyes and caressed his cheeks. "It's over, Curran. At last, I can lay the past to rest. And so can you. We have the present, and the future. And whatever comes, we have each other."

Curran could not speak for the emotions that welled inside him.

Bera took his hands. "Now help me up, husband. It's a beautiful day, and I want you to take me outside."

"How can you tell it's a beautiful day?" he asked as he helped her to her feet and steadied her. "And don't try to say it's the sound."

"It's everything: the light, the scent of the sun on the heather, the warmth of the air, the feel of spring." She smiled her secret smile. "I just know it, the same way I know you love me. By the light in your eyes, the scent of your flesh, the warmth of your voice . . ." She placed his palm over her abdomen. ". . . the feel of your seed growing inside me."

He kissed her slowly, gently, savoring the peace that filled him.

Bera was the one who pulled away. "About that council meeting," she said briskly. "Did you tell them I was a goddess?"

"No," Curran half-said, half-laughed.

Bera stripped her chainse over her head and stood there in all her storm goddess glory, an unmistakably carnal gleam in her eye. "Oh, well. You can tell them next time."

"Perhaps our outing could wait," Curran suggested, his manhood throbbing at the sight of her. "I believe I need to catch up on some worshipping."

epilogue

Eight months later at Pitlanric, Bera watched Curran cradle their daughter in his arms. "Yes, she's a strong girl, and so brave."

Katlan was strong. She'd cried lustily with her first breath, and grown stronger every day for the past four weeks. And she looked just like her father, with Curran's bright blue eyes, fair complexion, and golden hair. Her hair was straight, though, and stood out from her head like a baby bird's.

Curran hooked his finger against her tiny ones and she gripped against his pull. "Such a grip. So strong, just like her mama," he said in the adorable, ridiculous way of doting fathers. He held his little princess up and sailed her from side to side. "See, she can fly. Papa's princess can fly."

Warmed by Curran's devotion, Bera looked over from braiding her hair. "I wouldn't do that if I were you. She's just eaten, and—"

"Aack!" He barely managed to escape the inevitable eruption. "Katlan! Why would you do that to your papa?"

"Papa did that to Katlan," Bera said calmly. Finishing her braids, she arranged them in a halo, then secured them with silver pins. She wanted to look especially regal for the afternoon's bridal rituals. She rose. "Watch after her, Curran. I'll be with The Wives."

"Wait!" Curran held Katlan gingerly, lest she erupt again. "I can't watch over her. I have to be with the brothers. Grooms have rituals, too."

"I know that," she said. "I just wanted to see the panic on your face." She took the baby from him. "Come to Mama, my little dandelion." Bera checked Katlan's clout. Finding it dry, she wrapped the baby in the warm bunting she had woven, then placed her in her carrying basket amidst a nest of furs. "I'm still amazed that Diedre agreed to submit to the bridal rituals. As a widow, she could have demurred."

"She's wise, as you were, so she agreed," Curran said. "And probably for the same reasons you did."

"I like Diedre, Curran. She seems different now, at peace."

"So I'm told."

"You like her, too. Admit it." Bera picked up the basket and approached Curran for a kiss.

He circled her with powerful arms. "Yes, Weaver. I like her, too."

Curran kissed her, and her stomach flipped just as it had the very first time. "I'll see you at the wedding feast."

That evening, the two of them sat side by side at the center of the highest table. Angus and Moina were on Bera's left, and beyond them sat Murdoc and his new bride, Kenneth MacAlpin's niece Sine. To Curran's right, Diedre wore her bridal crown over her silver coronet, and Evan sat proudly beside her.

Everyone was laughing and talking and drinking. Becan and Boyd were singing their wedding songs, accompanied by lute, pipes, and timbrel. Platters of hot roasted beef and honeyed cakes were circulating, and wine was flowing free.

Under the table Bera took Curran's hand, and he squeezed hers. "Thinking about our wedding feast?' he asked.

"Aye." She smiled her secret smile. "It's almost the same. But this time, there is no sword hanging over us, and Pitlanric knows plenty again. Diedre's dowry will take us all comfortably through the winter."

Curran nodded. "Ironic, isn't it, that we share the same anniversary month as Evan and Diedre."

"This is November, Curran." Bera swatted him in mock outrage. "We were married in January. January twentieth, to be exact."

"Well, I was close." Unrepentant, Curran grinned. "It was cold. I got that right."

"You'll have to make it up to me," she said loftily. "At the next council meeting, you'll have to tell them."

Curran laughed aloud. "Tell them yourself," he retorted good-naturedly, just as he always did when she demanded that he tell her brothers she was a goddess. "I shall never reveal your secret."

Bera granted him a regal look, then turned to Angus. She hadn't had a chance to talk with him since he, Becan, Roy and Fidach had at last returned home, bringing Diedre with them for the wedding. "Angus," she called over the roar of laughter and conversation. She watched him excuse himself from his conversation with Murdoc, then slide close to her.

"I've missed you, Little Bit." He put his arm around her and gave her a hug. Then he waved a hand over the feast. "What think you of all of this?"

"I think Kenneth MacAlpin is a very wise man," she leaned close to answer.

"Aye." Angus lifted his cup to Murdoc and his shy young wife. "That match was a stroke of pure genius," he observed. "All of us, including MacAlpin, knew that Murdoc wanted to marry Diedre once Drust was out of the way. But MacAlpin was clever. He enlisted all of us to fight with him, including Murdoc. Once he saw what a skilled and clever warrior Murdoc was, he introduced his pretty little niece to the big, brave hero. The next thing we knew, MacAlpin had given his consent for them to marry. By then, Drust's chieftains had had time to accept their thane's death and Diedre's alliance with MacAlpin. Only then did MacAlpin decree that Diedre and Evan must be married." Angus shook his graying head in admiration. "As you said, a wise man indeed."

"You might have sent us word sooner," she chided. "A week is scarcely time enough to prepare for a royal wedding." The grain and wine and cheese of Diedre's dowry had made the preparations easier, though. As had the forty head of highland cattle.

"As I recall, we only had a day or so to prepare for your wedding feast," he reminisced fondly. "You and Curran must have spoken only truth at your own wedding feast. The two of you seem very happy. And Katlan—what a blessing."

"More than I could ever have imagined." Bera looked over at Evan. "How do you think they will fare?"

"It's a true love match," Angus said. "I got to know Diedre very well when we were all with MacAlpin. She is a brave and intelligent woman. I came to admire her, and understand why Evan loves her. They both deserve some happiness." He smiled. "Diedre certainly thinks highly of you."

"That's not what she said this afternoon when I was scrubbing her back," Bera said with a grin. She sobered. "I'll miss Evan terribly."

"We all will." Angus gave her shoulders a squeeze. "But Burghead is not so far away. They can come visit, and we'll visit them."

A shiver of foreboding passed through Bera. "I cursed that place, Angus. The well is evil, and I cursed it, too.

I did not know that Evan would be its thane."

Angus laughed. "If curses really worked, you'd be long dead, and all the brothers, and all our wives." He flicked her chin. "You're not the only one who's let fly with a curse or two. Fortunately, the Good Lord usually ignores us."

Bera kissed her brother's cheek, then turned back to her husband.

"Bera!" Evan shouted over the din. "Now that the baby's born, are you planning to go back into training?"

Diedre grinned, looking twenty years younger than she had at Burghead. She winked at Bera, and Bera winked back.

"Of course!" she bellowed in the spirit of the jest. "At least until there's another princess in the making!"

Curran recoiled in flustered horror, intensifying the hilarity.

"Keep her on her back, Curran!" Becan shouted.

Airell chimed in with, "Chain her to her loom!"

"Anything, to keep her from clobbering us again," Cusantin added.

Curran drew her close and peered into her eyes. "You aren't serious, are you?"

"No," Bera reassured him. "Not exactly."

"What do you mean, not exactly?" he asked askance.

"Well, Diedre and I were talking this afternoon. She's learned of several places on the coast where the Vikings have been hiding. If we combined forces with hers, we could confiscate their supplies and barricade the caves. It would only take a few weeks. They wouldn't be expecting us if we went next month at the Saturnalia—"

"*You* are not going anywhere, Little Mother," Curran said tersely. "You're staying home where you belong."

"Oh, no I'm not," she shot back, the old juices flowing.

Angus and Evan exchanged meaningful glances, then burst out laughing.

"Oh, yes you are," Curran bit out through tightened lips.

Bera smiled. "You forget yourself, sir," she purred. "Remember, I am a goddess." She stroked a loving hand along his jaw, matching his angry look with a smoldering one. "We shall see who rides against the Vikings next month."

Curran did his best to stand his ground as thane and husband, but he was clearly losing the battle to lust and his own perverse pride in her determination. He snatched her into his arms. "Aye, we shall see who rides next month." And then he kissed her, full and hard, in front of everyone, prompting cheers and jeers and laughter.

When he was done, she drew back dazed upon his knee, but no less resolute. "Just this one last time," she told him. "Then I'll settle down."

Curran dropped his forehead to the table and pretended to bang it on the wood. "Blast, Bera. You are the stubbornnest, most perverse woman in all of Christendom."

"Only when I'm right." She threaded her fingers into his thick, golden hair and drew his head aright to gaze into his beloved face. "Would you have it any other way?"

"Ask me in twenty years," he shot back wryly, his rancor gone.

"I will," she said, fully intending to do so. "And I will ride beside you against the Vikings, just this one last time." Before he could protest, she kissed him ferociously, with all the fire and will that drove her soul.

Damn, but it was glorious to be alive.

She would do as he asked, lay down her sword, but

only after she'd helped to banish the Vikings from their shores.

Aye, then she'd behave herself in a proper, wifely manner.

Maybe.

author's note

Though all the characters in this book but King Bred and Kenneth MacAlpin are the product of my imagination, I have made every effort to depict accurately the culture and complex tribal intrigues of the ninth century in what is now Northern Scotland, including married priests, execution rituals with their pagan roots, and codes of honor more often broken than kept.

It's popular among today's historians to take potshots at the Venerable Bede's history of early medieval Scotland, but I see no logical reason to doubt his detailed accounts of the cultures of Caledon and Dalraida. So I have depicted Caledon (described by the Romans as the land of the Picts) as he did: a tribal warrior culture in which both wealth and royal status were passed down through a line of princesses. I was fascinated to learn that women figured so prominently in Scotland's early history, and that they often fought alongside their warrior husbands to protect their lands and families. Caledon had no ruling queens, but only the sons of princesses were eligible to try for the crown over the seven minor kingdoms within its borders. That kingship was won by strength and prowess of the individual contestants, but not passed on to the king's heirs.

In the neighboring kingdom of Dalraida, the sons of

kings, not princesses, were eligible to vie for the crown. For more than a thousand years it was so, with the two nations at odds until Constantine and his brother Oengus ruled both rivals in the early ninth century, calling the unified nation Fortren. But as often happened in Scottish history, tribal rivalries and Viking attacks splintered the fragile union. Enter Kenneth MacAlpin, the lawful issue of a marriage between a Dalraidan king and a Caledonian princess. In addition to holding a rightful claim to both thrones, Kenneth MacAlpin was a brilliant warrior and statesman. It was he who united Caledon and Dalraida for good, ruling for sixteen years and putting an end to the epoch of the princesses.

That didn't stop the women of Caledon, though. Like my ferocious fictional characters Bera and Diedre, they continued to fight beside their menfolk for freedom, hearth, and home.

Haywood Smith

"Haywood Smith delivers intelligent, sensitive historical romance for readers who expect more from the genre."
—*Publishers Weekly*

SHADOWS IN VELVET

Orphan Anne Marie must enter the gilded decadence of the French court as the bride of a mysterious nobleman, only to be shattered by a secret from his past that could embroil them both in a treacherous uprising...

SECRETS IN SATIN

Amid the turmoil of a dying monarch, newly widowed Elizabeth, Countess of Ravenwold, is forced by royal command to marry a man she has hardened her heart to—and is drawn into a dangerous game of intrigue and a passionate contest of wills.

**AVAILABLE WHEREVER BOOKS ARE SOLD
FROM ST. MARTIN'S PAPERBACKS**

HAYWOOD 11/97

A SCINTILLATING NEW SERIES OF MEDIEVAL WALES
FROM AWARD-WINNING AUTHOR

REXANNE
BECNEL

THE BRIDE OF ROSECLIFFE

Randulf (Rand) Fitz Hugh, a loyal warrior and favorite of Henry I, is sent
to Wales to colonize for his King. When he meets an English-speaking
Welsh beauty, Josselyn ap Carreg Du, he hires her to teach him Welsh. The
attraction between them is undeniable. But can love overcome the bitter
enmity between their two worlds?

THE KNIGHT OF ROSECLIFFE

Young Jasper Fitz Hugh is to guard his brother Rand's family in the half-built
Rosecliffe Castle. Attempting to keep rebels at bay, Jasper doesn't expect his
fiercest enemy to be a beautiful woman—or one who saved his life when
they were children. Now the two are torn between their growing desire for
one another and the many forces that could keep them apart forever.

THE MISTRESS OF ROSECLIFFE

Rogue Welsh knight Rhys ap Owain arrives at Rosecliffe Castle to reclaim
his birthright and take vengeance on his hated enemy. Rhys plans to seize
Rosecliffe and his enemy's daughter. He has everything planned for his
siege—yet he is unprepared for the desire his beautiful hostage will ignite
in him...

AVAILABLE WHEREVER BOOKS ARE SOLD
FROM ST. MARTIN'S PAPERBACKS

LET AWARD-WINNING AUTHOR

JILL JONES

SWEEP YOU AWAY...

"Jill Jones is one of the top new writing talents of the day."
—*Affaire de Coeur*

THE SCOTTISH ROSE
TV host Taylor Kincaid works on a top-rated series that debunks the
supernatural. But her beliefs are challenged when she travels to
Scotland, in search of Mary Queen of Scots' jeweled chalice, The
Scottish Rose. For there she meets Duncan Fraser, a man who helps
her to find what she seeks—and to understand the magic of love.
0-312-96099-9___$6.50 U.S.___$8.50 Can.

MY LADY CAROLINE
During a séance, Alison Cunningham encounters the spirit of Lady
Caroline Lamb, a troubled apparition whose liaison with Lord
Byron ended bitterly. Compelled by the spirit, Alison purchases the
London manor where Byron's secret memoirs are hidden. But
Alison isn't the only one searching—so too is a sexy, arrogant
antiques dealer whose presence elicits not only Alison's anger, but
the fiery sparks of attraction.
0-312-95836-6___$5.99 U.S.___$6.99 Can.

EMILY'S SECRET
Handsome American professor Alex Hightower has always been fascinated by Emily Brontë and her secrets. Alex journeys to Haworth,
the village where the young writer lived and died, to discover more
about her. But while there, he discovers another mystery—a beautiful gypsy woman named Selena who also ignites in him a passionate curiosity.
0-312-95576-6___$4.99 U.S.___$5.99 Can.

AVAILABLE WHEREVER BOOKS ARE SOLD
FROM ST. MARTIN'S PAPERBACKS

JONES 3/00

Enter the World of #1 Bestselling Author

BRENDA JOYCE

The Most Passionate and Powerful Voice in Fiction Today

THE RIVAL

Lady Olivia Grey and her daughter both possess the "gift" of sight, and it is a vision that drives Olivia from a loveless marriage directly into the arms of Garrick De Vere—handsome heir to a scandal-entrenched legacy. But Olivia and De Vere soon find themselves at the heart of a bitter rivalry—as dangerous lies buried secrets and ancient passions threaten to destroy their love.

SPLENDOR

Under a male pseudonym, Carolyn Browne lampoons London society with her scathingly witty columns. But one day, Carolyn throws her barbs at the wrong man—the enigmatic Russian prince, Nicholas Sverayov. Nicholas, outraged to be the target of such derision, uncovers Carolyn's true identity—and starts a sparring game of deception, pride…and passion.

THE FINER THINGS

Violet Cooper came from the streets—an orphan who married into the posh world she had previously only dreamed about. But when her elderly husband died, Violet became the object of cold stares amidst whispers of murder. Theodore Blake has no regard for the rules of Victorian society—or the rumors swirling around the beautiful young widow. He only knows that he is completely compelled by her…and will stop at nothing to have her.

AVAILABLE WHEREVER BOOKS ARE SOLD
FROM ST. MARTIN'S PAPERBACKS

JOYCE 4/98